Praise for Award-Winning Author C. Hope Clark

Hope Clark's books have been honored as winners of the

Epic Award, Silver Falchion Award, and the Daphne du Maurier Award.

"Packed with plot twists, suspicious new characters, and the Edisto Beach community readers have come to love, C. Hope Clark fans will be cheering."
—Julie Cantrell, *New York Times* and *USA Today* bestselling author of *Perennials* on *Badge of Edisto*

"An addictive page turner."
—Jan Tangen, Netgalley Reviewer on *Edisto Heat*

"I am grateful that the mayhem of the Edisto Island Mysteries is restricted to these enjoyable works of fiction, and I am a big fan."
—Former Mayor Jane Darby, Town of Edisto Beach, SC

"A cannot-put-down mystery."
—Brenda Burke, Amazon Vine Reviewer on *Edisto Heat*

The Novels of
C. Hope Clark

The Carolina Slade Mysteries

Lowcountry Bribe

Tidewater Murder

Palmetto Poison

Newberry Sin

Salkehatchie Secret

The Edisto Island Mysteries

Murder on Edisto

Edisto Jinx

Echoes of Edisto

Edisto Stranger

Dying on Edisto

Edisto Tidings

Reunion on Edisto

Edisto Heat

Badge of Edisto

The Craven County Mysteries

Murdered in Craven

Burned in Craven

Badge of Edisto

Book 9: The Edisto Island Mysteries

by

C. Hope Clark

Bell Bridge Books

Bell Bridge Books
PO BOX 300921
Memphis, TN 38130
Print ISBN: 978-1-61026-182-1

Bell Bridge Books is an Imprint of BelleBooks, Inc.

Published in the United States of America.

We at BelleBooks enjoy hearing from readers.
Visit our websites
BelleBooks.com
BellBridgeBooks.com
ImaJinnBooks.com

10 9 8 7 6 5 4 3 2 1

Cover design: Debra Dixon
Interior design: Hank Smith
Photo/Art credits:
Seascape (manipulated) © Michal Bednarek | Dreamstime.com
Badge (manipulated) © Theaphotography | Dreamstime.com

:Lebh:01:

Dedication

This book is dedicated to Phylis Weeks,
whom I seriously miss so much.

Chapter 1

Callie

CALLIE MORGAN stretched her sweater and tucked the ends under the thighs of crossed legs stiffened from a self-imposed vigil by Michael Seabrook's grave. Seabrook's wife lay in the next plot, and Callie almost resented her being that close to him. Then she thought of Mark Dupree, bless him, who was every bit as loving and supportive to Callie. Not to mention alive. A man who worried himself silly about her these days . . . even knowing that her latest habit was to slip away to the cemetery to talk to her former lover.

She wasn't stupid. Being here was more an attempt to touch base with her former, better self—that seemed well beyond her grasp—than an attempt to hold on to his memory as one of the loves of her life. His memory was all wound up with an earlier time when she'd found herself, rebuilt herself, and become someone she could respect. Become someone the community could respect.

These days, well, she wasn't sure what to do with the kind of days she had now. Days she'd brought upon herself.

It was October, but Edisto's jungle shrugged off fall with barely enough hardwood trees for color, with the moderate coolness giving contrast to the long tourist summer. The orange, rust, and gold wreath on the Presbyterian Church door did more to announce the season than the woods surrounding the sanctuary's ancient graveyard. Breezes tunneled through the paths separating blocks of old family plots . . . the Seabrooks and the Jenkinses, the Townsends and the Mikells.

For two years Callie hadn't been able to make herself visit the Seabrook family congregation of graves, but once she'd done so, a visceral need to confess kept her coming back. She just hadn't said it aloud yet. She wasn't leaving this time until she did . . . though she said that every time.

But a woman had arrived fifteen minutes after Callie, and Callie's thoughts were too raw to confess with any chance to be overheard. If the woman didn't leave in the next fifteen minutes, Callie might leave and come back another time.

The woman had parked herself beside one of the few cradle graves in the cemetery, remaining far enough away not to be a bother but close enough to remove any sense of privacy. Grandmotherly in age, could be in her fifties or as old as seventy, the lady's caramel skin was smooth and cared for. She kneeled, hands covered in dirt from methodically culling dried remnants of flowers. Beside her rested a new flat of blooms Callie couldn't identify. Snapdragons, maybe? A dish towel draped across the lap of her skirt, catching stray soil while giving her a place to wipe her hands. It was an old grave, as in almost two centuries, and for a second Callie pondered the need to tend it, but only for a second.

The grave before Callie deserved more of her attention.

She stared at Seabrook's headstone, then slid her gaze to the grass, familiar enough to almost recite the number of blades spouting from the St. Augustine cover. She whispered, "I screwed up, Mike."

She'd finally said it.

Nothing happened. She swallowed and said it again. "I really screwed up."

Voicing the words launched a tumbling, avalanche of feelings. Bowing, she laid her forehead on the cool, damp sod and whispered, "I'm so sorry. To you, to Stan, to Jeb . . . to everyone." Hands drawn up beside her temples, she breathed into the sod. "I'm so lost, Mike. You trusted the chief of police job to me, and I ruined it." She sighed a shaky sigh then surprisingly had no more words.

She waited for redemption, forgiveness, a better sense about herself. All she got was hot silent tears. Professing into the dirt hadn't done her a damn bit of good.

Bottom line, she'd been the guard at the Edisto gate, left her post, and allowed the enemy to overrun the castle. Since she'd handed in her resignation as police chief, she'd been unable to look at herself in the mirror, much less at friends and neighbors of Edisto Beach.

Death had been no stranger during her tenure, a couple of men dying by her hand, not that she regretted those. One tried to kill her son. The other killed the man buried before her. Those she could live with, regardless of how any religion labeled her, but it had damn sure taken a toll.

In her last case, however, the arsons dredged up her fire phobia and knocked her off her game. She solved the case, but if she'd done so better, faster, cleaner, she might've salvaged three lives . . . and the careers of two officers who gave up and moved on. Way too high a cost.

She didn't even care that her physical house had burned down. Right now the smoking ashes of her metaphorical house were what she regretted most.

At her last "impromptu" town council meeting as chief, something had clicked in her. The vague idea of quitting became an instant reality as she chose not to endure Brice LeGrand and the town council in their never-ending public assassination of her as police chief. *I quit* came out at the time like the words were measured and meant to be.

How goddamn naïve of her to think that walking away mattered only to her. Like Officer Thomas Gage, her youngest yet favorite officer, had said, she chose herself over the citizenry, deceiving them by becoming a police chief they trusted before tossing the role aside, which gave some fool-to-be-named-later the incentive to take control.

Brice had pushed her until she caved, relieving him of the fight he might not have won.

She believed the changing of the guard since her resignation had been a clandestine takeover by Brice LeGrand and his crony. *Cronies* counting the two deputies that came in tow with Lamar Greer when he assumed the role within two weeks of Callie leaving. To Edisto, Greer initially seemed a timely dream come true. Callie, however, figured he'd been waiting in the wings all along, awaiting Brice's beckon. She should've known that her resignation had not been Brice's endgame.

Mark and her old, retired Boston PD boss Stan had said a cadre of residents wanted her back, but nobody had time to blink before Greer assumed the badge. Out of courtesy, she attended the new swearing in, but she couldn't have been greeted with more chill than if she'd spit on the uniform and peed on the badge she turned in, because that's what it felt like she'd done as soon as Greer started instigating change. Change which happened to coincide with a rise in crime, blamed on Callie's leaving more so than Greer's arrival. More thefts, burglary, and vandalism for the most part. Vehicle break-ins. The changes allowed more criminal activity, everyone murmured, some murmuring rather openly. She had been tough. Greer was not, they said. Callie wasn't convinced they were wrong.

But on the other hand, Greer had clamped down on weed. Beaches like Edisto were laid back. People visited to forget the madness of their day-to-day. That often came with recreational users, something Callie hadn't bothered policing as long as they didn't drive. But the new zero-tolerance policy hadn't been contested, at least not yet, for fear of the contesters being labeled as users.

Edisto Beach's aura was changing, as her yoga friend Sophie would say, and not in a good way.

Callie stayed home mostly, so Mark brought her groceries and the Mexican cuisine from his establishment El Marko's so she didn't have to appear in the grocery store. Stan checked on her for other needs. Sophie rocked with her on the porch swing several times a week, urging her to come to yoga.

Callie hadn't seen her son since she'd resigned, unable to put into words why she did what she did. Lucky for her, their burned home and content loss seemed the only concern at the time. The tragedy meant a total loss of her things, his things, except what she had in a couple suitcases and what he had in his college dorm. But she wouldn't hear of him missing a semester, so she sent him enough funds to replenish whatever he needed, promising him she'd be fine.

Last time she'd lost face in his eyes, he postponed those education plans. That wasn't happening again.

They phoned periodically, though, texting every other day, her telling him she was good and that she should have left the job all along. He didn't relish her being in law enforcement anyway.

One look into her eyes now, and Jeb would recognize the fresh lie and old ways, which were part of the reason she didn't often let Sophie into her home, either. Part of why some days she didn't answer the door.

Part of why she left her phone charging in another room most of the time, or like now, in the car.

She drank strategically. The gin came from Charleston, not local, and she only imbibed once per day, when whoever checked on her was gone for the night. The nights she spent with Mark were the best . . . and the worst since she hadn't admitted to him she'd slipped.

What she hadn't wrapped her head around was how she had screwed up beyond correction and why she couldn't put her finger on the reason she'd so easily walked. Sure, the pressure of public opinion weighed heavy with so much loss of life and property, but in hindsight, she had thought she was stronger than that.

People assumed she would move. Why not? With no job, no house, and her only child in college, she'd tossed any and all reins holding her to Edisto Beach. People started over all the time.

So why was she stuck here? The coward paying penance? The lost soul preferring gin to facing an interview having to explain why she'd quit?

Or was it Mark?

The hand on her back sent her own hand to her hip for a weapon she no longer carried. The older woman didn't fret at the reaction, even when Callie leaped to her feet. Cheeks reddening, Callie reached out to her. "I'm terribly sorry if I startled you."

The woman smiled understandingly. "I'm afraid it was I who startled you, dear." Then after a pause, added, "Are you all right?" and returned a light touch to Callie's shoulder.

Callie started to answer yes, but somehow felt the woman would read the lie. "I appreciate you asking."

"You were the police chief, right?"

The shock passed quickly. More people knew of Callie's plight than she cared to admit since rumors traveled like mosquitoes on this island. "Yes, ma'am. But you have me at a disadvantage, and my apologies if I should recognize you."

She'd forgotten how pleasant a normal conversation could be without the nuance of a stink-eye look or pitying stare.

"Lumen Townsend," the woman said.

"Oh," Callie replied, registering this was the so-called Witch of Edisto, whom Callie knew of only through gossip and Sophie's stories. But while Sophie was outgoing and spiritual through her yoga, sage smudging, and obscure communications with the dead, Lumen was more akin to a folktale. Independent and self-sustaining, she existed off her own resources by curing with herbs and offering advice from her home somewhere along Blue House Creek. The distance was walkable from the church if one was fit enough to do a mile, which she appeared to be.

A fragrance of herbs Callie couldn't name softly reached her.

Lumen smiled, and there was nothing wicked-witchy about it. "Seems we recognize each other after all. Seriously, can I help?"

Callie shook her head. "No, ma'am."

Lumen didn't ask for details. "We all pay for our choices." She spoke without the first hint of sanctimony, delivering one of those rare gazes that warmed with reassurance.

Anyone could look at Callie and spot unease, but Lumen's words sounded deeper and more aware than that, prompting Callie to say, "What's done is done."

"No." Lumen shook her head, her salted black hair curled, coiled, and shifting across her shoulders with the motion. "You left what you loved." She winked, soft and positive. "You miss your *errands of mystery.*"

"And she quotes Virginia Woolf," Callie said, her grin feeling foreign yet warm.

"You have a keen ear, Ms. Morgan."

Callie wasn't sure how to respond with the quote, only one of a couple she recalled from college lit class, but she was hungry for dialogue not tainted in judgement. "Is the grave a relative? It's rather old, I'd say."

"I assume I'm related to her," Lumen replied, glancing over to where she'd been working. "The tradition is almost gone to tend a cradle grave, but I like to think the family looks down and approves. It's an old white man's practice, but I'm still a Townsend, which means lots of white in my veins. That one is a child. The other two are grown, but the small one receives most my attention." She led them to the small plot. "J.R.R. Tolkien and his wife have cradle graves. We're called taphophiles, you know." When Callie clearly didn't grasp the meaning, Lumen added, "Cemetery enthusiasts."

Seemed they both enjoyed nonjudgmental chat.

Callie tipped her head. "May I help you finish?"

Not much was left to do, but Callie aided in the last of the planting and then the cleaning up and caught herself humming along with the woman when she recognized the hymn. All too soon, Lumen Townsend rose to her feet and announced it time to go.

"When do you usually come out?" Callie asked. "I'd like to help with. . . ." She read the grave closely. "With Caroline's resting place."

"Saturdays mostly, so she and the others look good for Sunday services. This time of year doesn't amount to much work once the roots take hold. These like the coolness. But I come about this time of day."

Her tools gathered in a woven vegetable basket, the flat of plants empty and held by a corner, Lumen readied to leave. "Thank you for the help."

She walked off, only not toward the parking lot, and it was then that Callie noted no car. "May I give you a ride?"

The woman declined. "I need the exercise. You're welcome to weed whenever you come talk to Mr. Seabrook, though."

She released that knowing smile, turned, and navigated the cemetery. There was no clear path, and like smoke, Lumen Townsend disappeared into the woods behind the Julia Legare mausoleum and was gone to the point Callie wondered if the witch rumors were true.

Her gut felt better. Her mind wasn't such a fog. She hadn't climbed completely out of her misery, but meeting Lumen made for a better day.

Callie'd confessed to Seabrook and met a friend. Baby steps.

She almost wanted to go tell Mark, then changed her mind. *Hey, I told Seabrook I screwed up, and then I met a witch. I feel so much better.* Here was Mark tending to her daily, and yet she felt better confessing to a dead man and a stranger. The realization immediately sucked away some of the joy.

She trod up the main path to where she parked just as an Edisto Beach patrol car sped by heading toward the beach, then put on brakes. Darting between headstones toward the church, she flattened against its wall.

Stupid. *Stupid.* She could've just waved. He was one of the new o-fficers and might've stopped and spoken, but that could've been awkward. He turned his vehicle around, yet she still held her breath he wouldn't spot her, feeling even more foolish. The officer returned from whence he came. He must still be learning the lay of the land, she guessed.

Once he was out of sight, she went to her car and checked her phone on the seat. Sophie had tried to call several times, but Sophie did that. Not checking voice mail, Callie left the phone and pulled onto Highway 174 south to the beach.

It was almost three. Too late for lunch and too early for dinner, so she opted for the seclusion of home, or rather, what she deemed home for the time being. Seabrook's parents graciously rented his beach house to her these days since hers was an ashy footprint on a now-bare lot.

After a month tied up in insurance claims and the arson investigation, she received the go-ahead to clear the debris. She culled a list of contractors down to one. Bureaucratic finalities kept her from signing a contract just yet.

Or so she told herself.

Truth was she'd become rather comfortable at Seabrook's place. The habit of turning onto Jungle Road toward *Chelsea Morning* had dissipated, a fresh habit of taking Palmetto Boulevard to *Windswept* in its place.

Autumn sun had an angle making it the brightest of the year, despite what tourists thought, and she donned sunglasses to avoid the glare discoing through the oaks. Back at the beach house, she parked underneath the bottom floor and took the two flights of exterior stairs. Inside, she hung keys on a hook in the kitchen, wondering if the breeze was too cool to fix shrimp and eat outside on the porch swing.

Did she dare have a drink this early? No, eat first. A handful of boiled shrimp later, she stooped to her knees and pushed pans aside, laying her hands on the Blue Sapphire bottle behind a pressure cooker as if she'd earned the reward.

Bang. Bang. Bang. "Callie?"

She nearly came out of her skin at the frenzied repetition of knuckles on glass. Like a teen caught in the act, she released the bottle, hopped back, losing her balance to land butt first on the linoleum tile.

"Callie? It's me."

Damn it. She knew who it was. Nobody else was that spastic in announcing herself.

Callie clamored upright and peered around the archway to see Sophie's cheek smashed against the etched glass. "Let me in," came the muffled voice. Distorted shadows behind her said she wasn't alone.

Opening the door, Callie found herself glaring at someone else, Sophie having stepped aside. "Um, what are you doing here?" she stammered.

"Lovely seeing you, too, honey."

This unexpected woman hated the ocean, so the only reason she was here had to be she'd been beckoned. "Sophie," Callie said in warning, "you need to learn to keep your mouth shut."

But Sophie pushed past them all, giving Carolina Slade clearance to waltz in, too. Wayne Largo, Slade's fiancé and federal agent cohort, in his slower-moving, six-foot, bearded self, shook his head. "Sorry for not calling." Yet he entered as well, cowboy boots clomping the floor, leaving Callie in her own open doorway which she wasn't sure she wanted to close just yet.

If this wasn't an intervention, nothing was, and her temper started to simmer.

"They've been waiting at my house for, what"—Sophie looked at Slade—"two hours? Where have you been?"

Slade walked through the living room, taking in the layout. "Not quite. What is this?" She spread her arms out, emphasizing the need for explanation.

"It's my home for now," Callie said, tight jawed.

Slade spun and strode past the federal-blue linen sofa and back up to Callie. "Not what I meant and you know it. Why did I have to hear from Sophie that you lost your home and threw away your badge?"

Sophie's nose rose, owning the accusation. Slade scowled. Wayne moved to the window to give them space, but even his expression expected a reply.

Slade and Wayne handled federal investigations under Agriculture's umbrella and lived in Columbia. They'd clashed then bonded with Callie over two prior investigations in the Lowcountry. One Slade's and one Callie's, each having played Robin to the other's Batman.

"Wish you'd have told us, Callie," Wayne said.

Callie had reduced her world to a precious few people, and some days even those were too many. "I'm dealing with stuff."

"We've all dealt with stuff," Slade said. "Hurts like hell you didn't call."

"Hurts like hell to do just about anything right now," Callie murmured, and Sophie raised a pointed, scrutinizing, well-sculpted eyebrow.

"Drop the drama, Soph."

"Bite me for caring."

Still standing in the doorway, the blue flash in the corner of her eye spun Callie around, her instinct still intact. An Edisto Beach patrol car approached from five houses away. Just as Officer Thomas Gage pulled parallel to the street, Callie covered the stairs to the front yard to meet him.

She fought the urge to order Thomas to report . . . like she ever had to. Through habit and respect, however, he did so, as if she'd never left the job. "Report is that Lumen Townsend was just found dead in the woods behind the Presbyterian Church, Chief."

Chapter 2

Slade
2 hours ago

WHEN WE CROSSED the big bridge onto the island, my nerves got antsier the closer we got to the beach. The sun shone bright as though promising life was good on Edisto, but I wouldn't have ridden two and a half hours on a moment's notice if I thought all was well.

The Callie who Sophie described wasn't the Callie I knew anymore. Sophie came with embellishments as part of the package, but the concern in her voice rang truer than the dramatics of her call.

The scenery swam by, and ordinarily I'd sit back and bask in the ageless oaks and marsh inlets, the egrets and herons, trying to read whether the tide was coming or going, but my friend weighed heavily on my mind. Law enforcement did *not* quit law enforcement. Well, not real law enforcement people, not without something damaging involved, which had my brain hurling what-ifs in a million directions. Sophie said Callie wasn't physically hurt. At least that was something.

Hanging up from Sophie's call, I'd rung Callie once with no answer, so I sent a text asking how she was doing, not revealing I'd learned something was up.

"She couldn't have at least called?" I spouted after a twenty-mile silence. "She couldn't have run her options by us? I know we don't live near, but damn, we'd become friends." Or so I thought.

"She's embarrassed, or angry, or . . . lost."

He wasn't a wordy guy, but I agreed. Wayne Largo's worry had worn ruts in his forehead as he played out possibilities as well. He was the real agent, but I had enough skillset developed in my quasi-invest-igative work with Agriculture to run alongside him pretty well. My mini-badge might only take me so far, requiring me to call in his shield and firearm and pass the baton once things got criminal, but our tag-team experiences over the last few years had honed a synchronicity between us. Our personal relationship abetted those talents, the diamond on my finger clinching the fact that our shared wavelength was damn tight.

Wayne hadn't blinked an eye when I said he could come or stay behind, but I was headed to the coast. He threw a gym bag together. Both of us called our respective employers and hit the road. Thank God for my sister taking care of my kids, but that was part of the price Ally Jo paid living with me. I supported her butt while she cooked and babysat, and the kids gained a fun aunt to gang up with against me. At times like this she was a lifesaver, and she'd told me in her redneck, loving way to go take care of my friend.

Wayne drove an SUV. I owned an F-150 pickup. We took my vehicle. He drove.

On the right, we passed the road to that frightening plantation we once investigated with Callie, where we met her. Three times in that case I'd found myself in the water. I was an anomaly in South Carolina . . . a native who hated the beach.

The closer to Callie's, the more nervous I got. From our lake outside Chapin, in the middle of the state, we had dared the drive without letting Callie know of our arrival. We'd bonded with her, at first tentatively, on that Indigo Plantation case, then more intimately at Salkehatchie. Wayne Largo's respect for her grew exponentially there when she showed her chops in helping solve his partner's murder. That's the Callie we liked to envision. Strong, methodical, keeping her personal to herself because Edisto Beach merited a reliable chief of police.

We reached Scott's Creek causeway, docks poking out from the long string of beach homes, the marsh giving me a shiver with water on both sides of the road. Once across and inside the town limits, we rounded the curve past the Pavilion to run parallel to the ocean on Palmetto Boulevard for the ten blocks or so Sophie said would take us to *Windswept*. The simple fact Callie was unemployed and living in *Windswept* bothered me deeply. That boyfriend was dead. I thought she had someone new. Where was he?

She hadn't even called us when her house burned to the ground, for God's sake.

Wayne parked in *Windswept*'s vacant drive, and I ran up the stairs, huffing and puffing by the time I made it to the top landing and banged on the door. Nothing. Wayne rested his forearms across the top of the steering wheel watching as I came back down to the truck. "Thought Sophie said Callie was practically a recluse?" he said when I got back in.

"She did." I pulled out my phone and called Sophie. "We're on the island, but she's not here. You sure you aren't exaggerating all this?"

"Positive!" Sophie's indignity was clear. "I'll just call Mark to see if she's at the restaurant. In the meantime, come over here. We'll find her. She can't be far."

We headed to Jungle Road, but the image of what greeted us, the scorched earth and an oyster drive to nowhere, hit hard as the only remnants of Callie's beloved *Chelsea Morning*. A hard lump lodged in my throat. "Oh, Wayne. Look at this."

An angry impotence filled me over her having lost so much all at once. My chest hurt. Tears pricked my eyes. "Sophie said the fires sucked all the life out of her. Seeing this hits so much harder than hearing it."

He reached over and took my hand. Words weren't needed.

We pulled next door to Sophie's place, *Hatha Heaven*, and rang the bell. She greeted us with, "Nobody's seen her. Mark said he'd help hunt for her."

Mouth flat-lined, Wayne peered down at her from his height difference. "Tell him no. Unless you're not telling us everything, we don't know enough to be worried yet. Should we be worried?"

Sophie caught her breath and thought a sec. "I don't think so."

"Then there you go," he concluded, quashing her flamboyance.

I wasn't comfortable in how to read someone who claimed to feel spirits. Her drama ran too deep for my taste. She'd always had dreamy eyes for Wayne, so best to let his effect rein her in.

Sophie texted Mark not to set up a search party quite yet. "There." She held up the phone so we could read. "Happy now?"

To think this was Callie's best friend on Edisto Beach. That had never made sense to me.

"She can't have gone far," Sophie said in a nervous titter. "Come on in. Sit a spell, and I'll pour you something to drink. She'll show up." She skittered off to the kitchen, leaving us in the hallway, so we helped ourselves to her living room and in our passing, noted her tiny self tippy-toeing to retrieve glasses in the kitchen.

About the time we relaxed on a white sofa with cushions that sank all the way to China, she appeared with three glasses of something carrot-y, with a celery stick poking out the top. I left the celery in the glass, thinking of the demon that would be released if I dripped orange all over that white sofa.

Without prompting, Sophie launched into a description of a Callie I didn't recognize, some remarks I'd already heard over the phone . . . some different ones making things worse.

"I don't always understand her cop stuff," she elaborated, "but this time she acted like she couldn't catch up, couldn't do right, couldn't figure things out like she was supposed to. It was those fires, I'm telling you. She moved here an alcoholic and afraid of fire. Edisto, its people, its spirit . . . mended her. You've only seen the good Callie. You never met the ruined one who arrived, nor the shattered one after Seabrook died. She's tough, but nobody takes it and takes it and doesn't pay a price. Seabrook tried to get her to AA. I once mentioned a shrink. Stan scolds her, and Mark runs around caring for her not knowing what else to do."

Callie Jean Morgan was heavy-duty. I could never have weathered what she had. Her loss was unfathomable, the deaths around her enough to unravel most law enforcement, much less a layperson, but she always bounced back with fresh scars and a wisdom that made her an even keener investigator. The best investigator I'd ever met . . . well, short of Wayne. But still, the person Sophie described sounded insanely broken.

I toyed with the diamond on my finger. Wayne played with the celery in his glass. We'd invested emotional stock into Callie. He'd proposed to me the night his partner died, and Callie'd been the one to convince me that the memory of trauma was not strong enough to come between the love we had. I accepted her wisdom, accepted his proposal, and he'd moved into my place on Lake Murray. Unfortunately since then, we'd been tossed from one case to another, him in the Smoky Mountains for six months. Me in Aiken, Chesterfield, Dillon, and a couple other short-term cases in small, obscure South Carolina towns. Sexting had become a thing I'd never thought I'd come to understand.

He came home one time suggesting we get married in Pigeon Forge, and all I could envision was a Dollywood wedding, so I threw out Asheville and Savannah as options, in an attempt to add taste to our nuptial exchange. I remembered the night I called Callie, telling her that a second wedding ought to be little more than a garden and a justice of the peace, but she told me to humor the romantic nature of the Lawman and give him his shindig, even if it turned out to be in downtown Dollywood with a barbecue rib reception. She'd laughed at his interest in details, and my lack of, then promised to be wherever we held it.

That's who I wanted to see today. Wouldn't it be nice for her to show up dressing me down over our wedding delay? But according to Sophie I would not be seeing that Callie. Instead, I'd be jumping in *her* business and demanding some answers as to why she'd gone off the rails. It was the only way I knew to deal with things. Head on. Still, I feared I'd break her more.

She's too sturdy a person to break, I found myself repeating. Because if she could, I could. Wayne could. I wasn't ready to accept that sort of reality.

Later, having worn out the subject of Callie, Wayne, Sophie, and I sat around the glass coffee table. A granite circle rested in the middle with fist-sized crystals I couldn't stop looking at. One does anything to pass empty time, and I kept wondering how one dusted the crevices on those things. Our carrot juice gone, our celery sticks and hummus consumed, even our hostess groped for topics to bide our time.

"My ex-husband was NFL," she said.

I scrunched one eye in attempt to pull my focus from the crystals and grasp the NFL train of that thought.

She saw me. "The stones," she said. "They are crystals, and this set cost him a fortune back when he thought I walked on water. I had to specify it in the divorce decree or he'd have sold it. Poor sap never appreciated universal powers which was most of why we parted. That and catching him boinking the team's physical therapist."

Wayne and I nodded from our puffy sofa places.

Sophie scooched forward on her chair, pointing. "Rose quartz offsets negative self-talk and welcomes kindness."

"Pretty," I said, checking the horoscope clock over the mantel for the umpteenth time.

"Red agate is for balance, but it also ignites passion. Aids the sex organs," she continued.

Yep, one of those was going in Wayne's stocking at Christmas, for no other reason than to share the joke of this moment.

The tiger eye was cool, with me being a Clemson Tiger fan, but I zoned out after amethyst. Likewise, Sophie ran out of talk after the blue stone, whatever its name.

"If we had called, Callie would have told us not to come," I said. "Text her once more, and if she doesn't answer, we'll head to El Marko's and grab a bite. We haven't even met Mark yet."

I rose to take the empties to the kitchen and almost dropped them when Sophie screamed, "She's there. She's at the house."

"Jesus, Sophie," I fussed. "Tell her we're—"

"Don't tell her anyone is coming over," Wayne said. "She might bolt."

His comment stunned me, but I knew better than to query him in front of Sophie.

"Yeah," I said, as I rinsed glasses in the sink. "Ask if she needs anything because you're out running errands."

Sophie did as told and looked up. "Now what?"

"Now Wayne and I head over there."

But she leapt up, sliding her shoes back on from under her chair. "I'm coming, too."

Not what I'd prefer, but Sophie was Callie's friend as well. She would be less likely to pull the wool over our eyes with Sophie there, because this crazy yoga woman would call her out.

Sophie followed us to *Windswept,* and I breathed a sigh of relief seeing a vehicle in the drive. Sophie scurried up the stairs, banging on Callie's door before we could reach the top. For a moment longer than the norm, Callie didn't answer, but Sophie banged again, her cheek pressed to the glass. "Callie? It's me. Let me in."

Upon opening the door, I stepped in front of Sophie. Callie's surprise was fleeting. "What are you doing here?"

Wow. "Lovely seeing you, too, honey." On that note, I didn't even hug her. Not that I preferred her falling into my arms unraveled, but something along the line of *welcome* would've been nice.

"Sophie," Callie said in warning, "you need to learn to keep your mouth shut."

Whatever. Sophie beat me inside, her attitude on the level of mine. Wayne made minor apologies with a shrug for good measure. If he wanted to be the counterbalance to our annoyance, let him. We'd played yin and yang in so many situations we could pull off the ploy in our sleep.

"Where have you been?" Sophie asked.

I studied the place, taking my own tour through the living room, peering into the bedrooms, so that when I asked, "What is this?" Callie misunderstood. I wasn't talking about the damn décor.

Suddenly, she got it.

Wayne explained we were concerned and wished she'd have called us.

Callie generalized some sort of excuse about dealing with *stuff* then jumped on Sophie for scoffing at her reply.

Not the best reunion. My frustration rose, and I fought to contain it, but Callie's was worse. Sophie's splashed all over the place.

Thomas driving up telling us someone had died put our tit-for-tat to shame.

But Callie's flash of shock, disbelief, then sadness, washed us clean of our attitudes. She knew this person, and gracious, she didn't need this right now. Thank goodness we were here.

Chapter 3

Callie

CALLIE REACHED to lean a stiff arm on Thomas's patrol car. "Lumen can't be dead. I just came from there."

Thomas's slightly stunned expression was soon replaced by professional interest. "What were you doing in the woods?"

"I wasn't in the woods," she said. "I was at the cemetery visiting Seabrook."

Thomas's embarrassment shifted toward the ground. He missed Seabrook almost as much as she did and had witnessed firsthand how the loss almost decimated her. But when he looked back up, she glared. "Don't even think of me as a suspect," she said.

"I'm not."

But he had questions. She could see it in his eyes.

"Lumen came after I arrived, and we just talked," she said, to avoid his asking. "Then we cleaned up a grave. She left around three."

He waited as if needing more.

"What happened to her?" Callie shifted to her work face, compartmentalizing the theory and facts in one room, feelings in another, finding it more difficult than usual to keep those feelings locked down. She hadn't thought she'd be doing this anymore.

"Don't know yet," Thomas said. "And I don't care why you were there, Chief," he threw out quickly.

He would be the last party to call her Callie, Ms. Morgan, or anything other than Chief. She'd respect that until she died.

"Just don't tell anyone you were with her," he quickly said. "Not yet. Not till you have to." He paused. "Maybe not ever."

Wayne stepped up, and Thomas lifted a hand in acknowledgement. "Hey, y'all. Doing all right?"

Wayne nodded. "Hey, man, let's stay mute and hear what they find first."

"Yep, keep this on a strong need-to-know basis, y'all," Slade added from his side, then in afterthought added, "Hey, Thomas."

Sophie slipped in, having missed half of what was said. "What happened?"

"Nothing," they all said in a loose unison.

"Bullshit," she said. "Somebody died. I can see it on all of you. Or something illegal happened you don't want me to hear about. You can't even *try* to credit me with keeping a secret, can you? After all I've done for you, Callie."

Sophie was right in every aspect of her little rant. She talked too much, but she had a history of siding with Callie when it wasn't the popular thing to do, like the friend she was.

"Lumen Townsend died, Soph."

"What? How?" Then before anyone could answer, she narrowed her eyes and asked, "Why?"

Why, indeed. The question only made Callie wonder if her crossing paths with Lumen had anything to do with her demise. How could she not? A lot happened to a lot of people who had crossed her path before.

"We'll need to talk later about what happened." Slade tried to end things there on the street, her trust for Sophie not as true as Callie's.

"Nothing happened," Callie said under her breath.

How many people had to die because they knew Callie Jean Morgan?

And would that thought make somebody try to pin this on her?

"Well," Sophie said, shifting a hand to her hip. "Brice can't blame any of this on you this time, *ex-Chief Morgan.*"

As if Sophie read her mind.

Her tenure as chief had dumped a lot of blame on her for a lot of happenings. Victims and their friends and neighbors did that. Plus, these days, anything that went wrong under Greer's watch still seemed to be tagged to her by default.

She'd feel a sight better knowing whether the new officer who'd flown by the church in his cruiser had seen her or not.

Slade and Wayne studied her a bit hard, and she shifted to the here and now.

Thomas pulled off, leaning in to tell Callie he'd keep her updated, but from what she'd noted of the current chief, she sadly suspected Thomas hadn't access to details. Case in point, Thomas policed the beach while Greer or one of his guys checked out Lumen's death. The whole island recognized Thomas's loyalty to Callie, and Brice would've informed Greer of that loyalty. Greer's management style wasn't much of an open door from what she'd heard, and loyalty was more of an ultimatum-type affair that Thomas might not readily accept.

Still on the defensive, Callie's gut churned through a mixed bag of emotions. From gladness in seeing her friends, to regret she hadn't called them, to dislike for the sudden drop-in, which felt more like an intervention than visit . . . but mostly the fear and sadness about Lumen Townsend. No point standing on the side of the road for God and everybody else to watch her sort it out, though. She turned to retrieve suitcases from the truck and started escorting Slade and Wayne up the stairs to *Windswept*.

Sophie didn't follow, however, and remained in the yard, her size-ten feet still in those bejeweled sandals, regardless of the season, though her yoga tights were topped with a white furry sweater. Her highlighted pixie-do danced in the coolish autumn breeze in contrast to her still pose against her car. "I'm not coming up," she said, holding a pout. "I've got to go."

She spoke loudly, whether over the tide coming in, the wind, the distance, or disgruntlement, but Callie couldn't let her get away on a sour note. "I apologize for fussing at you. You're welcome to come up with us." She nodded up the stairs. "And thanks for taking care of these two. I really do appreciate you."

Sophie wasn't one to injure easily, which made her all the better buddy. A thank-you usually sufficed, but this time her attitude clung tight. She remained unmoving at her car as if needing more. "Come here," Sophie said.

Wayne ushered Slade up the stairs, with the latter peering over her shoulder. Callie set a suitcase on the step and walked back to Sophie, trying to second-guess her, feeling she at least owed her friend an ear.

Tiny, fit, her body and lifestyle coveted by male and female alike, Sophie flit around Edisto like a hummingbird, never lighting long in one place unless yoga was involved or the social setting intrigued her, like the hostessing job she did at El Marko's. But even Mark limited the energized woman to four-hour shifts. She'd entertained Wayne and Slade for two hours already, so her not coming up was not unexpected.

"You've had your time to heal," Sophie said about the time Callie reached six feet away. "Grow the hell up."

Callie stopped in place. "Excuse me?"

"Look at those two up there, hurrying here to check on your ass. Mark's in a dither about how to treat you, and Stan's pissed."

Mark didn't seem out of sorts. Admittedly, she hadn't seen Stan in over a week, but since when did he confide in Sophie?

The yoga lady closed the distance, and with her finger in Callie's chest, sea-green contact lenses sparking in anger, she tapped a rhythm to her words. "You were doing fine. But *you* quit. Now you act like somebody did something to you. Stop it."

Pulling back, Callie rubbed her front, irritation oozing. "I don't exactly see it that way, Soph."

Sophie spread her arms wide, as if all the houses up and down Palmetto Boulevard needed to see . . . and hear. "You solved the damn case, girl. We get it that you lost your house in the process and a dear old man died, but he was a thousand years old. *Boo* would have finished him off. You weren't the bad guy. And as to the woman burning up in your house, she was a lunatic."

"That's harsh even from you."

"Maybe, but harsh only seems to be what gets through to you. You've moped long enough. You should've cried a few days then gotten over yourself. *Damn!*"

Her hatha-preaching friend bit that last word with a passion Callie'd never seen. This wasn't the usual nurturing, humor-driven Sophie, but Callie hadn't shared all her darkness with her either. "That woman was not the first body to die in my house, Soph. That's part of the problem. Too many people have died on my watch, in my wake, in my life, within my grasp. That's not what Edisto's about."

"You idiot!" The yell spun Slade and Wayne around, and Sophie went back to hammering Callie's chest with a finger. "You didn't exactly send out invitations to the bad people. You are not the cause of all that goes wrong on this island. Do you know how many people thank the heavens that you were here when some of this crap went down?"

Callie pushed the hand off. "Stop it. You don't exactly have the right to—"

"The hell I don't!"

Callie glanced at nearby houses then up the stairs to the porch where her houseguests leaned over the railing.

"Go ahead," Sophie preached, her tone loud and edgy. "Look at them. Then go to El Marko's, the SeaCow, town hall, Wainwright Realty, and every other venue around. Those with any guts will tell you." Now she pointed angrily to the ground. "They all trusted you. They felt safer. And now? Everyone who lives at this beach, visits this beach, or works on this beach has the damn right to say you let them down."

"I've heard enough," Slade said from up top and started down the stairs, but Wayne held her back. She might've knocked Sophie a hundred yards into the Atlantic, and Callie was almost willing to let her.

Her heart in her throat, emotions balled in a knot, Callie tried to choose words that weren't too mean to say. In a silent panic she realized she could count her close friends on one hand, and the lady before her was one of the most reliable, but no way would Callie melt into a puddle, either.

Sophie stood there staring as if she'd practiced this speech for days.

Callie tried to hold down the breathing that would belie her galloping heart. "I'm sorry you think that way, Soph, but people like you don't understand."

Leaning forward, Sophie repeated, *"People like me?"*

Callie meant what she said. "Yes, people who do not understand law enforcement. People who have not pulled a trigger. People who have not had to make decisions that saved or crucified someone's future. That's an intense burden to bear, girlfriend. A horrible burden that I'm weary of carrying. No, you cannot understand, but you could sure at least try!"

Hands shaking, it was Callie's turn to stand fast.

The impasse was stifling.

Sophie yielded first. "But we thought you were taking care of us." The tender response pierced Callie as deeply as any knife.

Tears welled. "And that's the point, Soph. I thought I was, too."

"If you can't, who can?" Sophie almost whispered. "You were the best we've ever had." With that, she got in her car, and with no further eye contact, she backed out and drove off.

Callie stood stunned in the drive. She'd never seen Sophie shed a tear and wondered how close she'd just come to making her do so.

She'd go inside and finish that bottle of Bombay if she didn't have guests.

"Anybody else would've run through ten shrinks by now," Slade said, coming up on her right, slipping an arm around her. Apparently, Wayne had let her loose.

When Callie didn't joke back, Slade hugged her close. "Let's go back inside. Thought you were carrying my luggage for me. It's still on the step. What kind of hostess are you?"

Slade's sense of humor, sometimes timely, sometimes not, soothed the sting of the moment, and they retreated inside.

While her guests took their belongings into an extra bedroom, Callie waited in the kitchen, needing something in her hand to drink, a particular *something* still hidden behind the pots and pans. The *something* that shouldn't matter anymore if she wasn't on the job.

By the time the couple returned, she had three glasses filled with ice and the bottle of gin on the kitchen bar and rummaged in the fridge for the unopened bottle of tonic.

"Where's the Blenheim's ginger ale?" Slade asked, assuming her stool.

"All out," Callie said, closing the refrigerator door, going with the flow to avoid the inevitable questioning. "Give me a sec, and I'll scrounge you up some shrimp. Got some crab dip and crackers in here, I'm sure. Afraid I've ordered out a lot of late, so the pickings aren't plentiful."

She wasn't fooling anyone, especially two investigators. While their purview might be rural and agriculturally specific, they were savvy enough to recognize an alcoholic off her wagon.

"I'm not a gin fan," Wayne said.

"Summer maybe, but not in October," Slade stacked on, leaving Callie with the unspoken dare to go ahead and dive into the bottle without their aiding and abetting the crime. "What else you got?"

"Um," and Callie returned to the fridge. "Water?"

"Callie, come on." Wayne, this time. The more straight-laced of the two, his challenge made her take a breath to turn and face the music. "We're not judging," he said, recognizing her effort. "We're concerned."

Slade shot a can't-believe-this expression at them both. "You might not admit you're judging, but I sure will. What's with the booze? You'd licked it."

Then before Callie could correct her, Slade added, "I know, I know, an alcoholic is never cured, but you'd changed your habits. There. More accurate?"

"Yeah. I quit my job so I don't have to abstain anymore. I—"

"Lame excuse. It's not like you don't have money enough to tide you over. It's not like you even have to work. What drove you to this? Does Jeb know? Of course he knows. I'm surprised he's not camped out in the guest room, keeping an eye on you."

And there she was, cornered in her kitchen by someone who knew enough of her past and had enough guts to ask the right questions.

Though Mark was a ten-month relationship, about six of it conjugal, he didn't know much of her past, but he related somehow. He had a law enforcement past he hadn't revealed much of yet either. Probably why he kept checking on her.

Her old boss Stan knew all the skeletons in her closet, every damn scary one, but he'd given her distance after a lecture about getting her head on straight, only with a more gravelly style of delivery.

It was like she waited for people to call her out.

"No, Jeb doesn't know it all," she said. "He had to endure the loss of his father, his grandfather, and Seabrook, and he's in a good place. I'll figure this out."

Wayne leaned elbows on the bar, his bearded chin atop folded knuckles in analysis of her. Slade sat more draped in her chair, though her mind clearly was absorbed with what to say next. "Tell us about this dead woman," she finally said. "You look like crap, by the way."

Callie managed half a smile. "I just met the woman today. She recognized me. I recognized her once she said her name. Lumen Townsend. The Edisto Witchy Woman by reputation. We cleaned up a grave together. She walked off in the woods, and I drove away."

"Who saw you?" Wayne asked.

"Nobody I know of."

Slade sat straighter and pushed the bottle toward Wayne who reached his long arms over and removed the glasses and bottle to beside the sink. "Meaning someone *may* have seen you?"

"An Edisto Beach patrol car drove by, then turned around and drove back. Didn't stop. I don't think he saw me," she said. She hoped.

"Who's *he*?" Wayne asked.

"Jason Armstrong, one of the new deputies who slithered in with Lamar Greer," she said. "I figured he was lost. The other deputy they brought is a woman. Anna May Greer."

Slade exchanged looks with Wayne.

"Anna May is the new chief's daughter," Callie clarified.

Slade nodded. "Okay, while I'm dying to sit here and blaspheme the new chief and his entourage, I want to know how Lumen Townsend died," she said. "Nobody said anything's suspicious about her death."

"For a change, Slade is spot on, Callie."

Slade knuckled him in the arm. Their banter was refreshing.

"Let's wait for Thomas's feedback," he said. "Or you can check with your old people. What about Raysor? How's he doing, by the way?"

"Yes, Raysor." Callie's little piece of humor vanished. His situation hurt her as much or more than the resignations of her two officers. "One of the first things Greer did was change his status. He's on an as-needed basis. No more full-time liaison between the Colleton Sheriff's Office and Edisto. That man has served five Edisto chiefs in his career, with Greer making the sixth, not that you call what he does assisting anymore. They haven't called on him once."

Slade pursed her lips. Wayne scratched his head.

"Yeah," Callie said. "Sucks big time for him and for Edisto Beach."

A lot of people didn't understand that Edisto Island belonged to Charleston County while Edisto Beach was in Colleton County per a county line coup in the early seventies. To Raysor, the island was his history, regardless the county claiming ownership.

Then last November, using that intrinsic familiarity of the area, he'd assisted in the search for Wayne's partner's killer. He was mighty handy.

"With Edisto only a six-body police force, that's a helluva waste of a resource," Wayne said. "Makes me wonder. . . ."

"What's Greer hiding?" Slade finished but shook her head. "He hasn't been here long enough to entrench himself into anything sleazy, and it wasn't like he had this long-tail plan to infiltrate Edisto Beach. Nobody knew Callie would resign, right? A pure happenstance opportunity."

Callie's cheeks darkened. She had her own theories on how Lamar Greer planted his flag on this beach. "No, not right. Not anywhere near right."

"Fine, fine. Another topic for another hour," Slade said, appeasing. "So if I understand the territory correctly, explain to me why he's handling Lumen Townsend outside of his jurisdiction?"

If Callie had a dollar for every time she had to explain the relationships of the Lowcountry towns and counties. . . . "No different than Indigo Plantation. Lumen died behind the church, which is in Charleston County, but that sheriff hates sending deputies so far out in the sticks. A detective will eventually show, but they let locals do the heavy lifting."

"Right. How could we forget the illustrious Detective Chuck Roberts?" Slade mumbled, reminding them of the pompous, humiliated Charleston detective on the Indigo case. "Maybe he could be your inside connection."

Not a bad idea, but this was not her issue. "In the meantime, Greer gets asked to lock down the scene and canvas the area," Callie continued. "If Greer wants the case, they'll let him work it so they don't have to."

"Or task-force it like we did with Roberts," Wayne added.

"Right. But now . . . not our circus, not our monkeys."

Wayne gave her a delayed nod. Slade stopped herself from taking the issue further short of saying, "At least Thomas will keep you apprised. He seems like a sharp guy."

Callie returned the favor and stopped short of reminding them again about the circus.

Wayne rose from his barstool. "It's going on six. Where are we eating?"

Callie's pantry was bare, and Mark usually delivered later than this. "I could call out—"

Slade hopped up. "No, let's *go* out. We haven't met this Mark guy. You may not have told us much about him, but Sophie sure did. I hear he's a catch. Let's check him out in his native habitat. I adore Mexican."

Wayne rose, his height stretching five inches above Slade, closer to a foot above Callie. "Of course you do, Butterbean. Who comes to the beach and eats seafood anyway?"

"What's the fun in cliches?" she countered, slipping arms around his middle.

Their banter continued as Callie slipped into the bedroom to throw on better jeans, a fresher long-sleeved tee, and a fleece hoodie. From the crash of the tide coming in, it seemed the wind had picked up, and with it would come a ten-degree drop.

As she came out, the two parted from a murmuring exchange. Slade looked guilty as sin.

Chapter 4

Callie

KEYS IN HAND, Callie led Slade and Wayne to the car, Lumen's memory weighing heavy. Today sucked on an incredible level. Callie was tempted to have a couple of gins at El Marko's, to formally fall off the wagon just so she could drink in public and get over this covert living.

A text came across her phone as she slid into her front seat. *Come for dinner.*

Jesus Christ and all the angels. Callie almost dropped the phone in the cup holder to just ignore the message.

Her mother and mayor of Middleton, Beverly Cantrell, ruled Callie's hometown forty-five miles away. Her texts had become a daily ritual. *Daily*, for God's sake. It had gotten late enough in the day for Callie to dare believe she'd get by without one for a change.

Silly her.

Like Jeb, Callie hadn't done a face-to-face with her mother either, not that her mother hadn't been told the basics as well as heard from the eyes and ears she still courted on Edisto. She'd built *Chelsea Morning* and lived on the island as many as five months of every year going back to before Callie had arrived in this world. Like Biden always in Delaware or Trump at Mar-a-Lago instead of the White House, everyone knew where to find Beverly Cantrell if she wasn't in Middleton.

Busy, Callie texted back. *Maybe next week.*

Beverly was her non-biological mother, actually, but technically the only mother Callie knew until she hit forty and learned of another. She also learned Beverly had rolled with her husband's affair, even having the occasional dinner these days with his old flame. To Beverly, there were bigger issues at stake, like seeing that Lawton Cantrell's bloodline perpetuated the Cantrell political legacy. Callie's resignation had prompted Beverly into newfound hope that her daughter would return to the kingdom and run for office.

We have matters to discuss, Beverly texted.

Not now, Callie replied.

Let's carve a new career path, dear. You have an obligation.

The rest was etched and rote in Callie's mind, to include a *dear* or two, a word her mother used with ingratiating intentions that fell short on her daughter. Beverly was pushy, overbearing, and the woman who taught Callie to drink gin and make the most exquisite martini, but she'd failed to perfect her daughter's navigation of political social circles. Beverly was the highest functioning alcoholic Callie'd ever known and shrewd in the ways of small-town politics.

She presented as a more polished version of Brice LeGrand on Edisto, who was, coincidentally, her old boyfriend from her younger days.

Since Callie stepped down as chief, Beverly had been relentless, and Callie had been just as relentless with excuses. Too much longer and Beverly would show up unannounced and stick like glue until they fought.

Got to take a call, mother.

Come be my chief of police.

Callie's key stopped just short of the ignition at the fresh tactic. *That sure came out of nowhere.* While Chief Warren was senior enough to retire, surely Beverly wouldn't oust him to make room for her daughter. But just as quickly, Callie recognized she would.

"What?" Slade asked, peering over her shoulder only for Callie to clear the screen and drop the phone in her cup holder as she should've done earlier.

"I haven't been out to eat in weeks," Callie said.

"A special occasion then." Wayne sat in the front seat for the leg room. "Tab's on me."

The distance was barely two miles but too far to walk in brisk weather. Streetlamps flickered on. Dusk still raised Callie's adrenaline, a reminder of fire. That rash of arsons had renewed her phobia with a vengeance, especially with it having culminated in a barbecued body in *Chelsea Morning*. In her forty-four-year lifetime she'd had three people die in her home, two more than anyone deserved, the first being her husband.

Even she was amazed she hadn't cracked. *Are you sure about that?*

On the heels of that thought, she couldn't help but hunt the evening horizon for another ominous glow. Like the gin, fire was something she hoped she'd overcome.

Grateful to reach the parking lot, the relief quickly slid into regret as she hunted for a spot. The damn place was full. She hadn't been around this many people since the day Greer took his oath.

They entered the restaurant, the aroma of cumin accenting those of jalapeno, fajitas, and chiles. Sophie buzzed on the job, resetting a table as the customers beside her waited to be seated. Guess she did have someplace to be when she'd left so quickly. They had to wait for another table to clear. Sophie ran by fast enough to say, "Wait here."

She didn't say it nice.

Wayne cleared his throat. "Always a good sign when the tables are taken, I always say."

Finally, Sophie returned with a pasted smile and escorted them to a table, dropped three menus, and left.

"Yep, still a pickle, isn't she?" Slade said under her breath, grabbing the top menu. "What's good here?"

"Everything," Callie mumbled, feeling the stares as they one by one noted her presence. As chief she had access to Mark's small personal table near the kitchen to avoid attention, but tonight even that one was taken, and Sophie parked them in the open.

The silence came down hard. Diners who lived on Edisto hushed, which made the rest go silent in wonder who might be famous.

"Ignore them," Slade said, without looking up.

A waitress brought one of Mark's unadvertised sampling of appetizers, a treat reserved for his friends, dignitaries, or customers who needed appeasement, like the one day Brice had showed his butt to Callie, scaring half the room. Mark had seen Callie and her guests, probably too busy to cut loose from the kitchen to come out.

"Sweet," Slade said, snaring a mini quesadilla. "When do we get to meet this man of yours? So far I like him."

Callie managed a smile, but looking at Slade also created eye contact with a real estate agent behind her, and a retired doctor and his wife two tables over, longtime residents, all failing miserably to be clandestine.

The waitress arrived. "Your usual, Chief?" Then she turned red at the misstep. "Oh, I'm sorry, Ms. . . . Ms. . . ." Then she turned crimson. All she'd known to call Callie was Chief.

"Callie's fine," she said. "And the usual is fine, for both food and drink." Callie pointed at Slade to order, to take attention off the mistake. The waitress proved most efficient taking their orders then hurried off.

"Poor girl," Slade said, filching jalapenos off another sample and doubling it down on hers. "You've got this place in a tizzy. I hope you see you're missed."

"I'm a tabloid piece," Callie uttered.

"Well," Wayne said. "Tonight, just be a normal Edisto person. Eat out, speak to people, and enjoy not having to go to work in the morning."

Slade wiped his chin. "You've got picante on your beard."

She sure was enthralled with her man. Callie would be too, if she were Slade, but that wasn't a knock against Mark. That man was a gift from God.

And God was probably growing impatient with Callie for not embracing the second-chance relationship he presented. As destructive as her life had been to way too many, she wasn't ready to accept someone unconditionally into her world. Her world tended to destroy people.

"It smells scrumptious in here!" Slade said.

Callie smiled. "Always does. He's a good cook."

There was a reason Mark chose Mexican food for his restaurant, and the efficiency of delivery was one of them. They had their plates before the appetizers were half eaten. They dove in, the dialogue centered around which tasted best. New customers filtered in, the door's overhead bell just loud enough to be heard over the background guitar instrumentals. Callie cut into her enchilada, like Slade, appreciating the extra jalapenos, enjoying dining with friends, finally able to stop canvassing those coming in.

"I remember her," came the familiar voice of too much whiskey and cigars.

She tried not to drop her head in her hands, tried harder to pretend she hadn't heard.

The belly laugh clinched the recognition of Brice LeGrand. He waved at Callie over diners' heads.

"Damn, act like you've got some manners, LeGrand." Lamar Greer was sixty years old. Tanned, slim, mustached, and not bad looking in casual day uniform, he hooked a finger to draw a waitress. Sophie had somehow disappeared. "Little lady, how about finding another table to push together with those three folks over there. Nothing better than a good meal with good company."

The young girl scooted over, a hint of panic in her expression at the lack of tables available. Callie wiggled her own finger at her. "All we need is one more chair, honey, which I'll get. You just pour me a gin on the rocks, hold the tonic."

The drink arrived before the duo reached the table, since Brice introduced Greer like a United Nations Ambassador to every Edisto resident in the room. Callie's first sip fortified her like a dose of morphine.

Brice's chair scraped the floor before he plopped into it. Greer, however, had the manners to first shake each person's hand. "Chief Lamar Greer, my friends. And who might you be?" Of course he spoke to the man first.

"Senior Special Agent Wayne Largo." Wayne gave a slight rise from his chair, his tight grin confident. "USDA Office of Inspector General's Office, Criminal Investigation Division."

"Now that's a mouthful," Greer said, then turned to Slade. "And what would your fifty-cent title be, ma'am?"

"Carolina Slade, Special Projects Representative, likewise with the Department of Agriculture," she replied, enjoying the joust, giving his hand her own hefty squeeze.

"Never heard that one before. Now," he said, turning to Callie, his gray, curved-down, Sam Elliot mustache lifting on the ends with his grin. "No title needed here. How're you tonight, Ms. Morgan?" Palm up, he bowed, waiting for her to lay her hand in his.

She vise-gripped the shake, drawing him in over their appetizer. "Enjoying retirement," she said. "Forgetting all the skeletons."

He maintained his stare, his grin a little less. "Oh, every town has those, Ms. Morgan, and Brice seems to have a keen grasp of them."

Callie shifted her stare to Brice and held it long enough to make him uneasy. "Oh, I imagine Brice has a lot of skeletons to tell you about, assuming he wants to bare them all." Once Brice looked appropriately flustered, she let loose of Greer. "Have a seat," she said, motioning to the two chairs.

In spite of the verbal posturing, Greer seated himself with a gentility that made Brice come across as crass. Brice didn't even see it.

"Heard you caught a body," Callie said before either had a chance to put napkin in his lap.

"Still got your ear to the ground, huh?" said the chief.

"Witchy Woman died," Brice said, beating Greer to the punch.

Of course the son of a bitch had to belittle the deceased. "So she's real, huh?" Callie said.

"Used to be," Brice replied, then snickered. He was on his game with the chief of police in his corner. Sophie said the two knew each other from college. Callie wondered which one came up with the thought of ridding Edisto of her to make room for Greer. Might have been one of the reasons Brice rode her so hard these last couple of years.

Brice received his beer. "We can't stand to have another murderer roaming the beach. God knows we had enough of those under Morgan."

Slade's complexion darkened, and Callie bet Wayne kicked her under the table.

"Chief Greer didn't mention murder, if I understood him correctly," Callie said, keeping attention off her friends.

The chief shifted focus to her. "Absolutely right, Ms. Morgan. And no, Brice, no psychos at large. Poor woman died of a heart attack from all appearances."

A twelve-hour turnaround was rocket speed for examiners to determine a cause of death and this guy nails it in, what, four? She took a glance at Wayne who raised a brow back at her. He'd caught that, too.

Law enforcement didn't normally throw investigation facts around so liberally, but Brice was basking in his role as best friend to the most powerful person on the beach short of the mayor. The mayor would lose what was left of that control if he wasn't careful.

"Wait." Brice seemed keen to dominate the dialogue.

But then he paused, formulating whatever it was he was about to say, and Callie wondered if the idiot had lost his train of thought. "Still waiting, Brice."

"She died in Charleston County," he said, frowning at her for rushing him. Then to Greer, "Going outside the town's jurisdiction is something the old chief used to do way too much, Greer. We need our law enforcement on the beach. Council can't afford to hire more officers for you. That's what Deputy Raysor was for. Not that I'm sad to see him gone, but he filled a hole the town didn't have to pay for."

"You can't serve two masters," Greer said. "We'll call on him when we need him. Bad weather, a man hunt, something pulling us too thin in too many directions is fine, but last thing I need is a man working under me who I have no control over."

Nobody agreed with him. Nobody disagreed with him. The man didn't appear to be seeking validation on the topic.

Clearly, this was not a man of the people, and that saddened Callie. She'd at least tried to be. In hindsight, she'd had a better handle on it than these two put together. "Charleston probably asked for Mr. Greer's assistance so they didn't have to come out, Brice. They let him determine if they needed to waste manpower to travel so far. Standard protocol," she said. "It pays off in the long run when we need them in return. Still,"—and she turned to Greer, who seemed to enjoy being addressed by his last name—"that's pretty darn fast for a cause of death, especially for Charleston. Takes almost an hour just to get her body there."

Greer showed no reaction. He had almost twenty years atop her twenty; however, both of them knew each year of her career experience equaled four of his. But her forfeiting the job gave him the trump card.

"I was in Charleston," Greer said. "So I came in late in the game. My officer said she died at five after one, if we're being precise. Of course he jumped on it, came to a quick conclusion, and got Ms. Townsend to Charleston ASAP. The examiner determined everything cut and dried. I trust my officer."

"Now *that's* how you run a tight police department," Brice said.

Yep, that might be how Greer runs a police department, but there was nothing tight about it. He was lying, *to be precise*. Callie had left the cemetery at *three* in the afternoon, and Lumen Townsend looked alive and well when she walked into those woods two hours after she was supposed to have died.

Chapter 5

Callie

A PASSIVE AGGRESSIVE air blew across the plates of enchiladas, tacos, and fajitas, and before Callie could say it, Slade wiped her mouth and did. "Still, y'all got some damn efficient medical examiners around here. We don't get that kind of turnaround in Columbia."

Like Agriculture dealt with a lot of bodies, but Greer was local law. What did he know?

But Greer only waggled that mustache once and reached over for the hot sauce. "Oh, we've got no formal report, young lady." Slade stiffened at the diminutive reference. The man might be a generation's worth of years older, but she was past forty. Everyone had to be dense not to spot the condescension.

"Doesn't take much experience to tell the difference between murder and natural causes," he said. "She gave out in the woods, behind that cemetery with the spirits in it. Right?" He looked to Brice for accuracy.

"The Presbyterian Church," Brice replied, swallowing a mouthful of quesadilla with an equal one of beer. "The Legare girl's ghost, I think you mean. An ancestor, actually, back when they used a lowercase G in the name."

Greer acknowledged with a tip of his head. "Thank you. Anyway, nothing earth shaking. At least I saved Charleston detectives a trip. Case open and closed. No relatives to speak of, I hear." He shook the sauce bottle one last time.

A sense of distrust crept up Callie's spine and took up residence. The man had opened and closed a death case in four fictitious hours. And who's to say Lumen didn't have relatives other than the grapevine of old, worn-out rumor? Had they searched her house? Interviewed neighbors? Spoken to those at the church who knew her well?

Even before discovering that the Witchy Woman was a kind, thoughtful person named Lumen Townsend, Callie would've given her or any deceased more attention than this. Lumen was Edisto. She was a Townsend, an important surname from Edisto's history, a surname associated with the original ownership of land that eventually became part of Botany Bay wildlife preserve on the island, but how would Greer know that if he hadn't taken the time to learn who the person was?

In a matter of an hour, an hour during which Greer claimed Lumen lay dead in the woods, Callie had learned about cemetery flower beds and made a friend. The visit had nicely sprouted into something other than Seabrook apologies and handwringing. Callie had left with a desire to return with lunch next time and learn about Lumen's apothecary interests. Lumen had had a sweet wisdom about her that Callie could use more of.

"Surely, she has living lineage on the island," she said when Greer took a bite.

Her remark drew a guffaw from Brice. "She made potions and lived alone. Her lineage was no more than an illegitimate fling from six generations ago." Then he called aloud, "Hey, Sophie. Come over here."

Sophie tensed, left her hostess position, and strolled over at her own speed, clearly peeved at the summons. "What is it, Brice?"

"You're a so-called witch, per island talk." He tapped Greer on the arm. "She's the one I told you about who talks to dead people."

He baited Sophie, not that she could react. In this moment, she represented El Marko's as much as herself, which put her in an awkward spot.

"The Witchy Woman," he continued. "Her name was Townsend. Was she of *the* Townsends, or an import, or pretending she owned that name?"

Sophie's tiny nose turned up. "What does it even matter? Lineage does not make the man," she said. "We proved that a long time ago around here, or didn't you get the word?" She walked off.

Brice had ridden his great grandfather's laurels since birth. All of Edisto knew that.

Greer laughed. "She told you, my man. I think I like her." He looked at Callie. "Is she spoken for?"

Brice chuckled. Callie didn't answer, not wanting to aid Greer in infiltrating Sophie's life.

"No, I'm serious," he said, leaning toward Callie. "She's your friend, I hear," with a glance toward Brice, his apparent mentor for all things Edistonian. "Think you could fix me up?"

"Not in my job description," she said, finishing her drink. She nodded to the waitress for another.

"Didn't think you had a job description anymore," Brice said, but had to laugh solo to his own joke. Even Greer pretended he hadn't heard.

Slade silently mouthed from across the table, *Don't.*

Whether she meant don't mince words with these men or don't drink, Callie wasn't sure and didn't care, and she gave Slade a frown as if she didn't understand, lifted her glass, and drained the remnants off her ice.

Greer launched into stories of his past as chief of a little town called Pon Pon on the far side of another Lowcountry county. She hadn't heard of him, much less his escapades, yet she understood well the tendencies for law enforcement to talk shop, and he was dining with three people who'd had a heavy hand in the profession. He asked Wayne to contribute some of his experiences as Greer's enchilada plate arrived, making it no longer Callie's favorite dish

She nodded, and the waitress obliged with a third drink. She'd eaten, she had no place to be, and she'd be damned before she shared war stories with Greer.

As she lifted it, the glass suddenly disappeared from her hand with a substitute placed before her. "Thought you might need that freshened." The black-haired man with salt-and-pepper temples pulled up another chair and handed off the gin to the waitress behind him.

Callie assumed correctly that the low-ball glass disguised with a lime and swizzle stick was ginger ale, specifically the Bleinheim that Mark kept behind the bar. He leaned over and popped a kiss on her cheek. "Taking care of you, Sunshine."

Before Callie would react, Mark stretched out a hand to Slade first, like Greer should've done. "Mark Dupree. I own this place. You must be a rather special person for Callie to bring you in like this."

"Carolina Slade. Just Slade," she replied, beaming in an approving side glance at Callie. "Love the Hawaiian shirt, by the way."

"She's mentioned you," he said. "Fondly, I might add," then he continued to Wayne.

Gracious, courteous, and smoothly, Mark turned the topic onto food, then fishing, even getting Slade to admit to her fear of dark water, a phobia a Cajun like himself did not understand. Not a word about law enforcement despite the fact five of these six people had a past.

But work called, and after a half hour, Mark returned to the kitchen. Greer claimed to be an early-to-bed kind of guy, unless he could grab

Sophie, for whom he'd make an exception, he said, and Brice left with him like the groupie he was. Finally, back down to the original three, Callie suggested they head to the house.

Outside, she gave the keys to Wayne who didn't question why.

This hodge-podge mixture of tragedy and history, enemies and friends, was a far cry from the retirement routine she'd expected. Maybe she needed the outing, but Lumen's demise had thrown a wet blanket over any positive of the day. Callie found it easy to feel sad, yet at the same time riled about Greer and Brice.

At *Windswept,* she tried to judge what Slade and Wayne felt like doing, since as hostess she couldn't just disappear to bed unless they were of the same mind. She couldn't get Lumen out of her head, but she'd rather ponder the questionable death alone. Her feelings were just too raw about such things these days.

"Let's sit on the porch," Slade said.

"It's fifty degrees out there," Callie replied, reading her friend's need to talk.

"You got any blankets?"

Wayne threw in, "Coffee would be nice."

Before long, the women sat on the red porch swing, Wayne in a rattan seat against the wall, a boot on the swing to keep it in motion. The view took their attention across Palmetto, across a vacant beachfront lot, and to the Atlantic, and on clear moon-filled nights like this one, one could hear the sleepy evening waves, the whitecaps showing then dissolving into the dark.

"What did you make of dinner?" Slade asked, coffee cup in both hands, a navy and cream-colored nautical quilt covering both her and Callie, stolen off the guest room bed because lap blankets were never big enough, she said.

Callie shrugged. "Not much. Wish they hadn't sat with us. Wish Mark could've sat longer."

"I like him," Wayne said. "Retired SLED, you say?"

"Early retirement," she replied, a little proud of Mark's career with the state's highly respected law enforcement agency, happy to see Wayne impressed. "We haven't gone into details as to why. Just feel he'll cover that when he's ready."

"Saw the limp," he said.

"He hasn't explained that yet either."

"Why not?" Slade said. "I mean, why not just ask? You told him about your arm scar, right?"

Callie shrugged again, the unsaid being no. She hadn't told Mark her complete story about Boston or many of the details on how she came to Edisto nor the deaths that followed. She wasn't much into exposing her inner self anymore, period, and yeah, she recognized Mark deserved better.

Maybe once her new life decided what form it would take, they could have those types of chats. Speaking of new life, Callie had to admit that Beverly's offer of police chief in Middleton held a degree of quizzical interest. Having her mother as a boss would be the ultimate drawback, but she hadn't pondered taking up another LEO position after Edisto.

Nudging her under the quilt, Slade kept on. "How serious are you two?"

Figures Slade wouldn't let loose of a Mark discussion. "We're monogamous, if that's what you're asking."

"No, that's not at all what I'm asking."

"We spend the occasional night at his place," Callie said.

It went unsaid why they didn't stay at *Windswept* since it came attached with Seabrook's ghost.

"Well," Slade said. "He's clearly nuts about you."

Another unspoken choked the air. *What the heck is wrong with you?* But most of all, *Why did you quit being chief of police?*

Slade usually cut through crap instead of this gingerly tip-toeing line of talk.

"Give him a try," her friend continued. "A stronger try."

"Slade," warned Wayne from his silence in the dark.

Ah, Wayne had probably told her to behave tonight.

"Take a chance, Callie," Slade said.

Wayne's head turned. "Slade."

"Throw caution to the wind, girl."

"Slade."

"Let this guy—"

Callie threw off the quilt and hopped off the swing. "Stop it! You don't get it."

Wayne halted the swing and leaned forward, whispering, *Damnit.* Slade planted her feet on the plank floor. Neither said more.

"You have *not* lost what I've lost," Callie said, hands thrust out in front of her. "Your ex died after he tried to kill you. No love lost there, I'd say. Then you found Wayne. You still *have* Wayne. For God's sake you haven't married him when you should have ages ago. Lose him and you just might have a clue of the shit in my head, but I don't wish that on you. Never would I wish on you what I've lost."

Her pain hovered like stinging sparks in the night. Still nobody spoke. Callie moved to the railing, staring at the water, fighting to grasp back the numbness that usually kept her halfway sane.

Movement caught her eye to the east. A walker. Mark, per the mild limp, with a hoodie over his Hawaiian shirt. It must be later than she thought. Mark never came until El Marko's closed up at ten, the staff going home at eleven.

He climbed the stairs with his slightly off footfalls. "Hey, you."

"Hey to you, too," she said, hoping she'd cooled enough for him not to notice.

He held up something. Rarely did he appear without his signature paper sack. "Brought dessert."

She accepted his kiss but remained at the railing, still feeling the distance between her and Slade.

Mark shook hands again with the others. "Nice to *really* meet you." He handed off the bag to Slade before returning to Callie, reaching around her. "Sorry those two asses back there had to ruin your *coming out* dinner tonight."

"They're not worth the discussion," she replied.

Slade started to speak, but Wayne kicked her foot.

"No, stop it, Cowboy," Slade said. "We have three people here who care about this woman who's almost lost her friggin' mind. I, for one, want to lay it all out in the open."

Callie's initial reaction was to forcefully shut her down, but Mark's presence gave her pause before reacting so harshly. In a handful of deep breaths, a semblance of sense slid in, telling her to let Slade get it all out. When she didn't bark back, Mark leaned his backside against the rail, motioning for Callie to do the same. "Go ahead, Slade," he said. "I think she needs to hear this."

Callie gave him a sharp glance, then accepted the inevitable. Slade would speak her mind before she left. Now was as good a time as any.

Slade literally rose to the occasion, standing, though she kept the blanket around her shoulders. "She's afraid of losing you like John and Seabrook before you," she said to Mark, as if Callie weren't there. "People have died all around her. She saw the fires as a final warning that her career raised the odds for more of the same. The knee-jerk thing to do was quit the job. Like turning off a faucet against evil."

"Damn, Babe," Wayne whispered.

But Mark only drew Callie to him. "No, Wayne, I happen to agree. I just wish Callie'd talked to me before she took the leap, but trust me, I get it."

Nobody asked him how he got it. Recognizing the hint to his past, Callie eased nearer.

"Listen," he continued. "You turned in your badge, but you become like them if you blow off Lumen Townsend. Why not investigate her death?"

Wayne went back to his repose, boot on the swing. "I like that."

For a change, Slade remained silent.

Everyone tried not to stare at Callie but how could they not? The suggestion came from Mark, the most powerful voice in the group and who had deftly turned the discussion to the two other passions of her life—justice and respect for the dead. The silence which lingered after his question merited response only from her.

Callie hated that Greer had not treated the death with the respect it deserved, but she was naked without authority, no different than someone like Brice or Sophie deciding to crime solve behind Greer's back. Even worse since she was still viewed by the community as the standard for Greer to match.

But he'd fallen way short of her standard, in her opinion, and she couldn't get that out of her head. Much less his lies.

Chapter 6

Slade

WAYNE LOOKED at his phone and fell back on the bed, stripped to his gym shorts, the quilt they'd used on the swing thrown haphazardly back in place. "Damn, it's after two in the morning."

I had just washed off my makeup and sat cross-legged beside him, leaving the bedside lamp on. "We couldn't just jump up and leave. We had to give Mark time to work on Callie. She wasn't about to leave us and go to his place, and he hasn't been asked to spend the night here, so they needed time. Not sure which of them has the bigger issue with the house thing, but they need to get over that."

He threw an arm over his eyes. "Please don't tell me you feel like talking."

"How long can we stay?" My gears churned. We had four law enforcement types sitting around on their hands with an investigation at their disposal, but Callie called the shots. And we had no idea what that meant yet. She seemed fractured to me.

Since the death wasn't in Greer's jurisdiction, he didn't have a voice in the matter, but some people would perceive Callie having anything to do with Lumen Townsend as a slight against Lamar Greer. *I* would leap into this for that very reason and stomp all over public opinion, but I wasn't Callie. From the talk tonight, she'd developed an empathy toward Lumen, which could easily slide into a sense of loyalty that we all hoped would evolve into obligation.

Hey, we were on an island full of hoodoo and witchery. We could pray the woman reached out from the grave, maybe.

"Lumen Townsend deserves this as much as Callie needs it," I said, Greer's falsehood an irritation.

"Greer could get pissed," Wayne mumbled from behind his forearm.

I scoffed, showing him my opinion about that. "Assuming he finds out. Besides, might be entertaining watching him get stirred up about anyone second-guessing him. You know small rural towns. Bet his policing never got questioned in *Pon Pon*." I dragged out the name of the town of maybe three thousand people—no more and no less for at least twenty years. "There's a reason chiefs stick around a long time in a place like that."

Wayne rolled to his side. "Of course, some of these people are respected, trusted, and good at their job."

"So why did he leave?"

"One last fling. Change. Divorce. Salary. Bored. Who knows?"

I shook my head. "Kid me all you want, Cowboy. Good ones move up, not laterally, unless they are like fourth generation or something." Having overly pigeon-holed the stereotype, I tacked on, "Well, most of them."

He sat up. "This isn't about the man, it's about the case."

"It's about Lumen Townsend, yes, but his lie made this also about the man."

He nodded, giving me that.

"Well, it's Callie's to pursue," I said, scooching closer. "As much as I'd love diving into this—"

"It's not yours to dive into," he said.

"We're a team, though. This'll be our third joint venture if she takes it."

He shook his head. "Slow down. She's the one digging out of a hole. It has to be her instigating this. Not only is she the most knowledgeable, but she's a bit damaged from what I've seen." He tapped a finger on my forehead. "Help, but do not get in the way, Butterbean. She has to decide."

I grabbed his finger away from the annoying tapping. "It's not *getting in the way*. It's assisting. It's being a friend."

"And you are indeed a good friend," he said. "You're loyal to a fault, and it's one of the things I love about you."

She kissed his hand.

God, she hoped Callie lay in her bedroom thinking the same thoughts about Greer and Lumen's situation. Callie had a strong sense of right and wrong. "Something tells me she's in there thinking just like me," I said. Still holding his hand, my attention turned back to Wayne, with the sudden enchanting attraction of a strange bed beneath us. I drew his hand against my chest. "What do you think?"

He came toward me with a sleepy grin and used that hand to push me on my back. He lowered to kiss me, right before whispering. "I think she isn't thinking anything like you're thinking now."

As the lamp went out, I only wished Callie had Mark in the other room. She'd have better dreams.

WAYNE WOKE ME with the sound of his shower, and I lifted my phone and moaned at the time. Ten after eight. Less than five hours' sleep, and with the lull of the surf, I could've slept till noon. But we were in Callie's place, on Callie's time, and using the good manners my mother strove to drill into me, I threw on a robe my sister gifted me for my last birthday, a sister who knew I slept nude and needed something to keep me decent if woken in the middle of the night.

Like any hostess, if we were up, Callie'd want to be up and ahead of us, accommodating, so I slipped out of the room to see what stage of dress she was in. I'd been craving a SeaCow breakfast since we unpacked last night.

Callie's bed was made. I hoped to God she'd slipped out to Mark's place versus being unable to sleep. I could at least make coffee, but I hadn't finished rummaging around her kitchen hunting for cups and sweetener before someone fumbled at the front door, and before I could reach it, Callie came in arms loaded.

"A SeaCow breakfast," she said, setting bags on the counter.

"Bless you, bless you, *bless you!*" I said, diving into the huge assortment, wondering how the heck she expected us to eat this much food. "You could feed six people with this."

Bad me. I'd noted the food before noting her. She looked better than last night. Maybe we'd done her some good after all. *But damn, look at this spread.* We'd have leftovers for sure. I was already imagining microwaved biscuits and bacon for lunch.

She started laying out the plates. "Not six. Five. The three of us, Mark, and Raysor, who ought to be here any moment."

Before I could whoop and holler seeing my girlfriend come alive, a truck, from the sound of it, pulled in the drive. I scooted out in time to see Raysor pivot and slide his big, burly self off the front seat and onto his Timberlane boots, in civvies. If the man weren't so remarkably sized and shaped, I wouldn't have recognized him sans uniform. Mark exited the passenger side.

"Deputy Don Raysor!" I shouted. "You look no worse than last time I saw you."

The deep, Lowcountry drawl sounded up the stairs way before him as he took his time climbing those steps. "They'll let anyone on this island, won't they?" he yelled back. Finally at the top, he grabbed me for a bear hug, and I did my darnedest to reach arms around his middle.

Suddenly he let loose, his hands out to the side. Wayne had appeared in the doorway. "Didn't grope a thing, Mr. Special Agent Sir," he said. Then leaning in, he quietly uttered, "Girl, go put some clothes on. You aren't wearing a damn thing under that robe, and I don't want him to know I know that. Don't need your man trying to kick my butt because I'd hate to take him down."

Waggling a finger at him, I laughed and turned to sashay past Wayne, probably wondering what had been whispered in my ear. But as hungry as I was, I needed a quick shower before someone smelled Wayne on me. "Y'all don't eat before I get clean." I didn't want to miss anything.

"To the devil with that," Raysor said. "Eggs and pancakes go cold fast."

"Then screw the shower." I turned my back, retied my robe tighter, and spun around to assume my place at the bar.

Bless her, Callie had put together an investigative team while Wayne and I shagged in her guest room. Kudos to her. Maybe she did still have her head on straight, or so I hoped. We'd find out sooner or later, but enticing Raysor to visit had to mean something.

Chapter 7

Callie

"YEAH," RAYSOR SAID from behind a mouth full of biscuit, dripping with butter and strawberry jam, three drops of it already on his flannel shirt. His light-brown hair thinning, his physique caving to gravity, the fifty-year-old was Callie's dear friend. He'd been shot at twice over the criminal element on this beach, and you'd never know it.

He studied his food as he spoke. "Six weeks ago, I was dressed and ready to hit the road to the beach business as usual, when I get this call from the sheriff saying my services were no longer needed on Edisto."

He swallowed, then had to swallow again, and snuffled like it took effort to feed the likes of him. "I asked him why, and he said the chief doesn't have to say why, and this one wouldn't bother." He grunted. "Then my sheriff welcomed me back and put me on patrol. Hate policing my own people," he said. "They think they can get away with anything, then I wind up in trouble with an aunt or an uncle for ticketing their kid. . . ." Another bite. "Put a second cousin in lockup and see where that gets you at the Sunday dinner table."

His family went back for generations in Colleton County, resulting in his being related to ten percent of the population. Callie had used his familial connections a few times, resulting in his kin believing she had the hots for their man Don. He didn't mind it. Laughed about it often, but the rumor made her professional dealings with the county awkward.

Not that she had to worry about that sort of thing anymore. Maybe she was less marketable now . . . unless they saw her as better stay-at-home wife material. Who knew with those people.

"Well, I need you, Don," Callie said.

"My aunts and cousins will be happy to hear that." He chuckled at his joke and reached for the last biscuit, not asking who else might want it.

She let everyone finish their meal. Everyone needed their hunger sated first, because they might not necessarily get lunch, depending on how her plan spun out.

Greer might not appreciate her asking around about Lumen, but he had no authority to stop her or anyone else seated here. Over a meal, ever the Southern way, they fell into their old camaraderie, even with Mark. She was touched by their love, their original concerns being to tend her, which morphed into indulging her in her need to investigate Lumen. Things were a little odd, and her feelings might run sensitive these days, but her friends' natures could smooth her edges. They would gladly help in studying this case . . . couldn't call it a crime yet. That was yet to be determined, but the time of death sure made one wonder.

Bellies full, Slade disappeared to shower while Callie and Mark cleaned up. Eager not to miss a word, Slade was in and out in ten minutes, even drying her hair. She found them scattered in the living room, an Edisto map on the coffee table, steaming mugs in their hands. The seashell clock over the bar read nine forty.

"Lumen dying of a heart attack might be the truth," Callie began once Slade perched next to Wayne. "But it's subject to question since Greer lied about the time of death."

"Who has the best access to the Charleston medical examiner?" Mark asked. "I say start there."

Nobody had a direct line, per se.

Wayne did a scrunched-forehead thing. "If I call, grapevine will think it's a federal case."

Slade leaped in. "I could pretend I'm—"

Putting a hand on Slade's knee, Wayne answered, "No. We aren't into underground tactics yet."

"Wait, wait, wait," Raysor said. "Give me a clear overview of what happened, the details this time. Not that I mind dissing the new chief, but I'm coming in late."

Callie rehashed what they knew. "I went to the Presbyterian Church cemetery at 1:30 p.m. yesterday to see Seabrook."

"Yeah, sorry, Doll. I miss him, too." He turned to Mark. "Nothing against you, man."

Mark lifted his cup to him.

Raysor's pet name touched her, but Callie pushed through. "I met Lumen Townsend. We talked and cleaned up Carolyn Townsend's grave."

Raysor seemed to reach into his head for confirmation. He'd become a Colleton deputy upon completion of high school, was not an investigator and never claimed to be. His beat-cop persona fit him well, and that's what Callie would use him for, as well as respect him for all he was worth, which was a lot when it came to the history of Edisto and his skills with its people.

"A child's grave, Don. Dated back to 1840."

His frown eased in recollection.

"At almost three, Lumen and I parted," she continued. "She slid into the woods behind the Legare mausoleum, and I headed toward the front parking lot. At that time, Officer Jason Armstrong drove past in his cruiser on 174 south toward the beach, but he quickly turned around somewhere out of my sight and cruised back north. I backed against the church. To the best of my knowledge, he did not see me."

Mark raised a finger to speak. "Why were you hiding from him?"

The others looked at her with equal interest for the answer.

She sighed. "Have no idea. Gut reaction."

Slade shrugged like she didn't care one way or the other.

Callie continued. "Thomas came by here last night around six and notified me that Lumen died, but he had no other details." She motioned to Raysor. "Thomas might be on the force, but I get the feeling he's not in the inner circle anymore. He'll keep me apprised but not sure what that's worth. I assume you're aware since you two talk?"

Raysor slowly shook his head. "I'm aware and totally pissed."

More guilt piled up on her. Raysor would have his age-old job on the beach, and Thomas would be treated properly, if not for her. As Thomas had said in a spat of temper, she'd underestimated the impact of her resignation on the people.

Slade interrupted the lull. "Callie?"

"Yes," she said, a mild jerk at coming back to the moment. "We parted around three, but at dinner Greer stated Lumen died at five after one. *Precisely* was his exact word in reference to that time. At least two hours before I saw Lumen alive."

"Who saw her die to be so precise with time of death?" Mark asked.

She reached for her coffee cup. "Don't know. Now, let's also address the other issues that merit our attention, but before I go any further, I want each of you to understand you do not have to get involved in this. You can bow out at any time."

Before they could shake heads and pledge allegiances, she interrupted. She wanted to call each out by name. Friends could easily get caught up in group think, especially loyal ones.

"Mark, you have a business. Piss off Brice and Greer and they lean on you."

"Brice I've mastered before," he said. "Greer . . . we'll see. Don't worry about me, Callie."

Not using Sunshine, her new nickname, meant he was serious and didn't want to dilute the importance of his decision. Bless him.

She turned right to Raysor. "Don, you're protected in Colleton, but this could permanently shut the door between you and Edisto. Plus, Greer could backstab you to your superiors. I don't want your career hurt."

"Not an issue, Doll. That codger isn't dominating me in my neck of the woods."

The other two she could address as one. "Slade and Wayne. Y'all took personal leave to come dry my tears and baby me, not tackle what some might call a vendetta with Brice, now Greer. I love you for coming down, but you have federal careers to think of. If you—"

Wayne spoke first, cutting Slade off at the pass. "We're adults and we're professionals. We're good." As always, minimal word count.

Slade smiled in agreement, inserting, "People worse than this have come after us before. Besides, nothing I like better than an investigation."

The group awaited her plan, not wanting to rob her of the lead in any way and probably seeing this mission as therapeutic. Callie would humor them just as they were humoring her. She felt like Frodo in his reluctant quest to deliver the One Ring to the bowels of Mordor, and this diverse crew awaited their orders to that mission. The image of Raysor as Gimli the dwarf drew a small grin.

"These are the issues," she began. "Again, somebody has to talk to the coroner. I'm probably the last person to do that in light of the recent change of authority."

They studied each other, thinking, exchanging realities that not a one of them could request a report in any official capacity.

"Let me," Raysor said. "I have a relation in the admin side of the Colleton Coroner's Office. She's the mothering type. She can call and claim a distraught relative is asking what happened and called Colleton by mistake." He waved his hand. "Or whatever, but she'll do right by me."

"The first of many reasons we have you on board, Don. The date, time of death, cause of death. . . ."

"Yep."

They were off and rolling. "Next we dig into Lumen Townsend's life. What's the link that caused the lie?"

"Was she in the wrong place at the wrong time?" Wayne said.

"Which means what did she see that merited killing her?" Slade tacked on.

He turned on her. "We're not jumping right to murder, Slade."

"But you can't take it off the table, either, can you? You're dancing around it, so don't chastise me for keeping an eye on that possibility."

Everyone thought about that.

"If Slade is right," Mark added, "we could open up a whole different can of worms."

Callie wasn't interested in going down that rabbit hole just yet. "At which time we'll decide whether to continue. We are not cops."

The glances and raised brows around the coffee table shouted with opinion.

"Excuse me, but yes, we are," Slade said.

She was the least trained of them all, but her reputation carried proven skills. As an amateur too curious for admin work and too old to qualify for any program with a real badge, she'd strategically maneuvered herself into a civilian role to sleuth with the real agents. "Badge or no badge, we have the right to question if the badges in place are doing their damn job!" She escalated, and Wayne focused on his cup, letting her go for once. "I want the dirt on Greer," she said. "That was stupid for him to discuss Lumen with us at all. What was his motivation to lie? Cops don't shoot their mouth off to people without the need to know, but he almost went out of his way, Callie. The man either showed his ignorance or planted information with purpose. Loose lips come back to bite you, unless you're dropping clues."

Were they too early in this exercise to be second-guessing Greer that deeply?

"I'm glad we heard him lie, though." Again, Wayne nailed it short and sweet. "Callie, who else was at the cemetery? What other cars? Think back."

Callie reached into her recall. When she'd pulled into the parking lot, hers was the only car. Several cars passed while she sat at the grave but nothing to notice. Nobody parked. Nobody honked, waved, or made themselves known. Then Lumen arrived. Callie hadn't noticed how she came until she left, walking through the woods. No one seemed to be in the church or the fellowship hall. A mid-week, dead time of day.

"Nobody was on site but the two of us," she said. "And only my car. I didn't want to be seen, frankly." She avoided a look at Mark. "If Armstrong hadn't been driving an Edisto Beach cruiser, I wouldn't have noticed him. Seeing him twice imprinted on me."

"Well, we have a timeline," Wayne finished.

Mark spoke next. "I'll call SLED and see what kind of files they have on Lamar Greer, Jason Armstrong, and . . . who's the other one? She's a woman, I heard."

"Anna May Greer," Callie said. "Blond, late twenties. Lamar's daughter. She and Armstrong arrived in lockstep with Greer, and I heard they all left careers in Pon Pon."

Mark grinned and stretched his neck to the side as if preparing to tackle the task. "Nothing curious at all about three cops leaving a small-town police department. That represented a loss of half the force. I'm not seeing the lure of the beach being that strong, either. Certainly not the pay, from what you've told me."

Not enough pay to bait someone to pack up home and leave, and definitely not enough income to cover someone living on the beach. None of the police officers short of the chief could afford to live in town limits. The town preferred their chief live there, but that rank usually came with experience . . . and other income means, equity from another house, or savings, because the salary alone wasn't anything to write home about. Callie had inherited her family's house and acquired her dead husband's insurance. Seabrook had been a doctor before his wife's death, giving him a bank account.

Greer she wasn't so sure about. "See if they've looked at his financials," Callie said. "He's renting a condo in Wyndham for the time being. That's the cheapest way to live on Edisto Beach." She paused, thinking.

"What?" Slade asked.

"Something else that bothers me is the crime spree that's popped up since his arrival. Let's tuck that aside for further study."

"Ooo-kay," her friend replied at the unexpected twist. "Don't think I'll forget that."

They all thought it. Dirty cops often capitalized on the constituency in some manner or another, but the profession was slow to label someone *dirty*. Thefts and break-ins had decreased under Callie's tenure, but they'd risen thirty or forty percent since Greer, per Thomas to Callie in one of his drive-bys. All it would take was for one of those break-ins to involve a victim and the residents and business owners would want someone's head to roll. Usually, Brice led such a protest, but he'd been unusually silent about the rise in crime, not so quick to point fingers at his buddy.

She went back to Mark. "Whatever you can dig up on Greer would be appreciated."

"No problem. I'm on it."

Excellent. "Might be best you stay at El Marko's," she said. "By keeping a status-quo appearance, you can also run interference if anyone asks about us."

"And feed gossip back to us," Raysor added.

But it would take boots on the ground to check out Lumen. Wayne and Slade weren't comfortable with the lay of the land, but they still had the camouflage of being two friends visiting another who wished to see the island. "Slade, Wayne, and I will go to the cemetery," she said. "We'll go in my car. People know me, and these two will be just tourists."

Sweeping out his arms, Raysor asked, "What about me?"

She swatted him on his beefy knee. "You knock on doors. Tell them you just heard about Ms. Townsend. Let them miss her with you and commiserate about you not being on the beach anymore. Have coffee; eat their cookies. Ask what they know. That's your forte, Don. And it gives no connection to us."

Their cups emptied, she checked the clock. A quarter to eleven. She rose. "Let's do this."

Raysor patted himself on the chest. "I hope some of these people have a pound cake or something," meriting a few laughs. But before he left the house, he pulled Callie aside by the arm. "Thanks for involving me, Doll."

"Thanks for trusting me," she said and gave him a hug.

"Nobody else will tell you, but I sure will. If we find dirt on this chief, I'll be the first to campaign to have you reinstated."

She hugged him again. "That's assuming I want it."

"Oh, you want it," he said, serious and firm. "We wouldn't be doing this if you didn't."

Letting him loose, he left, as close to a spring in his step as his weight could handle.

His assumption threw her off balance but indeed stirred an issue. If they found something, what were they supposed to do with it? And was everyone else assuming as well that they were helping to pave the way to her reinstatement? That wasn't her aim.

"You gave him hope," Mark said, slipping up. "For you, for him, for all of us. Being cast aside hurt him, I'd say."

What a domino affair, with her being the finger that had pushed the first tile. She owed Don. She owed Thomas. What if she didn't want to be chief again?

"I feel rather foolish," she said. "This isn't to recover my job, Mark."

He took her to him. "This is you making amends, or don't you see that?" He dodged the job issue.

"Yeah. But I only want to do right by Lumen."

"I know."

This case had gone sideways even before they left the house; however, she meant what she said about unearthing facts on Lumen.

There was one person they hadn't discussed, though. "Should we question Sophie? In a way, she was Lumen's counterpart around here. I've used her often for intel on island people."

"No, not yet," Mark said. "Thought the saying was *telephone, tele-graph, tele-Sophie* out here."

"True, but she has incredible feelers."

Maybe she was the only one who respected that Sophie's far-reaching radar outweighed the odds of her gossiping. Callie saw her as more than the comic relief others did, but they'd already planned the day. Once they learned more, they could reconsider her. "I feel like we should've invited Stan, too. He'll be hurt being left out."

Her old Boston boss was rife with experience in some of the worst kinds of crimes. As retired captain of detectives from a substantial city, with a fair share of commendations for breaking serious cases, he had talent.

When Mark scratched his jaw, Callie hesitated. "What's wrong with asking Stan?"

"What does he know that any of us don't already contribute?" he said.

"Another viewpoint and a lot of police experience, but that's not the issue, is it?"

His lips mashed flat. "I was hoping Sophie told you."

"Told me what?"

He blew out a breath. "Stan is dating Sophie."

"He's *what?*"

Embarrassed, she reined in her voice, hoping Slade and Wayne hadn't heard. They'd stepped in the guest room to return calls to respective offices before heading out. "*My* Stan . . . and *my* Sophie?"

That sounded stupid once she'd said it, but Stan? Callie had almost slept with him. That's how close they were. After working together for fifteen years, he'd retired to Edisto because of her. He was a huge mentor. His breath smelled like cinnamon gum, and he'd adopted Hawaiian shirts as his uniform well before Mark. She'd come to like his outdated, close-cropped buzz cut.

But . . . Stan with Sophie and her Bohemian dress and scent of sage? She owned more colored contact lenses than she had shoes to fit feet as large as a man's. She painted her nails a signature coral color each and every morning and liked clothes that hugged her or swayed.

Nothing about them fit as a couple. "They're like a mishmash of *Blue Bloods* and *Charmed*. Sounds almost dangerous." She wasn't sure she could embrace the whacked-out images *that* union conjured. "Wait, is that my fault, too?"

Mark didn't hesitate. "Afraid so. They wound up at her place one night after dinner in El Marko's, trying to figure you out."

"Damn," she whispered, not sure whether to take blame or credit.

"Might be a blessing," Mark said, keeping the positive vibe.

Callie leaned against the wall to the kitchen, feeling like her butterfly effect was downright lethal.

Her phone rang. Thomas.

"Chief? You having a party at your place or what?"

"What does that mean?" She peered over at Mark and put the phone on speaker.

"I just drove past your house," Thomas said. "I mean, Seabrook's house . . . and saw the three vehicles, one of them being Raysor's. Should my feelings be hurt?"

She didn't want to risk his career by drawing him into their plans. "Raysor came to see Wayne and Slade, so I bought us all breakfast. You saw them last night. They're here for a few days."

"Well, I'd believe that, Chief, but explain why Armstrong's cruiser is parked at *Turtle Time* six houses down in perfect view of your place. Either he's staking you out. . . ."

"Or he's watching traffic," she said.

"But that's my assignment," he replied. "It's all I do. I've pulled two cars on Palmetto already this morning, both of them right under his nose, and he didn't budge. He's going to get a crick in his neck staring your way."

She was afraid to say much more. "You're a good man, Thomas. Keep me apprised."

"Enough said, Chief."

Callie walked out on the porch. Sure enough, Thomas was right. Without reservation she snapped pictures of the vehicle. At that distance,

Armstrong might not be able to tell, unless he had binoculars, in which case, he would see he wasn't all that when it came to surveillance.

His behavior only fueled her fire.

"Don't let him see you," Mark said.

"Don't care if he sees me or not," she replied.

Try to keep up, Armstrong. Try to keep up.

Chapter 8

Callie

CALLIE'S LOGIC CAP was on, her power of deduction engaged. This felt rather right, she thought, driving down 174 to canvas the scene of what could be a questionable death. Wayne rode in the front and Slade in the back. People noticed drivers, not passengers, and she didn't want her friends to stand out.

It wasn't far to the church, and if many people were there, she'd pass it by, maybe drive up Blue House Lane to Lumen's house instead. Being midday in October, there shouldn't be many people out and about. Low clouds in a hazy overcast replaced yesterday's sun giving the air a coolness that seeped through sweaters, so they'd donned their coats in preparation for a walk through the damp woods.

Barely a half mile past Scott's Creek, Slade cleared her throat. "Didn't want to bring it up in front of the others, but you left a big hole in your discussion back there."

Please don't bring up Stan. The couple had become acquainted with him during their first case with Callie. He and Wayne especially hit it off.

She still might find her old boss and have a one-on-one update with him, swearing him to secrecy. He could maintain a confidence, and not including him couldn't do anything but sting the man she respected with her whole being. If he hit it off with Sophie, as weird as that may be, why not support his happiness?

But Sophie hadn't said a thing about her new boyfriend. And how was she to trust Sophie to remain mum about any of this?

"Callie?"

She brought herself back around. "I'm listening."

"Brice," Slade continued.

Brice. Okay, Brice she could handle. "What about him?"

"Maybe I'm on the outside looking in, but he seems awfully chummy with Greer. Nauseating, from my vantage. Did he offer Greer something special to come to Edisto? I mean, should we be looking at Brice, too?"

"Maybe," Callie said, passing the post office, the real one, not the restaurant, then the Edisto Bookstore on the left, a banner broadcasting some author signing that weekend. Bad time of year for that. "But the pressure could've come from Greer, with Brice being naively taken advantage of. Let's check out Greer before Brice, who can be a wild card in any situation."

"Meaning he's stupider than Greer. Go with the smart one first."

Callie lightly snorted at the accuracy of Slade's satire.

Police chiefs didn't accept the position in a town as limited as Edisto Beach without reason, and it wasn't upward mobility. Either the job was their first role as chief, and they'd put in a year or two then move on, or it was presumed to be their last, an easy assignment as they slid into retirement policing the tiny, four-mile stretch of surf. Greer's age dictated the retirement category, but with thirty years entrenched in Pon Pon, why not ride into retirement there? Why give up all those connections and what had to be an effortless day-to-day existence?

The escalated string of small-time crimes made no sense to her either. Not in this short a time period. Did Greer not care enough to bother policing properly? Had some ill-sorted locals decided to take advantage of the new guy? The crimes weren't prosperous in nature. Break-ins, cars and houses, with low property loss value conducive to the thief who preferred low hanging fruit.

"Brice have any sort of relationship with Lumen?" Wayne asked. They passed the Old Post Office Restaurant, on the right, its lot empty.

These two were still focused on Brice. "He's not known for catting around," she said. "Those two lived in entirely different worlds. Honestly, I would think Lumen had more sense. Plus, she's noted for being a loner. Never married."

She slowed. There was only one car parked in the church's lot, closer to the office building than the cemetery. Someone working, no doubt. Nothing to deter the trio from stopping and playing tourist.

The breeze brisk, they buttoned up coats. Hands in pockets, they browsed headstones, wandering in and out of a half dozen plots, pointing at who was who, talking for talking's sake and for any eyes that might happen to be in the church beside them. Callie finally reached Seabrook's resting place.

A reverence washed over her, and emotion tugged.

What a shame he never met Slade and Wayne. He would've liked them. She took in the sight of his grave a moment, her friends not wanting to interrupt.

"Okay," she said, almost like an *amen*, and lowered herself to her knees. "I was right here like this when Lumen showed."

She studied the headstone a second more in respect, as if she wasn't already intimate with every etched letter, each swirl in the granite's design. Reaching to her own shoulder, she recalled Lumen's gentle touch. "She approached and sympathized with me."

Then standing, she took soft steps over to the Townsend plots, to the cradle grave. "Then we wrapped up her gardening here." The flowers had a hint of wilt but seemed to be living, best she could tell. "She told me about the child, Caroline Townsend, presumably an ancestor. We removed the dead flowers and planted these."

And she learned what a *taphophile* was.

"How pretty," Slade said. "Dahlia, snapdragons, and pansies. A perfect autumn mix."

Callie forgot Slade was agriculturally inclined. The woman could name every tree and plant in the Lowcountry, which had come in handy on the Indigo Plantation case. The flowers, the bushes . . . the poisons.

Wayne listened and studied the area, measuring with his eyes. "What did she bring with her? What was in her hands or on her person?"

Callie pictured Lumen standing almost where he stood, holding her basket, the lap towel folded neatly atop old tools. She described all down to the color and age of each, then recalled to Wayne the empty plastic flower flat balanced on her hip, the pulled-up plants piled smartly in rows with the dried roots toward one end.

"Then what?" he said.

"I went toward the parking lot." She pointed. "And hid against the wall there when Armstrong drove by. Lumen, however, went that direction." They swung around toward the ancient Julia Legare mausoleum, its reputation created from the tragedy of a comatose child accidentally buried alive, who attempted to claw through the door of her tomb.

This cemetery was plentiful with memories and feelings. A popular tourist stop. And if one tuned in hard enough, the attentive soul found sounds, visions, and scents to prickle the skin.

They strolled toward the small granite mausoleum, as if interested, then after some token peering and study, they slipped into the woods. Thirty feet in, Slade pointed to the ground. "Someone discarded dead petunias, cosmos, and white yarrow." Picking up a sample of one, then two, then a third dried bunch, she held them up. "Clearly nobody uses this path, but she had, taking care to toss these so that they weren't an eyesore to visitors, knowing they would decay quickly. Do they look familiar?"

Callie snapped phone pictures. Her horticulture knowledge fell way short of naming dried-up flowers. "I honestly can't say, Slade, but the theory fits. Let's go with it. Keep walking."

The path wove in and out of oaks and pines, cabbage palms and myrtles thick enough to stop the cold autumn wind. In a quarter mile, they exited on Blue House Lane, a narrow silt road about three-quarters of a mile west of Jane Edwards Elementary School. Lumen's house would be less than a mile further north, to their left. Callie'd driven on Blue House Lane only twice, down and back hunting for someone, never stopping, but common knowledge was Lumen lived up toward Blue House Creek.

"So where did they find her?" Slade asked, standing in the middle of the road. "Guess if they decided on natural causes there wouldn't be crime scene tape, huh?"

Wayne studied north, then south, scratching the nape of his neck. "Love the way you said *they decided*."

"How would you describe this?"

They studied both sides of the road a ways in either direction. "They said she was in the woods." Callie hunted for extra boot traffic or tire tracks from the three or four people and two or three vehicles that would've trampled the vicinity of where a body was found. There was nothing. "We walking or riding up the road? Anyone up for a mile?"

"Let's just walk it," Wayne said, and struck out.

"Wonder who found her?" Hand propped on an oak, Slade swiped mud from her sneakers onto a clump of weeds then jogged to catch up. "Might save us time talking to them."

"Let's hope Raysor solves that for us," Wayne said.

Not many houses occupied this road. Lumen and a few others still held onto their acreage with their small homes tucked in native plant growth and surrounded by a handful of high-dollar homes. Like all lanes leading to water, the well-to-do scooped up the land wherever they could see marsh or river.

The level walk took no effort, the coolness a perk.

After only a couple hundred feet, the land opened up on both sides in agricultural use, someone having planted a single row of oaks on either side of the road. "She had a pleasant walk to the church," Slade said, studying flat green land that Callie couldn't see held much interest.

"How much further until we reach woods?"

There wasn't much of the island's jungle along this road. "Tell you what," Callie said. "Since Raysor's talking to people up there, we need to go back to where we were and look the other direction. It's only a few hundred feet to Highway 174, but it's heavily wooded. We might have more luck."

The pair stopped and turned around. "We're not looking too sleuth-like here," Slade said.

"Nobody's judging," Callie replied, thinking the same.

Retracing their steps, they reached where they'd exited the woods. They kept going, and not thirty yards south, footprints trampled every-where. Five or six sets, maybe more. Tire tracks. Three cars had parked, turned around, and crisscrossed each other's trails.

"Here we go." Callie gave the evidence a wide berth, getting a macro view of the activity before violating the scene.

Slade peered up and down the silt road. "Why in the world would she be here? This is going away from her house."

Wayne walked the tree line.

Lumen would be friendly with whoever lived on the road, making Callie scan the other side. Across the road and up a ways was a lone rutted path, the mailbox reminding her of who lived reclusive in that jungle. Nobody else lived on this road for a mile on in.

"Here," Wayne shouted, and Callie spun. She had to hunt through the green to see his beige canvas coat. "There's a smaller path she might've taken."

The two women entered the woods where Wayne directed them, the ground lightly trod compared to the other, almost invisible with leaf coverage. This path took longer to navigate, with roots still claiming their dirt and vines accustomed to getting their way and discouraging foot traffic. Canvassing the path and its woody tunnel, a few yards in Callie caught a glimpse of something red through a greenbrier patch six feet into the brush.

Barely red, rather, and if she hadn't actually used the dang thing, she might not have recognized it. Faded paint flecked the wooden handle, the metal dull and well used. "That's her trowel," she said, gingerly moving around it, seeking other signs. A claw-like tool went with the trowel. Lumen had gloves, too. Dull green. None of them in immediate sight.

The basket, the towel. Where were they? "There." Wading further in, she found the flimsy plastic tray with small holes from where they'd teased fresh plants free.

Wayne took pictures from several angles, laying his keys in one of the photos for perspective. Slade and Callie continued scanning for the other items.

Callie built a scenario as she pushed aside weeds and foliage. She pictured Lumen on the main path, maybe sensing the heart attack, the pain creeping in. She might've second-guessed heartburn. A few steps more, a more serious pain gripped hold. She detoured to the closest possible help, which would be the house Callie noted across the road.

They thought they found where she'd fallen, the way the damp dead leaves bunched in places, a couple of rutted scars in the dark ground where heels slid after a misstep. With so much vegetation, Callie found it difficult to define anything exactly.

Wayne caught up to them. "You said she lives back up that way?" He pointed up the mile stretch they'd first taken. "Then why would she come here, further from her house, taking a more complicated path in almost the opposite direction?"

"If she had a heart attack, she tried to shortcut to that house across the road, maybe. Otherwise something diverted her attention," Callie said. "She didn't just want to walk further."

Slade squinted. "Or she went the normal way, then went to the house, then ran from someone." She inhaled at another thought. "Or she was killed and brought to the woods."

"You and your Hollywood scripts," Wayne said.

"We have to define exactly how she reached here," Callie said. "And why would Greer lie about time of death if that's all that happened? We have two discrepancies now. Place and time. What made her change course? Voices? Sirens?"

"Gunfire?" Slade spit out, her voice rising on the end.

Wayne stared. "She ran *toward* gunshots?"

These two souls offset each other . . . and yet complimented. Callie had witnessed the odd interplay several times. Slade leaned toward the more fantastic in terms of blatant clue-mongering, while Wayne stuck to the straight and narrow and obvious. Yet somehow their thought processes found ways to collaborate in a Nick-and-Nora Charles-type arrangement from the forties era . . . the wife as the outside-the-box gumshoe, the husband the by-the-book detective.

She was glad to have them with her now they'd found the site. Callie phoned Raysor while Wayne snapped pics. "Don? Where are you?"

"The other side of Lumen's house," he said, his words a tad

smothered. A gulp followed. "Just finished the best cinnamon roll. Why? What's up?"

"We believe we found where Lumen went down and where they collected her. We're missing pieces because it's not making sense. Think you can tear yourself away to come down here? I have a residence that needs your attention."

"I started up here since it was near her house," he said. "But I'll come on down. Where will you be?"

"On the same road, Don. North of you is water. South of you is us. Don't believe you can get lost."

"There's the old chief I've missed," he said, chuckling.

"You calling me old, Don?"

"Not in the least, Doll."

He was the only person who could get away with that moniker. He was also the best person to talk to ninety-year-old Truman Burnett, the owner behind that old mailbox and rutted path. Hopefully, fingers crossed, the senior may have seen Lumen.

At least she hoped he could tell the team the actual time all this had gone down.

Chapter 9

Callie

THE YARD LEADING to the old shack was more of a Caribbean jungle, the oaks older than time and the palmettos droopy and brown allowed to naturally shed than be groomed. Brittle fronds littered the jungle floor. Unidentifiable wildlife shuffled to safe places to watch as the four made their way up the rutted drive. Once they'd reached an unobstructed view of the porch and its door, Wayne and Slade stayed put, while Raysor and Callie approached the home of Truman Burnett.

Callie was so accustomed to wearing a badge and making this sort of approach that she reached spitting distance of the house before remembering she wasn't armed. Mr. Burnett, however, was especially noted for being so.

Raysor led the way up the concrete-block steps, their cracks and gaps filled in by hand with Quikrete cement, sturdy enough to handle Raysor's weight without the first sign of compromise. Welded lead pipes served as railing.

A couple of feral kittens scooted into crevices. Screen, rusted orange from time, bowed loose and ripped in corners, claimed to keep out mosquitoes.

"Who is it?" yelled a worn voice, crackling with rancor.

"Truman? It's Deputy Don Raysor. Came to talk to you, if you don't mind, sir."

Callie jerked as a dark image made a quick appearance at the window nearest her then disappeared just as fast, him equally frightened at being spotted up close.

"Who's she?" Truman yelled.

"A friend of mine," Raysor replied. "She's totally harmless, sir. She's a friend of Lumen Townsend."

The iron bolt clanked back in hardware as old as Callie. With a creak, the solid wood door opened a notch, then with a harder push by Truman, opened the rest of the way. The dull butt of an equally aged

Remington 870 rested on the cabin's hardwood floor, and the old man leaned on it like a walking stick.

"Don't worry," Raysor said under his breath to her. "He sleeps with the damn thing."

"What'd you say?" Truman ordered.

"I was admiring your shotgun," Raysor replied.

"Sure you were," the old man barked back. "I may be old but I'm not deaf . . . nor stupid. What the hell do you want, Don? I'm busy." Then instead of inviting them in, he let himself out on the porch. "Ain't been outside yet. Need to check the plot for tracks."

He pulled the door closed, and though he had a hitch to his amble and used the railing for balance, he made his way out and led them around the house, a lined flannel jacket already on him, an ear-flapped hunting cap loose on his skinny head. "Tell your friends to quit ogling me from out there and come on," he said. "If they came with you, they're likely to own a lick of sense." He teeter-tottered on, not caring if they followed or not.

Callie couldn't tell his race. Burnett was a Lowcountry name, but that didn't define color. He could've been dark from a lifetime of the outdoors or from heritage, and deep, dried wrinkles confused which. He lived alone, though, and had for some time. An old Datsun sat to the side, weeds hugging rotted rubber tires.

Past the back of his place, past a straggling stand of trees, they came out at an open field of corn stubble with a carpet of green beneath it. Truman walked the edge, studying the ground, muttering to himself when he spotted whatever he hunted for.

"A deer plot," Wayne said, easing up. "Is that turnip greens I see out there?"

Truman twisted around, his whole body turning as if his neck didn't work, and he gave Wayne a head-to-toe analysis. "And rye and a few other things. You hunt?"

"Yes, sir." Wayne stepped up to ingratiate himself as a like-minded enthusiast. "This is good weather for it, too. Don't like getting in a stand before nights get below fifty."

Truman nodded a string of little nods. "Yep, yep." He thought a second. "Been after this one buck for five years now. Maybe more," he mumbled. Using his Remington, he pointed to the back corner of the plot. "He hugs that line right there. He's a twelve-pointer. Maybe fourteen by now."

Wayne looked hard in that direction, as if he hoped to spot the big rack, catering to the old man.

If Callie'd learned anything about Wayne and Slade, it was that agricultural investigations had a flavor of their own, a different sort of people, and the two knew how to massage it to their advantage.

"Shot anything lately?"

Truman's shoulders bobbed up in a laugh. "Shot *at* something. Just yesterday."

"How cold was it that time of morning?"

But Truman shook his head. "Weren't morning. Happened to stick my head out after my afternoon snack and saw that bad boy standing in the middle of the damn plot. Had my hands full of dishes, so had to set 'em down and grab my gun. By then he was back to his corner over there, but I gave it a go. Missed the son of a bitch. It'll be a couple days before he's back, damn it."

Callie thought it before Wayne stole a glance at her. Gunfire reverberated out here.

Raysor caught on, too. "I came about Lumen, Mr. Burnett. Did you hear about her?"

The man's expression wilted. "Yes, I did. Afraid I had something to do with that."

All four of them stiffened. Callie craved to leap in with questions, but the two guys had Truman oiled up and talking well enough. No point ruining what worked.

"So you saw her?" Raysor asked.

"Sure I saw her, Don. She left here and died out there on the other side of the road in the woods, I heard. Within sight of my driveway," he said, motioning toward his drive and the road.

"So, you were there?"

Truman shook his head. "Nope. Just heard it. Like I told you, I ain't deaf."

"Mr. Burnett," Callie said. "I was in the cemetery yesterday with Lumen, tending graves. She was a lovely woman, and her loss pains me deeply."

His voice cracked. "I already miss her."

Callie's heart broke at the sound of the aloneness in his words, and she suddenly saw the man in a bigger picture. There was a threadbare tidiness to him, but his loss made the clothes appear looser. He was ninety. He lived a solitary existence, and Lumen was likely one of the few people he knew, and she had preceded him to death.

She could relate.

"Mr. Burnett," she began again after an extended moment of silence for him to collect himself. "Can you tell us what happened? The authorities collected her, but did anyone speak to you?"

His head barely moved . . . saying no.

"Does she have family?"

"No," he said, choking a bit. "We were alike that way. She had a fiancé a long time ago but never married. Had a sister, I think, but something tells me she died. Each was left a piece of land on this road, but the sister sold hers when she moved up north." He hung his head. "Have no idea if the sister had family. Might seem to recall mention of a niece. Not sure."

Time would tell if there were heirs. They tended to bubble out of everywhere when there was land to claim, and the parcel Lumen had would sell for a pretty dollar. Mr. Burnett, neighbors, and a lot of realtors would wonder about that side of things, but Callie's concern was elsewhere. "Can you replay what happened? Starting with her coming to see you?"

To that he gave a soft laugh. "Like she always does, when I fire off a round trying to shoot me a deer, she comes a running." More hoarse laughter. "She says she fears I'll kill myself, but she don't mind sharing the meat when I manage to put a buck in the freezer. We used to skin and butcher them together, but time wore on the both of us, so a fella' cross the bridge comes and gets 'em for me now. Lumen and I split the cost. A decent-sized deer keeps us in meat for a long while." A shadow fell over him at the fact that sharing such times with Lumen was over.

Callie attempted to bring him around. "She came to the house, I take it."

"Yes, yes, she showed, giving me the devil for scaring her. I asked her to stay here for supper, of course hoping she'd fix us something being the better cook. She called me out for it, too."

"What time was this, sir?" she asked.

"After three. I didn't check no clock, but my stomach told me halfway between lunch and dinner." He pointed back toward the road. "Sun shines up the drive the more it sets. That drive is almost due west. It's how I tell time."

"What happened next?"

His bearing then lost its starch. "We heard talking," he said. "Then we heard yelling. Men. Two voices. Out on the road. We don't get much foot traffic, so it caught our attention. We ignored it for a while, but then it came time for her to leave. I told her not to go out there. People don't like other people hearing their business, but she said she had to go home and wouldn't pay no mind to their squabbles."

Callie could see Slade itching to query him and holding herself back. Wayne eased closer to her. Both knew better than to disturb Truman's chain of thought.

Callie prompted him again. "So, she walked to the road. . . ."

"Yep." Truman peered in that direction, seeing yesterday again in his mind. "The arguing stopped. Couldn't make out much else since nobody was fussing anymore. I figured she went her way and they hushed, so I went inside. An hour later I heard more people. A siren whooped once, but not again."

The old man's Adam's apple bobbed as he stared up his drive. "I walked to the mailbox. There they were putting her in the ambulance. Nobody was in a hurry. That's how I figured she was dead."

Slade broke in. "Did they see you?"

He paused at this new woman interjecting herself. "Didn't want 'em to see me," he said. "Was prepared for them to come knocking on my door asking questions, but they never did."

Everyone wanted to ask the next incredibly important questions, but in an unspoken union, they gave the task to Raysor. "How many vehicles were there?"

"Three. An ambulance, an Edisto Beach police car, and a white Audi."

"Good catch on the Audi, sir. How many people were there?"

"Five. Two with the ambulance, one with the police car, two with the Audi. Just like I ain't deaf, I ain't dumb either, Deputy."

"My apologies," Raysor said and rocked on. "Recognize any of the people?"

Truman shook his head. "One of the ambulance people was a big woman my color. She seemed in charge of them two. One was an officer. I used to know the Edisto police, but no more. Heard they got a bunch of green ones now. They got rid of a few including that woman chief they had. Heard she wasn't bad, but them bastards in charge got the best of her. Makes you not trust police, Don. You know what I'm saying?"

Raysor cut Callie a look. "Yes, sir. I most certainly do."

"What about the other two?" Callie said. "The ones with the Audi."

Truman looked up from tapping his shoe with the butt of his shotgun. "Never seen the man in charge before. Middle-aged, half bald. Strutted like he was accustomed to being successful. The other guy, looked like a guy, stayed in the car." He stopped the tapping. "Do I know you from somewhere?"

She'd seen him but once, and she'd been in uniform. Civvies usually threw people. "I'm just a friend of Don's and a recent friend of Lumen's," she said. "But we thank you for your time. You wouldn't happen to have a key to her house, would you? We need to hunt for her will, maybe look for proof of heirs. Tend to her plants or pets."

His smile warmed at the proposed gestures. "Ain't no pets, but I got a key. Let me go back inside. . . ."

Raysor caught up to him in two steps. "I'll get it for you, Truman. Just tell me where."

"It's hanging on a nail in the kitchen near the refrigerator," he said, and Raysor eased past him and lumbered inside.

Truman rested in place, clearly grateful for someone else tending the task, but once Raysor got out of sight, the elder gentleman stilled suddenly and then turned to Callie to give her a knowing once-over. "You had a real good reputation, girl. You let 'em get to you. Don't let 'em rob you of anything else. Stand your ground and don't give up your sense of worth." He patted her. "Just you being here checking on Lumen says a lot about you. If she took a liking to you, I do. She told me about y'all's meeting in the cemetery. She liked you, girl."

Callie reached out to him and, like holding glass, she hugged him to her. Tears collected, and she blinked them back.

What was with her and little old men? In the fire case, she'd lost Dudley, a man of similar age to Truman. He was one of many reasons she'd resigned, feeling that her sluggish handling of the fires had expedited his fatal heart attack.

Though taller than she, Truman didn't weigh much, and against her his bones were angled and un-muscled. His skeletal hand rubbed her back. "Thank you," she said into his flannel coat smelling of wood-smoke.

"You're welcome," he said, drawing back. "Whatever you can do for Lumen, I'd be much obliged."

Raysor returned with the key. "Be assured I'll return it."

But Truman waved away the offer. "No, that's all right. The key's in much better hands than mine now. I'd never get down there to tend to anything."

Everyone shook his hand and left. They reached the end of the driveway with fresher perspective but far from conclusive.

"Y'all tell me if I've got this right. Lumen came to the end of the drive. . . ." Callie motioned toward the disturbed place near the woods. "And she was supposed to turn right to head home." She swung her attention the opposite direction, north. "So why, after telling Mr. Burnett that she didn't want to get involved in people's business, did she go left instead?"

"Unless they called her over," Wayne said.

"You're saying the police car and the Audi were there before she died," Slade said.

Callie wasn't liking any of this. "We can almost assume the police car belonged to Jason Armstrong then, since he's who I saw driving around about that time. He was alone. Since they heard multiple voices, sounds like he might've been meeting the stranger with the Audi. We're making assumptions here, but if they saw Lumen, and didn't like being seen, they might've called her over."

All four stared at the site as if images might materialize before their eyes.

Wayne scratched his beard. "Like I suspected, she might've been in the wrong place at the wrong time. These men were clandestinely meeting, not expecting to be seen."

"Please don't tell me they killed her," Slade almost whispered.

This time Wayne didn't hush her.

Callie walked toward the tracks again. "But we saw where we think she fell. Whether the two men called her over or she turned toward home, she wound up in the woods. Look at the difficulty we had finding the spot. Her tossed tools supported the location."

Slade covered her mouth then shook her head. "She ran, Callie."

Wayne nodded. "She attempted to lead them away from Truman while seeking someone at the church for help."

"And they tried to clean up the evidence," Callie said. "Taking her other tools, basket, and towel. Only they weren't thorough."

A frown coated Raysor's expression. Callie turned to him. "Don?"

"I'll call my admin friend and see if she was able to get a copy of the coroner's report."

"Thanks, but regardless how quickly Greer thinks coroners work, I doubt the report's completed."

"Yeah, but we might be able to get a loose opinion," he said.

Slade pushed out a big breath and spun toward Callie. "Is this Greer man an idiot or what?"

"Not sure about him yet, but Armstrong isn't much of a prodigy. Greer's used to getting his own way in a small town where he called the shots," she said. "And I bet his cohort is loyal to a fault."

"But who are the two other guys? Outsiders or Truman would've known them."

They were no longer just needing a coroner's report. They needed to go through Lumen's house before someone else did, then touch base with Mark tonight and see what he had extracted from SLED.

Callie'd sure opened Pandora's box when she handed in her papers. To think she'd hoped death would stop plaguing Edisto when she retired. She'd only lost the means to investigate them properly.

Even if Lumen died of natural causes, would she have died without Jason Armstrong arriving on Edisto?

Callie wasn't making this stuff up. Everything kept coming full circle back to her.

Chapter 10

Slade

AFTER PARKING Raysor's truck at the church, Wayne slid next to me in the back of Callie's car, and the four of us returned to Blue House Lane, Raysor pointing the way.

I saw no blue houses, though. The tires traveled almost silent on the silt, letting me read an app on my phone saying there used to be a blue house on what used to be Blue House Plantation. Someone chose to create a small development at the edge twenty years ago—the road taking its name from local parlance for the area. The site was nothing upscale originally, which on any sort of water still meant three-quarter million around here, or so Callie said. But we didn't make it that far, stopping halfway down at a rutted drive very similar to Truman Burnett's but a lot shorter. The mailbox was black, adorned with faded flowers hand-painted years ago, the real flowers of a trumpet vine still attempting to spit out blooms despite the cool days. The name said Townsend.

"She and Truman are the last of the older island residents on this road," Raysor said.

Which made us feel even worse for the nonagenarian gentleman.

Lumen's house dated back sixty years if a day. Plain red brick in a box-like shape, the plan looked awfully familiar.

Little grass grew in front due to the tree shade. "I'll bet money that Agriculture financed this place," I said as I got out with memories flooding in. I remembered my early days of checking out these homes when one was sold or needed repair or had an insurance claim, or many times even built brand new. I fell into the old habit of walking the exterior before stepping inside. These thousand-square-foot plans fell in one of five basic styles, designed for efficiency for lower-income rural folk who couldn't afford much. I knew them by heart.

My jaw dropped as I rounded the corner to the back. "Wayne, come look at this."

A three-quarter-acre garden of plants sprawled from the edge of Lumen's concrete pad patio to a lip at the river's edge. Rich, loamy dirt with enough sand in it to drain well. Simple irrigation tubing peeked out in places from beneath inches of mulch. A freeze hadn't reached here yet because the mint was still green. So were a few other things.

Some plantings were perennial and living, some dormant, some dead awaiting to be pulled up. A winter row of turnips, collards, and brussels sprouts popped healthy and luscious, the fall season vegetables too young to have budded yet.

Appearing beside me, Wayne scanned the plot. "Not sure what I'm looking at . . . except for that small patch right over there." He pointed toward a corner lit up like a stage spotlight with the afternoon sun accenting the lush green tinged with purple. The plants hugged the area nearest the house, obscure from the water considering all that grew in between.

"Pot," Raysor said, reaching them. "I'd heard she had some out here. Not sure what the rest is, though. I know about weed. How illegal is all this other stuff?"

I hadn't even noticed the marijuana because it's imprint on the garden was so miniscule. "Not illegal at all. The rest is natural."

I marveled at the science and the horticulture this woman had mastered. The afternoon was still young, but the sun fanned perfectly across the rows, giving that pot the daily six hours it needed and the collards and turnips enough to thrive.

"She wasn't selling," I said. "Not this little." I looked over the plot. "What a waste."

Raysor peered down his nose at me.

"I meant the whole garden, and, no, I do not smoke. I just know plants, you dufus."

"That she does," Wayne murmured, walking between the rows. He'd investigated farms long enough in his twenty-year career to recognize quality gardening even if he couldn't name the plants. "This is amazing."

Callie had used the key to enter the front, now poking her head out the back that opened onto a small concrete pad. "While you guys have been admiring weeds, I've found considerable more in here." She disappeared back inside.

"Weed . . . hah!" Raysor said, and followed her in.

But I couldn't take my eyes off this spread. Wayne waited by me. He was used to my quirks. "Do all these plants mean anything special?" he asked. "I mean, other than the pot."

"Means her working intelligence of medicinal and edible plants was damn rich," I said, unable to stop myself from inspecting closer. "Nothing is illegal. Like I said, even the pot looks like nothing more than personal use."

One of the herbs nearest to us was indeed a weed to the ignorant. Rabbit tobacco, introduced to me by a Gullah grandfather on Saint Helena Island when I was on a fraud case. I'd developed a cough, borderline bronchitis, and while interviewing him, he'd given me a small bag of it to make into tea. It worked, too.

Likewise, Lumen grew mullein, used for the same purpose, often smoked instead, considered the best base for anything turned into a smoking product. The more I walked and studied, the more Lumen's talents shined. Half of this garden was medicinal with a standard crop of vegetables on the side. Yep, there was coltsfoot, an expectorant, to my right. Several varieties of mint. Sage, of course. A couple of old rosemary plants on the edge. What I guessed was skullcap had already served its time and been cut close to the ground.

"Bearberry!" I noted, the orange berries identifying the woody groundcover noted for treating urinary tract infections. *"Uva ursi."*

"Now you're just showing off," Wayne said. "Come on. Callie called us inside."

I could hardly pull myself away. It had been a while since I'd investigated anything crop-related, and I had little time to plant a much-craved garden of my own. Her field peas strategically put nitrogen in the soil, and her compost pile off to the side looked sweet as hell.

Only then did I peer up at the small tributary off Blue House Creek that ran past a dock, the pilings ancient, the deck's safety questionable. But the view was breathtaking in mottled shadows and light. The sun had turned the marsh grass almost orange. I didn't need marijuana to be intoxicated with this place. Heirs, if any, would lose their minds having this drop in their lap, or at least I would as an heir. They'd likely sell it at the drop of a hat.

"Slade!" Wayne hollered from inside.

Tearing myself away, I entered the house . . . and hesitated. If I hadn't been stunned before, I was now. Another alternate universe stole my breath, as if that were possible after what I'd seen outside.

"What is this?" I said, slow and whispered.

If one could cross Bohemian and African, this would be the result. Paintings of animals, carvings, draped cloth of vibrant ethnic design, veils on lamps, beads draped here and there, some wooden and hand carved and inches big, hung wherever Lumen thought they might add a splash of attitude. A shawl swooned across an old sofa that could be either thrift store or vintage chic. Anything neutral wasn't allowed to stand alone, and the accent colors ranged from flamboyant to complementary.

The air hung thick with a lifetime of her. Books, some classics on one shelf, the rest appearing to be handwritten from writing on the spines, filled four shelves on a bookcase in the living-room corner with more perched like cookbooks on the kitchen counter. I rummaged through one in the middle, a journal. With a random flip of pages, I read how she'd visited a woman with arthritis, the same afternoon helping Truman put up deer meat, fixing a stew with enough leftovers to feed him for a week. Then, oh my gosh, she jotted the recipe.

Transfixed, I hungered to absorb this woman. Lost in her library, I refiled one book only to seize the next. She wrote about poetry on a page, then the exceptional coolness of the nights that week, listing the changes the weather dictated for her week in the garden.

"Are you touching potential evidence?" Wayne warned.

Um, guess I was. "My bad. But you ought to read this. Not sure these journals matter, though."

"No more," he said.

"Fine, fine," but I returned to the one in hand. Incredible writing. No end to the depth and breadth of wisdom. Lumen's soul was infused in these pages, and my heart ached at such loss.

Judging from Callie's pained expression, she felt the loss as much or more.

With the nib of her pen, the ex-chief slid items around, not daring to touch some of the décor with fingertips. She slowly toured the kitchen and living area, pausing, stepping lightly as if taking in a museum display. After making the circuit of the two rooms, she retreated into the back bedrooms. Three small ones with a hall bath, if I recalled this plan correctly.

"This is wild," I said with a reverence I wasn't sure I'd ever felt. This home held Lumen Townsend suspended in time. Her presence coated everything.

Raysor peered over bottles and boxes in a cabinet next to the stove. "I bet she had quite the occupation with this stuff."

All I could think of was *Kudos to her.*

An old-fashioned white, enamel scale sat on the table, empty glass containers still in an open cardboard box with spoons and a mortar and pestle at the ready. Small baggies. A cutting board. At the other end of the table, Wayne used a closed pen to turn the pages on what appeared to be another, recently consulted journal.

"Ooh, her records." That I wanted to see. I moved beside him close enough to touch, squinting to read the tiniest ornate cursive writing. The pages explained via sketches, descriptions, and measurements, the tested recipes using the myriad of growth out back. Years and years of trial and error for teas and smokes. Nothing registered illegal to me, but there were a lot of journals.

Lumen had drawn bookmarks with colored markers, a collection of which still stood on end in a pint-sized Mason jar, and the bookmarks noted purposes: lungs, headache, female, UTI, depression, and so on. A dozen additional bookmarks tabbed sections of the inch-thick journal.

"Not seeing a ledger of clients yet," Wayne said, heading to the books on the counter, assumed to be the most used.

"Bet she didn't have one," I said, hoping to be right, that the enterprise was more of an in-depth hobby or community service than a prohibited practice. Not that it mattered anymore.

Callie hadn't returned from the bedrooms, and she hadn't made a sound.

"Be back in a sec," I said to the guys, and tread softly down the short hall.

She sat on the end of the bed in what appeared to be Lumen's bedroom, holding a scarf. The furnishings were every bit as avant-garde in trinkets, clothing, and throws. A broken rosin lamp sat on a hand-painted dresser, the chipped damage touched up with hand-painted filigrees and flowers.

"Can't really tell if she was Gullah," Callie said, looking up at me in the doorway. I had cultural knowledge of these Carolina islands, and she was right.

It was difficult to tell. Maybe if I read more of the books. . . .

She stroked the scarf. "She leaned a little gypsy, too, didn't she?"

Surely, Callie wasn't feeling guilt over this woman's death. "She was awesome is what she was," I said, with a perkiness to offset Callie's gloom. "I would kill to read all that stuff she recorded and practiced and experimented on. I might borrow one of those books, if you don't mind."

When she didn't respond, I sat beside her on the too-soft mattress. "Please tell me you aren't taking this personal. I know you're down, and that your resignation sort of backfired on you—"

"Not just me," she said. "The whole island."

I shrugged. "So what if it did. Lumen is not on you."

She was wilted but remained dry-eyed. "We believe Jason Armstrong may have confronted her." She raised her gaze off the floor onto me. "He was in the patrol car I saw. Armstrong came to Edisto with Greer. Greer came because I resigned. What if—"

"Jesus Christ, Callie, you're damn smarter than this. You're stronger than this, too. Quit looking for reasons to take on more blame. I ought to call your mother *and* your son and rat on you. Get off this pity train."

"How do you *really* feel, Slade." Her question came out flat but fell short of being insulted.

I would've felt better if she *had* been insulted. In polar opposite to this house, Callie'd lost some color. In her complexion . . . in her life. This investigation was supposed to jumpstart her back to normal, and it seemed to have only dumped more on her shoulders. We had to get her off this hamster wheel of seeing everything as her fault. "Where we headed next?" I asked, knowing what I would do.

She possessed more crime-solving skills than I did, but she'd have to be brain-dead not to see this case as more than a random heart attack. Lumen had run into the woods, tossing her gardening supplies around. But Callie had to come to any conclusions herself.

"What next?" I asked again.

"Cause and time of death need to be confirmed," she said. "I believe I'll be contacting the coroner before we leave this house."

Needing the cause and time of death made sense. On that we were in sync. But her *making* the coroner call? "Thought you said someone else ought to call him and you wanted to stay in the shadows on that part of things."

She laid down the scarf, then picked it back up to shove it in her pocket. "Didn't you hear Mr. Burnett?"

Every word, but her logic eluded me. "Maybe not what you heard. Tell me."

"Her only relation, a sister, is likely dead."

"Right."

"There's nobody to claim the body."

"Okay."

"That's just not right," she said, voice rising on the end.

Where was the detective I knew? The one who didn't let emotion cloud her investigative choices? She hadn't really been the old Callie since we'd arrived, and this flash of emotion underlined my concern. I kept seeing little fractures in her and had hoped chasing a case would glue those fractures back together, at least making a start down the path toward whole again. I wasn't sure what to say.

She continued instead. "Nobody goes in a pauper's grave anymore, and it won't take them long to cremate her and put her on a shelf. I've been down this road already and not that long ago. A man in his eighties died at the beach, Dudley Vaughn, and I stepped up for him. Wife already dead, no kids we knew of. I owed the guy for what happened to him. He died because of my last case."

She hesitated. That last case had about done her in with three deaths. I'd heard about the bad guy and the one who set her house on fire but not this one. She took this Dudley to heart, and as seemed her norm, she blamed herself. Damn it, this woman and her incessant acceptance of guilt.

"So what happened to him?" I asked, needing to know more to best understand what there was to fix.

"We cremated him. Held a little ceremony on the water. I asked to manage his estate, but a relative came forward, so I didn't get too involved. Thank God, too, since he had a place of some value." She hesitated, started to say something, then didn't.

I wasn't sure how to word this. "You met Lumen once, Callie. She isn't the same as your little old man. You had nothing to do with her death, and I bet you didn't cause his either."

She acted as if she hadn't heard me. "This house would go to shambles, Slade. People would rob it down to the foundation. Truth is, sometimes probate goes to the effort of finding next of kin but most of the time they don't. They might accept my offer to be conservator for her and her belongings."

"Which means what?" I wasn't estate savvy.

"Meaning they'll tell me anything I need to know about time and cause of death if I'm in charge of her affairs. I'd be doing a public service."

I got that part. "And with your professional background to boot, they'll confide in you right off the bat."

"Well, Charleston's coroner *is* a woman."

Her mild chuckle didn't ring true. Callie Jean Morgan was a lost soul, trying to find her way, without a compass. She wasn't sure what was right, what was wrong, and what mattered anymore. She didn't even recognize herself and seemed to be grappling at making some sort of difference. I wasn't sure what to do about that.

Wayne's boots in the hallway stepped loud against the silence. "What're we doing now?" he asked, pulling the same trick I had earlier in letting Callie call the shots. "After listening to Mr. Burnett, I say we have several angles."

I stood as Callie pulled her phone out of a pocket. "Let's go, Lawman," I said. "We'll ask neighbors if they've seen anything strange out here. There's only a handful, and Raysor already spoke to one."

"There are three," he said, taking a back glance at Callie, "and they're several hundred yards away on the other side of the trees."

Was the garden a problem? "What if they're aware there's pot?"

"We tell them they're mistaken and no trespassing," he said.

"I say we say nothing and let them dispose of the evidence," I said. "Come on. We got some neighbors to chat with, and Callie's got a call to make." Walking past him, I paused long enough to slip past the Dickinson, Austen, and Woolf books and slide three of the journals out of the bookcase, then closed the one on the table and added it to my clutch. "We'll just need to put these in the car and check these carefully later for any mention of relatives, right? Besides, we wouldn't want these magic formulas to fall into the wrong hands," I said, hoping nobody asked for them back.

Chapter 11

Callie

CALLIE WAITED ON hold for the third time, getting impatient. She hadn't enjoyed reliving Dudley's death with Slade, but hopefully the brief explanation made her friend understand. Slade had watched her like a mental patient throughout the explanation.

The Charleston coroner's assistant finally came back on the line. "Heart attack," she said.

Even after three transfers, Callie marveled at the ease in which she'd gotten through and received information. She hadn't even filed papers with probate yet, only called, stating to the probate judge's office that she'd be by tomorrow. Then she'd gotten this lady at the coroner's office and, having bet on the low-odds chance they didn't want an unclaimed body on their hands, had surprisingly acquired the cause of death.

"Nice of you to step up to tend a friend," the assistant said.

"She was a sweet person and doesn't deserve to die untended," Callie said. "I saw her the day she died. We visited the cemetery together."

"Aww. That is so sad and so sweet at the same time," the woman said.

"I keep thinking what if I'd stayed longer?" Callie gave the woman more to sympathize with, not that Callie hadn't seriously weighed those words a zillion times. "What if I'd been there for her? Can you please tell me the time of death? So I can believe there was nothing I could do? I can't help but blame myself. . . . I mean, she didn't act like she felt bad when we parted."

"Oh, honey." Fingernails clicked on a keyboard. "Keep in mind that's probably a rough estimate on the time considering how long it took to get to her, but she was pronounced at five fifteen. Death occurred roughly around four per the notes, unofficial, mind you. That island's a long ways out from here. Even if you'd been with her, not sure you could've done a thing, hon."

Callie sighed for the woman's behalf, a little for herself. Clearly an hour or more had passed between hers and Lumen's goodbyes and the estimated time of death. "What are the chances for a tox screen?"

"Zero to nil, hon. Heart attack. No investigation pending. No family doubting cause of death, and no law enforcement asking questions. But we'll hold her until you can claim her." Empathetic or not, the woman hadn't forgotten her job. "If you don't claim her in a few days, nothing against you, dear, but you know how slow probate works, then we cremate her. That's not against your wishes, is it?"

Seated back down on Lumen's bed, Callie studied the room, the kitchen and backyard still vivid in her mind. The day was aging, but the western angle of the sun came straight through the window. A ray touched the small glass lamp on the nightstand, and a prism of color came to life to decorate the ceiling as if Lumen's spiritual nature smiled down.

"No, she'd prefer cremation," Callie said, imagining the ashes scattered in the back, part in Lumen's precious garden, part in Blue House Creek, maybe across the Townsend graves. She'd have to be awful discreet about that last one. "Can you do me a favor and ask the coroner to give the body a second going over? For bruises or needle marks?"

"Hmm," came the reply. "That's highly unusual."

"She died alone with nobody in her corner. I'm not just her friend, I'm a retired cop. The least I can do is stand by her and ensure no questions get left unanswered." She sniffled again.

"Well, I'll ask. No harm in that."

"Bless you," Callie said, breathless for effect. "I'll check back in a day or two."

She hung up, having confirmed and validated that Greer had lied.

The first question was why. The second was whether to do anything about it. Lumen's death by natural causes appeared an inconvenience to the Edisto PD, for undefined reasons worth bending the truth around. Of course, if confronted, he could just say he misspoke or made a mistake.

Callie dialed again, more nervous about this call than the one to the coroner's office. "Soph?" she asked when it sounded like her friend picked up and waited.

"Yes?"

Crisp. Yep, she was still ticked off.

"May I ask you a spiritual question?"

"Depends." Softer. Soph hadn't expected that.

"Lumen Townsend."

Sophie's tone softened more. "A good, good person. Some of the best pot I ever had."

"Didn't need to hear that."

"Then pretend I didn't say it." Her tone hardened again. "What's your question?"

Callie had to be careful how she touched on this, not wanting to spark a rumor that the ex-police chief had misrepresented Lumen's death for reasons yet to be determined. "Don't you think Lumen would prefer to be cremated rather than fixed up and buried?"

The raised voice surprised her. "Absolutely. Nobody should be embalmed. Lumen would not want anything but cremation, because it reduces the body to a natural form. She needs to be honored properly. Oh my," she said at a revelation. "She had no family. At least none she spoke of. What do we do?"

"I'll check," was all Callie cared to say.

But Sophie had gone all a flurry. "This has me worried now. We might not have practiced our spirituality the same, but we had like minds in a lot of ways. I stand firm on this. Cremate her. And spread her ashes. Don't stick her on a mantle someplace, you hear? Return her to nature, like she'd want."

A big, one-breath message.

"Thanks, Soph. I really appreciate it."

A long moment of silence hung on the phone. "I'm glad you're the one taking care of her," she said.

"I'm not exactly. . . ." but Callie stopped, rethinking how to say this. "I said I'd check. No promises. There are legal obstacles."

"But you know how to navigate those."

Sophie expected Callie to handle matters, and Callie wasn't up to disappointing Sophie again. She loved her friend. Callie remained puzzled about the Stan relationship, though, especially with it still secret, but that was another issue for another time. "Thanks for confirming my thoughts."

"Want to come by?" Sophie blurted.

Like water running to level, Sophie's nature returned to her default setting. She couldn't stand animosity for long. No wonder everyone loved the woman.

But Callie had to be careful. Her friend knew everyone. . . . "I'm out showing Slade and Wayne parts of the island. Are you working at Mark's tonight?"

"Supposed to but don't have to," she said.

And that was Sophie, too . . . walking through life with her trademark flippant manner, living in the moment. So what if Callie wanted to bring Mark with her to see Sophie? That left the restaurant untended. "If Mark doesn't mind both of you being gone from El Marko's, sure, we'd love to come by."

"Bring Slade and Wayne. The more the merrier. See you at seven," she said, hanging up without a goodbye.

"Wait. . . ." What about Raysor . . . and what about Stan?

And how was Mark to run the restaurant without his hostess *and* himself?

Callie sighed. *That woman.*

She pushed aside the tiny social train wreck and returned her attention to the here and now.

"Doll?" Raysor appeared in the bedroom doorway.

"Coroner's best estimate around four," she said, showing him her phone, meaning she'd called. "Cause of death, heart attack."

"So why the lie?" he asked.

She stood from the bed, systematically reaching to smooth out wrinkles. The prism lights had faded. "Alibis would be my guess, Don."

"For who? For what?"

"For whom," she corrected. "We can't tell yet. For Greer, for Armstrong, for the Audi guy . . . for people yet to be determined. You don't lie for the sake of it."

"Do we investigate or not?"

Her brain grappled over her options.

Greer was none of her business. What he did wrong was on Brice and the town council, but they were oblivious and would not care since Lumen wasn't one of theirs. She was an inland islander, not an Edisto Beach native, making her a non-issue for them. And if Callie reported the falsehood, the blowback could be intense. Jealous agitator, troublemaker, sour grapes all came to mind.

Though no longer chief, however, she resided on Edisto Beach with a respectable toolbox of investigatory skills. If she looked the other way while a government official strayed in his duties, what did that say about her?

Not the least of reasons would be what would Lumen think? What had she said over Caroline's grave when Callie said, *What's done is done?*

No. You left what you loved. Then in remarkable literary prowess she'd quoted Virginia Woolf and winked.

But the *no* was what resonated, as if Lumen had felt Callie's life still held options.

She gave the bedspread another swipe and noted a book on the nightstand. *Letters of Emily Dickinson.* Amazing that Lumen read classics written by depressed white women.

Callie moved to that side of the bed and opened to an herbal decorated bookmark. Lumen marked in her books, too. Flipping through pages, Callie's eyes gravitated to the assorted underlined wording until her gaze stuck on a line.

After great pain, a formal feeling comes.

The title and first line of a short poem. Only three stanzas. The ending stuck most, and Lumen had underlined it three times.

As Freezing persons, recollect the Snow —

First – Chill – then Stupor – then the letting go –

As if back in the cemetery, she could imagine Lumen reciting these words like she'd recited Woolf. Same theme about overcoming life's problem. Did she struggle with issues of her own, or was this reading to gather means to assist others?

"Doll?"

She snapped back to the deputy.

He leaned on the doorframe, fat fingers in his pockets. "Just waiting for you to wrap your mind around your thoughts." He shifted upright. "You're fighting with yourself. It ain't my decision to decide to investigate. Not my jurisdiction, not my province, *not my circus and not my monkeys,* as I heard you say. I have no more authority than you. Frankly, I came here *for you,* not the case, so tell me what you need. Get off your ass or send us packing."

He hadn't spoken gently, and his scolding slid under her skin a bit. "Hush, Don."

"Nope. You're getting in your own damn way. Decide. There's no such thing as middle ground here."

He was right. Investigating was an all-in or all-out activity.

Apparently, he wasn't done, either. "This isn't just on you, Callie." Not Doll nor Chief. Her real name caught her off balance, and when she reacted, he stared back like a parent waiting for the kid to come to their senses after a lecture on reality.

"You sound like Thomas," she said.

"I sound like everyone who ever met you on this beach and across this island, but you don't listen. We're sick of this limbo shit."

"Excuse me?" Now he sounded like Sophie. She didn't need this.

The familiar clomp of cowboy boots came through the back entrance. "Callie?"

"Back here, Wayne." She spoke firmly, eager to move past Raysor's version of a discussion and past the glare between them.

"Get out here." The Lawman sounded worried.

Callie eased past Raysor, turning his wide girth sideways to let her by, a grunt sounding in her ear. She met Wayne and Slade at the front of the hall, their attention on the front window. "What?" she asked.

Both of them breathed heavy from running. "Greer's man just drove past, slowed, probably noting your car," Wayne said.

Armstrong must have followed from the beach. He'd been diligent doing it, too, because after parking at the church, they'd traversed the woods, and practically hid out at Truman's house for almost an hour. The officer hadn't been around long enough to know the minor trails of the area, unaware one could get to Blue House Lane from the Presbyterian Church. He had probably waited around for them to exit the church or pastor's office, when instead they'd slipped cleanly into the woods in case people were watching, unaware of Armstrong canvassing .

Good thing they'd retrieved Callie's car, and Raysor had ridden with them, his car parked at Truman's. Nothing Armstrong could do about Callie, but he could make trouble for Raysor.

She kicked herself for not expecting his tail.

From Truman's accounting of yesterday's events, Lumen had seen Armstrong on the road. Once he found out where she lived, he'd have assumed she just walked down Blue House Lane to Truman's house, unaware of her visit with Callie at the church. Still, nobody aware of what she knew and how she knew it.

His surveillance broadcast his concern about their activities, though. "Did he see you and Slade?" she asked the Lawman.

"No," he said.

Slade brushed a tress from her forehead, still catching her wind after the run. Her fingers found a twig in her hair, and she picked it out and pushed it in her jeans pocket. "Nobody was at the closest house," she said. "When we returned to the road to find the next house, we spotted the patrol car and darted into the bushes. He crept along, hunting. He'll be back. No doubt he saw your car."

Callie hurried to the front window, grateful for the three levels of veils and sheers. Armstrong pulled in behind Callie's SUV. "There he is. Let him only find me. Y'all scoot out back. Now!"

Raysor didn't argue and left, but Slade stood fast. "Why can't you have someone here? He's aware we're staying with you. Maybe omit Raysor so he doesn't get in trouble, but we don't matter. We're visiting friends."

The locked front doorknob rattled.

Callie wasn't convinced. "You told Greer who you work for. Get out of here."

"I'm staying," Slade said, then motioned wildly at Wayne. "Go outside. He'll feel less threatened with two women."

"Hello?" Armstrong yelled. "I see the car, Ms. Morgan. You in there?"

With no more time to argue, Wayne darted outside, and Callie opened the door. "What can I do for you, Officer Armstrong?"

Armstrong had too much chin to be handsome, his eyes almost black and too cool, with a slight air of contemptuousness. A pair of moles near his hairline. Generally, a miniature visual of Raysor and almost the same age.

Seeing him in the familiar uniform rubbed Callie wrong, but she self-corrected.

He used his traffic-stop voice. "You are aware that the owner of this house is recently deceased?"

Callie had her array of cop voices, too, but this wasn't the time to brace a cop. "I'm very much aware. The surprise about knocked me down. She was a friend, and she never complained about her heart. It was a heart attack, right? I heard someone with the Edisto Beach PD was there, but you're aware of how reliable street talk can be. Was it you by any chance?"

"I cannot confirm nor deny that sort of information, ma'am."

"Not to give me, her friend, some solace? Did she go peacefully?"

"I repeat, Ms. Morgan. I cannot—"

"Well, I did," she said, tired of his crap. "Confirm, that is. After speaking to probate to be Ms. Townsend's estate representative, I spoke to a very nice woman at the coroner's office."

She took a breath, letting her firmness fall over him. "I'll be handling her affairs. I'm taking inventory and making sure nothing valuable remains as temptation for thieves, not that she had much. On the contrary, she was one of the most non-materialistic people I've ever known."

After that soliloquy, she poised, waiting for his response to a scenario he clearly hadn't expected.

Slade chose the moment to make herself known. "Hey, officer.

How do you do? I'm Carolina Slade, close friend of Ms. Morgan. I didn't want her coming alone so close to her friend's passing, but she was concerned. It's just so rural out here, but you need not worry about her."

She rubbed Callie's back, then in a dramatic afterthought peered at Armstrong. "May we have your card? I mean, in case we need anything? Or anyone breaks in or vandalizes the place?" She held out her hand.

Armstrong couldn't quite decide which woman to speak to, much less what to say. He reached into his front shirt pocket and hesitated before choosing to give the card to Slade.

"Jason Armstrong," she read. "What a strong name. Sounds like a good name for a policeman, doesn't it, Callie?" She used the card to cover her mouth. "Wait, is it police person? I get so confused these days."

"Officer is fine, ma'am."

She snickered. "Of course it is, and you'd think I could figure that out." She slipped the card in her back jeans pocket, sobered, and eased closer to Callie in a sign of protection.

Both stared with scripted patience and innocence, waiting for the man's next move.

"You've applied with probate then?" he asked.

Callie dipped her head. "Made the call. They require the death certificate to make it formal, and the coroner said that could be arranged as early as tomorrow. Trust me, I was not expecting that level of expediency."

He seemed to hunt for more to be skeptical about. He peered around them, and Slade stepped aside, following his gaze, making a path for him to inspect.

"Just us girls," she said, then shifted to a slight indignance. "But you're welcome to inspect if you don't believe us."

Callie sniffled and wiped an eye with the heel of her palm.

"Oh, honey," and Slade reached around her shoulder, drawing her up close. "I know this is difficult. You take as long as you need." Then she anchored a stare on the officer, telepathically indicating his presence no longer needed.

"Well, secure the doors when you're through." Armstrong raised a brow. "You do have a key, don't you?"

Callie retrieved the key Truman gave them from her front pocket. Locking the lock from the inside, she then unlocked it with the key, proving it indeed belonged to the house. Then she planted her own glare on him, daring him to question her more.

"Okay, then," Armstrong said. "I'll leave you to it." Then he added, "My condolences."

"Much appreciated," Callie said. "You be safe out there, Officer."

Against each other in the doorway, the women watched him leave, enjoying the fact he knew they watched him. They gave him a minute, then shut the door.

"You're dangerous," Callie told her friend.

Slade smiled in thanks but sobered fast. "No, I think *he's* dangerous. There is no need for him to follow us. If they hadn't lied about the time of death, we'd have been none the wiser. Now they don't trust *us?*"

"You're assuming Greer is in on this."

She grimaced. "You're assuming Armstrong is flying solo?"

Callie had to agree. "Can't say either at the moment. Go tell the guys we're good."

By the time Slade reached the back door, the two men had slipped in. Raysor still gave Callie a wary eye, and Wayne waited to be told what to do. Callie assumed they'd hugged the outside wall listening.

The consensus was that the new law wasn't to be trusted, and her friends chomped at the bit to prove why.

But as Callie had previously pondered in the bedroom, they remained at a crossroads. Time to dive whole hog into this case or turn their backs and let the heart attack stand.

Callie had never let a death go un-avenged, but she had no hard reason to think it deserved avenging. What obligation did she have? On the other hand, Callie had lost a lot, and this loss seemed to cross the chasm reaching out to her.

She had let her guard down and dared a friendship, and, God help her, had dared hope this woman could help her move on.

Maybe this day meant Lumen still tried from another world.

And what about her lonely, age-old friend, Mr. Burnett?

"If I'm standing up for Lumen," she said, "we find her will, assuming she has one, and search for an address book or indication of family. We use the probate laws on the books."

Relief shined on the three faces.

"Good going, Doll," Raysor said. "We don't need badges to search for truth and justice."

Slade wasn't so jolly. "But the badges sure seem at odds with us. That man tailed us, and we need to learn why."

Yeah, yeah, Callie got it. Armstrong wasn't comfortable with Edisto's ex-chief coming out of her hole and returning to life, and professional jealousy didn't quite fit the bill.

"Let's talk to Mark," she said. "Treat this like you would a legit case, people."

Callie and her entourage gave bookshelves, drawers, and kitchen cabinets one last going over for a will that didn't seem to exist. Sad how lifetimes got so easily erased, people so quickly forgotten.

Chapter 12

Callie

THEY RETURNED TO *Windswept*. Callie didn't bother telling the others about Sophie's evening plans, because she'd had to cancel them in a text. Once the team declared they'd pursue Lumen's death, the unsaid was to restrict details to a chosen few. Socializing with Sophie would not work. She'd ask questions. They'd either lie or change the subject. Sophie might get pissy. Stan would smell something. Callie's familiarity with the players wrote the script in her head, and she hadn't the energy for another controversy.

The silly thing was she wasn't sure how to approach her old friend Stan with his arm around Sophie. She remained a little hurt not having been brought into the loop of that affair and was still unsure why that bothered her. Stan was platonic to her, and Sophie her girlfriend buddy.

To be fair, Callie hadn't looped them into the Lumen investigation, either.

Sophie returned the text. *How dare you leave me high and dry.*

Three emojis trailed behind the words: frowning, scowling, and crying.

Sophie hadn't time to go to much trouble for the event, and she would've slipped snacks out of the restaurant anyway. People brought their own bottle to friends' socials, and with Callie supposedly sober, few would imbibe alcohol. Nobody was put out. This was Sophie feeling jilted, and Callie figured her friend was testy as much or more because she wanted to talk the latest on Lumen.

Callie didn't like doing this to her. She'd invite her to a private lunch later to make up. Maybe even with Slade.

Callie tried to explain. *Doing something with Slade and Wayne.*

The little dots flashed indicating Sophie typed. Then they stopped. Then they started. About the time Callie put away her phone, the text came through.

I promise not to be the fifth wheel. I'll bring a date.

Ooh, close. *Anyone I know?*

You'll see, came a swift reply.

"What're you so engrossed over?" Slade said, peering at the screen, not caring she wasn't invited to do so.

"Sophie," Callie grumped and typed, *Mark won't come if you cancel hostessing. Let's plan another time.*

The yoga mistress spat back. *Go talk your precious police business. Don't let us cramp your evening.*

No more flashing dots. She was gone.

Callie sighed and slid the phone in her pants pocket. *Son of a bitch, Soph.*

"Mark?" Slade asked.

"No, Sophie. Speaking of Mark, let me text him about meeting tonight." El Marko's was too open, too nosy, and too full of Sophie. Mark might've unearthed discovery that eager ears shouldn't hear.

Raysor and Wayne had reclined on the back porch, away from being seen on the road. Everyone took casual glances outside to Palmetto to see if Armstrong had resumed his surveillance up the street.

Around five, a knock sounded at her door. Callie'd sent Slade to the grocery store, her ability to remain incognito far stronger than Callie's, and she returned with a snack spread that would complement whatever Mark brought from the restaurant. One might expect a body to tire of Mexican, but Callie hadn't reached that saturation point yet.

Hands wiping on a dish towel, she answered the knock. She froze, stunned at the uninvited guest. "Thomas?"

"Mind if I come in, Chief?"

She let him through. "What's up?" Before closing the door, she glanced up and down Palmetto. No sign of a parked patrol car.

Without his vest and uniform, Thomas appeared smaller. One could see more of his youthful fitness beneath his long-sleeve Henley shirt. "Raysor called me. Said y'all had a meeting I might like to attend."

So much for limiting the number of people involved.

"Wayne and Raysor are out back. Beer's in the fridge."

He did a double take, stopping himself from going to the refrigerator. "Not funny, Chief. I'm not drinking a beer in front of you."

"Wasn't trying to be funny. Just trying to be a good hostess," she said.

After Seabrook, back when she wasn't too regular on the wagon, the only way she could put her demons to bed was gin and late drives along quiet streets. With people asleep and the roads empty, in her mind she hurt no one. Thomas had pulled her over and caught her lacking in sobriety. After stern warning, her baby officer checked on her nightly for weeks, relegating the task to Raysor when Thomas was otherwise occupied. Admittedly, she'd learned to think twice before getting behind the wheel.

"If you get caught these days. . . ." And he trailed off but came back with, "They'd love to catch you."

She motioned to the back. "Under control, Officer."

"By the way, I parked a block over to not raise suspicion."

She returned to the door and peered again for Armstrong.

"He's rolling this time," Thomas said. "Probably worried you'd see him."

Armstrong's curiosity was piqued. Made sense he changed his surveillance tactics.

Thomas grabbed a water and found the men.

"Just waiting for Mark now," she said, returning to Slade at the sink.

"Are we being watched? Not that I give a damn."

Callie shook her head, scrunching her nose as if the topic was childish.

After rinsing her hands from slicing up veggies, Slade reached for Callie's towel. "Nobody's drinking around you, so quit offering."

"Why'd you buy beer?" Callie asked.

"You told me to. When we leave we'll take it."

Callie tried to joke. "Enabler."

"Lush," Slade replied. "Take the tray to the porch."

A tap on the door told them their last participant had arrived. "You go ahead," Callie said. "I'll get him." She wanted to warn Mark about Sophie's behavior of late.

He came in with multiple sacks this time, kissed her quickly, and took charge in the kitchen setting up the spread. She enjoyed watching him work.

In the midst of his staging, he handed her a Bleinheim without mention of her drinking the night before.

"They're quietly shaming me," she said. "Nobody's drinking."

"Good people." He pushed the odds and ends on the bar to the side, laying out platters. "How about putting these on the table."

That small gesture . . . the one of not scolding her for last night's triple gin. The gentle strength, the unspoken but smooth expression of his caring touched her, and each time she wondered if he ever felt he gave more than he got.

He talked on about work while his hands prepped food, joking about a disgruntled diner whom he'd won over with no more than an extra taco. She laughed at the right moments and wished she could break down that wall that kept her from giving him all the sentiment he deserved.

A flush of blame shot through her after he flashed her a sideways smile, his attention quickly taken back to his work. She raised the ginger ale to her cheek and temple to quell the feeling.

"You okay?" he asked.

"Yeah," she replied, lowering the glass. "Can't wait to catch you up to speed."

"And vice versa." He laid down his utensils, about done with his work, and wrapped arms around her, the drink pinned between them. "Listen, the badge doesn't make you the chief, Sunshine. All this does. The questioning, the artful watching—"

"The snooping."

He gave her his lazy smile, the one that meant nothing else was on his mind but her. "Yes." He squeezed her once more and let loose. "The woman who held the job is still the same woman who doesn't. I want you back to feeling good about yourself."

She wanted the same. Every time she turned around, someone mentioned how things used to be, what had happened since she left, what wasn't being done anymore . . . what people missed or what wasn't done right. "Part of everyone's problem is they don't like change."

He nodded. "Of course it is."

"You forget they have a chief, and there's no easy way to ask him to leave. He's hired, not elected." Her sarcasm rang in a lone clipped laugh. "And good luck convincing Brice to oust his buddy."

"Enough of that. Go get your posse. Mexican food isn't worth a damn cold, and that chilly porch isn't the place to eat it."

Not to be prompted twice, the crew piled in easily enough once Callie opened the door and the aromas beckoned. Soon they sat around the dining table, chat directed to food. Mark had set up fast food to look like cuisine on real plates, with real utensils.

In remorse that Stan and Sophie were missing, Callie remembered she hadn't told Mark about Sophie's temper after the shirked dinner. "Sophie covering for you at the restaurant?"

"Yes, ma'am. Came in moody, but I'm accustomed to her drama. I never ask why."

"Smart," she said, taking the passing plate of tacos from Slade.

Thomas fit in like he belonged, and theoretically he did, but Callie had wanted to keep him safe, which meant distant from Lumen's case. Of the group around this table, he had the most to lose and was the one most prone to lose it. He was also the most eager to speak up, eating the fastest and cleaning his plate first.

"Armstrong has made you his project," he said, wiping up salsa with the last bite of a burrito. "Not sure about Greer, but those two spend an absurd amount of time together discussing how to police the town." He shrugged. "Or so I assume that's what they talk about. We don't have staff meetings. We only get orders. It's the Pon Pon people"—he held a palm up flat to his left—"and the rest of us." The other hand went up on the right.

Callie noted he didn't call his new boss *chief* and took some selfish pride in it. "Anything else?"

His eyes switched, just like that, from confident to defensive. "I mentioned your name one time and was told you were history. Marie keeps her mouth shut, nose to the computer, arriving at eight and leaving at five."

"So Armstrong's his right hand?"

"For sure. I'm almost in the way, assigned whatever they don't want to do. That promotion to sergeant you put me in for never made it through, either."

"Say what?" She stared around the table, seeing if the others considered this just as obscene as she did. Thomas's promotion had been her last official act. "They give you a reason?"

"Budget," he said. "Council said it cost so much to hire the replacements that they didn't see a promotion in the cards quite yet."

Gobsmacked, she knew the math, and it didn't add up, unless. . . . "They lost a chief and two officers. They hired a chief and two officers. What am I missing, or should I ask?" The only answer to the equation being that the replacements cost more . . . thanks to Brice.

She looked at Raysor, the seasoned Edisto cop at the table. "Don?"

"What are you staring at me for?" the deputy said. "I don't read the budget."

Her temper simmered like a smoldering campfire waiting for someone to throw pine straw on it. "You always know everything, Don." She'd spent all day with the man, and he hadn't mentioned this?

"I got dumped, remember. Plus, it's *his* story!"

"I told him not to tell you," Thomas quickly said.

Son of a bitch. Had her resignation ruined *everyone's* lives? On autopilot she rose from the table and marched to the front porch, absolutely disgusted with Greer, with Brice . . . with herself.

Before her husband died, she'd reigned as a Boston detective. Life was good then, she thought, staring down to the ground eighteen feet below.

Or was it? She lived for work, not her marriage. Stan would vouch for that. He'd been there, righting her compass at every turn after listening to long tirades about how she had to shield her son from all the bad in the world. . . . Stan reminding her that he'd learn about it sooner or later. But when her daughter died of SIDS at six months old, what remained of her marriage withered to nothing, only she wouldn't accept it. Neither would her husband. It was just neither one of them understood what to do next.

When he'd died, they'd been giving each other the silent treatment for days.

She'd escaped to Edisto, at her father's direction. Being here was supposed to put her back to right. Since then . . . so much more loss.

The screen door creaked. She glanced back to see who had drawn the short straw to put her pieces back together and retrieve her, but nobody was there. Must be the breeze.

She wasn't ready to say life held no redeeming qualities but couldn't deny an unexpected emptiness these days. The retirement from cop to benign citizen, who no longer had to feel guilty for the bad things or deal with politics and idiots like Brice, had instead morphed her into a guilt-ridden nobody whom everyone hated, pitied, or cared less about.

Was she still running from life and the bad things that happened on her watch? Like she had when she ran from Boston after her husband died?

Hands rubbing her face, she took in she had no place else to run. Then she remembered Beverly's offer to be Middleton's police chief. How insane was that? Or was it? Just saying she took the offer, would she be running away from Edisto, or toward opportunity?

Crap, she couldn't tell.

Jesus, was she seriously deliberating working for Beverly Cantrell? What new kind of hell would that be?

An Edisto cruiser rolled the speed limit from her left, four houses down, her old habits having honed her traffic awareness.

She wasn't running this time. Straightening, she stiffened her arms against the railing, watching him. Armstrong slowed but kept moving, observing her hard, then the cars in her drive, the house, then back to her.

Callie put on a smile and waved.

That wasn't running away, was it?

Chapter 13

Callie

ARMSTRONG CONTINUED trolling east on Palmetto Road, Callie's triumphant front-porch moment gone. After scratching into her hair, her fingers ran down to rest on collar bone as she pondered how to go back inside where her four friends waited for her to get over herself. A nip traveled in off the water, and she shivered.

She was better than this. When she returned inside, she needed to have a plan so that she hadn't just run outside to be dramatic. Blowing out, temper in check, scouting the road one more time for Armstrong, she counted her blessings Sophie hadn't been here. Her performance atop Callie's would've been unbearable.

Plan, Callie. What's your plan? Retrieve your senses and walk back in like whatever show you just put on is regretted and gone, the energy redirected into a concept they could use.

She could offer to speak to Greer head on about Thomas, but the young officer would ask her not to. She had no clout. She had no pull. Like a high schooler asking his mom not to talk to the teacher, her assistance could prove more toxic than helpful.

She'd ask Thomas's and Raysor's opinions first. They'd been the most affected so why not shift attention to them. She'd been a fool robbing them of it.

With a big inhale, she returned inside.

The table had been cleared down to glasses, and Wayne had fixed himself a coffee.

"Chief," Thomas said, when she reached the table, "please don't worry about me."

Raysor peered at the junior officer. "She ain't worried about you, kid."

Wayne tapped fingers on his coffee cup. Elbow on the table, Slade leaned, chin in her hand. Mark piddled around with details in the kitchen.

She could see they felt sorry for her. What did she expect inviting them over only to lose her cool when the banter soured. Not soured, exactly. More like turned serious, speaking of the obvious. Change had happened. Change that Callie couldn't readily fix now.

For a moment, she wondered what Seabrook would think, then in an instant felt horrible for Mark. But Seabrook understood the town's dynamics, its personnel, and had held the talent to smooth anyone's ruffled feathers. Mark had been state law enforcement, but he'd had less exposure to these sorts of shenanigans from the internal side of things.

Damn it all, she couldn't have a single thought without wondering what was wrong with it.

She peered over at Mark. He was right here. He was safe. And he hadn't covered what he learned from SLED. "Mark? Let's start this mess over. What did SLED have to say?"

"Wait," Thomas interrupted. "I didn't cover everything before you . . . earlier."

Apologetically, she turned to her favorite officer. "Sorry, Thomas. Finish."

"Greer and Armstrong asked about Wayne and Slade."

That woke up Slade, and before Wayne could ask for clarification, she did. "I knew we shouldn't have told Greer who we were last night at dinner." She turned on Wayne. "How many times do I have to say we function best on a need-to-know basis? We are Callie's friends. That's all they needed to hear, but no, you had to spout off you were Senior Special Agent blah-blah-blah."

Nobody dared remind her that she'd coughed up her credentials as well.

"The head cop of Edisto was at our table," he said. "You don't go into someone else's territory and not let them know. It's professional courtesy."

"We were here for personal reasons," she said. "I wouldn't have spoken up if you hadn't, and I wasn't going to be seen as just the girl on your arm. But, Lawman, Greer used our titles to remind Callie she no longer had one." Her arms crossed. "I felt bad for her."

She spoke as if Callie weren't there, and Callie wasn't comfortable being made the victim There'd been enough attention on her already. "What did you tell Greer?" she asked Thomas, to avoid reliving last night's dinner. All that was water under the bridge.

"I said they were just friends until, like Slade said . . ."—he waved a finger at the Agriculture duo—"he repeated what y'all told him at dinner. He asked was I aware the feds had shown up on Edisto's doorstep without giving him the courtesy of notification."

Wayne gave an I-told-you-so look at Slade.

Thomas continued. "I repeated they were old friends, there as civilians. I'd heard they were getting married and were probably visiting about that. Maybe planning something at the beach."

Slade drank on her ginger ale, turning it up as she mumbled past the bottle, "With all this water? Hunh, last damn place I'd get married at."

Everyone at the table had witnessed firsthand Slade's fear of dark water on the Indigo Plantation case where she'd avowed herself a died-in-the-wool landlubber.

"But he didn't buy it," Callie finished.

Thomas shook his head. "No, ma'am, he didn't."

"When did he talk to you about all this?" Wayne asked.

"Last night. He called me at home. Y'all definitely have his attention."

"At home?" Slade said. "Why would our being here rattle him unless he feels guilty about something?"

Callie turned to the only person who might have an answer for that. "Mark? You got through to your people?"

"Oh yeah," he said. "I got through. There's history between SLED and Pon Pon."

"The town of Pon Pon or the PD?" Wayne said. "What county is that?"

"Craven County," Slade said first. "Not much there. More of a wedge of ground between Charleston and Colleton. Some agricultural value, but I've not had a case down there as of yet."

Mark nodded. "SLED has had eyes on Pon Pon's PD. It's not the quaintest nor the cleanest of the state's small towns, but nothing serious ever came of complaints."

Slade squinted. "Unless I'm mistaken, the fact SLED just looked at them says something."

Grinning, Mark nodded once. "Yes, it does. Let's start with our friend Armstrong."

Everyone hung on his words, some over the table, others resting back, each hoping this would be good.

"Three excessive force charges," he said. "All were dropped by the complainants. The guy I spoke with says no doubt there were others not reported. Armstrong is a *strong-arming* sort of person, to repeat his assessment."

"To think I told him what an appropriate name Armstrong was," Slade said. "Surely, there's more than that on him. Any of us could warrant that."

Wayne laughed. "Says the lady without a badge. Excessive force isn't like on TV. You get charged with that and it rides your record. Mine's clean. I bet Mark's was clean."

"It was," answered the retired SLED agent. "But I left before things got heated between politics, the public, and cops."

"Anyway. . . ," Callie said, drawing the group back since they were finally getting somewhere.

Mark read notes on his phone. "Greer came to Armstrong's defense every time, but what my man said was that the shooting was particularly notable."

Raysor frowned. "Shooting?"

Callie'd fired her weapon a few times in Boston . . . a couple times in Edisto. That was way more than the average LEO, so she just listened. Wayne did, too, having been in her shoes as well. One of his bullets had crippled his ex-wife per a late-night chat Callie had had with Slade. The woman had turned criminal, but criminal or not, how did one handle that burden?

"SLED got involved with the shooting," Mark said. "Armstrong ran down a fentanyl dealer who turned mouthy. Armstrong swears he thought the man was armed."

"He wasn't?" Raysor asked.

"One would think he would be. The guy went for Armstrong's weapon. They fought. The gun went off. Greer said he saw it all. No other witnesses."

The group-think silence said each person could see how such a situation might play out. They also recognized potential for easy cover-up. "That's it?" Slade asked.

"On that, yes. Unofficially, as you might deduce, Armstrong is a hothead. The guy I spoke to says he's frequently a loose cannon in Pon Pon but loyal to Greer who cleans up behind him. Greer may have a habit of covering up."

Nobody interrupted.

"A judge in the area is a sot," he continued. "He hit a motorcycle and killed a kid. Turns out the kid was drunk and had weed on him, enough to distribute. Greer investigated the scene, then called the Highway Patrol who couldn't dispute Greer's report. The kid had no record. The family made some noise then suddenly didn't. The judge is still on the bench."

"And beholden to Greer," Raysor said. "Some of my kin have tried to pull that with me. Cover-ups, I mean. I no longer get a Christmas present from a couple mommas."

"Moving on," Mark continued. "The talk is that there's a protection society of sorts in that area. The police, the mayor, a county council member, and certain business owners and landowners. They run things in Pon Pon."

"What about the sheriff?" Callie asked. In a rural county, the sheriff often wielded the most power, and while they didn't always have control of towns and cities, a bit of a pecking order evolved. Said power impacted elections, funding, formal and informal politics. Craven County's sheriff had been there for decades. He wasn't so clean himself per the rumors she'd heard growing up in her father's politics.

"Nothing said about the sheriff," Mark said.

This story was as old as the hills. There wasn't a small town in the world that didn't have a firm coterie in place, an inner circle that managed the law, politics, and economy. Sometimes those cliques served the greater good. Sometimes they protected individual interests. They were big fish in small ponds where nobody on the outside cared enough to do much about. Like the infamous Severs case in Aiken County, it took multiple murders atop of someone growing too big, too pompous, too greedy, and over his head in million-dollar debt for state law enforcement to step in. That family had flaunted their power *ad nauseum* to the point they made mistakes, so they got caught. The fallout of that clique of folks remained ongoing and would for years.

Thomas hadn't worked anywhere but Edisto, though. "Don't we have sort of a closed group? Why wouldn't the law enforcement and politics and key businesspeople be leading a town? That's how we run Edisto."

"It's a fine line, son," Raysor said. "Used for good or used for bad, and you can cross the line in a heartbeat."

"Whatever it is any of those guys"—Callie's voice pulled gazes back to her—"and their cronies have going on—"

"Had," Slade said. "They're not in Pon Pon anymore. Which is weird."

Callie continued. "They could have had their hands in anything from land development deals to drugs to internal protection of each other's worlds to kickbacks. Could just be nepotism, or as crooked as skimming public funds. Who you know is a very real deal."

"Like we have Brice," Thomas said, still trying to define the black-and-white of it all.

He lifted a chip from the bowl Mark left in the center of a placemat. Raysor sucked on his teeth, his thinking trait. Callie couldn't read Wayne, his modus operandi, but what he didn't express, Slade always did.

"Still not getting this," she said. "Let's say they had this little kingdom in Pon Pon, South Carolina, and these guys built this mini mafia. All these men . . . I assume they are all men?"

"As far as we know," Mark said.

"Okay, we have this mini redneck mafia. I bet they grew up in those parts and spent their lives there. Probably have parents if not generations planted in the local cemetery."

Mark nodded. "Correct. Born and reared there."

She threw up her hands, holding them out wide. "Then why do you leave a place where you have it made, in the autumn of your life in the case of Greer, in the prime of your career in the case of Armstrong? Bottom line, who pulls up roots and unties all those connections to move to, of all places, Edisto Beach? What am I not getting?"

Raysor did a little mouth shrug. "It's rather bigoted not to wonder about the girl, too, you know."

Callie chided herself for the oversight. "You're right. We haven't discussed the woman on that team. Where does Anna May Greer fit in?"

Slade fell right back into her rant. "Anna May leaving Pon Pon makes more sense than the men, but even so, she would be a legacy in Pon Pon and as a woman, an easy shoo-in for future chief. Did she come along because she's *that* connected to her daddy? That's a little weird."

Thomas proffered an answer. "She's not so bad. And I think her father didn't want to leave her behind. She lives with him, you know."

Slade panned the crew. "How old is she?"

"Twenty-nine," Thomas replied. "Old as me."

Slade winced. "That's a little old to still be living with daddy. Either he's really protective or she's not a very strong cop."

Wayne just shook his head at the quick analogy.

Mark scrolled his phone. "We checked her out, too, y'all. Word has it she got the job as a favor to her daddy."

"Like we said, mini redneck mafia," Raysor repeated. "Bet however they functioned in Pon Pon just shifted here."

The incredulity on Slade's face drew a smirk from Wayne. "Please tell me she's not involved with Armstrong. How long's she been a cop?"

"Almost a decade," Mark replied.

Slade shook her head in disbelief. "They sound rather incestuous to me."

"We have no proof of any of that," Callie said. "Doesn't matter though."

"Not sure it doesn't," Mark replied. "Bedrooms make for unusual allies . . . and enemies."

"I'm not feeling that vibe," Thomas said. "Sure she grew up around the guy, but not sure that carries into the sexual. Not feeling that at all."

Callie sighed. "Well, you would know better than us."

Everyone took a second to think about Anna May. Sounded like Brice had asked Greer to relocate, then Greer asked for the rest of his team to fill the other empty slots. Stereotypical behavior standard of small-town living. Slade's incestuous remark rang closer to truth than not.

Slade feigned a shiver. "Girl may not have her head on straight, if you ask me."

"I haven't had a problem with her," Thomas added, almost defensive.

"Of course you haven't," Raysor said, prompting snickers around the table. Thomas wasn't nearly the gigolo folks professed him to be, but he looked cute enough to give people the thought. "She's a looker. You're a flirt. When you taking her out?"

Thomas reddened. He blew out hard and crossed his arms, refusing to answer.

The guessing game continued though. Suppositions ran rampant, each talking over the other. Callie deduced it all in a one-liner. "Like I told Raysor, motive for lying is invariably rooted in a need for alibi. We just don't know for whom and about what."

"Other than that ass Armstrong," said Slade. "Subtle as a damn hand grenade."

"The white Audi guy, too," Mark added. "Meeting on a secluded dirt road screams secrecy."

"And who says Greer didn't send those two to communicate so he had culpable deniability?" Wayne concluded.

"Wait, wait, wait." Slade fanned her hands, palms up. "We're treating Anna May like she's ignorant, y'all. A tool of the men. I'm proof you do not underestimate a female. If she isn't covering for them, she has to have organic knowledge of Pon Pon dirt."

Thomas twisted his mouth. "I don't know. . . . If we talk to her, she'll talk to Armstrong or at least her daddy. I'd bet money on that."

The unanimous deduction, however, was this. Greer and Armstrong had left behind muck in Pon Pon. The why eluded them. Did that make them good guys evading something, maybe still stuck with old Pon Pon habits, or bad guys wanting to do their own thing on fresh turf?

Edisto held no clear attraction for the two men that anyone could see, and nobody cared to paint Anna May with as broad a brush. She was young and kept her head down doing her job as Thomas kept saying.

"I went out there, by the way," Thomas said. "Where Lumen died. Just wanted to look for myself since they'd shut me out."

The remark turned all heads. "And?" Callie replied.

"Hard to read what happened, but there were several different tire marks on one side, like they'd parked there. No houses within sight. No telling what happened. Sort of sounds like Armstrong's brand, doesn't it?"

Callie wasn't sure that helped much. She'd tell him later how they had already canvassed the scene without him.

As to Brice, a catalyst to all this if one thought about it, his driving force had been to replace her with a comrade, but she doubted Brice understood Greer and Armstrong as much as he thought he did. He hadn't a cop mentality, and he was an easy dupe.

"Brice isn't the brightest bulb on the tree," Raysor said, surprisingly in sync with her thought. "So he doesn't know shit."

Thomas spat a chuckle at that. "Duh!"

While Brice was not her favorite person, and maybe her opinions were clouded by their history, he helped run Edisto. His decisions impacted the whole town and reflected on his judgment. Excited about the luxury of a friend in power, he might not try to understand the oddity of a chief leaving a thirty-year position in a legacy town to start anew in an even smaller town.

A lesser option, one that natives presumed an automatic attraction for any chief fifty or older, was retirement. A chief could put in a year or two then sink bare feet into the sand for the rest of his life. Pure myth, though. Nobody before Callie had retired and remained in town. Made Callie wonder for the first time if Edisto had washed out more police chiefs than her.

There was also the outside chance Greer had an ailment and sought a simpler slide toward the autumn of his life, but would Armstrong and Anna May tag along for that? Were they that unable to stand on their own two feet back in Pon Pon without Greer?

A hard fist fell heavy on the front-door glass. Everyone jumped.

Callie's first thought went to Sophie, with Stan in tow. He could pound like that, and she glanced over the bar to measure the leftovers. She would welcome the couple, endure the dressing-down, then pull up chairs, and fix them a plate. Best get this over with. She rose to get the door.

But when she entered the hall, she hesitated, at first not recognizing the man behind the glass.

Then she did.

He banged again.

Stealing herself, she opened the door. "Yes, Officer Armstrong. What can I do for you?"

A couple of chairs scraped behind her. They'd heard.

The timing gave her an eerie sense Armstrong was aware what they'd been up to. He looked angry enough to have heard it all.

Chapter 14

Callie

ARMSTRONG WORE a hard stare, his serve-a-warrant stare.

The officer wasn't tall, but his vest atop his stoutness shouted a willingness to tackle anyone of any size, and Callie's diminutive stature only seemed to empower him.

Mark touched Callie's elbow, letting her know he was there.

"I need Thomas Gage," Armstrong demanded, his toes almost on the threshold.

The squatty man spoke with a force that stabbed Callie wrong, and when he moved to step across uninvited, she moved in sync, blocking his effort. "I don't recall asking you inside, Officer Armstrong."

His complexion darkening, he stood fast, hands on his utility belt as if the shift in stance would make a better statement. "An officer of the law is asking admittance for official reasons. And right now I need to see Officer Gage, so that gives me—"

"No right whatsoever," Mark said, then caught himself. "Sorry, Callie. This is your home."

He'd come to her defense before, in public, back when she was in uniform, and it had been a temporary rub between them. The apology made up for it, especially in front of Armstrong.

"We're eating dinner, Officer Armstrong," she said. "Is this an emergency?" She didn't offer to get Thomas, invite Armstrong in, or assist in any manner. If this wasn't an official visit, whether Thomas was there was none of his damn business.

By then, Raysor had made his own hefty presence known. He was built like Armstrong, only thirty percent bigger, and he threw his shoulders back to show his awareness of the difference.

Thomas appeared on his own, though. "Yeah, I'm here. What is it?"

"Chief needs you."

"What's up?" Thomas asked. "I'm not on duty, but if there's an emergency—"

"I don't make the chief explain himself. He just said he needs you, Kid."

The condescension sent a hot rivet of anger through Callie, but this was Thomas's play.

Thomas read his phone screen and held it up. "He hasn't tried to get in touch. We're not big enough on Edisto for—"

"Do what you're told, Gage." Armstrong had no grasp of nuance, his brow furrowed deep giving the order.

Raysor moved in closer, the doorway becoming snug with bodies. "Wait a damn minute."

"Excuse me, Chief," and Thomas moved forward, between Callie and the officer. "I don't work for you, Armstrong. This ain't Pon Pon, and you're not assistant chief."

From behind, Callie laid a hand on his shoulder blade and whispered, "Thomas."

As she expected, Armstrong wasn't having the lip. "Boy, don't buck the boss. He needs you at the station. If you came to fetch me, saying the boss beckoned, I'd jump up and go. You best do the same."

The porch light came on, by Mark's hand. Now Armstrong was lit up for the Palmetto Boulevard population to see. Wouldn't take long for people to begin flicking on their porch lights and notice the police car.

"I'll message him I'm on my way," Thomas said, and turned to Callie. "Thanks for having me to dinner, Chief." Then to Mark, "Appreciate the food, man." He moved out, nudging past Armstrong to the stairs.

"I'll escort you—"

Thomas spun back around. "The hell you will. You did your job, and you're no part of mine. Unless this situation is an all-hands call, you did what Greer asked, and you're done." Then he left the porch and trotted across Palmetto toward wherever he'd left his old lightweight pickup, the night swallowing him up.

Armstrong started to leave, without as much as a thank-you or goodbye, but Callie wasn't having it, not after that inhospitable demonstration, plus, Thomas needed time to leave without being followed. "Armstrong!"

"Callie, don't," Mark whispered.

"Hell, let her," Slade said from somewhere behind them.

The officer turned to the crew, saying nothing, but his rutted brows almost met over the wide nose, waiting for whatever Callie had to say.

"Thomas is an excellent officer," she said. "He'll work with you if you give him half a chance."

The man only stared.

"He was dining with us because my friends are in town."

The man still didn't respond.

"What the crap is wrong with you?" she asked, tired of the game.

"Why would Gage park a block over if this was only dinner?" he said.

"Because you've been stalking me, and he wanted to save me the trouble of having to deal with you. What is your problem?"

What brand of paranoia was this? She started to lay into the guy with a scalding rant, but she'd rather not waste her time, nor give him any further suspicion or reason to make Thomas pay.

"Good day, Mr. Armstrong," she finally said and shut the door.

Armstrong clearly cherished being Greer's errand boy. Callie had no reason to believe the man hadn't come at Greer's direction.

Armstrong had been the one on Blue House Lane speaking to some unknown entity, doing something questionable enough to lie about. He had no need to be at Lumen's house later, either. And for some reason he was tailing Callie.

"He's Greer's flunky, all right," Slade said.

"Makes one wonder whether the Blue House Lane meeting was Armstrong's idea or Greer's," Raysor added.

Standing in the hallway, Slade, Raysor, and Mark discussed interpretations of the moment, with Wayne having hung back the entire time, ever quiet. Callie, however, moved through them, without engaging, and sat back at the table, finding her phone.

While they hadn't designated him as such, Thomas was an inside source now. She wouldn't be able to call him off now that he had the bit in his teeth either.

Be careful, she typed.

She got a thumbs-up.

Let me know if Greer really asked for you.

Another thumbs-up.

Do you know where Armstrong was yesterday?

He replied, *AM on traffic like me. Disappeared after lunch. Radioed him once, but he was off island. He had Anna May assist me.*

What time?

He replied quickly. *Three-ish. Can confirm with the ticket I wrote.*

She mentally dropped that into the timeline.

Slade spoke over her shoulder. "Not sure that helps us."

"Except to validate I did see Armstrong about that time," Callie said, putting away the phone.

The group had quieted, pondering how to delve deeper. The dinner was supposed to be time to map things out. Instead, tonight had turned into little more than a flurry of conjecture. Heart attack didn't speak to anything nefarious, but the damn lie about the time of day did. Truman Burnett said Armstrong had clandestinely met someone at the same time Lumen died. Callie wondered if Armstrong had a wife . . . or ex-wife who hadn't gotten over him, though God only knew why. The Audi man could have been an attorney, or a private investigator, a whole potentially different explanation, the issue maybe more personal.

The simplicity was that Lumen died in the woods, and she had to travel past Armstrong to do it.

"Lumen or no Lumen, something isn't right with that man," Wayne said, breaking the silence. "Lumen just put a spotlight on him." He spoke as if he'd been reading her mind.

Slade was quick to add, "Not that Wayne's belittling Lumen's death, Callie."

Callie waved her hand, assuring both she hadn't heard him that way. "Mark? Can you dig deeper with your contacts?"

"I can try," he said. "I left enemies as well as friends at SLED, and I don't need the two to clash."

"Who couldn't love you?" Slade said.

His grin held a darkness. "Trust me. There are a few."

This was the first time he'd mentioned enemies. The longer Callie spent with Mark, the deeper his history sounded. He held a reluctance to talk family other than his origins being Louisiana Cajun. He deflected during pillow talk when Callie dared inquire. Probably why he asked little about her past since to do so meant he had to share. Such secrecy would ruin other relationships. To her, that kept their relationship noncommittal and safe.

A voice spoke from the other end of the table. "I'll make a call or two."

Everyone turned toward the federal agent. "You sure?" Callie asked. There was a reason people joked about making something a federal case. Once they got involved they didn't back out.

"I'm sure," Wayne said. "Better me than Slade. She's more vulnerable in her job than I am."

Slade frowned. "Not really. I just don't have his connections."

"Thought you were buds with the governor?" Callie prodded in jest.

Slade repelled the thought with an animated grimace. "You want him in your business?" She didn't let anyone answer. "No, you don't. You involve those types, and you owe favors."

Raysor's brows piqued. "You owe the governor?"

"No, meathead," and Slade flipped her hand to brush away the thought. "He owes me, and I'm not ready to cash in that chip just yet."

"Damn," he replied.

"Don't listen to her," Wayne said, turning to Raysor. "Hey, you know everybody in this region. Do you reach as far as Pon Pon?"

Callie got up to refill her glass, her mouth dry. "It does seem that clues lead us there, Don."

He mashed his mouth tight, as if he had to think harder than normal. "Might know people who know people, but I've got no strings to pull, if that's what you mean. Nothing like your lady friend there." He reared back. "The governor, huh?"

Callie opened the fridge, reaching for the ginger ale, thirsting for the gin. "Anyone need a drink?"

"Seriously? A real one?" Slade said, clearly judging.

"Whatever you want." Then to spite Slade's babysitting, Callie went for the gin in the freezer, and before anyone could judge, she poured two fingers in her ginger ale glass and carried the bottle to the table, setting it with a *thunk* for the others. She sat, the first swallow of gin going down so damn smooth before she had a chance to cross her legs under the table.

Slade looked shocked. "I didn't mean for you to—"

"What's the plan?" Mark asked, taking the bottle, pouring himself a splash, then setting it further from Callie. He wasn't allowing the alcohol issue to sideswipe what they were there for.

They couldn't guard her twenty-four seven, but bless Mark for the discretion in her own house . . . or rather Seabrook's. Shaming filtered through at the thought. Seabrook had tried to get her into AA to the day he died.

She shut down the memory. "In the morning, I'll be at Charleston probate when the doors open to start the paperwork," she said. "Wayne and Raysor can visit Mr. Burnett again. See if he remembered anything after we left, but more importantly, tell him to call us if someone harasses him. Armstrong reeks of bully. Lumen exited his drive, so Armstrong might go back."

"I was thinking that," Mark said. "I'll remain behind at the restaurant, business as usual again, but I'll make one more call to SLED."

All had stood except Slade. She laid elbows on her placemat. "What do I do? Hang out with Mark all day? I'm feeling rather left out here." Mark had started clearing the remnants of utensils and glasses, and she lifted her glass before it was taken. "Why can't I go with Wayne and Raysor?"

"From what I saw earlier today, the old man will talk easiest to us," Wayne said. "He's old school, Slade."

Mark called from the kitchen sink. "You're more than welcome to hang at the restaurant. I'll snack you to death."

Slade sucked the last of her gin off an ice cube. "At least *somebody* loves me."

The four made light jokes about activities she could do like swimming, kayaking, fishing, all involving dark water, but nobody came up with an investigative task.

"I won't be long at probate," Callie finally said. "You can ride along, but there won't be much to do."

Raysor made his way to the living room and flopped in the armchair. "Sorry but I'm already doing my Lumen casework while on the sheriff's time clock. Mascots not allowed."

That prompted a round of laughs.

"So how is Wayne going to meet you?" she asked, joining Raysor on the sofa.

He doffed his head toward the others. "He'll have to meet me out there . . . say, around ten? To give Truman time to wake up?"

"I can do that," Wayne replied.

"Leaving me with no car." Slade's sigh rang dramatic. "Oh, I'll be fine." Another sigh, making Callie smirk. "Since none of you needs a sidekick, that leaves me to wander the town looking for trouble."

"A natural talent of yours," Wayne said, coming over to give her a quick hug to his side. "Pick up shells for the kids and get some exercise. A mile on the sand is a heck of a lot harder than a mile on a track."

"Who says I can do a mile on a track?"

More laughter. Between the drink and the jokes, Callie's spirits rode higher than they had since she'd quit. To be honest . . . before she quit.

"So what'cha actually going to do with yourself tomorrow, *Green-bean*?" Raysor said loud enough for all to hear, aiming at Wayne's nickname for her.

"It's Butterbean," she said. "He calls me Butterbean. And I'll do the beach thing, probably. As long as I don't have to get wet, I'm good. I live on a lake, you know. Water's pretty as long as you're looking at it from the land."

"Chief Brody . . . from *Jaws*," Mark said.

She shook her head. "Nope. *It's only an island if you look at it from the water.* I'm not about to get on or in the water. But you're right. Me and Chief Brody are like this." She held up crossed fingers.

More fun. Callie wished she had something to assign to Slade, and she regretted leaving her friend alone. "Sure you don't want to come with me? I'll buy you breakfast in Charleston. Ever eaten at Toast? Breakfast all day long." She'd enjoy girl time with Slade. They could talk the pending marriage that seemed to be ever pending. Callie'd just have to weather the counter queries about her and Mark.

Slade winced. "I don't know. What time are you leaving?"

"Seven, most likely."

"Which means getting up at six." Slade scrunched her nose. "I believe I'll hang here. Besides, someone will be back by lunch. First one here feeds me."

"First one back might be waking her up," Wayne said, sliding in on the sofa beside her.

Again, Slade raised her hand with crossed fingers. "Me and Churchill, too, I'm telling you. We hate mornings. Bet you didn't know he ran England from his bed until eleven, so y'all don't bash genius."

When Callie finished laughing, she went to fold up the dish towel at the sink, finding Mark watching. "I love seeing you laugh."

Admittedly, she felt good doing it. "That woman cracks me up. I'm so happy she dropped in."

Slipping his arm around her waist, he beamed. "I'll have to get her to give me lessons, Sunshine."

She slipped her arms back around him in kind. "You're good in your own way, Mr. Marko. Don't think you have to change. And I'm sorry I've not been much good to you lately."

Leaning in, he went for a kiss, soft and simple. "We're getting there, Sunshine. We're getting there."

She returned one of her own, relieved he felt they were making strides. She couldn't remember when she'd ended a day on a note as good as this.

THE NEXT MORNING Callie left early, no sign of movement from the guest room. Even with eggs in the refrigerator and bread in the pantry, she expected Slade to head to SeaCow for her breakfast. There wasn't a better morning meal on the beach.

She stepped out with shades on. In August, a sun this bright would be a killer scorcher, but in October it coated the day in a soothing warmth. Tide out, the ocean murmured lazily, matching the lack of human activity. Too early. This almost-off-season time of year gave Edisto a softer, homier, less commercial feel.

Tourists were an economic necessity. She appreciated the financial support they provided. They paid her salary . . . *used* to pay her salary; however, she didn't have to love the chaos they brought with them. These people traveled from far and wide, bringing their cultures and habits and love for creature comforts with them. Some enjoyed the elementary lifestyle of Edisto while others loved the thought of it, becoming bored three days into the stay. They soon hunted for chain restaurants, Uber, bars with all-night music, and plug-in stations for electric cars, finally heading to Charleston for more upscale entertainment. Visitors trying to make their vacation livelier on Edisto often became those the police visited most.

Out here, when sidewalks rolled up around nine, many families wondered what to do with one another.

No, this place wasn't the standard vacation, and never a weekend-type getaway. It was a week-long break of doing nothing but sinking into nature and one's own mind. Not everyone had that level of patience in them. This solitude was what Callie appreciated most.

But today merited leaving paradise. She rolled past Blue House Lane with a twinge of sadness and quickly passed Seabrook's grave at the Presbyterian Church.

Death. She despised it. Some days it consumed more of her memories than the opposing bliss of friends and family everyone preferred to brag about. Her scales weighed heavily in the opposite direction of most people. Today, she made a conscious effort to push through those feelings, because she was accomplishing something, and God had gifted her a beautiful day to do it in.

Morning rush hour caught her on the outskirts of West Ashley, and she synced into the start-and-stop behavior, reaching downtown about the time she expected. Still taking a while to park on Broad Street, she was happy to find a place on the street and not in a garage two blocks away. She took her time walking. Pastels of coral, beige, and cream reflected the morning sun on pre-Civil War properties adjoining each other like Legos, wrought iron on some windows, flower boxes on many, balconies hanging over the tops of small shops. People paid a fortune to rent above those shops in order to claim they lived in down-town Charleston.

The Holy City had become a tourist mecca for the world. To some like Callie, the growth saddened her. A lot of the genuine Southern gentility had been replaced by the force-fed feel of imported commer-cialism. To natives, Charleston would always be the touchstone by which the South defined herself, the good, the bad, and the ugly, and would ever be remembered as it was before the traffic and bustle of the modern world invaded.

She entered the building at 100 Broad, smack-dab in the middle of the downtown peninsula. She entered the quasi-modern building in an old-town façade, how everything in Charleston tried to present, and after asking directions, she took her seat behind two others, ten minutes after the place opened.

She scrolled on her phone to see what she needed other than a death certificate. In a city as large and synchronized as this one, surely they had online access to the coroner's office. Guess she could have done a lot of this online, but her experience was that eye-to-eye netted more results.

She approached the counter, expecting the place to smell stale and oppressive from the continual cattle drive of people attempting to wind up death, manage demented seniors, commit the mentally challenged, and oddly enough, grant marriage licenses. Sophie would cringe at such a confusion of kismet. Surprisingly, the place smelled pleasant.

A gentle-looking woman in her forties smiled, making Callie wonder how many times a day she offered condolences. "May I help you?"

"I'm here to open probate for the estate of Lumen Townsend of Edisto Island."

The lady slid a form to her, listing all the forms and documentation necessary, the first being the original death certificate. After that, forms depended on how many creditors, the value of Lumen's assets, other heirs. . . .

"She has no will, and there are no heirs," Callie said. "At least that we can find."

The lady wasn't obstinate or rude, just robotic. Callie hunted for a name to even the playing field and become more personable. *Lane Abernathy* said the name plate behind the window.

"My friend died day before yesterday, and she had no family. Her name is . . . was . . . Lumen Townsend, on Edisto Island." Wait, she already said that. She sounded nervous.

Out of nowhere, a feeling of selfishness zinged into her about what anyone might deduce about her not being family, maybe sensing materialism. People could be ruthless about death, but Ms. Abernathy hadn't given the first micro expression indicating such. Then an ache about Lumen being gone too young sprung up along with a melancholy that Callie might be the only person who dared come into this place and inquire.

"She has real estate, right?" asked the woman.

"Um, yes." Odd assumption. Not everybody owned property.

"Does she have creditors?"

"Um, not sure."

"Why is it you are filing probate again?"

Callie's opinion of the office slipped a bit. "One, because she's dead. Two, because I'm her friend. Three, because her closest friend is ninety years old. Four, there isn't anyone else."

Ms. Abernathy's expression slipped, too, showing a shadow of doubt. Understandable since she'd seen fraud and attempts at fraud waltz up to this counter a zillion times. Death brought out the greed in folks.

"That's odd," Ms. Abernathy said, in a practiced, safe demeanor. "Someone just called about her, and I mean like they hung up two minutes before you walked in."

"Seriously?" Damn, the woman could have led with that remark. If there was an heir, then fine. In that case, Callie could be grossly overstepping. Her intention wasn't to capitalize on a thing. "I'm sorry but can you say who? I wasn't aware of any heirs, and I'd be happy to get in touch with her, him, whomever. I just didn't want Lumen to be forgotten . . . wanted to give her a respectable send-off and ensure her belongings were treated properly. But if someone is related. . . ."

As soon as she spoke, Callie worried this woman had probably heard that spiel before, and she started over. "Let me try again. I'm Callie Jean Morgan. Just retired from police chief of Edisto Beach." she said, hopefully infusing credibility. "Lumen and I spent the day she died cleaning graves at the Presbyterian church on the island. I feel obligated, if that makes sense."

Ms. Abernathy's smile hung like a mask. Either she had a trained habit or a sincere concern for people who came in at their most vulnerable, but it was trained enough such that Callie couldn't predict the woman, raising her heartrate a notch. With Ms. Abernathy being people's first impression to Charleston probate, she'd skillfully learned to keep the public settled to avoid the emotions of loss, injustice, or in this case, embarrassment.

"As a matter of fact, the caller was your successor," the woman said.

"Police Chief Lamar Greer?" Callie added.

Ms. Abernathy nodded.

Callie gave her best smile of relief.

"Yes, he's not long been in the job. This is his first death since he arrived. They are aware I knew Lumen."

But a shadow fell across the greeter's expression. "He warned me you'd be coming."

Callie's smile fell at the word *warned*. "Why would he do that?"

"Not sure," Ms. Abernathy said, "but he didn't sound too happy about it. Warned you were taking advantage of the situation, seeking personal gain."

"He what?" spilled out of Callie before she could catch herself.

So much for giving Greer any benefit of the doubt.

Chapter 15

Slade

THIS WAS THE morning of all mornings when I could lie in bed until noon, as Wayne joked last night. I'd intended to do just that, but between Callie rising pre-dawn and Wayne's shower not long after, sleep escaped me. Eight o'clock wasn't early but was still a far cry from what I intended.

"Sure wish I could go with you and Raysor," I told the Lawman, joining him on the porch. His lack of answer was his answer. He could look so chilled, and coffee cup in his hand and boot propped on his other knee, he seemed the epitome of cool, calm, and collected. The slight squint of his eyes and the crease on one side of his mouth told me otherwise.

Even if I didn't dare dip a toe in it, I'd learned that damn ocean could be mesmerizing, but he wasn't studying waves. "What're you thinking about so hard?" I asked.

"Everything," he said, taking a sip, his gaze affixed on the water, no doubt Greer and Armstrong on his mind.

"We have a body dead of natural causes, with no empirical evidence to the contrary," I said. "You sure these guys aren't just assholes?"

While I served as the girl who described situations in dramatic movie scenes, also as Wayne loved to say, our brief bit of detective work remained mired.

"There's nothing altruistic about these guys," he said. "And there's no need to lie, that we can see. Unexplained acts like that drive an investigator crazy. Dig, dig, dig . . . you gotta know why. There's something we aren't seeing."

His spider senses churned.

"The who, what, when, where, why, and how," I said. "And we're missing the *why* most of all. Like Callie said, somebody needs alibis. Guess that means we're missing a *what* or two as well."

Lawman went back to watching water.

"They aren't used to being clandestine, are they?" I said, preferring he interact.

"They aren't used to being called out, you mean. We are an unexpected fly in their ointment." Finally, he let loose of his stare and focused on me. "Don't go off half-cocked on any of this, you hear me? Something about all this bugs me big time, and I don't need to worry about you amidst it all."

Boy, had we parked at this crossroads a number of times in our history. He tenses up on a case, tells me to back away, only for me to find a reason to delve deeper. He knew it. I knew it. We discussed it often, but nothing ever changed. We both wondered if it deterred our wedding plans, too. Yet he had moved in with me. What difference did a piece of paper make, for that matter?

Why was I so nervous about setting a date?

Not going down that path, I tugged my phone out of a too-tiny sweatpants pocket and flipped through my contacts.

"Who're you calling?" he asked, meaning in other words, *What are you up to?*

I quit letting his wariness upset me a long time ago. He knew me and my reputation well; plus, he cared for me almost to a flaw. There were worse relationships. "Texting Sophie. Might tag me a breakfast buddy. If she's already eaten, maybe lunch."

He rose. "Be careful. If you see Brice, Greer, or Armstrong, do not engage, please."

"Not my turf, Lawman."

"Since when do you observe property lines?" He ran a finger up my chin and tugged my earlobe. "Just be careful."

"Yes, sir," I said, feeling the text come through on my phone. Instead of reading right away, I watched him leave. I always liked watching him walk in those boots. "Be careful out there with Raysor."

Walking away, he gave me a loose wave of assurance. So damn sure of himself. I loved that, too.

Back to the phone, Sophie's text took a different turn than I expected.

Yoga at nine. Will go to SeaCow after, but only if you come work out. Got a mat for you.

Well, that most certainly backfired. I could run, though not as well as in my younger days. I could even play a decent game of tennis, or had until about four years ago. Dang, had it been that long since I'd formally exercised?

The only leggings in my suitcase came with a long tunic and a small hole that severe stretching might exacerbate into revealing my assets. Touching my sweats, I was wearing the only other option. Gray sweats and a long-sleeve Clemson tee.

Whatever. This was the beach, and off-season at that. To see Sophie, I had to run as is . . . after brushing my teeth.

"Wayne! Wait!" Luckily, he heard and dropped me on his way off the beach, or I'd have never made it.

Sophie trended high on Edisto's coolness list. First, nobody looked as trim or acted as expressive, however hard they tried. Yoga gave her a lithe, easy appearance . . . and the honed fitness infused her with energy. She made everyone feel the center of attention. Secondly, she taught yoga like no one else, going all out with candles, bells, and her outfits a sundry of sultry colors, tights, and bracelets. She was a wonder to watch, and more than a few men, and women, attended to behold her.

To the tourists, her classes at the Pavilion, a bar by evening, with its doors and windows open to the gulls and waves, made for the primo yoga experience and a great touch to a vacation. Students were already seated cross-legged on mats when I rushed in, trying to gulp down my panting from running up the steps. Candles flickered, and music lightly hung on the air. Our instructor dipped her chin and made a gentle fluid arm motion toward an empty mat right in front of her. Weaving in and out, I made my way, and as I plopped onto the mat, Sophie began her lesson.

Yeah, make it obvious I was the late one.

She opened the class with calming, deep breaths. Then she told us to stretch legs straight out for a forward fold, tapping into our heart chakra, she said, telling us to mentally say positive things to ourselves. Whatever. I could barely keep my huffs and puffs in check. She eased into poses I couldn't name, the first couple within my realm. The half-spiral seated twist should have warned me. Downward dog was harder than it looked. Thirty minutes through, sweat trickled down my jaw. This crap was hard!

Tree pose. Warrior this and warrior that and planks. Half locusts. More downward dog and something called a half monkey.

Wondering if I was the only oddball, inept girl in the room, I glanced at my fellow contortionists when a twist or turn or almost-standing-on-my-head move allowed me to, wishing my butt flaunted itself to the wall and not to everyone behind me. I reached harder around my shoulder, trying to show some sense of agility while taking count. Thirteen women and two men, from thirty to sixty-plus.

Sophie winked to me, then shifted her eyes down the line I was in. Giving personal attention, I guessed. Or rather giving me credit for not having passed out.

We started another pose, something to do with a boat, and in my reading her for the right move, she winked again, progressing down the line again. She wasn't winking at anyone else.

On the next pose I thought my pelvis would crack in two on something innocently named pigeon pose. No damn pigeon ever looked like this. A vertebrae popped in protest.

Sophie rose and made rounds amongst the students. When she reached me, she lightly pressed on my lower back, indicating I could take it lower. When my hips snapped out of socket, maybe she'd see the insanity of her demand.

Nobody else grunted.

Sophie moved in closer, voice low and soft like with everyone, only she got right next to my ear. "To your right," she said, and left.

She continued on, and I eased a glance to my neighbor. Pretty, female, blond, thirty. She struggled way less than I did, but the glisten on her upper lift gave me satisfaction. What was I supposed to be looking at? Maybe a role model not too incredibly out of my league?

Not soon enough, we relaxed into Savasana, meditating. A seated position, breathing, hands over our heads. That one I mastered.

"See y'all next time. *Namaste*," Sophie said, smiling, nodding to each student leaving using a tranquility I'd never witnessed in her. She really loved this stuff.

The blond next to me rolled up her mat.

Sophie doffed her head toward her. Okay.

"Hey, I'm Carolina," I said to the stranger, using the name only my mother used. Slade was too memorable and events too tense on Edisto these days. "I'm visiting this week. How about you?"

The girl smiled, her manners on a rein, without expecting to follow through on a friendship. "Just moved here."

"Lucky you." I showed the appropriate astonishment, having learned a long time ago that not everyone uprooted and moved to the beach. Natives carried a slight sense of royalty about them, the ones who legitimately acted on their dream.

"Nice to have met you."

Still no name. She watched the last people exit and started to do the same when Sophie stopped her. "Coming to breakfast like last time?"

The woman glanced at me, as if she wished I hadn't heard.

Sophie noted. "Her? She's coming, too. She's a friend."

I tried again. "Like I said, my name's Carolina. . . ." partly so Sophie heard.

"Y'all come on," Sophie said. "Help me put away the candles, and we'll head on over to SeaCow."

Just like that, we were roped together. *Slick, Sophie.*

Sophie drove me to the restaurant one block over and two blocks down, her antique, powder-blue Mercedes convertible barely ten years younger than I was. The girl followed in a white Kia maybe five years old which told me she was a resident but not wealthy, or else she tooled around the beach in a backup vehicle. Salt air wreaked havoc on a car, so anything expensive was a waste.

With the weather too cool for the screen porch or open deck, Sophie ordered a table inside, all the SeaCow staff welcoming her, with Sophie asking each about their boyfriend, child, or health issue. She had the charisma to be mayor, just not the desire. Nor did she possess the necessary discretion regarding fragile situations. although Brice's existence called into question whether discretion in a public official mattered all that much.

Even with the air filled with the aromas of bacon, coffee, and syrup, Sophie ordered a yogurt. Our friend chose two eggs and wheat toast. I took the oinker route of a full omelet breakfast. Exercise gave me an appetite.

We sipped on coffees, waiting. "What brings you to Edisto?" I asked. "You're too young to retire. Sorry, but I missed your name." I was going to get it one way or the other.

"This is Anna May," Sophie inserted. "She's one of the new police officers. Isn't that great?"

Oh wow. What were the chances? "Yes, female police officers would be a real asset here." Suddenly, Sophie's winks and nods made sense. Duh on me. "I work for USDA. My fiancé and I are visiting friends for a few days." No point in revealing details, and hopefully Sophie understood to play along. USDA meant food inspections to most people.

"I'd ask who your friends were but not sure it would matter. I'm still learning my way around," Anna May said. "Carolina, you say?" Maybe fishing for my last name.

"And Anna May, right?" Doing the same.

I don't give you my last name if you don't give me yours. Thing was I knew hers.

"I come here a few times a year," I said. "And I have to eat at SeaCow just about every morning. Note my fiancé isn't here. He's off with a buddy, so I called Sophie to see if she wanted to hang." I scoffed. "And she ropes me into yoga!"

Sophie gave me a light pat on the hand. "You need to take it up permanently, Carolina."

I shrugged. "I keep saying I will, but. . . ." Then to Anna May, "You seem to do okay on the mat. You done this long?"

"No, only my third time. Sophie talked me into it. Said I'd learn more about Edisto and fit in with the crowd better."

"Sophie's queen of this island," I said, to which Miss Yoga shot us a plastic grin. "Where are you from?" I asked.

"Probably never heard of it. Pon Pon?"

My turn to grin. "Gotta remember who I work for. Agriculture. Of course I've heard of it but can't say I recall anything remarkable. No offense."

Anna May laughed. "None taken. I was all too happy to leave Hooterville. At least here I'm nobody's daughter or second-grade student or the cheerleader who split her panties in the game against Beaufort High."

"Escaping, huh?"

"You have no idea," she mumbled, and I took note.

"Like the sand better?"

"It's a job," she said.

"More crime here or there?" I wasn't letting her loose. "You hear nothing around here. I mean, I've seen lights and heard sirens, but it's always much ado about nothing."

"That's pretty much it," she said.

"When's the last real crime around here?" I turned to our mutual friend, as if Anna May seemed too green to know.

Sophie leaned in over her cup. "Witchy Woman died this week."

I reared back. "Say what?" I turned to Anna May for elaboration.

"Heart attack on one of the island roads," she said. "Not sure about the witch part, and not labeled a crime."

To which I laughed and tipped a chin toward Sophie. "Trust me. If there's another witch in these parts, *she* knows." Back to Soph, I sobered. "Were you close? I'm sorry if you were."

"We had a union, Carolina. Sometimes I swore we mentally connected. The afternoon she died, I sensed this, this. . . ." Her hands spread clawed like she groped for words. "Darkness."

"Ooh," I said, urging her on. Anna May tried to pretend she wasn't all ears, her gaze in her cup as if something swam in there. "Was she calling for help?" I whispered.

Sophie leaned in closer after peering at neighboring tables. "As clear a cry for help as I've ever experienced."

"See?" I said to Anna May, then back to Sophie. "When did she die? Did you check on that? To see if what you felt matched?" But before Sophie could answer, I asked Anna May, "When do they think she died?"

"I have no idea!" Her snap shut us up.

Food arrived. Sophie and I sat back. We ate in silence until almost done, hoping our officer friend would come around.

"Don't see many bodies, huh?" I said to her, hoping that leaving a piece of toast on my plate reflected some degree of abstinence. "Not like television?"

"Sorry," she replied. "They don't let me work those cases."

"Oh, honey," Sophie said. "All-male club, huh? Our old chief used to feel that way. I was close to her."

Anna May shook her head in short twitchy bursts. "Not allowed to talk about Callie Morgan. I can't do more than traffic, but I'm the least experienced. Every place has a pecking order."

"Unless you like swimming with the dolphins, not sure why you moved here, then," I said.

"Looking for a way out, ladies. Just looking for a way out." She peered around the room. "Do they bring you a ticket or what? I've got to go."

"On me," I said. "You go on. Thank you for your service."

Her expression hung on the edge of uncertainty, but when Sophie patted her hand, she succumbed to a smile and left.

"What have you been up to, yoga lady?" I asked my new partner in crime.

"No more than you, *Carolina.*"

I gave her my best smirk. "My, my, my, look at you and your sleuthing. Where did this come from?"

"Never poked my nose into Callie's and Mark's detective work. Didn't think they wanted me to. Didn't think I wanted to, really." A roguish little spark flashed in her azure contact lenses.

"But?"

The most devilish leer crept in behind that spark, and up went a well-penciled brow. "But when you sleep with a certain ex-Boston police captain, you sort of take more interest. *Detectiving* can be a turn-on, if you catch my drift."

Chapter 16

Callie

"I UNDERSTAND THAT this Lumen Townsend owned real estate on the water?" Ms. Abernathy asked.

Now how would the probate lady know that? No way she knew if not for Greer's preemptive phone call. "Yes. That's why someone needs to step up and handle her affairs. We can find no heirs, but that doesn't mean we aren't searching high and low for a will, a journal, birthday cards, old tax returns. Everything we can think of."

"We?"

"Other friends." Callie's pressure rose. "The woman didn't live in a vacuum. Are you telling me I cannot file to probate her estate? That house you're so intrigued with will deteriorate if it sits empty, and with nobody handling affairs, with her having died intestate, the paperwork would take years. Correct me if I'm wrong."

"Intestate means without a will."

Yes, she knew that. Ms. Abernathy remained stoic, but Callie noted the most minute little expression to the right of the woman's maroon lipstick. "But you are correct in that no will and no executor drags things out."

We agree on something!

"For years," Callie repeated. "Please hand me the papers, please."

"They're on the website along with the steps and the costs. A hearing will have to approve you. People can contest your request." She nodded toward the one-page sheet of instructions still in Callie's hands.

Callie wasn't going to argue with the woman. She left with her instructions. Apparently, you could file online, though the death certificate was not allowed to be electronically transferred, and they preferred you be an attorney to use the online system.

She thought she had a solid respect for the probate process, but she'd just learned how they could be or not be your friend. First impressions were important, and Greer had fully capitalized on that fact to give Ms. Abernathy the wrong first impression of Callie. There was no reason for his doing that. Or rather, no honest, pure reason.

For a second, but only a second, Callie pondered if she should even expend the effort of applying as executor, but the audacity of Greer to lie for no apparent reason and Armstrong's tactics of late nudged her to remain on task. Greer's preemptive shout to probate said he didn't like Callie's dabbling. That alone made her keep her nose to the scent.

Took her more time to walk back to her vehicle than the appointment had taken. Her next step would be the Charleston Coroner's Office.

Like she had with the probate office, Callie held the Charleston Coroner's Office in high regard. She'd at least dealt with them once on an older case. Out of 266 board-certified Medicolegal Death Investigators in the country, South Carolina had seven of them, four in Charleston. They were savvy at cold cases, murder cases, and efficient at processing any case. There was a lot to be said for bigger city resources.

Nothing like Boston, though. As chief of Edisto, she missed many of the cutting-edge tools that her old detective days afforded her. Boston had 2,000 uniformed officers. Eight hundred admin types. Labs and forensics out the wazoo.

All the cities in South Carolina combined didn't measure up to the population and means of Beantown.

Still, Charleston sprawled monstrously in comparison to Edisto Beach, making her grateful that Lumen lived on the island instead of the beach, putting her in Charleston's territory. Whatever the coroner's office said about Lumen, Callie could run with. Not that Colleton was slack. They just operated with less.

Just past nine thirty, Callie planned to boogie to the coroner's office in North Charleston, hoping to find her faith in them still preserved. If she'd learned anything from her experience with Ms. Abernathy, however, it was to call first. Kudos to Greer for that lesson.

A good thing she did.

The pleasant young man answering the coroner's office phone would only tell her that certified copies of death certificates came from DHEC, the Department of Health and Environmental Control. Out of luck there. He was kind but clearly a by-the-book first line of defense. Doubted she'd get past him to see the coroner without an appointment. She had originally planned to show up pretending not to know about the death certificate issue and attempt dialogue with an assistant coroner, or maybe a friendly admin type, but without any sort of authority she had no power to work with, and there was no point in compromising some-one's job.

"Sorry for your loss, ma'am. But you don't have to drive all the way to Columbia where they handle the death certificates." He did have a kind voice. Ms. Abernathy could learn a thing or two from him. "The funeral home usually takes care of that."

She didn't bother to say there wasn't a funeral home. She kicked herself for it not crossing her mind. There needed to be, though, didn't there? But if Callie wasn't family, would they let her pick one and see things through without a will? Without being executor?

"So if there's no funeral home yet. . . ."

"Coroner takes care of her in the meantime. After a certain amount of time they might cremate her and hold her until the family comes around, in which case you really don't need the funeral home."

Callie'd wondered how many people died like this, without family to tend to affairs. She guessed not many, and even then not many with assets. The dang bureaucrats sure made dying a pain in the ass.

Two more phone calls to make. DHEC and a funeral home. At this rate, she'd have to feed the parking meter. She could've stayed home and made phone calls over breakfast with Slade. DHEC bounced her to two extensions, and after holding for several minutes for the second one, a voice older than Jeb but younger than Callie answered.

"It takes five to seven days for a death certificate if ordered online," the person said. Callie couldn't quite determine male or female, as if it mattered. She just liked putting imaginary faces to voices. "Are you a relative?" the person asked.

"No, I'm a friend. Lumen didn't—"

"Sorry, but if you aren't family, we can't release an actual certified copy. Instead, you'll have to request a non-family statement that the death occurred, including the date and county. Probate ought to take it, but don't rely on that."

Smart disclaimer. They hadn't dealt with Ms. Abernathy. Callie bet the woman knew about this obstacle, too.

"But anything is quicker if you just go there and get it," they added.

The first common-sense statement made all day, but Callie wasn't heading to Columbia quite yet. She Googled *Charleston funeral home* and called the first on the list, a creepy sensation of quivery nerves accompanying the task. Nobody called a funeral home without reluctance.

As she expected, if she walked in and said she was the long-lost friend and there were no relatives, but most of all, if she had the means to pay the bill, she could do what she wanted with Lumen's remains. The problem was she wasn't family and couldn't name the first family member, who her parents were, or her birthdate. How would that look? Plus, they'd make her sign something stating she held the authority to make these sorts of decisions, and she didn't.

By ten thirty, she sat in her car pondering the difficulties of death, much preferring real bodies in the field to this bureaucratic craziness of the afterlife. Again, she wondered if she ought to become involved in Lumen's estate.

Her mother had handled her father's death. Seabrook's father handled his. In Boston, Callie handled her husband's, but that was Boston, not here, and she didn't half remember much of that year after John's murder. Stan helped out so much back then, plus the both of them had connections in Beantown, and she bet that eased her plight a lot.

But if she didn't handle Lumen's estate, who would?

In hindsight, she should've invited Sophie to the house last night. If anyone knew Lumen, she did. Sure she was flighty, but her motives were pure. Most of the time.

A will would help. Especially if it pointed to a family member who could take this over and hopefully do right by Lumen. She and her crew had looked through Lumen's house but not thoroughly. They would now. That was a good Slade task. Lumen's horticulture talents were right down Slade's alley, and in exchange for reading the journals, Slade could hunt with her for a will.

Her stomach gurgled. She really wished Slade had come, because she craved one of those delish stuffed French toast plates from Toast.

Then it hit her . . . she had an appetite. She hadn't craved food in ages.

She tried to call Slade, to see if she was up. No answer. Probably still sleeping like Wayne said.

Grabbing coffee and four chicken tenders from the closest drive-through, Callie aimed her car back toward the beach. Three bites into tender number two, she received a call and put it on speaker. "Hey, Thomas, what's up?" Her young officer was calling the chief, just like old times.

The four-letter expletives flew like angry seagulls robbed of a meal.

"Whoa, whoa," she said. "Start over." His loathing of Armstrong came through loud and clear. He spit out obscenities like bullets to make his main point. He was likewise ready to feed Greer to the bull sharks in Big Bay Creek.

"I'm banned from being seen with you," he said. "That's why Greer wanted to see me last night. They can't do that, can they?" Then before she could answer, he shouted, "Stupid sons of bitches can't own my life, but Brice gives them power so who knows what they can do, or what they've already said to him, or what plans they have for importing some other damn bully in here in my place. Really, they can't fire me for speaking with you, can they, Chief?"

"Take a breath, Thomas. Take a breath."

South Carolina was an at-will-to-work state, good for some and bad for others, with the bottom line being that employers could terminate an employee at any time, with or without cause, with or without notice. The paperwork that officers signed coming on board the Edisto Beach Police Department made that clear.

"You better?" she asked when he no longer panted like a dog on a trail.

"Just pisses me off," he said.

"I know. Me, too." She knew he awaited a reply, but she hadn't a good one to assuage his worry. "Listen, Thomas, without going into all the details of labor law in the state of South Carolina, I gotta tell you this . . . they can terminate you regardless of what you do, for any reason or none. But if you don't do as they order, they'll terminate you for insubordination. That doesn't look good on anyone's employment reference."

"You're *shitting* me!"

"Where are you, Thomas?" She wondered who could hear him. Who could rat on him.

"In my patrol car, parked at the marina. Just grabbed lunch, and I'm sitting here trying to hold it down."

"Nobody with you?"

He laughed with bitter sarcasm. "Afraid to be seen with anyone. What kind of crap is that, Chief? We're here *for* the people, not in spite of the people. You and Mark and Sophie and Stan . . . you're all part of Edisto's people. I can't talk to some and not others."

Her heart pounded for him, knowing full well his ran like a racehorse. "They can still fire you, Thomas. You need to be careful."

She guessed the dull thud in the background was his fist on something . . . the dash maybe. "For how long? Like, forever?" he asked.

"Until we learn more about them," she replied, the best she could do. "Lay low and avoid me. If you text or email, keep a tight grip on your phone so nobody reads it, but you might just speak to Raysor or Stan for the time being. Hold on, Thomas. Hold on."

He threw a few more expletives around his front seat then silenced.

"You better?" she asked.

"I just wish—" but he drew himself up short.

"Yeah," was all she could say. The rest of the sentence went unsaid. *I just wish you hadn't left, Chief.*

"You wouldn't consider coming back, would you?" The question had no answer, because there was no job to come back to.

"Watch your back, Thomas."

He hung up. She couldn't tell if he did so miffed at her or not.

During some of her weaker moments, she pondered if her mother's offer of Middleton Chief of Police held potential. How was she supposed to hang in Edisto if the good folk like Thomas only saw her as a quitter at best . . . a betrayer at worst . . . selfish most of all.

She phoned Slade to decide her next move.

"What is it?" Slade answered, voice low.

"Just checking in. I didn't wake you, did I?"

"No. Spending time with Sophie. She's opening my eyes, girl. Don't feel like you have to rush back."

Curious. Sophie could open one's eyes about a lot of things. "Listen, have you heard from—"

"Gotta go. Talk later." The call ended.

So, no rush to get back and tend to her house guest. With it being after ten, and Wayne and Raysor scheduled to visit Truman Burnett about this time, it was too early to check in with them. That left Mark who, this early, prepped food fast and furious for his eleven o'clock opening. He was calling in favors with SLED by querying them, and no doubt he called them early, but none of them could expect them to jump fast in response.

She almost called Marie to check in at the station, like the old days.

With a good forty minutes or more left in her drive, she phoned home, meaning her old Middleton home, which meant her mother, which meant city hall. Beverly Cantrell lived at city hall. To wait and call her at home carried high odds of finding the woman still in her suit, jacket thrown over the sofa, her gold lamé slippers on still-stockinged feet dangling off the edge of a cushion, three martinis into an evening. Sinatra or Neil Diamond on her sound system. Dinner was optional, depending on how big a lunch she'd had at Oscar's with a political ally. She only sipped coffee with her enemies, ordering cheesecake depending on the results.

Callie couldn't believe she was making this call.

"Callie, dear, where are you? On your way to see me, I hope."

Of course that's what Beverly would think. Why wouldn't she since Callie infrequently called, and when she did, it was to drop in. Beverly occasionally came to *Chelsea Morning*, also unannounced, but mostly they texted. The texts came at least every other day. Their visits in a year could be counted on one hand, despite living only fifty miles apart.

"I'm on Highway 17," Callie replied. "On my way back from Charleston." She wouldn't go into the Lumen situation. Her mother rarely cared about a case, and without mention of the suspicious nature of the death, Beverly would pepper her with all sorts of sage advice about why she shouldn't bother about a woman she'd just met. If Callie did mention her concerns about Lumen's death, that would be interpreted as Callie clearly needing the job in Middleton to fill in her days if she had to go looking for cases. Besides, Beverly would say, her daughter hadn't said no to the job offer yet.

"Good," Beverly replied, "then you aren't on the island. Come here. Meet me at Oscar's. It's not like you have anything obligating you at the moment."

Muting the call, Callie sighed loud and hard and . . . unmuted the phone. "Okay, lunch only."

Beverly laughed. "Don't make it sound like it's such a burden, dear. Every daughter needs the occasional lunch with her mother. See you there in an hour. We'll beat the rush."

The call ended. Beverly always had the last word.

Chapter 17

Callie

OSCAR'S HAD BEEN a mainstay eatery since before Callie arrived on this earth. Upgrades changed it here and there throughout the years, an outdoor section under patio lights added as well as a private area for parties, but the main dining room—still flaunting its original walnut paneling and booths, low light and white table linen, soothing music piped in as if time had stood still since the fifties—served as the go-to for Middleton's socially conscious. Ministers, business owners, politicos, and blue bloods dined regularly, most in no need for a menu.

In broad daylight, without the ambient lighting, the place showed its age, much like the regular diners, many of whom belonged to families dating back generations. Worn flooring and nicks in the tables, the occasional crack in the booth seating, but there was a certain respect to the place which attracted a crowd that liked respect, too.

Beverly sat at her regular, four-person table in the middle of the dining room with coffee on a saucer. Anyone coming in had to almost hug the wall to avoid speaking to her. One didn't ignore Beverly Cantrell. She sat there as mayor, holding informal court, noting everyone who came in and with whom, reminding herself whom she needed to call when she got back to the office. To be fair, the diners usually chose Oscar's to be seen, the result being eleven a.m. to two p.m. serving as the restaurant's showtime, the main dining room discreetly reserved for the usuals.

Beverly had no alcohol today. Callie wasn't sure if the coffee was a good sign or not. Could be Beverly's nod to her daughter's effort to abstain. Could be Beverly's way of showing the world she could turn the drink on and off at will, like most functioning alcoholics thought. Could be someone else would show up to join them since Callie's appearance was rather impromptu.

The aromas clung so familiarly to her bringing memories of so many meals under this roof. Something about the seasonings. Not spicy, not fried, not ethnic, just memorable. She spoke to three tables before weaving her way to Beverly, the regulars still honoring Callie as a legacy of the Cantrell clan. Finally, she slid into a chair. "Hello, Mother."

Beverly raised a finger, didn't even lift her hand. The waitress brought a water and hot coffee for Callie, a fresh coffee for Beverly, leaving with the used cup.

"I assume you already ordered for me," Callie said, when the waitress didn't ask for her preference.

"That menu hasn't changed in twenty years. I know what you like."

Her mother wore a soft gray suit, the cream in the blouse to match the pearls, and hair coifed by Nancy's on Doty Avenue once a week. She adhered to a certain formality in her office, and though some could say outdated, others admitted the attention to dress emulated the attention to standards expected of her office by the citizenry.

Few could criticize that. Middleton had been run like a well-oiled machine by a Cantrell, in one role or another, since just after the Civil War. One of Callie's Southern ancestors had managed to recover the town from the control of carpetbaggers. Cantrells had always been known for their negotiation skills, with her father's talent the most respected of all. His funeral had attracted both U.S. senators, the lieutenant governor, and hundreds more. Callie remembered it like yesterday. The guy who'd run her father off the road had killed him to spite her.

"Coffee's really good today." Beverly sipped from hers, set down the cup, and eyed her daughter. "You look better than I expected."

"Well, thanks a lot for that, Mother," Callie replied, choosing to drink the water just because her mother praised the coffee, recognizing instantly the old pattern of obstinacy between them. This was the typical Beverly and Callie show. Nothing casual. Usually reactive. Yet, like the mayor's office in its formality, the mother-daughter duo maintained a public display of honor in the name of family.

Every eye in the room took turns studying the pair. They weren't often seen together in public.

Callie smiled at her old school principal, who remained school principal. He had to be eighty years old, and she wondered how in the world he handled today's technology, gender diversity, and the drug sophistication that escaped even the best of cops.

"Who are you smiling at?" Beverly asked, not wanting to look over her shoulder.

"Mr. Brighton," she replied, then focused on her mother. "I hope you don't interview people out in the open in here. Or talk shop. It's rather cruel putting people on the spot like this."

"It is Middleton, dear, and you of all people ought to understand." She set her cup down with nary a sound. "Speaking of interviews, did you come to discuss my job offer?"

Callie wasn't sure how to answer. Or if she had come for that discussion. "What about Chief Warren?"

Raising her brows once, Beverly leaned in. "I'm liking where this conversation is going."

"Don't get ahead of yourself, Mother."

The waitress brought their plates. It hadn't been five minutes. Crab omelet for her mother and a BLT for Callie. The omelet almost disappeared under the béarnaise sauce, and the BLT stood double stacked three inches tall, held together with decorated toothpicks with beads on top. Callie already knew the bacon would be perfectly crisp, the tomatoes from a local greenhouse, and the mayonnaise only Duke's. This place would go down un-budged from its Old South roots.

The sandwich would taste damn good, too.

They ate for a couple moments, smiling at various folk coming and going, Beverly occasionally nodding or raising her fork in acknowledgment.

Callie finished a quarter of her sandwich and wiped her mouth. No way would she finish this meal. Maybe Beverly could take half home with her.

While the earlier chicken tenders robbed her of appetite, the thick air of nuance stole more. What was she thinking entertaining Beverly's offer, because it did hit her that that's exactly what she was doing here . . . weighing her options. She'd thrown away Edisto. Where else was she supposed to go, assuming she was missing law enforcement? She had no suitable skills for other careers.

But there was Mark. Also Sophie and Stan. The choice seemed to boil down to doing nothing on Edisto while remaining close to friends or leaving her friends to return to law enforcement. That separation might as well be two hundred miles, though. Look at how often she came to Middleton now. But then, other factors fell into place there.

She corrected her posture, then hated the stiffness of manners that snapped back into place by being in Beverly's presence, a taste of what would become habit if she considered this job. Even as police chief, she'd never escape being the mayor's daughter, and how did she ever expect Beverly to give her the respect she needed to get the job done right? God, she could already recite the names on the mayor's untouchable list.

"I can almost hear you think," her mother said, dipping a bite of omelet in the sauce. "You might as well say it aloud."

So Callie spoke outright. "You'd hamstring me in this job."

Beverly scoffed in a dainty yet firm manner. "Since when do I stop you from doing what you want to do? You've also never worked for me, dear. A totally different relationship. Middleton comes first."

Such words would sound trite from the average politician, but the priority of Middleton and its people was not a pretense in the Cantrell family. The town did take priority, to include *over* the Cantrell family. Town events, council meetings, and ribbon cuttings came before birthdays, anniversaries, and family gatherings. Callie leaving South Carolina after graduation to marry, God forbid, a Yankee in Boston, had rocked that family. Her not returning home to learn how to handle the reins upended generations of expectation.

Which was why Beverly leaned on Jeb to come visit so often, to learn the family ways. Yes, even grandparenting came second to the Middleton calling.

To think Callie had a perfectly good biological mother back on Edisto. A fact kept secret from her until a year ago . . . in the name of managing the Cantrell legacy.

"How do they make the bacon the same every time?" she said, to dodge the chat.

"It's called tradition and adhering to what's important. Much like accepting one's calling," Beverly replied, and Callie sensed none of her remark had a damn thing to do with bacon.

"You give me a headache, Mother."

"Ditto, Daughter."

More people focused on meals, murmurs keeping the room at a low buzz. Callie attempted a second quarter of her sandwich, but when she wiped off mayo from the corner of her mouth, instinctively glancing up to see who might've noticed, her gaze froze on two men entering the room. Both in uniform.

Callie stopped chewing, the bread half eaten in a wad on her tongue. *What the ever-lovin' hell?*

A slow burn began in her belly and worked its way into her throat. If she hadn't been followed, God and Fate and Sophie's heavy-duty Karma had teamed up against her. She dropped the sandwich, forced a swallow, and darted her attention back to her mother who appeared to have been watching the whole time.

"What is Lamar Greer doing here?"

Beverly only raised her penciled brow and reached for her cup.

To which Callie added, "And don't tell me you didn't know he was eating with Chief Warren."

Beverly grimaced at the coffee and did her finger thing for the waitress. "Warren told me he'd be here with Greer. And Greer was kind enough to phone me in advance. From what I heard, your agent friends didn't exhibit that level of courtesy when they came to Edisto Beach."

Heat rose into Callie's cheeks. Good thing the lights weren't bright. "My friends came to see me and me alone. Is Edisto reporting to you behind my back, Mother?"

Beverly shook her head. "No. Just Greer. I like him."

"Of course you would. He's one of your ilk."

Only one brow raised this time, and Beverly twisted one side of her mouth, an expression Callie despised because it meant her mother felt she had the upper hand.

"They reported to you that they'd be eating at Oscar's for what, to get your approval?"

"No, dear," and Beverly pasted on her best welcome smile and made eye contact with the men. "To see if we could do lunch together. Who'd have thought you would show up, too?" Her smile reached her eyes. "Why, hello, gentlemen. Won't you have a seat?"

Damn her. Callie almost rose to leave. Almost. She needed to know how this gathering happened, and she hoped to learn a tad more about Greer. Some suspicions were gelling, coming together like a loose collection of gases before they formed a star, and if she walked off now, she'd accomplish nothing. Worse she'd leave them to interpret her action as petty, as holding a grudge, her jealousy out of control.

The men studied the table, Warren choosing Callie's left and Greer to her right.

Why not attempt some intel gathering? Why not play the very people who she assumed were playing her? At least Beverly was. That was her way.

"Gentlemen," Callie said, welcoming, then to Greer, added, "Let Mother order for you. The menu hasn't changed in ages, and she knows everything on it."

Greer grinned wide at Beverly. "I'd be honored, Ms. Cantrell. I'm sure your tastes hold more talent than mine."

He showed no surprise at the comment of Beverly being Callie's mother.

Chief Warren was someone she'd trusted, lost trust in, then started to trust again between her high school years and present, each and every test ending in the conclusion that his decision began and ended with the simple fact he worked for Beverly. Maybe he was tired of that equation.

"You're thinking of hanging up the badge, huh?" she asked Warren.

He didn't flinch. "Retirement's been crossing my mind a lot these last few months. Wife's leaning on me to travel before we get too decrepit."

Seemed she was the only one in the dark, but Beverly hadn't known Callie would drop in. Or had she? Someone better not have tagged her vehicle, but if she brought it up, everyone would deny and label her paranoid.

"Don't retire on my account," she said, a darting glance from Warren to her mother.

"Well, would be nice to know who'll fill the shoes instead of leaving the town exposed too long," he said.

Greer nodded, nonchalant, in agreement at the logic. Three people, each old enough to be her parent, acting as if they mentally communicated on a level which left Callie too young and inexperienced to keep up.

Her job offer wasn't an unexpected blip on anyone's radar. They all knew Beverly had offered Callie a seat in the kingdom, and the universe had decided in an incredible matchmaking twist to deposit Callie in the middle of a luncheon with all the important players in the drama.

She'd still check her car for bugs.

Time to sit and let the others take it from here, and while she was mostly full, she lifted the half-eaten quarter of the BLT and took another bite. Funny how thick the air got with nobody talking.

Somewhere between the silence, the casual mention of traffic control changes for the high school football games and the need for at least two more patrol cars, the men's meals arrived. Venison burgers with fat, fresh-cut, home fries thicker than Warren's plump thumb.

Callie ordered a to-go box for her sandwich before the men finished half their burger. "While this has been fun, I have guests at the house."

"What were you doing off the island, dear?" Beverly asked.

"Running errands," Callie replied. No way would she mention she'd been to the probate office, which would only open up Greer's warning to them about Callie. She started to push her chair back.

Warren laid a hand beside her plate. "I'd appreciate it if you'd replace me, Callie. Honestly, I would be damn honored for a Cantrell to assume control."

"See?" Beverly said, having been more quiet than her usual. "Told you I wasn't pushing him out. Come work for me. We're all aware you're not in love with politics, and I'm not holding my breath you'd replace me in my role, regardless the family history."

Callie passed a cynical eye roll toward Warren. "Please don't lie to me and tell me this could work . . . me working for Mother."

"I wouldn't be lying," he said, and she felt he meant it.

"I wouldn't be lying either," Greer added.

Heat climbed up her collar. How did he think he was entitled to an opinion? He hadn't been Edisto Chief for two minutes and had probably met Middleton's political duo just today.

This was enough. "What exactly is your role in this lunch drama?" she asked him. "Y'all couldn't possibly know I was headed this way, so this was something proactive on your part, Chief Greer. Reaching out to my mother to find a place for me somewhere out of your hair, I assume, to get me out of your way."

Her mother frowned. "Callie."

"I'm not employed by nor beholden to anyone at this table. I'll say what I please, especially when it comes to you butting into my business."

Greer's arms crossed his chest. "You obviously left the Edisto position prematurely, Ms. Morgan. While I'm not trying to push you off Edisto Beach . . . wouldn't dream of it . . . your presence unnerves my people because they were so loyal to you. If you held some other law enforcement role, I believe all our problems would be solved."

Beverly seemed to enjoy the explanation, her expression softening in agreement. Warren, however, remained rather benign. She'd appreciate him looking more uncomfortable than this, though.

"So I'm a problem," she said, homing in on him.

Greer didn't respond.

"Mr. Greer, you—"

Beverly did a limp finger thing toward her daughter. "It's Chief, dear."

"*Mr.* Greer," Callie continued, after a long stare at her mother. "You don't have the power to run me off Edisto Beach."

Clearing his throat, he tried to repeat himself. "I said I wasn't trying—"

"And the only people you seem to show loyalty to are your own officers you dragged from Pon Pon, and from their behavior, I don't unnerve them one bit."

"Callie," her mother said, brisk and curt. .

Callie held up a hand to her, still talking to Greer. "And my career choice and personal decisions are none of your frickin' business."

Pulse up, she started to tell him she'd confirmed Lumen's four o'clock time of death, well after his one o'clock report. She started to leap into his warning to probate. She yearned to chew him out for killing Thomas's promotion, and she chomped at the bit to scold him for casting Raysor aside.

But she didn't.

"Quit having me tailed," she said instead. "It borders on harassment, and I don't think you have many friends at SLED as it is . . . Mr. Greer."

The others at the table lost their facades, expressions sliding into disbelief.

Greer wavered a moment, but he wasn't a novice in the game, even if he did come from Pon Pon. "Callie, I understand you wish you hadn't given up the job. . . ." With a sympathetic look, he chose to leave the sentence unfinished.

She almost asked if he got that tidbit from Brice, but the remark would only underscore his stance and erode hers. So all she did was turn to her mother and ask, "Would you allow me to pay for lunch?"

"You know it's already covered, dear."

Yeah, a lot had been covered before she got to Oscar's, most of it having nothing to do with a meal. If she wasn't curious about Lamar Greer's motives before, she damn sure was now. Time she seriously learned what kind of life he'd led in Pon Pon.

Chapter 18

Slade

I FROZE AT SOPHIE'S remark, the murmur of SeaCow diners and the clink of their dishes fading into the background as I studied my breakfast partner, attempting to digest this fresh, boggling piece of dating news.

But she didn't give me enough time to collect myself. "Yep. Stan and me are an item," she said.

"I've gotta have another cup of coffee to take this in," and I raised my cup to catch the attention of a waitress.

Sophie wasn't one to sit and sip, though. When words popped into her head, they got said. "I just kept thinking what was the deal with being with a cop. You, Callie, Mark, that luscious cowboy of yours . . . and Seabrook, of course. You didn't know him. Lord Almighty, I wanted to date that man the whole time he was here on Edisto Beach, but along comes Callie and nips that option in the bud. She didn't even want him at first, but he only wanted her. The whole island kept waiting for them to get together. Damn, that was a sad story."

She took a breath. Yes, terribly sad. I was familiar with the whole Seabrook history and didn't care to discuss it.

Sophie kept going. "Then Stan literally moves to Edisto when he retires, to take care of her, like she needed taking care of. Then along comes Mark. I ask to work for him. I do everything in my power to latch ahold of him, but, no, he takes to Callie like a magnet to a car door. Finally decided I need to get me some of that, that . . . whatever it is."

I went for my coffee black this time to get the caffeine in me sooner. Callie warned me Sophie was an acquired taste. She clearly loved to color outside the lines.

At last I squeezed in a few words. "Please tell me that you aren't screwing Stan just to see what it's like to be with a cop." Poor Stan. If that was the case, he'd be hurt, and Callie would be livid at her mentor being taken advantage of.

Hand on her chest, Sophie pouted. "I'm sort of hurt you said that."

No, she wasn't. "Just answer the question, Sophie."

The yoga lady's voice hardened a bit. "Didn't *hear* a question, Slade."

Would Sophie act this ugly in front of all those zany mood rocks on her coffee table and mess with the karma or chakras or whatever it was that she claimed inhabited her place? She always said she didn't allow negative under her roof. Guess it was okay under others.

I leaned in toward her. "Do you really like Stan, or is this a badge bunny thing?"

A glower twisted Sophie's expression so silly I busted out laughing. "You don't know what a badge bunny is?" God, I wish I'd nabbed that picture.

"Cannot imagine," came the reply, her confused expression saying she wasn't sure if the designation was a good thing or not.

"It's someone who pursues sexual relationships with cops."

Sophie's forehead smoothed then twisted up in an even more comical contortion. "More than one?"

"That's the question you ask?"

"Seems like the obvious one to me." Her eyes wide, her little toned body hunched over the table, Sophie sought to understand.

I could not believe the definition remained unclear. "One at a time or several at once, doesn't matter. Bunnies go to bed with cops just for being cops. You're not using him just because he was one, are you? Just answer that."

Sophie shook her pixie shag. "No. Listen, we just sat down one night not long after Callie resigned. At El Marko's. We were all, like, stunned, you know? He wondered what I knew. I wondered what he knew. Every single one of us was in the dark. Mark wasn't saying much, and probably didn't want to say much in front of me, so he wouldn't sit with us. Everyone thinks I spread gossip, you know. I'm aware. I'm not stupid."

There was no replying to that without stepping in something nasty.

"I chatted with Stan for *an hour*," she exclaimed, "which had never really happened before. I mean, one-on-one. Once we analyzed Callie, we ordered drinks. He laughed at me. I laughed at him. It was like a release." She paused. "Okay, if I understand it right, I admit I may have had a badge-bunny moment, just wondering if that cop dominance carried into the bedroom, and I may have used my come-hither talent on him. He bit, I took him home, and, amazingly, we had a good time. We're still having good times." She leaned in tighter. "He has like six years on me, but have you ever noticed how he's built? I mean, what does he do to stay so . . . firm?"

Hands up, I saw where this was going. "Nope, don't need the details."

Sophie smiled, pleased with my reaction. "We like each other. Seriously. It's been maybe three weeks? Going on four. We've hit his house or mine at least three times a week. The first time was immensely entertaining, but the second? God, there was even one night. . . ."

I slapped hands over my ears. White-haired ladies at the table next to us glanced over, their radar pinging, so I dropped the dramatic air and simply shook my head in disbelief. "You like him?" I said, low. "I don't mean as one of your bedroom toys, but as a person."

"I believe I do," she replied, not recoiling in the least at my use of the word *toy*.

"Does Callie know?"

From the eye darting, Sophie's exuberance slipped, and the quick forced smile back at the white-haired ladies told me she didn't want others to hear. She ran her finger around the remnants of her yogurt bowl. "Um, I haven't told her."

"Has Stan?"

"Don't think so. She seems too delicate, he says."

I understood that part. Wasn't sure anyone wanted the burden of putting more negative on our friend's shoulders, with everyone assuming she would see the Stan and Sophie union as negative. Nobody wanted to test those waters, was my guess. Mark maybe. Could explain why Callie said she excluded Sophie *and* Stan from the Lumen maneuvers at *Windswept*. From what I'd seen of Stan before, Callie relied heavily on his advice, but if that now came with Sophie attached . . . ?

"You need to tell her," I said.

"Nope. You do it."

"Me? Why me?"

She licked her yogurt finger. "That would let her get over the shock factor before she sees me. Then she'll confront Stan before me. All that diffuses that fire."

Damned if that didn't make sense. "She'll respect you more if you tell her."

"Honey, please."

The ladies next door must've heard that part because they got still. Sophie dipped her finger in her water glass and wiped her hand on a napkin. "She doesn't *always* take me seriously. If I tell her, she'll ask questions just like you did. If Stan tells her, she'll hear it with a different ear. Stan has been her rock, seen her through a lot of crap, and if he tells her, it sounds more solid." She shrugged. "Trust me, I've thought about this a lot."

"Does Stan know the burden's on him?"

She sucked on her top lip a second. "Don't think so."

"Soph."

"He's smart. He'll figure it out."

God help us. God help Callie. And God help Stan. I doubted he fathomed what he'd gotten himself into.

Sophie's phone rang, and a smile spread over her like the butter that had run off my long-ago-eaten grits. "Hello, lover."

Yep, Stan.

Then my phone rang. Instinctively, I noted the time and identity before answering. The caller Wayne. The time eleven thirty. Breakfast had turned into lunch. "Hey," I said, holding back *Lawman* or *Cowboy*, not wanting to sound like Sophie. He and Raysor were supposed to meet Truman Burnett around ten. "Y'all done?"

"I'm done," he said, none too happy. "They ordered me back to Columbia."

Investigations didn't give notice, so I wasn't surprised about a new case rearing its head all of a sudden. We'd grown accustomed to last-minute changes to a schedule.

"Any chance this case is with my agency or is this from someone else?" I asked, trying to predict if I'd get a phone call, too.

"There is no new case," he said, emphasis on the word *no*.

A little zing of déjà vu coursed through me of the times he or I, or both, were chastised for exercising a bit of creativity in our investigative work. Sometimes politics came into play. Sometimes we got more creative than others. "You're not in trouble, are you?"

"Someone would like to think so."

What did that mean? Recognizing a pissed-off Lawman, I tried to make light. "You're snarling."

Ordinarily, he was about as level as they came. The hierarchy of the federal government could get under his skin at times, but that skin had toughened over the years. Usually, *he* toned *me* down, not the other way around.

"On your way here?" I asked.

"Yes, start packing up, please. I have to be in Atlanta for an eight a.m. meeting, so as soon I get to Columbia, I'll repack and hit the road.

Be there in a minute." He hung up.

Wayne wasn't wordy on a phone. He wasn't wordy, period, but he'd spill all this when we were in the truck headed home. However, I wasn't sure I wanted to go home yet.

The silence at my own table suddenly caught my attention. Sophie had hung up before I did, her jovial grin and twitters gone, a frown in their place. "What?" I asked. "By the way, I gotta go. That was Wayne."

"And mine was Stan."

Duh.

"He's trying to calm down Thomas."

That's not good. I pulled out my credit card and took both tickets as thanks for Sophie taking us in the other day. "What's got Thomas upset?"

"Greer banned him from seeing Callie."

"He did what?" Did I hear her right?

"Just what I said. Thomas told Stan he might resign. Stan's trying to talk him out of it." She flounced back in her chair. "Callie screwed so much up around here."

Oh hell no. Surely I didn't hear *that* right. "No, ma'am, you do not get to blame Callie for this. If you blame anyone, it's Greer. No, even better, you blame Brice LeGrand. He hired him."

"But none of this would've happened if she—"

I narrowed a squint on her. "She saved your ass, if I remember correctly. She's sacrificed more for this beach than any hundred people combined out here." I raised a finger, jabbing it at her. "To include you." I didn't pull my punch. "Despite professing to be some kind of warrior for the positive in the world, you sure have sent some serious negativity to your friend. When push came to shove, you turned on her, same as the rest."

"We needed her," she said, loud enough for the entire room to hear. "She deserted us."

"Y'all used her up!" I stood. Even if I'd wanted to fight this fight in public, I didn't have time. Wayne would be waiting.

She popped to her feet ready for battle, but this time I was the faster talker. "You ought to be ashamed of yourself, Sophie Bianchi."

"We need her as chief," she replied, sounding almost as if she recited a mantra.

Then a thought flew all over me. "Is Stan blaming Callie? On that call, did he ridicule her?"

"No, he didn't," she said, craving to be in the right on at least one aspect. "He wouldn't."

But with him sleeping with Sophie, I wasn't so sure.

"She deserves better than this," I said.

Wayne would beat me to Callie's at this point, so I dropped twenty-five dollars on the table not knowing if the bill deserved more or less. Sophie could deal with it.

On my way out the door, it hit me . . . I came with Sophie. Trotting, I cut through the nearest cross street, Mary Street, and a quarter mile down turned right on Palmetto. Damn it, I couldn't even see *Windswept* from here. What block was it on . . . eighth, ninth? Wait, someone said ten blocks from the Pavilion.

Dark clouds threatened, pushing a surge of cold air. The jog would do me good, but I still prayed Wayne hadn't gotten back yet so he could pull up alongside me and shorten the trip.

Didn't take me long to pant like someone who hadn't run a mile in a couple years. By the time I'd walked, run, stumbled, and jogged to within a block of *Windswept*, my phone rang. Worried it was Wayne or Callie, I stopped, breathing heavy, and wrestled getting my phone out of my sweats pocket. If this was Sophie, I'd let it go to voice mail.

But it was Monroe. My boss, Monroe Prevatte. I thought Wayne said there was no new case?

"Hey, Monroe. Guess you forgot I was at the beach."

Monroe was the state director of my agency and one of the dearest friends I'd ever had. He'd hit on me a few times in the past, but once Wayne became a fixture and Monroe my boss, like the gentleman he was, he declared me romantically off limits. Made me appreciate him all the more, not that we didn't pick at each other like an old married couple.

"No, I didn't forget," he said. "Afraid this isn't a good call, Slade."

I cleared my throat and tried to take a deep breath to regulate the stupid, all-over-the-place breathing I was doing. "Why?"

"Were you . . . running?"

"Yeah, but don't worry about it." Another breath. Frankly, the breathing thing had lowered my blood pressure from that wacky breakfast with Sophie.

"There's been a complaint," he said.

"About me?" My thoughts went to my last case, but everyone had seemed rather relieved at its findings. Maybe the one before?

"About you and Wayne."

A loose pattern was beginning to take form. "Who called you, Monroe?"

"Jesus, Slade, you didn't even ask why, which tells me you've been up to something. You're on vacation, for God's sake. Can't you give trouble a rest for that long?"

Hand on my hip, my blood pressure spiked back to Sophie level. "Who was it, I said."

"The police chief of Edisto Beach. Seems you've met him. He claims you've interfered with police activity down there with no authority to do so."

What the ever-loving hell.

"I'm asking you to come back," he said.

"Which you have no authority to do," I spouted, fully understanding the division between the professional and personal when it came to federal employment.

Plus, I hadn't interfered with squat.

Lumen died of a heart attack. There was no official crime.

Now I was pretty damn sure there was.

Chapter 19

Callie

CALLIE LEFT HER mother with Chiefs Warren and Greer at Oscar's along with the half-eaten BLT. What minimal interest she'd held for the Middleton chief of police role had burnt to ash with the realization the trio had corroborated to relocate her out of Edisto. The move would get her out of Greer's hair, give Warren a good reason to retire, and return Beverly's prodigal daughter to the political fold.

She felt like such a fool.

Her mother schemed as usual. Warren . . . just seemed tired. Exhausted from working for Beverly, no doubt, and no way would he contest the mayor's wishes. But what business was it of Greer's other than, as her investigative crew suspected, he hid something smelling a bit illegal that Callie might be too shrewd to overlook?

Politics and law enforcement often bled into each other, like this very lunch. All too often for her tastes. She had always avoided those events like the plague. She would count her blessings she'd left that environment if a spark of regret didn't burn deep.

She reached the outskirts of Middleton, having veered off Highway 17A almost to Clubhouse Road, the back way and quickest to reach Edisto Beach. She wasn't in a rush but had taken the route out of pure habit, the less traveled roads always her favorites. It was not quite one in the afternoon and her day was practically done. It began full of opportunity, ending early with obstacles everywhere she turned.

Her phone rang. This time Slade. She smiled, wondering how her friend's day had gone, hoping she could provide some comic relief. "Hey," she answered. "Did you get your beauty sleep?"

"No." Phone on Bluetooth, Slade's voice echoed in the confines of the vehicle. "Wasn't sure how long you'd be gone, Callie, but this couldn't wait. Where are you?"

Callie slowed on the two-lane. "Why? What's going on?"

"I need to meet you, wherever you are."

"I just left Middleton. Long story. I'll tell you about it—"

"Where's a good place to meet you and still be on Wayne's way home to Columbia?"

Slade spat out some mighty angry words, clearly preferring to meet in person and ASAP at that, but what was this about Wayne leaving? Surely, they hadn't fought over something.

"It's only twenty minutes longer for me to just come home. Can't it wait?"

"Nope." Terse. "Wayne has to leave now. We need a discussion, which I intend to cover with him in the truck."

Sounded like a lover's fuss.

Callie pulled onto a hunting cabin road to focus. "I guess Jacksonboro would be the best place," she said. "There's a diner there. Jackson something or other. There's a small billboard on Highway 17, on your way. It tells you where to turn. You won't miss it."

"Good," she said. "We're leaving now. Meet you there. I'm riding back with you."

Contact ended.

Strange conversation.

At the rate this week was going, she wouldn't blink if Armageddon rained down. To think she expected her life to simplify once she put law enforcement behind her.

Callie returned to the road. She could've suggested Ravenel or Adams Run, but the way Slade sounded, they were hitting the highway hard, and Jacksonboro would prove more efficient to Wayne. At least they could talk over coffee.

The day had been steel-gray cloudy since the outset, making light thoughts an effort, so she concentrated on Slade and Wayne and what she might've missed between them. Maybe Wayne had a real emergency with his agency. A sudden case. But Slade remaining behind felt like a problem of some sort.

What the devil had turned the world upside down in such an incredibly short period of time? With everything abuzz, she was glad she hadn't had much Sophie in her world of late. She would claim Callie had ripped open some cosmic veil and released hordes of ill-willed spirits or something.

While her circle was a far cry from a Marvel Metaverse, she admittedly had sucked in her friends like some vortex of doom. It was up to her to rectify at least some of these issues.

She turned on the same highway she described to Slade and kept watching her rearview mirror to catch sight of the F-150 somewhere along the way.

Her phone rang through her vehicle. *Jeb?*

"Hey, son. What's up?"

"How are you doing?" he asked.

How was she supposed to answer that? And why was he really calling? Now, of all times, too. Who had he spoken with, and why?

"Fine, I guess," she said, seeking a level, normal tone. "How are you doing?"

She wasn't sure how normal that sounded. Wait a minute. She got it now. She would bet a hundred bucks on whom he'd spoken to and give the other person ten to one odds against her being right.

"I'm good," he said. "How would you like a guest for a few days?"

He hadn't been home from college for an overnighter since before the house burned down. He'd given her the space she cryptically asked for, with her assurance she'd call when her life was better organized.

"What about classes?" she asked.

"I'm ahead in some classes, and we have a long weekend coming up. Sprite wants to see her mother, and I thought maybe I'd like to see mine."

Suddenly, she was driving through tears. "Would love to see you, too."

Was now a good time, though? However, since when did a mother tell her son any time was not a good time? "I have house guests, but there's another bedroom."

There was a short moment of obvious silence. "What kind of house guest?"

"House *guests*. Wayne Largo and Carolina Slade," she said before remembering Wayne was packed and gone. "You've heard me mention them."

"Do you *mind* me meeting them?"

"Of course not," she said without hesitation.

"Good," he said. "Done deal. We'll be there either this evening or in the morning."

"Um," she started.

"Um?"

"Not sure when I'll be in. Hopefully before you arrive. If I'm not there, go with Sprite to Sophie's. I'm sure the other momma will take care of you until I return."

"We can make anything work," he said. "Where are you?"

He didn't need to hear about her day, especially the part about despising his grandmother. Once he got to the house, however, he'd sense something. He might not like the cop world, but he had inherited the keen senses of both his law enforcement mother and father.

But Sprite's mother Sophie could also spill her guts to them in her multi-colored, off-balance manner which would then require Callie unraveling the comedy from the tragedy to get the story straight.

"Had errands to run in Charleston then had lunch with your grandmother. On my way to Jacksonboro right now to meet a friend."

"Good," he said, really sounding like he meant it. "Sounds like you're staying busy. Can't wait to see you, Mom. Drive safe."

"You, too, son. Love you."

She hung up feeling like the kid who'd told half-truths to keep parents out of her business. Her twenty-year-old often changed roles, with her being the underling and him the overseer, and she kicked herself black and blue every time he felt the need to play the part. Like now.

She pulled into the parking lot of Jackson Hole, a bar slash diner from the neon in the windows. A few cars in the parking lot, but it was two o'clock, give or take, and lunch time was over. A Craven County cruiser parked off to the side, clearly with a desire to be seen, like most cops working off-book to add a protective presence. A condition of the part-time, private security work most uniforms performed to make up the difference for low salary.

No sign of Slade's truck, but Callie hadn't yet reached the entrance before it popped gravel and slid up beside her. Engine still running Slade spilled out of the passenger side with nothing but her phone in hand.

Wayne saw that Slade reached Callie and started to leave.

"Wait a minute!" Callie shouted darting to him. "What's going on?"

He pointed at Slade. "She'll have to tell you. Gotta get to Atlanta tonight and make a few calls along the way. If you think of anything I can research for you, let me know."

Callie blinked fast, trying to catch up. "How long—"

"A few days at most. Will be back no later than Saturday or Sunday, I expect." Then with a sheepish sneer, added, "Sorry to dump her on you like this. Her choice, by the way."

Slade scooted over to him and gave him a kiss. "Bite me, Cowboy."

"Not here," he said and left them breathless in a dust cloud.

"Well?" Slade pivoted and eyed the building. "Some of my favorite diners are in the middle of nowhere. Every county has one, and I make sure I visit one every chance I get in the field. Let's see if this place passes muster."

But Callie grabbed her arm. "Y'all aren't fighting over something, are you?"

Looking puzzled, Slade tried to put pieces together. Then the furrows smoothed out. "Oh. You think. . . ." She pointed at herself, then in the direction Wayne disappeared. She laughed. "No, sorry, I've had time to chill since I called." She inserted her arm in the crook of Callie's and headed inside. "Still not happy and you won't be either, but we can talk over wings, or burgers, or whatever this place specializes in."

"So you're less mad," Callie said, stepping inside, squinting, then widening her eyes at the darkness of the interior.

"No, just decided I didn't need to explode all over you about it." The door shut behind them. "Where do we sit?"

"Booth or table?" asked the pleasant, middle-aged woman, two menus in her hands. Her complexion was dark enough to have appeared beside them before their eyes adjusted. Her red apron had *Lenore* embroidered across the bib.

"Booth," both said, making Lenore smile at the unison. She led them to the closest one, leaving menus on the table. "Take your time, ladies."

The dark wood and red seats made the room feel more bar than a mid-day eatery, but Callie appreciated the secrecy feel of the place. Slade went straight to the menu, while Callie scouted the room.

A sprinkling of late lunchers sat at four-person tables, with a lone man at the bar. A deputy in khaki uniform. A big deputy. Dark and handsome, maybe six or seven years younger, giving Callie a senior feel. Lenore went to him and asked a question. When he nodded, she pulled his head down and kissed him on top.

That explained the cruiser outside. A relative, most likely a son. Wasn't long before Lenore slid a plate under his nose and scooted to their booth, hands twisting in her apron.

Callie hadn't thought about eating.

Slade took the lead, plopping the menu on the table and leaning on it with elbows. "What's your specialty?"

"Today it's chicken-fried steak, skillet potatoes with onions, and fried okra. Of course, you can substitute if you—"

"You had me with chicken-fried steak, ma'am."

"Make that two," Callie said, not wanting to be the hold up.

"Sweet tea or water?"

Slade's expression turned impish. "Love your style. Unsweetened tea isn't worth the trouble, is it?"

Lenore grinned back. "No, you just look like a sweet tea girl."

"And me?" Callie asked, loving this lady.

The waitress narrowed one eye. "Water," she guessed, "though I imagine you'd splash it with something of substance given half a chance."

Callie nodded at the choice, uneasy a stranger had identified her thirst. Lenore left, not having written down a word.

Like twins, the two women hugged the table toward each other, Callie motioning first. "Did she just say I looked like a lush?"

"No, but she pegged you rather well, didn't she?"

"Hmm," she replied, watching the deputy at the bar. "I'll be back in just a minute." She slid out of the booth.

"Sir?" she asked, easing atop the stool beside him. "Opportune we caught you here."

The man made a conscious effort to wolf down the forkful of potatoes he'd just put in his mouth, wiped hands on a napkin, and held out a hand. "Deputy Tyson Jackson. What can I do for you?" Deep voice.

Callie introduced herself. Her name felt empty without a title.

The deputy filled in, though. "Used to be chief of Edisto Beach?"

"You got me," she said.

"Pon Pon chief took your place," he added.

"Yes, sir."

He studied her. "How's that working out for y'all?"

She'd hoped to slide into baited chatter with the man, not hit the ground running. "Not sure I'm an impartial voice in the matter. Glad you broached the subject, though. I came to speak to the sheriff about our new chief, something I'd rather not have spread around, but since you seem familiar, and Pon Pon is in your county jurisdiction, I'd love to hear your take on him."

The chuckle came out low, deep, and ended on an edge. "I'll let you know when we get a good taste of what replaced him. The devil you know versus the devil you don't, and all that."

Curious. Not willing to commend him nor crucify him. She began to like this man.

"Think the sheriff would be willing to chat with me about Pon Pon history?"

He shrugged. "I don't ever try to speak for Sheriff Sterling, ma'am.

That kind of thinking lands you in hot water pretty damn quick around here." He gave a slight wince. "Not sure he'll be too open talking with you about him either, and if he was, Greer would be aware before you could get back to the beach."

Callie nodded once in understanding. Any discussion with Sterling would not be confidential. "You don't know how sorry I am to hear that."

He gave Callie an appraising stare and then shot a quick glance to a booth in the back. "Go eat your lunch and take your time, and I might find you someone just as good to talk to."

"Here or by phone?"

"Here," he said. "Nice talking with you, Chief Morgan," and he winked.

Yeah, she did like this deputy.

Returning to the table, the drinks in place, Callie hoped the deputy didn't send some guy from the chamber of commerce or the local mayor. She didn't trust politics. Even sheriffs could be cagey and only quasi-trusted, depending on how much politician they were versus cop.

"What was that about?" Slade whispered.

"I asked him about Greer," then she pushed back as Lenore appeared with two steaming plates. Her third meal of the day, Callie doubted she'd be able to eat much, but she hadn't finished anything she'd eaten. One chicken tender, two quarters of a BLT.

Callie lifted her fork when a tall young woman appeared. "Scoot over," she said, then when Callie didn't, Slade did, shifting her meal further down the table with her.

Lenore showed out of nowhere and sat a bowl of fried okra on the table. The young woman took ownership of it. They exchanged no words, as if this were their ritual.

Even in the dark Callie registered the red hair, the tanned and toned physique making her guess the woman lived a lot of time outdoors. Callie smelled law enforcement of one type or another and waited for the woman's next move.

"Hear you want to talk to the sheriff," she said, her attention on Callie, a breaded okra nugget in her fingers. She popped it in her mouth once she spoke.

Slade remained quiet.

Callie gave her response a moment of introspection first, casting the impression she didn't trust just anyone, especially someone who chose to dominate so quickly.

"Sorry," the woman said, wiped her hand on a napkin, and reached over for a shake. "Name's Quinn Sterling. I'm the niece of the illustrious sheriff, hold no loyalties to him, and have sure heard about you, Chief Callie Morgan. Now, what's the Pon Pon police done to muck up your Edisto world?"

Chapter 20

Callie

CALLIE STOLE A glance at Slade who leaned on her left elbow, blatantly giving this Quinn Sterling woman an up-and-down analysis.

Ms. Sterling caught the look and tossed back a lighter version. "Y'all go ahead and eat. Don't mind me."

"We sort of have to mind you," Slade said. "You invited yourself to our table. That and you're like a foot taller than either of us. Just who are you again?"

The sass teased a smile out of the new woman about the time Callie remembered. "I've heard of you," she said. "Private investigator."

"And farmer," Quinn said. "I own—"

Slade sucked in a breath and pointed her fork. "Sterling Banks Plantation," she exclaimed. "That place is historic. Agriculture, that I work for, by the way, has never had to loan you a dime. Well managed. Second biggest pecan operation in the state."

Funny how Callie had heard of the law enforcement side of the woman while Slade knew of the agricultural. They'd have more to talk about on the way home.

"Enough of my teasing," Quinn said. "Seriously, Deputy Jackson and I are old friends. Go on and eat, please. Lenore's cooking is marvelous. Don't let it go cold on my account."

Slade obliged, and through a bite of steak and gravy told Callie, "You're in charge. You talk to her."

Callie took a bite of the steak herself, then the potatoes, and finally the okra, doing a double take on the okra. She gave the guest a slo-mo surprised look. The okra came with a kick.

"Good, right?" Quinn said and pointed to her own bowl. "It's brain food for me. She brings me a helping every time I come in here. Now, down to business. I might be able to help you instead of you bearing the brunt of my uncle's notorious misinformation. "

Callie noticed Ty peer over. Quinn gave him a nod. "So it's true,"

Callie said. "You operate out of a diner."

"Yep. Beats renting a place and wasting time and money. I work when I choose, picking clients I prefer, and I don't prefer them at the farm. My turn," she said. "Lady, you had a reputation for solving some serious cases, here and up north. Why'd you quit?"

Callie's respect for Quinn dimmed a little, not too keen on justifying herself, especially on that topic. "Why'd *you* quit?" she asked in return. "Being FBI?"

Quinn chewed on that question long enough for Slade to do a back-and-forth between the two. "We're here about Greer, girls," she said, and popped an okra in her mouth. "Accept the touché, Miss Sterling, and let's move on."

Slade was right. "Sorry," Callie said. "Quinn, I assume you know everything there is to know about Craven County."

"Lived here my whole life as did my father, grandfather, and others who go all the way back to 1700. Sort of makes me an expert, I'd say."

"Which means you're familiar with the town of Pon Pon."

Quinn narrowed one eye, weighing how to respond. "I know what I hear more than what I've seen firsthand."

"Well, Lamar Greer isn't doing the job we expected," Callie said.

"Armstrong's as bad or worse," Slade added.

Quinn pointed with an okra morsel. "He's more your problem, if you ask me. Let me enlighten you a bit, but first, elaborate the why of all this. What have they done?"

Callie glanced over at the deputy. "Who will you relay this information to once we leave?"

"Nobody but Ty," she said.

"And who will he talk to?" asked Slade.

"Nobody but me. Not my uncle, either. Ty and I have an arrangement." She crossed her heart. "You have my word."

Callie needed to lighten up. If the universe was throwing an informant in her lap, she needed to accept the gift. "We had a woman die on Edisto of a heart attack," she said. "And Greer is lying about the time of death when there isn't an obvious reason for him to do so. My interest has Armstrong tailing me."

"He tail you here?" Quinn asked.

"Haven't seen him," she replied. "I've been to Charleston, Middleton, and here, and so far no sign of him. His tails seem to be limited to the beach and island." She had several questions and pondered which to ask next. "Is your sheriff uncle a friend or foe or uninterested party when it comes to Greer? Their ages are about the same, and with both being deeply entrenched in their territories, their paths have to have crossed, and crossed often."

"Yes, Uncle Larry is a Greer fan," she said. "That's why Ty gave you to me. Chief Greer helped mold Pon Pon. Uncle and Greer stay out of each other's way while patting each other on the back."

Slade stopped and sipped her tea. "Is that a good thing or a bad thing? I don't know your uncle, and I've only heard enough about Greer to be skeptical."

"Let's just say Greer gets his way. And those he favors get their way. Have they done anything illegal?" Quinn let that question hang a second. "I doubt he has the stones to cross the line for anything horrendous, but I wouldn't put it past Armstrong." To Slade, she said, "Between you and me, I believe Greer tries to keep Armstrong in check."

Then she seemed to recall the earlier comment. "You said he lied about time of death for a heart attack victim. How do you know that?"

"He told us," Slade answered. "Then Callie double checked with the coroner's office."

Quinn's head slightly nodded, accepting. "Who worked the death?"

The question prompted a fresh angle Callie should've considered before now. "Armstrong."

Armstrong could've told Greer wrong on purpose, and in Pon Pon style, Greer went along. Aware or unaware of the time shift, who knew? Sounded like scratching each other's back may come with Pon Pon's territory, and the unquestioned credo may have gravitated south to Edisto. But in the absence of evidence to the contrary, she assumed Greer was a knowing and willing participant.

"There's just no reason to lie about time of death," Callie said. "Unless someone needed an alibi. Are you familiar with a middle-aged balding man who drives a white Audi? He was seen with Armstrong and has not been seen on Edisto before, at least per the description by people in my circle." No way was she giving up Truman Burnett's name.

Quinn snagged more okra and sat back in the booth, thinking. About that time, Ty waved, done with his meal. "Hey, over here," she said just loud enough.

He moseyed over, not disturbed, not curious, just a cop going where he was needed.

Quinn described the white Audi man. "Ring a bell?"

He raised his chin. "Sounds like Troy Fox."

The farming detective's eyes narrowed. "It does, doesn't it?"

"Fox is still in Pon Pon, head of town council," he said to Callie.

"If it's him," Callie said, "then he met with Armstrong about the time a woman died in their presence, and they're lying about the time of death."

The big man scowled, his mind working.

"What do you think Armstrong's up to if he's secretly meeting with Fox?" she asked him.

Ty peered once over his shoulder across the mostly empty room. "The bigger question is why did Armstrong follow Greer to Edisto?" Then to Callie, said, "Not my business why you left the job, but why'd they hire Greer in the first place, Chief Morgan?"

"He's tight with Brice LeGrand, head of our town council," she said. "Believe they went to school together. LeGrand pretty much spearheaded the anti-me show at the beach for the last couple of years."

Someone came in, and they let Ty look over for risk assessment. He turned back to the ladies, unimpressed by whoever it was. "I just know they kept their business to themselves in that town and ran it tight. Sheriff Sterling told us to let 'em be, but there were times we got calls from Pon Pon people about Armstrong's heavy-handedness. Greer consistently took up for Armstrong, though, creating a sort of mob feel about the town."

Mark had mentioned Armstrong's overbearing reputation. Callie loved hearing it confirmed. "What did people complain about?"

"Excessive speeding tickets. Excessive use of force claims. Excessive interpretation of harassment. Excessive most anything that served Armstrong's purpose or someone in the inner circle."

"Uncle Larry doesn't stir trouble," Quinn said. "*Their turf . . . their responsibility*, he says."

"Why did they leave?" Callie asked. "Who has that level of control, clearly autonomous in its power, and goes a county over to police a place he has no history? Unless he wants to start over. Unless his history is worth forgetting. And more," she said before they had a chance to reply, "he takes two officers with him, Armstrong and Anna May. For a town the size of Pon Pon, the exodus of three officers had to seriously damage that force."

Ty nodded. "It did. They're still trying to find replacements."

Slade piped up. "Have they replaced Greer?"

"They promoted an existing officer to chief. About thirty-four, thirty-five?" Ty said. "They grabbed some kid out of high school to fill that guy's place." He frowned. "Who is Anna May?"

"You know Anna May Greer," Quinn answered, giving him a look he quickly read, as if the two of them held a mind-melding talent.

"Ooh, yeah, Anna May," Ty said, making it appear his light just came on. "That's on Quinn. I gotta go before the sheriff comes looking for me. Nice meeting you ladies." He dipped his chin and left.

"Wow, he's nice," Slade said, watching him leave.

"Yes, he is," Quinn replied, doing the same.

Once he was out of sight, Slade returned to Quinn, Callie patiently waiting for the information Ty said Quinn would deliver.

"She's Greer's daughter," she said. "At least formally. He raised her since she was born. But y'all know that."

"Not sure we do," Slade said slowly, suspecting a story. "I mean, she's a Greer, but that's the limit to our knowledge."

Callie grasped firsthand about a real parent not necessarily being the one who reared you. "Who's her real daddy?"

"Troy Fox," she said.

"So now we worry about all three of the Pon Pon cops," Slade concluded. "That's just great."

Quinn squinted at the remark. "Better raised by Greer than Fox."

They needed to take the discussion back a step. "About Fox, what's his history?" Callie asked.

"A major businessman in Pon Pon. Tight with Greer only to a point. When it comes to Anna May, Greer keeps Fox at arm's length. Before Anna May turned eighteen, things got testy. Fox ran for county council about that time and won. Didn't last but one term, supposedly because he hated the fishbowl it put him in. That was maybe ten years ago."

"Yeah," Callie said. "From our research, Anna May joined the Pon Pon force about ten years ago."

"And isn't exactly loving the job," Slade said, and when Callie looked questionably at her, added, "I had breakfast with her this morning."

Another topic Callie'd discuss with Slade on the way back to the beach. "So why stay in a job you don't like?"

Slade frowned. "And, Jesus, why hang with a man like Armstrong? Surely, they don't have a thing."

Quinn shook her head. "She doesn't like Armstrong. Nobody does. Fox joined county council the same year Greer hired her on the force, in my opinion, as much to protect her and keep her close as anything else. Fox tried to flex a lot of muscle back then."

"And couldn't pass muster?"

"Right."

Slade was eating up this new information. "You said Armstrong and Greer ran the force, right? Why would she transfer *with* those two when she had the chance to enjoy the shift in power in their wake back in Pon Pon?"

"Unless to get away from Fox," Callie said.

Slade draped over the table, excited about these angles. "Okay, then change gears. Why would Armstrong leave Pon Pon? He could vie for the chief's job since they apparently replaced Greer with a youngster," Callie added.

"Oh . . . well, let me tell you a little about that," Quinn said. "Damn, I'm out of okra."

Slade pushed her plate back and waved to Lenore. "At that, I'll get a go-box, Miss Sterling, and pay for another round of okra for you. I don't want to miss a word."

CALLIE AND SLADE didn't leave Jackson Hole until the early dinner people started filtering in. The additional talk with Quinn took a half hour to tell and a quarter hour more to clarify.

"Fox is Anna May's daddy, not Greer," she repeated. "The mother is dead. Of cancer, I believe. Guess everyone kept the affair secret for her. That's when the gossip started leaking out. Supposedly, even Anna May didn't know till then."

They'd covered all sorts of talk about Pon Pon politics and culture, which boiled down to little more than that of most other small Southern towns. There wasn't a one without its skeletons, and it was usually the families with the most skeletons that ran the towns.

They plowed through an obscene amount of okra, and Quinn let three calls go to voice mail, but by the fourth said she had to go. Something about goats and a cantankerous woman back at Sterling Banks spewing obscenities about orders pouring in. The three ladies parted, vowing to meet up again sometime. The beach, the farm, or the lake, each had a place worth the trip. Time would tell whether the promise held substance, but Callie added Quinn's business card information to her phone contacts regardless. One never passed up on a credible contact.

Quinn left them with a warning to be careful of Armstrong. Not Greer but Armstrong. Callie, however, was too keen to write off Greer just yet. Not after the warning from Quinn's deputy friend and especially because of Greer's all-too-commonly known support for Armstrong. Of course, there was the biggest glitch, the lie about Lumen.

Slade's phone dinged. "Wayne made it back to Columbia. He's about to leave for Atlanta."

"Before we talk about Greer—"

"And Armstrong and Anna May. That little po-dunk town has its history, doesn't it?"

Callie finished her sentence. "Wayne first. I assumed y'all fought or something when you first called, and you sounded like you'd bite nails in two. I now assume he got called to headquarters, and he was none too happy about leaving you. Is there a problem?"

Like instant replay, Slade's feathers ruffled. "Damn straight there's a problem. The Atlanta OIG received a complaint about Wayne flexing federal muscle around Edisto, interfering with an official investigation over which he held no jurisdiction. And it wasn't just one call. It was two. Greer for the police department and Brice for the town."

Callie's right tire hit the edge of the asphalt. "They did what?"

"Wayne tried to explain we were just on vacation, a friend of yours died, and we were helping you with the formalities of it all, which is the truth, but, oh no, those two asses filed a formal complaint, which made Atlanta yank him in." She had to stop and take a breath.

A burning climbed up Callie's throat. There wasn't a cleaner, more solid investigator than Wayne Largo, and to think these idiots sought to tarnish his professional reputation made her want to drive straight to Dock Site Road, to Brice LeGrand's house, to call him out to the curb in front of God, the tourists, and natives alike. She wasn't sure what she'd do then.

"What about you?" If they called Wayne's bosses, they had certainly called Slade's, too.

"They tried, but my boss doesn't have quite the power over me that Wayne's does over him," she said. "I refuted the complaint, told Monroe I was still on vacation, and reminded him I only investigated Agriculture's internal issues, and anyone trying to say I threw a badge around didn't remember I don't carry one. I'm civilian, and for a change, glad I don't carry a badge. At least a real one. Not sure I even brought that plastic thing with me, to tell you the truth."

"So you chose to stay here? With me?" Then Callie repeated, "Me over Wayne?"

Slade's chuckle came out dark, but she smiled, nonetheless. "I love you and all that, honey, but I can't do beans about Wayne in Atlanta. I can be of some good here or go home and fret about Wayne, which would let them believe they hurt me, too."

Callie mashed the gas, the speed used to assuage her anger. All those associating with her were paying a price. Some like Slade would let it roll off, but someone like Thomas had to toe the line to keep his job. Raysor had returned to his neck of the woods, not devastating, but a degree of bruising came with the directive since he hadn't worked his home area full-time in years.

Which made her wonder how they'd lean on Mark.

"Callie!"

Oh. This wasn't the first time Slade had called her name. "Sorry, what?"

"Anna May. You believe all that Quinn said?"

"I don't know."

Slade watched the old housing in Ravenel go by, most of it older than she was. "Quinn gives off a decent vibe to me. FBI agent, private investigator, a sheriff uncle she and Deputy Ty hide details from all the time. Shrewd lady in my book."

"You just like the pecan farm," Callie said.

Slade winked. "Can't lie about that, but that's not your normal farm. That's one smart cookie running the illustrious Sterling Banks Plantation. I can't help but respect her."

Truthfully, Callie did, too. "Still how does a secret like who your daddy is stay buried for almost three decades?"

Slade feigned shock. "You're asking me that? You, the woman with two mommas who was forty before she learned it?"

"They were fifty miles apart in two different towns, and they had an agreement." Sounded asinine once Callie said it so succinct and loud.

Slade continued. "You keep a secret like that by weaving it up in half-truths and innuendo. You make shit up so it sounds better than the real story."

"Sounds to me like they just honored the mother and vowed silence." Callie scoffed and glanced over. "But listen to you. Makes me worry about what goes on in that brain."

"Hah, you're no different than I am in twisting things around for safekeeping. I'm just louder than you are." She poked her on the thigh. "You're more devious than I am. I'd bet money on it."

Callie wouldn't call it devious.

"Anyway. . . ." Slade dragged out the shift in topic. "Quinn told you why it's not much of a secret anymore. With the mother gone and Greer and Anna May not in Pon Pon any longer, talk will die down."

"Except Fox has supposedly made an appearance on Edisto. Why's that?"

There was so much more to these people than what was on the surface, and Quinn did say there were many more layers than Callie's team had imagined.

"So why did Armstrong come with them?" Callie asked.

"Loyal to Greer, and to watch over Anna May."

"And why did he feel the need to do the latter?"

Slade rolled her eyes. "Because Troy Fox wanted him to?"

The Pon Pon team presented as a mixed-up mess, that's for sure. She wouldn't care except they'd spilled onto Edisto.

The big bridge would be about a mile up ahead, and Callie couldn't get there fast enough to talk to Mark. To check on Mark. To run all of this nonsense by Mark to see if it matched anything he'd heard from his friends with SLED.

On one hand, she worried gossipy hearsay learned in the diner only served to distance them from the real issue of Lumen, which is what mattered most to her. Greer didn't appear to have made the scene at Blue House Lane. If Armstrong lied to him about the time, he could've lied about more, to include meeting with Fox, a man not a fan of Greer's. And in protecting secrets, what if he'd intimidated Lumen, unexpectedly doing something to exacerbate Lumen's weak heart?

He was probably glad she died of natural causes. Saved him the trouble of having to deal with a witness.

And what did Troy Fox have to do with anything? Assuming he was Audi man. Was this nothing more than a biological father inquiring about Anna May? Didn't seem likely. That's what phones were for.

Callie hit the bridge. Halfway across, she pieced together a thought. She'd suspected someone needed an alibi. What if it wasn't Armstrong? What if it was Troy Fox? And what kind of crap was he bringing to her island? She didn't see this as being just about Anna May.

Chapter 21

Callie

CALLIE STOPPED BY El Marko's first. Worry niggled her. No, maybe a little more than a niggle. That nagging sense of trouble she used to pay keen attention to had taken up residence at the base of her skull. She hadn't felt it for quite some time, but she knew better than to ignore its presence.

It had saved her life before. That's what worried her. Why was it there now?

She and Slade went inside the Mexican restaurant. Though five thirty and dinner time, no way could Callie eat.

Slade had her Jackson Hole Diner go-box in the car. "Big breakfast, heavy lunch, not sure I can tackle a meal, Callie."

"We're not here to eat," she replied. "I just need to talk to Mark."

They waited at the hostess station. No sign of Sophie. Mark came out of the kitchen and motioned to his private table, and the two women zig-zagged to the back near the kitchen access. About half full, the restaurant wasn't hopping, but it would be in another hour.

He met them halfway. "Everything okay?"

"Got a lot to tell you," Callie said. "What about you?"

"Ditto," he said. He motioned to the table. "What can I bring you?"

"Ginger ales," she said.

"And a small plate of nachos," Slade tacked on. "We had a big lunch."

He winked and left.

Music played softly in the background, and the crowd was dull.

"I could get used to having a boyfriend as a chef," Slade said.

"You'd be big as a barn."

"Good point." Slade quit panning the room, seeing nothing or no one worth studying. "Things have gone pretty sideways today. Three down and three to go on our team. What next?"

"Besides worrying when they come after us?"

The drinks arrived via waitress. "Here you go, Chief."

She'd decided to quit correcting people on the name.

"They already tried coming after me," Slade reminded her. "It didn't work."

"Which leaves Mark, since Greer has already tried to sabotage me as Lumen's executor. I wish we could find a will. That would at least handle that issue. But the fact she had no one makes me wonder why she'd bother with a will. A lot of people don't. Do you have one?"

Slade did a sideways thing with her mouth. "Yeah, but it's old. Still has my dead ex on it. Planned to write a new one once Wayne and I got married."

"Speaking of which—"

"Don't start."

Mark arrived with the nachos and took a seat. "What a day."

Callie leaned in. "Tell me about it."

"You, too, huh?"

"No. I mean, yes, but what happened with you? I mean, you first."

Mark gave her a skewed look.

"I mean, has anyone leaned on you?" She finally got the words out straight and filled him in on the team. Wayne leaving, Thomas warned off, Raysor stopped. Slade's office trying to reel her back, and Greer trying to interfere with Callie in Charleston. Her half-circle spin of a finger motioned to the three of them. "It's down to us."

She had this creeping sense of impotency taking hold and didn't like it.

Then together they spoke of Quinn Sterling and the quasi-gossip intel of Craven County. About Anna May's questionable heritage, Armstrong's aggressiveness, and Greer's dominance. Then the unknown man named Fox.

A coffee cup in his hand, he listened, taking a glance over Callie's shoulder to survey his domain. Though an excellent listener, he never sat in El Marko's without one eye on the room. "Pon Pon drama comes to Edisto Beach," he said. "Just confirms what I heard at SLED. Tried to ask one agent friend in particular to dig a tad deeper, but I'm not expecting much. Especially once Brice showed in here earlier mouthing off."

He wasn't smiling. He didn't make light of the remark. He rarely worried hard or made a big to-do about anything, his laissez-faire attitude being one of his most admirable traits to Callie, but there was a darkness behind his eyes.

"What did he do?" she asked.

Mark didn't immediately reply. Callie'd seen him worry about her and click into action on several situations when he had accompanied her armed to check out some call or case that took a scary turn. He was a very capable man.

"Mark?"

Slade melted into the background, moving nachos through cheese.

"Greer or Brice, or both, called SLED, asking if they could file a complaint about me interfering with police work down here."

That snatched Slade alive. "They can't do that. You're retired." Then she checked herself. "Sorry."

"Slade's right," Callie said.

"Theoretically, but I still have connections with SLED."

"They're cops, Mark. Surely they don't take these kinds of people seriously. You wouldn't. I wouldn't."

He set his cup down, offering a quick return wave to a lady who came in the door. "Yep, and apparently it didn't get him far. I might not have known if my buddy hadn't given me the heads up and a warning that he needed to steer clear of my requests for a while, so there's my best lead dried up. But since that didn't work well for Brice, he hung up and dialed the state liquor license people, hinting I might be serving to minors."

"You'd never. . . ."

"And he can't prove it," he said. "But he said as head of Edisto Beach Town Council, he was concerned that I also readily served to overly intoxicated people then sent them out drunk to drive home. He said drunk driving statistics were way up, and the tourism of Edisto could not afford that sort of reputation."

"Jesus," Slade said.

"So somewhere there's a note in my file," he concluded.

Infuriated, Callie scooted her chair closer to him. Mark had enough on his plate without someone in the room hearing her temper. "Let me guess. He threatened to bring it up at the next town council meeting."

Mark lifted his cup at her, saluting her thought.

Brice's favorite ammunition. Flaunting to the Edisto population someone's flaws, taking fiction and weaving it into accusations. Nobody expected the head of town council to blatantly lie. Surely, there was some truth in whatever he spun or he wouldn't be in the job.

"He has to have proof," she said. "There is no proof. You're meticulous in here. Damn, Mark, last December you cut *him* off for being too intoxicated, and I was forever watching him so he didn't drive that way."

He took in a breath and turned full focus on her. "He said you used to cover for me when you were chief and that I used to feed your drinking problem in return."

Slade's mouth fell open.

Callie gasped. "That son of a bitch."

Her mind went back to the other night when she'd had those three gins. Had Brice noticed? Of course he had. Her behavior had probably given him these asinine ideas.

She rubbed her forehead, coming down to rest over her mouth. The message was being painted loud and clear . . . steer clear of Greer. Don't question his people, his methods, or his motives. Or else.

The average person would listen to the warnings. The average person in Callie's shoes would say *not my monkeys, not my circus*, as she'd quoted just two days ago.

Greer had demonstrated he had reach, and Brice had underlined the beach's support for however he wished to use that reach.

Slade finished the nachos. "I'd get drunk under normal circumstances," she said. "Hmm, guess that wasn't funny once I said it. What now?"

Callie wasn't sure. She needed to think. She needed to go home and jot the day's activities down and study them. Attempt to connect the dots and strive to identify any weak links of Chief Lamar Greer.

Mark took Callie's hand. "Maybe we ought to let Lumen die her natural death. There's just no teeth to this thing. They altered her time of death, but there's no rhyme or reason why, and actually, no harm done." From his resigned expression, Mark didn't like making the suggestion, but she couldn't deny the logic of it.

Slightly disappointed but mostly in agreement, she sat there unsure what to think. "I'm totally stumped," she said. "There has to be something off color here or these asses wouldn't be trying to shut us down."

Slade sighed. "Yep."

They sat in silence, each mentally rehashing, neither of them able to offer a direction, much less a solution.

It was six thirty. The room had begun to fill with hungry people.

Callie rubbed Mark's forearm, running fingertips under his three-quarter sleeve. "Let's give it up for the evening," she said. "We aren't thinking clearly."

"Wait," Slade said. "Forgot to tell you what Wayne found out from Mr. Burnett."

That ten o'clock meeting Wayne and Raysor had on their agenda this morning seemed like days ago.

"Make it quick," Mark said. "I need to be in the kitchen."

"Armstrong visited Mr. Burnett."

Callie stiffened. "When?"

"After we left Lumen's house yesterday. I think he waited until we were gone."

"And?"

"Armstrong asked him about Lumen. Mr. Burnett played old."

Mark grimaced. "He *is* old."

"I know, I know, but he acted like he had dementia. Like he couldn't remember the time of day or who Lumen was. Armstrong left his card. Burnett acted like he couldn't read it but kept it as proof."

Good old Mr. Burnett.

"Wayne told him to call one of us if anyone else shows or makes him feel uncomfortable," she finished.

One of us, Callie thought, shaking her head. Which one of them would that be? One by one they were being excised from the equation, and what would they do if they got there? They'd willingly come to the man's aid, but exactly what was it they were supposed to do when they arrived?

The Pon Pon uniforms they'd mistakenly labeled Keystone Kops had discreetly and neatly assumed the upper hand by eroding every person's authority. By researching each member of the team, they'd meticulously stolen their power.

"Again, let's just give it a rest tonight," Callie said. "Mark, don't break your neck coming over once you close up. We might make an early night of it."

"I have things to do, trust me, but you sure?" he asked. "I might do paper then hit the sack, if you don't mind."

Slade laid a hand on her girlfriend's shoulder. "I got her. Nothing will happen."

Like I need babysitting, Callie almost said, but truthfully she'd given them all reason to worry of late, and she wasn't proud of it. "We'll have our girl time we haven't had yet."

"Without booze," said Slade.

Mark smiled, rose, leaned over for a kiss from Callie, and left.

Slade looked at Callie. "Guess it's just us."

"We can make that work."

Unless Jeb comes in, Callie thought, but for now she could stand to just grab a coffee and, regardless of the chill in the air, sit on *Windswept's* red swing.

Wasn't long before they were home and changed with Slade back into her sweats and Callie into hers with a hoodie. Slade had stumbled out to the porch with two of the four Lumen journals she'd pilfered and the blanket from her bed. Callie carried the coffees, and they settled into the swing. Since Slade's legs were about four inches longer, Callie let her keep the sway going.

Slade read silently then would read aloud passages from the journal. "Here she quotes Dickinson, *That it will never come again is what makes life sweet.'* Then she adds a note to herself, '*Fine phrase to cite to whomever is facing anything in life, from simple choices, to the ultimate highs, and poignant lows. It's beautiful and makes anything bearable. Most of the time that's all folk need. Perspective. It's never all good or all bad.'*"

Slade peered up. "That's just beautiful, isn't it?"

Callie gave her the obligatory nod of agreement, and Slade went back to reading.

"Want to go with me to Lumen's tomorrow?" Callie interrupted a few quotes later.

Slade put down the journal. "You giving up on Greer?"

Was she? The group had received a lot of blowback today, a lot of warnings, and the situation still just looked like the old chief jealous of the new chief. In reality, Callie saw it more the other way around, but she wasn't in the driver's seat. Greer was.

"No," she said, "just think we need to think . . . plus without a will, this estate stuff is a bear to deal with. Don't want Lumen's place to fall prey to vandals because nobody took initiative."

"Yeah," Slade said, going back to the book. "We can do that. Might steal a couple more of these journals to read."

"You can't keep those, you know."

"Who'll miss one?"

"I will."

"Hmph."

Callie wondered how Thomas was doing. He took this pushback the most personal. Stuck in the middle of people who didn't like him because of who his old boss was, he couldn't possibly enjoy much of the job these days. If the beach lost him, the whole flavor of the police force would be replaced by something foreign. The tourists wouldn't care, but the natives sure would.

"They got it in for you," Slade said, not looking up. "They fear your abilities."

"And why would that be? What is there to fear?"

"You're a hard act to follow."

Callie felt more like she'd been neutered.

Slade kept eyes on the pages. "You're flogging yourself. You're using Lumen to pay some sort of penance. You're dying to make amends without knowing how."

A little flash of temper flared, but Slade's attention was in the book, not up for the debate. Not that she was done talking. "You're doing this two steps forward and one step back thing," Slade added. "And you want to feel better but don't feel you're worth it."

Who made her the island shrink?

But then, why did Slade's observations strike so close to home?

"I swear . . . ," Slade started again.

Callie stretched a leg out and kicked her friend in the thigh. "Stop analyzing me."

Slade popped her on the ankle. "You haven't denied a bit of it, have you?" Her stare hung on Callie now, and Callie pulled her leg back under her and returned to searching the water in the dark.

"You ought to read the other book I brought out here," Slade said, turning yet another page.

Yeah, Callie might see that Slade acquired one of those journals after all. She'd appreciate them more than anyone else. Lumen at least deserved that.

Slade sat up from her slouching and stopped the swing. "Callie, look at this."

She wasn't up to another health potion recipe. "Mark the page. We'll look at it in the daylight. Right now I just—"

"Shut up and look at this." Slade thrust the book over to her, keeping her finger in the crease to avoid losing her place until Callie got a firm grip.

The porch light was bright enough but nothing like sunlight. Callie squinted and held the book out, then closer, finding the sweet spot of being able to read.

"You need readers, girl," Slade said, scooting over, reading upside down. "Just look there." She ran her finger across the page for Callie to follow the words: *The last will and testament of Lumen Amber Townsend.*

"Oh my God," Callie whispered, beginning at the top and reading all the way through. Lumen wrote her will longhand in the middle of a journal. Simple. She designated her sister as executor . . . who Mr. Burnett said was deceased. She left her belongings to three entities . . . half the journals to the Edisto Museum, half to the Edisto Library, her seed inventory to Clemson University, and the house and land to the sister.

She scanned to the bottom, seeking a date and validation, not believing what she saw. Lumen's signature sloped elegantly, dated five years ago, witnessed by Mr. Burnett . . . and Sophie.

Chapter 22

Slade

THIS WAS THE juiciest damn journal I'd ever read that didn't mention sex. Lumen's concoctions were exquisite, and I was dying to test out a few, maybe on my sister when I got home. She was game for anything. Made me wonder if this was where Sophie got her pot. No way she didn't do weed.

Occasionally peering over the edge of the book, I watched Callie spending too much time in her own head. I'd mention this or that, but she didn't half hear me. I talked until she did.

Then I turned that page.

Who wrote their will in the middle of a journal?

"Is this legit?"

Callie read every word which drove me nuts. We could do that later.

"Is it legal?"

She flipped to the second page—there were only two pages to it—and ran her fingers over the notary seal in slow motion. I swear she held her breath. "I believe it is," she said, then she flinched.

"What?" *What had I missed?* Truthfully, though, I'd pretty much just seen Lumen's name and immediately handed it over.

"Sophie witnessed Lumen's signature. Her and Truman Burnett."

My jaw dropped. Here we'd been running around like idiots, seeking a will, wondering what to do about Lumen . . . and had cut off our noses by omitting Sophie from our resource group. I felt stupid. Callie, however, would take it personally and throw more guilt on the mental pyre she kept stoking.

She hopped up and went in the house. Of course, I followed.

She began taking pictures of the journal. The cover, the first page . . . then every page.

"Why not just take pics of the will?" I asked.

"One, probate will need this will for a while. Second, we need to keep copies of the entire *document*." She did document in air quotes.

"Third, I imagine you would like a copy of all this from the way you *oohed* and *aahed* on the swing."

I gave her a double thumbs-up. "Rock on, my friend."

"What's a seed inventory?" she asked.

"Lumen kept track of the seed she planted, maybe even crossed. If she was agriculture-savvy, she might have cultivated certain characteristics of vegetables and herbs or maintained some serious heirloom varieties."

"Pot too?"

"Yes, even the pot. Clemson's agriculture people would have to determine the value of it. Not in dollars, mind you, but in usefulness. They have a pretty big inventory of seed varieties in the state."

Click, click. Callie was more than halfway through. "Well, you have your will. Now what?" I asked.

"Mr. Burnett said the sister was dead, but who knows if that's correct. We need to ask Sophie. If she was close enough to Lumen to witness her will—"

"And buy her pot."

Callie paused. "Maybe . . . but she might know more about this sister. At least we have a name now. Lovey Townsend Walker."

"Lovey and Lumen." The names just matched. "Love and Light. How cool is that? Makes you wonder what their mother was like."

A few more minutes and Callie was done. She uploaded the pics to the cloud. "I'll save them to my laptop later."

"You're pretty thorough," I said, thinking more along the line of obsessive.

"This summer I dropped my phone in water . . . twice. Thus"—she held it up—"the new phone. There, done. Go change . . . unless you want to go like that." She measured me up and down, hinting my sweatpants weren't exactly for public appearance. Didn't tell her fifteen yoga people had no problem with them this morning.

By the time I changed clothes, she had as well. I assumed we were taking the new information to Mark's place, and I vowed not to eat a bite. My jeans pinched my naval after today.

But she headed another direction out of the driveway, which I might've assumed was toward the station once upon a time. "Where are we going?"

"To talk to a person I should've talked to before, Sophie. I should've trusted her. I do not understand where my brain is anymore. I don't . . . whatever."

170

She went quiet, navigating the streets like the car was on autopilot. How many issues was this woman carrying around?

"We can talk about Anna May, too," I added. "Quinn told us stuff that I bet Sophie doesn't know."

"No doubt," she said.

Which was about all we had time to say before we pulled into Sophie's drive. The house wasn't lit up, but enough light seemed on inside for someone watching television. A little early for my bedtime but late enough for some. "Any chance she's gone to bed?"

"Very doubtful."

She might be at Stan's place, though. I would be. The man was a decade older than Callie and me, but he still represented a fine specimen. Besides, Sophie was five years older than we were.

The porch lights were on, and we climbed the stairs. Callie tapped on the door. I stood to the side, the journal clutched tight. I didn't want to drop it, bend it, let anything happen to it.

Nobody answered.

Peeking in the window, I saw only the stove hood light on in the kitchen and a lamp on further in the living room like I would do if I were going out. "Want to go to Stan's?"

Callie tried the doorknob. The door eased open a couple inches.

Okay, maybe she was there. "Maybe she's expecting someone."

Callie shook her head. "Who knows? She never locks her doors. Windows either. Bad mojo, she says." She went on in.

Sophie was a weirder witchy woman than Lumen, in my opinion.

The place smelled herbal.

"Sophie?" Callie called two steps in. Even in the shadows, she moved as if she knew the place.

Scuffling sounded from the back of the house. Callie assumed her sideways defense pose, hand out to keep me behind her. I wasn't about to argue. My heart had already leaped into my throat, and I fought hard not to breathe scared and be heard.

Callie had no weapon. I never carried, my position not allowing me to.

Now what?

She eased forward, hugging the wall, easing around a credenza and reaching the railing leading to whatever was upstairs.

A thump sounded, definitely from a bedroom. Feet shuffled on carpet. Another bump.

"Stay back," she mouthed quietly when I inched forward to see, and

I wondered how she sensed to turn around and tell me.

"Don't shoot!" came a voice from the next room.

I jumped. Callie flinched and molded against the wall.

Sophie came out the bedroom door, a satin robe barely closed, loosely tied. "Doesn't anybody knock anymore?"

Shoulders settling, Callie relaxed. "I did knock, and most people lock their doors."

Sophie heaved an irritated breath. "Well, you should know me better by now."

With hands to the side Callie shrugged, acknowledging truth. "Sorry to wake you. I really am. If you want us to leave, we can talk in the morning. If you. . . ." Movement caught her eye, and her focus made me do the same.

"Oh good God in heaven," she mumbled.

Stan walked out, barely in his khaki shorts, the button undone, the zipper half engaged, his feet and chest bare. "Nothing you ain't seen before," he said, which sent color into Callie's cheeks, visible even in the dimness.

Had to admit the curled white hair on his chest was a bit of a turn-on. And those shoulders.

Sophie popped me with her robe sash. "Quit coveting my man. You've got a good enough one of your own."

There we were, accepting conjugal visits between these two as a new normal.

"Well," Stan said, walking past while finishing up his pants closure, "if this is a social call, we might as well fix something to drink. Who wants carrot juice?"

Callie followed him. "Since when do you drink that stuff?" Sophie caught up to her and popped her on the rump.

"Never mind," Callie said, understanding transitions had to be made in the name of sex and social compromise. She turned to Sophie. "Are you naked under there?"

"Honey, we were buck naked with me on top and him gasping for air when you helped yourself to my house."

I almost choked on my own spit.

Stan beamed.

Callie backhanded his naked bicep. "Oh, stop it."

"And you're showing," she said, waving at Sophie's robe, which was a bit gaped in the chest.

Sophie untied the sash, opened the robe wide for God and everyone to see, then rewrapped it tighter around her. "Now, what's so important to start a party? You didn't invite me last night, but you need me tonight. What's happened?"

"This happened," I said, handing her the journal, one of Callie's old business cards holding the will's place.

Taking the book, Sophie went to the living room, flipped on the lights, and lowered herself like water into her recliner, feet tucked beneath her. "I forgot about this," she said, caressing the handwritten words. "We met at the Presbyterian Church. She brought us this crispy green-bean snack she baked, and we sat around talking about, of all things, weed. For about an hour." Crushing the book to her body, she gave a breathless revelation. "Were y'all aware the irreverent reverend used to smoke? Don't know about now. Don't tell anyone, though. He'll deny it."

"He's a preacher," I said. "They don't lie."

"The hell they don't," she replied, returning to read the will. "Hmmm." She turned pages and sank into the other words. The philosophies and lessons. In that moment, I wanted to be in there with them and felt more akin to the woman than I thought possible. Odd yet peaceful at the same time.

"Is the sister alive?" Callie asked.

"She was then. Have no idea about now," came the reply. "We never spoke of her sister again after that day. I just know she wanted her will in place because she was afraid she'd pass on and someone would just steal her land, turn under her garden, and cram two houses on the place, taking out the trees. She said her sister regretted selling her land way back when, plus she was her only relative. The sister had no children either."

The Carolinas, both North and South, were undergoing an explosion from people who had tired of their state and its taxes, politics, and snow, each pushing in tighter, nary a one realizing with each new house came a small piece of destruction of the very environment they wanted to live in. Residents worried about becoming another island like Fripp, John, or Kiawah over the next ten years with taxes raised as development continued, running the old-time residents away.

Same deal was happening on my lake in the middle of the state.

Callie slid an ottoman over in front of Sophie and sat. "Anna May," she said.

Sophie looked up. "What about her?"

"What's she about? I mean, really. What's she doing here?"

Sophie closed the book, carefully marking the will's place. "Thought you'd be interested more in Lamar."

Lamar. Greer probably told her to call him that, too. She had that way with people.

Made sense Sophie had scouted him out. Maybe even flirted to learn more about him. She yearned to understand every green resident and adored being the go-to person on who was who on the island. She was good at it, too.

"What're you up to, Callie?" Stan asked, moving in and sitting on the sofa's end. Now they sat in a triangle affair, heads together, totally forgetting me. But my ears still worked.

Stan understood Callie best, and Sophie wasn't as dumb as she could act. If that helped Callie gather information or come to any conclusions, more power to her, to them.

I listened from the other end of the sofa, trying not to be hurt. This wasn't about me.

Truth be told, this was about Callie more than Anna May or Greer. This was Callie attempting to protect her beach, because no doubt she felt it vulnerable right now. She'd protected it well before, and while she wasn't admitting so, she regretted opening it up to the likes of Greer and Armstrong. Right now, she wondered which side of this fresh evil Anna May stood on, because if she wasn't loyal to the two men, she was open for Callie's use.

I was just damn happy to see her so concerned.

Chapter 23

Callie

CALLIE TOLD HERSELF to get over herself when Stan walked out of Sophie's bedroom in the semi-buff. He deserved love, in whatever form it may present as, from whatever partner he chose, and not in something or someone she'd necessarily approve of. While she might not have partnered the Boston police captain with the Edisto yoga queen, they were very much adult. She hated picking up the pieces if it didn't work out, though. Then in an almost-smack of reality, she recognized that both of these people had picked up her pieces in the past. She could keep her mouth shut.

But not about Anna May.

Sitting in her friend's living room, Sophie having validated the will, Callie, Stan, and Sophie had unwittingly assumed a circle of minds. Callie regretted having left them out of her other circle, proof her head still wasn't on straight. She had to work on fixing that, and she could start here.

"What are you up to, Callie?" Stan asked.

"I just have a lot of questions about this trio from Pon Pon," she said. "And don't go saying I'm jealous or vindictive or anything else. Don't even start." After that last statement, she recognized she sounded exactly like that which she described.

"You're not a jealous person," he said. "But you're stirred up. You're gnawing on a bone you can't put down, while telling yourself you're not. So, Chicklet, what's up?"

She started to tell him not to use the pet name, not after screwing Sophie, not sitting in Sophie's house, but what did that matter? He had used her nickname strategically. He knew it. She knew it. And she could use his thoughts on this loose sort of road she traveled on in her attempt to learn about the Pon Pon cops. He'd keep her thinking straight. He'd recognize when she headed off the rails.

"What do you think about Anna May?" she asked, starting with the question unadulterated so as not to influence either friend one way or another. Sophie could be easily swayed, and at times, would aim to please.

"Well," Sophie started, holding the closed journal to her chest. She unfolded her legs and scooched to the edge of the recliner. "She hates being here."

"Wait," Stan interrupted. "How do you know that?"

Slade slid further down the sofa, next to Stan. "Let her talk. I had breakfast with both of them this morning, and Anna May definitely doesn't see Edisto as the paradise y'all do. Go, Soph."

Sophie gave Slade a hard glance at the abbreviated name Callie often used but went on. "She came out of loyalty, I believe. She loves her daddy and is loyal to Armstrong but dodges questions about work." She snorted. "There's a lot of backstory with that girl. Imagine being stuck in the middle of two alpha males. Greer thinks he's boss, and Armstrong is an ass."

Stan cocked a half smile. "Greer *is* the boss."

Sophie squinted back at him. "But what kind of boss? There are mafia bosses, Callie bosses, and stereotypical sign-the-paycheck bosses. I peg him as the first."

Stan chuckled, which would have insulted Callie if she were in Sophie's shoes, but the yoga woman only cut him a sensual sneer, as if they'd just played a game the rest of them had no clue how.

"Armstrong, on the other hand," Sophie continued, "came to see her after her first yoga class, and I swear, he was checking out where she was, what she was doing, and who she was doing it with."

Slade grumbled. "Are we sure they aren't dating?" Then she had another thought. "Is she, like, under his control?"

"What," Sophie said, "like her daddy is letting her be a perk for his officer? That's just ewww."

"She needs to transfer somewhere else," Slade said.

And so they headed out on a tangent. "Makes no sense why she came here to start with," Callie said. "Unless she feels obligated to Greer."

Stan remained rather stoic, like some sort of moderator.

"What else did you read from her, Soph?" Callie said.

"No doubt she has some kind of plan. I sense it. And she's not happy about her lot in life. I started to ask what specifically she grappled with but figured that too nosy too soon, you know?"

Very un-Sophie-like. "Imagine that," Callie said and smiled at her friend. Sophie gave her a saccharine grin right back.

Callie stood, needing to pace. "If we talk to Anna May, we likewise show our hand to Greer. Maybe Armstrong, depending on that relationship. But she's the only loose thread we have, and it's up to us. Our guys are out of commission, except for Stan here."

"Oh, I'm one of the guys now?"

She'd apologize for months for leaving him and Sophie out of things. "Yes, you are. But from what you ladies tell me, Anna May isn't the most trusting soul."

Both shook their heads.

"But she's the strongest hope we have to dig into Greer and Armstrong."

There. She'd said it. The expressions on her three friends reflected they heard it, too.

"You're investigating," Sophie said with a breathy whisper.

"You're back to protecting Edisto," said Stan.

Callie gave an abbreviated chuckle. "Someone's got to," she said. "Nobody else is left since Brice has his head up his ass."

Slade looked person to person as if they called on her next. After a pregnant dose of silence, she shouted, "The bitch is back!"

Callie dropped her head in her hand at the round of laughter, which so helped. She lowered her hand unable to hide the smile. Nice, but they were still stuck as what to do. All leads had rather dried up.

As though all of them were missing gray matter, Stan looked puzzled. "We've left out Thomas. He's your CI, Chicklet. He's—"

"Banned from contact with me," she finished. "The whole department, not just him. He's caught grief for being a fan."

Stan planted palms on his thighs. "Are you kidding me?"

"Just what we said," Slade said. "She's off-limits because Greer's afraid of her, I say. She's powerful. She has sway with the island."

Sophie pointed in confirmation. "Damn right."

Callie loved her cheerleaders, and without a doubt they pumped energy into her, but the strength they thought they were infusing wasn't taking them one step further into solving their questions.

Narrowing her gaze, Sophie rose, catching her robe and giving it a billowing air-borne toss for effect. "Hand me the phone. I'll get Miss Anna May's behind over here, and we'll get her to spill herself." She shot her nose up. "I've seen y'all do it. How hard can it be? She trusts me."

"No she doesn't," Stan said.

Like her beau had thrown water on her, she eased back to the recliner. "You haven't seen her."

"You'd know more if she did, Bug. She hasn't let you in. Not really."

Slade mouthed *Bug* to Callie, who had to admit the nickname fit. The surprise wasn't in the name but in the fact they'd progressed to that level of intimacy. She wondered what Sophie called Stan.

"So, whatcha thinking, Cap'n?" Sophie asked, unknowingly answering the question, and using the same nickname Callie'd called her father for his boating skills. Stan's reflected his former position in Boston.

Instead of turning to Sophie, *Cap'n* turned to Callie instead. "Regardless what they told him, you need to call Thomas. He's your only viable source. Let him decide if he's up to violating Greer's orders."

If she were in Thomas's shoes, Callie would step forward without a blink, but she had years under her belt, and the young officer did not. "Not sure that's fair," she said. "He'd feel obligated to me."

"He'd be more hurt if you didn't," Stan replied. "Just try to tell me I'm wrong."

She'd hurt Thomas most by resigning, and sheepishly admitted she hadn't given him or any of the other remaining officers a second thought before she'd dropped that bomb and walked away. She hadn't weighed the resignation properly or surmised the repercussions of doing so on anyone else but her.

Stan was right this time.

"You're second-guessing yourself," he said, watching. "We're private here, Chicklet. I'll say it. You fucked up turning in the badge."

Sophie gasped, hand to her robe, drawing it closer. Slade shifted attention elsewhere.

His bluntness pierced Callie like a scalpel, but she accepted his critical stare.

She had no retort. She had no excuse.

"What has you worried?" he asked.

"By thinking only of myself, I allowed something potentially nefarious to infiltrate this beach," she said. "Might be nothing or might be Armageddon. Might be little more than nepotism by Brice, or as much as cracking open Pandora's box." Everyone waited. "But whatever it is that came to Edisto only came in because I allowed it to."

"We've been here before," he said, as if nobody else was in the room.

At that moment, to her, nobody else was. Captain Stan Waltham had mentored her for over a decade on the job. Tough love was his thing. She'd hated him for it at times, sorely appreciating it later.

He'd helped her stay sane on more than one occasion. He'd mitigated her annihilation tendencies and made her a better person.

She always wondered why he tried so hard to mold her. His answer was always that he saw her potential and he wasn't letting it go to waste.

Yet how many times had she wasted those efforts and gone down the path of self-destruction regardless?

"Déjà vu," she said.

"Déjà vu," he agreed.

This wasn't Boston, and nobody was murdered. She might not wear the badge anymore, but everything else about her remained intact.

She could ignore Greer and let the chips fall where they may, or she could move forward and seek answers. Throughout her law enforcement career, she'd often developed a gut feeling about investigations that Stan labeled as keen. She was made for investigations, he always said. She'd learned she could no more ignore that feeling than she could ignore the love for her son.

Stan's head cocked to the side, as if watching her more intently from one eye. She knew that look. He was watching her thoughts sift out of a whirlwind to come to order.

"So call Thomas," she said.

One brief drop of his chin. "Call Thomas."

She found the officer's contact and hit dial, moving toward the kitchen for less noise . . . and to do this right.

"Whoa," Sophie said to the others. "That was almost . . . spiritual."

"Some serious mind-melding going on there for sure," said Slade.

Stan fell slowly back into the sofa, as if relieved.

"Wait," Sophie said, eyes traveling from her new lover to Callie. "You sure you two haven't been a thing in the past?"

"Oh, we've been a thing," he said, his smile clearly cradling memories. "Just not in the sense you think."

Stan acted like he'd locked that door. Sophie fought to hold herself in check, uncertain if his response was good or bad. "What about—"

"Drop it, Sophie," Slade said.

In the kitchen, Callie waited four rings before Thomas picked up. "Chief?"

"Before you say another thing, you don't have to talk to me. I won't hold anything against you if you—"

"Shut up, Chief. We need to talk. I swear the universe must be trying to hook us up."

"Go ahead."

"I don't think it wise to come to *Windswept*, though," he said.

"That's good," she said, "because I'm at Sophie's."

"Give me thirty minutes, and I will be, too."

She hesitated at the odds, not daring to look back at Sophie.

"Seriously, I was just about to call you," he said.

She assumed he was done when he said nothing else, and she started to hang up.

"Chief?" he blurted out.

"Still here, Thomas."

"I'm so sorry. So damn sorry I got mad at you. It wasn't my place, and I'm afraid I made matters worse speaking up in front of Greer—"

"Thomas, Thomas," she said, the mother hen in her oozing back. "You did nothing wrong. It's all on me."

She almost swore she heard a sniffle.

"Look forward to seeing you," she said. "You know how to not be seen. Be careful."

"Ten-four, Chief."

The call disconnected, and she sniffed, her nose running, too. She rummaged around the kitchen for a tissue, finding nothing but dish rags and paper towels, when a big double grip turned her around and pushed one in her hand.

She mashed herself against Stan, naked chest and all, trying hard not to get his chest hair wet as he cradled her to him. "We'll fix this, Chicklet. We'll fix this, too."

"We ought to be hardcore by now, Stan. None of this crying crap." She backed up half a step and blew her nose.

"Not seeing any crying, Chicklet. And I don't need Thomas seeing me like this."

Stan disappeared a moment and returned with all of his clothes back on. "Bug, you might want to get dressed."

Peering over herself in examination, she asked, "Why? It's Thomas. He's like . . . family."

"He's young. You're the sexiest thing on this beach. We have issues to discuss—or rather, Callie does—and we don't need to distract the boy with the way that robe hugs your curves. Not fair to him."

She sashayed over in Vivien Leigh fashion. "Worried you'll get jealous, big man?" She winked over at Slade.

"No," he said. "We need him focused."

Out came the signature pout.

His tone changed, and he halfway begged. "Sophie." Having gotten what she wanted, she carried her sashay into the bedroom.

Slade waited until the door clicked shut. "You sure you aren't in over your head, *Cap'n*?" "Time will tell, Slade. Time will tell."

The half-hour wait Thomas promised seemed like way more, the tension so thick that when the knock came at the door, each jerked, looking at the other.

"Heavens," Callie said. "Look at us. It's only Thomas." She went to the front door, peeked through the etched glass for identity, and seeing the officer, opened it wide.

"Tho . . . mas."

The name descended into a whisper.

"Hope you don't mind I brought Anna May, Chief," he said, holding her hand.

Chapter 24

Callie

CALLIE WASN'T SURE how to react but retrieved enough sense to say, "Of course, come on in."

Thomas let Anna May enter first. He slowed going by Callie. "You need to hear this."

"Just hope Greer doesn't hear about this when she goes home. I'm relying on you." Not that she had the right to ask anything of Thomas, but this move struck her as too bold by risking himself, Callie, and everyone in the room. Greer and Brice could make their lives miserable if they learned of this meeting . . . or worse, its purpose. Thomas would lose his job, maybe Sophie her location to teach yoga. They'd return to Slade's employer and somehow crucify Mark to the liquor board. God knew what else they'd try.

"What is this?" she heard Slade say to them before Callie could shut the door and follow.

Thomas started explaining. "She didn't have to come, you know. This also puts her in jeopardy."

"She could be scouting for the enemy, too," Slade said, standing. They'd all stood by now.

Stan studied Anna May, his thoughts unreadable, while Sophie called herself playing intermediary, arguing this was her home and she would decide who was welcome under its roof.

"Stop!" Callie reached the cluster and motioned to the furniture. "Everyone, sit."

Everyone did.

"Chief—" Thomas started.

"You too, Thomas. Hush a moment."

He did.

Anna May, dressed in capris and tee-shirt, flip-flops, and with her blond hair down and brushing her shoulder blades, could pass as a college coed. Callie hadn't seen much of her on the beach except shoulders up in a passing patrol car, hair tucked in a bun. Under normal conditions, she would welcome another female on the force, but she couldn't let loose of the suspicion that the new chief's daughter sat here undercover. The odds were too great. Girls didn't often go against their fathers.

Callie's concern was how to let this go down with Anna May in the room. Callie and group could pretend they only invited Thomas over as a friend, with nothing planned. Or they could open up more and give these two the fifth degree about recent events. Or they would remain silent and make Anna May validate why they should've let her in.

Truthfully, Callie had zero trust for her. As the daughter of the enemy, her loyalties were torn at best. Worse, she could be using Thomas and his kind heart. They were the same age. She could align with him, win his trust, then funnel intel to her father. If Callie were Greer trying to overcome Edisto's past and dominate over the way things were always done, she'd do just that. Hadn't Thomas been anti-change? She could smooth some of those wrinkles.

"Callie," Sophie warned, but Stan laid a hand on her leg to shush her.

Anna May looked scared. Maybe not an act. Sharing the sofa, she sat closer to Thomas than a co-worker would. She'd either become more than an acquaintance to him or had weaseled her way into his sympathy for some opportune plan. Hard to tell. However, coming here tonight was a gutsy move, and the young female officer played the role of someone needing assistance quite well.

Decision made. Best to start this business with Anna May.

"You go first," Callie said welcoming but meaning business. "Explain why you're with Thomas, and what brings you here."

But Thomas chivalrously inserted himself. "Chief, I told her to come. She didn't ask. She didn't expect any of this. She was already over at my place . . . crying."

Anna May remained silent and damn pitiful looking.

"Don't trust her," Slade said hard under her breath.

The last person standing, Callie pumped the air with her hand toward Slade, keeping her gaze on Anna May. "I believe she understands the circumstances. No point threatening or bullying her before hearing what she has to say. Put yourself in her shoes." Everyone hushed and waited.

The silence shook Anna May even more. "Thomas, maybe we shouldn't have come—"

"No, we *did* need to come," he said, taking her hand. Callie noted.

"You can trust these people, Annie," he continued. "With your life. If you trust me, you trust them. They can help."

Annie.

The crew waited for Callie to steer the direction of this unexpected arrangement. Occupants filled every seat. Callie went to grab one of the barstools, but Thomas leaped up to move it for her, to in front of the fireplace, next to Sophie in the recliner, across from Stan, Thomas, and Anna May on the sofa. Slade had slid into a rocker to the left, her distrust of the two newcomers loud and clear.

Callie thought Anna May the best source of information but hadn't expected to be so suddenly face-to-face to get it. Hopping up to assume her seat, Callie crossed a leg, phone in hand in case she needed a recorder, and took a loud, visual sigh, hoping it made everyone do the same.

In an instant, she changed her strategy. "Thomas, I had questions for you, but this surprise sort of changes the plan. Anna May appears shaken, and you seem to understand the why. How about educating us?"

Anna May took in each of the others. "In front of everyone?"

"Yes," Callie said, leaving no option. "Carolina Slade, whom you seem to have met this morning at breakfast, is a fed. I have worked with her in the past." She motioned with her phone to Stan. "Mr. Waltham is a veteran captain from Boston PD with a damn fine record. He's rock solid and highly respected." She made the round to Sophie. "Ms. Bianchi you've met. She's a friend to have, believe me. She's aided me on several occasions and knows this beach like the back of her hand."

Anna May studied the crew, and after a moment returned a micro hint of a nod to Callie.

"Good," she said. "Now, Thomas. Proceed."

"From the beginning, Anna May was by far the nicest of the three Pon Pon arrivals," he said, "and I think our similar age helped. The others were downright mean at times, like I was a threat."

Anna May winced. "Daddy didn't mean—"

"We get that, Thomas." Callie noted Thomas's loyalties remained intact, but she especially noted he was willing to bash the father in front of the daughter. That mattered. "What brought her to you tonight?"

"Fear, Chief. For herself and her father. She's gotten herself into something thanks to Armstrong, and she needs guidance on finding her way out of it." He peered over at Anna May to see if he got that part right. She gave a slight smile in affirmation.

Now Anna May was almost too docile to suit Callie. "Let's let her describe this trouble firsthand, Thomas. And please, Anna May, start at the beginning. Maybe even what brought you here since it wasn't that long ago. We'd really appreciate it."

The girl cleared her throat and removed Thomas's hand from hers, as if stepping on stage. "I came to Edisto at the request of my father. My mother died two years ago. Cancer."

Consistent with Quinn Sterling's story.

"Sorry," Sophie said, the others murmuring the same. Anna May nodded in thanks.

"But before she died, she told us I wasn't the daughter of Lamar Greer. I was the product of an affair with a man in our town named Troy Fox." She exhaled through pursed lips. "Not fun to hear, believe me." Another little sigh. "Daddy suspected, maybe knew all along, I don't know, but it pretty much rocked my world."

"I guess so," Sophie said, on the edge of her seat, caught up in the story, oblivious to the bigger purpose anymore.

Per Quinn, things got weird between Greer and Fox when Anna May turned eighteen. Sounded like Greer was fully aware of Anna May's DNA, and since the mother was still around back then, might be what fueled a bit of a fire. Fox went to county council, and when that fell through, he came back to rule Pon Pon on town council. Somewhere in the next four years, the mother got sick, which more than likely cooled the animosity. One would hope. There was a book in all that, especially if one included Armstrong and all the trouble he caused.

But what did heritage have to do with the present? With this much history, it had to come into play, but she didn't ask, having told Anna May to start at the beginning. So she listened.

"Not sure what you know about Pon Pon," the girl started, then seemed to hang up on a thought.

"A bit," Callie said. No point in revealing the day's okra lunch with Quinn Sterling.

"Troy Fox might not be mayor, but he runs the town. Kinda like Mr. LeGrand."

Guess the girl wasn't so empty headed after all.

"Fox turned my stomach before I learned who he was to me. For years I thought he flirted with me, when in fact he was going through the motions of trying to get close to his daughter."

"Ick that you couldn't tell the difference," Slade said.

Everyone had been snagging glances at Callie throughout the storytelling.

Callie could relate, and they knew it, only with two moms. If her father hadn't been dead when she learned, she would've torn into him for his choices. Sounded like Anna May had a similar but far worse experience.

Quinn and Ty made Fox sound pretty sleazy. If Fox was the guy Armstrong met on Blue House Lane, then Anna May might be involved somehow, but it sounded like she was clueless.

Or at least so far.

Sure Greer knew of his wife's indiscretion. In a town that small, how could he not? No other brothers and sisters, this baby girl coming out of the blue, questions came to mind about how Anna May grew up, who in the community suspected, how Fox treated Anna May.

But then Callie'd had no clue of her own lineage for forty years either.

"Go on," Thomas urged his friend.

"Um," she said, and Callie felt her slipping away.

"Whose idea was it to move here?" she asked, to regain the momentum.

"Daddy's," she replied. "To get me out of Pon Pon, I think. To get me away from Fox."

Stan stole a glance at Callie, speaking what was on his mind. "Exactly what's wrong with Fox?"

That's right. Stan and Sophie were just hearing of Fox and had heard nothing of the day's lunch with Quinn.

"He wheels and deals, and Daddy never lets me near him. When we got a complaint about him, which was rare, Daddy handled it personally, and he forever told me to steer clear of the man. Whether because he was my real father or because he's the kingpin of Pon Pon, I'm not sure, but Daddy said Fox had a side I didn't need to brush up against."

Having raised Anna May, Greer would be protective. She wanted to ask if Greer was in cahoots with Fox over anything. What was their conjoined baggage? But they had to remain on Anna May's side to get anywhere. If any slights were made against her father, she could close ranks, clam up, and leave. Worse . . . inform her dad. This was the best lead they'd had into Greer since he arrived, and they needed to milk it best they could.

"It all sounds shady to me," Sophie started, only for Stan to squeeze her knee again.

"Yeah, and this meeting is starting to feel awfully one-sided," Anna May said. "Maybe I shouldn't have—"

"You're right," Callie said. "Give-and-take only seems fair. First, do you need anything to drink?"

Slade got up. "I'll get it. Unfortunately, there's only carrot juice and water."

"Y'all cleaned me out of carrot juice, remember," Sophie said.

"Then water it is." Slade left the room, soon returning with a filled iced glass.

Callie let Anna May take a sip, then two, then half the glass. She was nervous, attempting to hide she was scared to death. Thomas cut Callie a look. This meeting had dragged out too long.

"My interest is Lumen Townsend," Callie said. The others stiffened, subconsciously easing back to give Callie the floor, making Anna May's attention fell on her. "She was a friend. We met at the Presbyterian Church and visited graves in the cemetery."

"I've heard of the place. People say it's haunted," the girl replied.

"It is," Sophie said.

Callie tempered that assessment by saying, "Some think so. But we met there the day Lumen died."

"I didn't know that. Were you with her?" Anna May asked. "I mean, when she died?"

Neither Greer nor Armstrong had filled her in. The Pon Pon habit of keeping Anna May in the dark had continued in Edisto Beach. Callie wondered what Armstrong knew and didn't know.

Mostly, wondered why he had met with Fox on Edisto Island.

"No, I wasn't with Lumen when she died," Callie continued. "I left and she died about thirty minutes later." She paused. "Around four o'clock."

Callie waited for the reaction . . . and got none.

Thomas, however, showed puzzlement. "Your dad told everyone she died around one, Annie." Which he couldn't have known without Callie telling him.

Anna May waited for the rest of the story. She wasn't getting it.

"Annie," he exclaimed. "Your dad and Armstrong lied about when the woman died. It's been confirmed with the coroner. Why would they cover up?"

Her eyes widened. "Are you saying they killed her?"

Thomas turned, silently pleading with Callie. He wasn't sure where to take this.

"No," Callie said. "She had a heart attack. That's been confirmed, too. The time of death is what caught my attention. She died at four, while your father told me one." She motioned to Slade. "Spoken in front of witnesses."

Anna May shrugged. "I'm at a total loss."

"I have a question," Slade said, raising her hand.

Callie wasn't sure now was the time, but they didn't need to squabble in front of the young woman.

When Callie didn't kill the request, Slade rolled into her concern. "What's your relationship with Armstrong?"

Anna May hadn't expected that. She did a thing with her mouth, a shrug of sort. "He's Daddy's right hand. He's always been an uncle of sort. He's rough around the edges, but I've been raised to listen to him. That's why . . . that's why I'm. . . ."

Thomas finished. "That's why she came to me. Armstrong has coaxed her into something that isn't savory. She isn't sure how to get out of it, or who to pass on what she's seen. It has the potential of being something bad, Chief. Like nothing-we've-ever-had-on-Edisto bad. "

Thomas's read on the danger made Callie leery about who should remain in the discussion. Not a soul was active law enforcement except Thomas and Anna May who were the ones asking for advice.

"Sophie." Callie started with the most civilian of the civilians. The one least likely to understand the need for secrecy, the one most likely to share before catching herself.

"No, you wait a damn minute," came the reply. "None of us other than these kids are cops. You have no more right than I do hearing this."

Callie was ready to carry this meeting elsewhere, but Thomas spoke up. "Miss Sophie. This is life-or-death stuff. If any of us talks, someone could die. To include us."

"Oh no," Stan said, gripping Sophie's hand. "She doesn't need to hear this."

"Don't piss me off, Stan."

So much for the snuggly nickname.

"The more you know the more at risk you are," he said. "Best you not be here."

"It's my house!"

"Then best *we* not be here," Slade said. "Listen, if Wayne were around, he'd usher me out the same way."

"So why aren't you being put out?" Sophie asked, her hair dancing with each word.

"Wayne's not here."

"Well," Callie said. "I have a solution. Stan and I will talk to Anna

May and Thomas at my place."

"Sounds best," Thomas said, standing and motioning Anna May to leave.

"Ride with me," Stan said to Callie.

But Slade rose, shaking her head. "Armstrong's already been watching your place, Sherlock."

"Then we'll go to my place," Stan said, which shut everyone up. Callie doubted Armstrong knew Stan's last name, much less where he lived. He was the old retired guy from Boston. Yes, Stan's place was best.

Again, Keystone Kops came back to mind, but right now Callie would take what she could, however she could get it. There was a stench in Edisto's air that just kept getting stronger.

Chapter 25

Callie

IN AN UNEASY silence, the four rode in Stan's vehicle three short blocks over to his place, *Gang Plank*, a small two-bedroom affair on Pompano that he leased with the option to purchase but hadn't bothered to yet. He'd fallen headlong into the slo-mo style of Edisto, and the owners hadn't pushed the point.

He ushered them into his rustic living arrangements. "Sit. Wait."

Not asking who might want what refreshment, he retrieved four soft drinks of his choosing and posted them on coasters, sitting guests around his small kitchen table. "Now, get to Armstrong. He approached you, Anna May. How and when?"

Callie counted having her old boss here a blessing. He knew how to arrange a talk—the clustered seating, no chance for interruption, only the trusted parties present. The bowed heads emphasizing the need to remain clandestine seemed to give Anna May a more trusting posture. Callie should've known. As usual, Stan tweaked her ways, and always for the better. She chastised herself for omitting him from the start.

Anna May's voice came out more level than it had at Sophie's. "A week ago, Armstrong cornered me in the office. Dad had a meeting somewhere, and Marie had already gone home for the day. He pushed me, and we wound up in Dad's inner office. I had no idea how to react."

Callie's old office.

"He told me about some rich people coming in, and he wanted a uniform to be with him, to make security look better."

Callie tensed. How many of her old officers had been sucked into this? "Who else did he line up?"

"Just me," she said. "He didn't trust anyone from the *old regime*." She paused at how that sounded. "Sorry, but that's what he said."

"No problem," Callie replied, grateful for her old staff staying out of trouble. "Is this meeting in the future or has it already happened?"

"Already happened. For the first time. They'll be flying in several times a month, each time a last-minute notification."

Callie stiffened. "Flying? We don't have an airstrip on this island."

Thomas spoke up. "We do now, Chief. They carved out a small landing strip off Marsh Landing last week."

Staring at him as if he'd spoken Greek, Callie replied, "That quickly?"

"It's doable," Stan said, "but I'm dumbfounded none of us knew. Somebody would've talked about it, or at least one would think."

"Well"—and Thomas looked sheepish—"y'all have been outside the circle lately. Me, too, for that matter. The shift in the police force preoccupied us all, plus it was outside the town."

Callie motioned to the girl. "Let Anna May finish telling this."

"Like I said, Armstrong's like an uncle to me, so when he asked for assistance, I said sure. But when he said Daddy wouldn't approve, I got nervous. Then he offered me two thousand dollars to sit in the car on the outskirts of the landing strip for only two hours, guarding the gate, so I went along."

"Went along, as in agreed?" Callie asked. "Or went along as in you already did it?" She recalled no gate out there, either, but apparently a lot had happened in the last few weeks.

"Did it."

The rich didn't carve out their own airstrips out here. Honestly, the rich flew into the better facilities in Charleston and were secretly chauffeured in with nobody the wiser but the police chief and the broker handling the rental. Or that was how it used to be. The less splash the better.

This worried her. "What time of day did you do this?"

"Two in the morning," Anna May said.

Odd, unless they were that self-conscious about being seen. "Where did y'all take them, meaning where did they stay?"

"Charleston, or so I assume."

"Then why not fly into Charleston?"

Anna May tried to clarify. "All I know is they came here and then left the island."

Yea, she got that. Callie slowly shook her head at Stan. Whoever this was moved in fast, taking advantage of the shift in power. These weren't typical rich people on holiday.

Her first instinct was drugs. As long as she'd been on Edisto, she marveled that drug trafficking wasn't more prevalent. Coastal islands were primo geography for illicit covert activity with a shoreline filled with nature's nooks and crannies, inlets and marshes.

She could ask a lot of questions, but Callie preferred hearing this organically from Anna May, telling the story from her perspective, which thus far felt rather innocent. The trust factor here was huge, the situation potentially critical. "Okay," she said. "Start from the date Armstrong recruited you, and bring us to when you went to Thomas for help."

"Four days ago," Anna May went on, "Armstrong asked me to do what I told you."

That was the day before Lumen died.

"The middle-of-the-night meeting was the following night."

The same day Lumen died.

Callie built the timeline. This was also the same afternoon Slade and Wayne had arrived, and also when, at dinner, Greer told them Lumen had died at one.

"I asked for the nighttime shift, along with Russell, making sure he had the furthest end of the beach, giving me the ability to leave the town more easily for this gig."

Russell Wiley, Arne Webb, and Thomas were the remainder of the old staff. Russell was mediocre in his performance, and he'd be the last on the force to question how someone else did their job. He was the one voted most likely to park and doze. Though he hadn't been caught, he volunteered for night shift more often than the others. Anna May couldn't have picked a better night partner to not interfere with hers and Armstrong's plan.

"At one thirty in the morning"—Anna May's voice dropped, giving an ominous, secretive sensation to her story—"I drove to the site and parked, as he told me to, remaining on the lookout for anyone on Pine Landing Road. These people should not be seen, he said. Armstrong showed, repeated my job was to stay in the shadows, stay alert, open the gate for any vehicle to exit, close the gate, and disappear." She hesitated to see if everyone understood. Each nodded.

"Sure enough, a small engine plane appeared and landed. A van came out of nowhere to collect the passengers, guess it arrived before I did. Armstrong was somewhere along the strip, but he'd told me from the outset that his location wasn't my problem, so I didn't try to find him."

Callie watched Thomas as well as the girl. He listened, adding nothing, thus far seeming to hear the same story he'd been told.

"I heard the van coming my way—"

"Did you see who got in? Get a good look at the driver?" Stan asked, but she shook her head. He motioned for her to continue.

"It was pitch, which I imagine was the reason for that particular evening," she said. "The van approached, no plate visible, driven by someone who appeared to be Hispanic."

She paused. Thomas scooted closer. "Go ahead."

"I can't believe I participated in this," she said, the sentence reducing to a whisper.

Callie didn't push her, coax her, or do anything to influence her. She almost hit the record button on the phone in her lap, then decided against it. If Anna May admitted all this here, she'd repeat it later, plus, she'd already told Thomas. No point in ruining cooperation.

She also wanted to smack the young lady for blindly involving herself in something she hadn't vetted. Especially if someone as scummy as Armstrong, uncle figure or not, asked her to.

"I held the gate open, backed into the bushes, so I'm not sure they saw me or not." She took a swallow of her Sprite. "Surprisingly, the piece-of-crap, dirty-rattle-trap of a van wasn't a panel van. When they passed by me, I saw." Another swallow. "The driver had his window down from talking to the pilot and whoever else was out there, and I saw at least six girls, maybe more, inside. One spoke Spanish. He replied to them harshly, just two words."

The three of them hung on her telling of the tale.

"He said, *Callate putas.*"

Stan gave a deep groaning breath. "We know what it means."

Callie's heart broke. Child smuggling, girl smuggling, human smuggling of any kind represented the worst one could do to a person. The people snatching these poor souls represented the worst of humanity. She'd lose sleep for nights over the hopelessness those girls must feel, and the impotency at not being able to do much for them. Those girls were gone, off the map, no telling to what part of the country, continent, or the world, for that matter.

Anna May scanned her audience, a pleading urgency in her eyes. She'd walked into trouble, participated in this heinous venture that would haunt her for years. Now she was lost and, now that others were aware, she could hold back no longer. Silent tears spilled, and Stan handed her a napkin from the counter behind him about the time she broke down and sobbed.

"I didn't know what to do." Her voice trailed into more sobs.

Tears welled in Callie's eyes. Atop everything, Anna May suffered through her own trauma. Her father wasn't her father while her real father was a sleaze. Her uncle figure was embroiled in crime, and she'd been uprooted from a lifetime home to a foreign place.

She had nobody but the people around this table to come to for help, and to admit to them she'd veered off the straight and narrow had to feel desperate.

"God, I'm a mess," Anna May said, cheeks and eyes red. "But think about it. Is Daddy involved? God, I already know Armstrong is, and that tears me apart." She sucked in a few shaky breaths. "I've trusted him my entire life!" She blew her nose. "Is he still a good guy, just protecting my dad from whatever he got involved in, or is Daddy clean and looking the other way about Armstrong? I don't know."

Thomas curled his arm around her. "Anyone in your shoes might've fallen into that, Annie. The good thing is you came to me and I brought you to them." He turned to Callie and Stan, his gaze seeking direction.

"Did he pay you?" Callie asked.

"Yes," she said. "But it's in a shoebox in my closet. Cash. All hundreds. I'm not spending it. Wish I hadn't touched it." She sighed. "Wish I'd turned it down."

"No," Callie said. "You'd have been targeted at that point. You had knowledge and they'd think you couldn't be trusted. When did he pay you?"

"Drove by the gate after the van, handed it through the window, and put a finger over his mouth to be quiet. Then he left."

"So he said nothing?" Stan asked.

"Told me to shut the gate. I haven't spoken to him since." She sniffed and wiped her nose again. "Actually, I believe he's avoiding me."

It appeared the girl had been raised right with a sense of morality still in place, but where had she acquired it? Her mother? Curiously, by Greer? Maybe the man operated with two ethics—the one at home and the one on the job. No matter what he knew about this most recent mess, his history made it clear he had looked the other way for Armstrong on enough occasions.

"Are you sure you haven't spoken of this to your dad?" Callie asked. Anna May shook her head.

"And haven't spoken to Armstrong since the flight came in?"

Again, a negative shake.

To obtain and maintain the officer's cooperation, they had to gain her trust. Thomas carried her halfway there, but they had to overcome Anna May's lifetime of relationship with the two Pon Pon men to do anything about this.

"Annie." Callie dared use the familiar name, to align with Thomas, and to differentiate this group from the old Pon Pon group. "I told you about the time difference for Lumen's death."

The girl nodded.

"We believe someone needed an alibi. Someone didn't want to be recognized on Blue House Lane at four in the afternoon when Lumen saw them . . . when she really died."

Stan hadn't heard all this before, and he listened just as hard as Annie.

"If Lumen died, how can you know she saw them?" the girl asked.

Callie held back a second.

But Stan didn't. "The chief can't tell you. Not without exposing someone. That would be my guess."

Stan had guessed correctly. They still had Mr. Burnett as a witness. The man was too old and feeble to get wrapped up in this, and while Callie read the man as mentally stable, his age alone would nurture doubts. He'd be easy to dispose of and attribute the death to natural causes. Without relatives, he wouldn't be missed. Like Lumen, there'd be nobody around to claim otherwise.

Except Callie.

For Lumen and for Mr. Burnett, she was in this for keeps now, and she'd have to be careful who learned what from this point on. Knowledge was vulnerability for each and every person who was aware.

In her head, she had envisioned Armstrong as head of security but not chief of a smuggling operation. He marched around as the muscle, not the brains, and she would've suspected Greer as the honcho of the op if Fox hadn't made his appearance. Still Greer was too seasoned to be entirely ignorant. He left Pon Pon for a reason.

In many of these situations, the bosses don't get directly involved in the operational end. Which meant that Fox was likely just a local flunky who could accommodate someone with a place and time to pull this off. He'd be the big fish in a small pond, so to speak. The man in the plane was low-level, too. Things like this had layers of overseers, people who the low-levels had only heard of by name, if they had heard of them at all. Like they'd paid Anna May, these deals were about money in palms and no questions asked.

Callie decided to bring those around the table farther into the situation. "That afternoon on Blue House Lane, Armstrong, Fox, and some unknown in the car thought they'd slipped off the highway to a place nobody traveled," she explained. "Ordinarily, they would've been safe. Fate happened to place Lumen on the road, walking home."

Stan showed doubt. "And you're sure nobody killed her?"

Anna May's eyes widened at the possibility.

"Unless they scared her to death, no," Callie said. "Coroner's sure."

"The family might contest it if she hadn't been ill," he added.

"I haven't been able to find family," she said.

His expression fell. "So that's that about Lumen."

"I'll tend to Lumen. Let's focus on Annie right now. Here's what I think. Armstrong and Fox were lining up security for the incoming flight. I suspect the unknown person in Fox's Audi was affiliated with the plans. Lumen just showed up out of the woods, walking home. They were nervous. They didn't think clearly. Fox was afraid of being seen on Edisto, and Armstrong was afraid of being seen with Fox. The third party wisely remained in the car."

Thomas could guess the witness, but thank goodness he kept his mouth shut.

Annie waited for whatever else was to come. She'd grown up in a small town where, in her experience, drunks, speeders, and domestic spats represented the worst of the worst when it came to crime. Greer had handled everything else, and from the sound of things, using Armstrong as his lieutenant. If there were worse crimes, nobody was the wiser. Sounded to Callie like there might've been more going on in Pon Pon.

"Two mornings later, your father sabotaged me at the probate office when I tried to file for Lumen's estate. He called them ahead of time, painting me as a money-seeker. He went to my hometown and supported the mayor offering me a job, to get me off the beach. And that was *before* any of this." She took a breath. Annie didn't budge. "Armstrong harassed me at home, on the road, and at Lumen's. They threatened Mark, trying to sabotage his liquor license, and they called Slade and Wayne's employers and lodged complaints."

Annie dropped her head in her hands.

Callie reached over to the girl, hand on her back. "We get proactive now. Don't talk to Greer or Armstrong any more than you have to. Restrict talking to Thomas, which will look normal since he works with you, and like he said, y'all are the same age."

"We're making her an operative," Thomas said.

"For the time being, but I'm calling this in to higher powers. This stuff is way out of our league."

"Who are you calling?" asked Anna May.

"Just don't worry about it," Callie said. "You'll learn what you need to soon enough. The less the better for now."

Anna May shook her head. "I already know more than I want to."

Callie patted her once more and slid her chair back from the table. "We all do, honey. We all do. Now we push through and hope we come out on the other side . . . unscathed and with answers. We're in too deep to back out now."

Chapter 26

Slade

I PEERED THROUGH Sophie's kitchen blinds again. Callie and crew had been gone well over an hour, and the longer they stayed gone, the more I worried how much I didn't understand. Being in the dark didn't run natural through my veins, and once intrigued, my curiosity saw things through . . . or drew its own conclusions.

It's how I'd learned to live life after a nasty marriage, after almost losing that life following the proverbial rule book.

It's also how I often tripped over trouble.

With it approaching midnight, I peeked out once more, having gone in the kitchen in the guise of getting another drink of water.

"Can't believe I'm more patient than you are," Sophie said from her recliner, holding out the remote like a sci-fi stun phaser. She watched exercise channels, making approving or disapproving throat noises at the instructors.

Of course, Sophie wouldn't be too terribly disturbed. She observed law enforcement from the outside looking in, not concerned about how things were done, only the results. Sound-bite crime.

I'd been stabbed, tied up, and chased . . . almost drowned twice in the name of cases. For some strange reason I didn't worry about such things until they confronted me eye-to-eye, then there was no telling how I'd react. Thus far, I'd come out on top. My behaviors drove Wayne mad. They were normal to me. I wasn't a big *what-if* person.

"You're too quiet," she added, muting the television. "What are you thinking hard about?"

I returned to the living room. "How nasty things might be. How much we don't see and they won't let us know."

Sophie shifted to her other hip. "I follow the Serenity Prayer, girl. You might do the same."

Grant to us the serenity to accept what cannot be changed, courage to change that which can be changed, and wisdom to know the one from the other.

I sorely lacked in the wisdom department.

What nagged me most was ignorance of who the bad guys were. Or people. Bad guys were non-gender-specific. I still wasn't sure Anna May was on our side or theirs. Callie ghosting away the discussion gave me paranoid thoughts that she didn't feel I'd agree, or cooperate, or . . . something.

"It's nothing personal," Sophie said.

"Oh, it's extremely personal," I replied. "This has criminal written all over it, and whenever it does, the badge folk throw up walls and pretend we don't have sense enough to come in out of the rain." A sore spot with me.

I'd scooped her and me into the same category. That felt incredibly weird.

"Or maybe we don't know how to dodge bullets as well as they do," Sophie said. "I can live with that."

Probably some of the smartest words I'd ever heard her say, but I wasn't telling her so.

I returned to the kitchen, unable to sit and watch people way more fit than I assume impossible poses. Suddenly, I heard tires on gravel, and I turned back to the blinds. Stan's car was back. *Good.* Thomas and Anna May walked to Thomas's vehicle to leave. In the dim streetlight of Jungle Road, I could make out Callie on the passenger side. The interior lights were still off, and they weren't getting out of the car.

Their not totally confiding in Sophie and me, especially me, bothered me, but the emotion didn't rise to the point of anger. I had to trust them. But to sit on the sofa and wait to see what intel they chose to feed me didn't sit well. I had to do something, but not something to hurt whatever they were doing. So I called Wayne.

I woke him up. "Hey, it's me. Are you in Atlanta?"

He yawned, groaning at the end. Made me wish I lay there with him to talk instead of this long-distance nonsense. The image of him alone in a hotel room, knowing how little he wore to bed almost took my mind off things. "Yes, I'm in Atlanta." Then he snapped to attention. "Why, what's wrong? You okay?"

"I've been sidelined," I said.

He friggin' laughed. Not a chuckle, but one of those long, reach-in-your-chest ones that meant the joke was really good. "Good for Callie," he said, then he chuckled, coming down off his high. I wasn't willing to share the humor with him.

"Why?" he asked. "Was it what you did or what's happening?"

Then he totally sobered. "Anyone messing with y'all?"

"Not yet, but I'll be surprised if they don't. Details are coming to light, Lawman. As Thomas put it, *Like nothing-we've-ever-had-on-Edisto bad.*"

"Don't dangle crap out there to me like that, Slade. Not when I'm so far away. What's going on?"

"Anna May ran to Thomas, upset that Armstrong got her into something that's very illegal. She hasn't talked to Greer about it because she isn't sure he isn't in the middle of it. So Thomas brought her to us. Once Callie deduced whatever this was had a serious undertone, she and Stan took Thomas and Anna May to his house. Rather insulting, in my opinion, but the girl was ready to spill her guts, Wayne. I didn't want to mess that up."

"Well, kudos to you for that, Butterbean. Where's everyone now?" She heard rustling, betting he was sitting up, discarding the covers.

"Stan and Callie are outside in the car talking. Thomas and Anna May just left. Sophie and I are in her house twiddling our thumbs." I didn't like the fact the posse chasing this . . . whatever this was . . . wasn't active LEO. We couldn't go to Edisto Beach PD, that's for sure. "Wish you were here. They aren't going to tell me everything, and you—"

"I'm calling Callie," he said.

"Then you'll tell me."

"Then I'll decide what I can tell you."

"You're as bad as they are," I said.

"I'll take that as a compliment," he said, before hanging up with, "I love you."

Chapter 27

Callie

STAN SHUT OFF the engine. "We can't handle this ourselves."

"And it's a given we can't deal with the Edisto Beach guys. Not sure we can even mention it to the sheriff's office," Callie said, staring straight ahead, assuming Slade or Sophie, or both, watched from a window. "Human traffickers are the worst kind of humanity, Stan. You remember."

"Yeah."

They'd broken up a couple trafficking rings together in Boston. The whole damned lot of them would kill any breathing man, woman, child, or dog that got in the way of their business. Or have them killed. Young women and children were no more than a commodity . . . chattel trucked to the next livestock juncture. The few whom Callie and her peers had saved were scarred for life. All too often they fell into step with wrong types again, or prostituted themselves, feeling being trafficked was their fault for living wrong or making wrong decisions. It was a hard hole to dig out of.

But at least when they were saved they had a chance to try. When authorities like them took down one ring, that was at least a few who didn't get snatched. The weight of this new reality took Callie down.

Stan reached over. His big hand enveloped hers. "Stop it, Chicklet. If you're going to help right this wrong, you can't do it with a yoke around your neck. This isn't your fault."

She knew better than to fuss back and say, *So whose fault is it?* because she'd done it before. *It's the bad guys' fault*, he always answered, because it always was.

"This is opportunity," he said instead.

Here they go. "How is this opportunity?"

He didn't bat a lash. "These people had an enterprise long before tonight, before Anna May, even before Troy Fox. Am I right?"

Of course he was, but Stan loved the rhetorical and she didn't reply.

He rolled on. "They came here because you weren't in place. They would not have come otherwise."

"Exactly," she exclaimed.

"If you had not resigned, they would not be here, and they would be slipping around someplace else . . . maybe at a place where they had a lesser chance of getting caught."

In an odd, backhanded twisted sense of logic, Stan made sense. Question was, without any sort of authority anymore, where did she go now? ICE would be the logical choice.

Her phone rang.

"Wayne?" she answered. "Everything all right?"

"You stole my line," he said. "Slade phoned me, and in her oddball roundabout manner told me things had gone south over there. What's up?"

She put him on speaker to include Stan.

"Karma must be working overtime tonight," she said. "I was just running through my head how in the world we'd contact ICE about what we knew. You might be what the doctor ordered."

"ICE?" he said.

She explained Anna May's dilemma, which had now become Edisto's dilemma, which immediately meant she considered it hers. "We don't have a lot of facts yet. The plane in the dark, the van nondescript, and unidentified people, referred to as *putas*, who have come and gone."

"You still have players on the ground," he said. "Anna May, Armstrong, and Fox. Maybe Greer. We know who and where they are. Listen, I have a meeting with the higher-ups in my agency tomorrow to clear up the damage Brice and Greer caused, but telling them this changes the entire picture. We'll do our best to bridge something with ICE, then I'll be back in touch tomorrow. I'll drive back the second I can. Tell Anna May to lay low until she hears from federal people."

"And Thomas," Callie added.

"For sure."

He didn't hang up. She didn't hang up. "What're you thinking?" she said.

"I'll do my best," he said, as if he had to add a disclaimer.

"Meaning they may not listen to you," she said.

"The good thing is I'm an agent coming to ICE, not a civilian. And there's an LEO asset inside the operation. That's the way I sell it. We can only hope ICE already has some sort of feelers out for activity in the Lowcountry, and we offer potential. If they've heard nothing about this operation or these people before . . . just saying I'll give it my best."

"What if they say no?"

"I tell them I'll go to the FBI."

LEOs and their territories. "My second biggest concern is that they ignore all this."

"I can guess your first."

"That in the middle of trying to get someone interested . . . someone gets hurt."

He sighed heavily into the phone. "Y'all be damn careful." He went quiet for a moment then cleared his throat. "Callie? Thanks for keeping Slade out of this. She means well, and most of the time she's an asset, but there comes a point when. . . ."

"She's not trained for serious stuff. I get it. I got it earlier tonight." She gave him a low short laugh. "Now wish me luck going back inside to explain she can't be brought up to speed."

He gave a small grunt. "I'm just glad it's not me for a change." Then he called, "Stan?"

"Yeah, still here."

"Take care of them, please."

"You got it, my man."

SLADE HARDLY SPOKE to Callie on the way back to *Windswept*. As they pulled into the drive, her guest managed, "Just because you tell me the details doesn't mean I jump in guns blazing."

"We're not blazing anything," Callie said. "It's a quarter to one in the morning. Let's go to bed." She had no idea what tomorrow would bring, whether Wayne could convince his agency using third-hand information, and if so whether they could convince ICE to pay attention to Edisto Island. Thomas and Annie—funny how that name had stuck—relied on her. Annie was in a pickle otherwise, and if she didn't find the gumption to back out on her own, she would eventually wind up in trouble.

Callie could call Knox, her FBI buddy in Charleston, but like Wayne he'd have to convince higher-ups as well. No, she'd wait to hear from Wayne first.

Callie just could not fathom any enforcement being aware of trafficking on Edisto and looking the other way. She had to think hard on this. Wayne, Mark, and Stan hopefully would come up with a plan B or C. This sitting on the sidelines waiting for the badges to decide if this merited attention did not agree with her, but she could do it. For a day. Maybe two.

The problem for her was knowing those kidnapped girls endured the same days only under nasty, degrading, hope-sapping conditions, totally at the mercy of scum. Their futures stolen, they could not envision how to get through the next hour, much less the rest of their lives.

It had been a long day, but Callie had no right to feel tired compared to them.

Annie said that activities would occur a few times a month. Too much activity and you drew attention to yourself. Having carved out a short airstrip for a small plane already looked odd, for those who were aware, which wasn't many, apparently. Marsh Landing wasn't on the main thoroughfare, a few miles off the highway, used mostly by hunters and farmers only, ever since Indigo Plantation went under last year.

"Are we ever getting out of the car?" Slade asked.

Callie reached for her purse. "Sorry, lost in my thoughts. For some reason Indigo came to mind. You remember, right?"

Her head rearing back like a chicken sizing up something new in the coop, Slade narrowed one eye. "You're kidding, right? First case we worked together. I bumped into a body in the marsh on what was supposed to be my vacation. Had to swim in dark water . . . twice. Dark water and dead people, two things I don't take kindly to. Why?"

Those people arrested at Indigo were nailed for trafficking drugs up the waterway. What if these new people were an arm of the others, and during that case they'd recognized the beauty of that landing strip locale?

"Never mind." She'd already said too much. She'd have to watch her brainstorming in front of Slade.

They exited and started up the stairs, Slade scurrying behind like a puppy waiting for a treat. "What's the plan tomorrow?"

"Tomorrow is a waiting game. Hopefully, we hear that it's someone else's problem. I might go out to Lumen's again and take inventory. Want to help?"

"Wayne called you, didn't he?"

"Yes."

"I told him to, by the way."

"I figured."

"He's making connections," Slade added.

"Yes, he is."

"He'll be coming back early."

"Maybe yes."

"You're full of conversation tonight."

"That's because it's now tomorrow morning. I'm spent." Callie unlocked the door and entered, expecting Slade to lock up behind her. She did.

Callie headed for her bedroom.

"You're not going to tell me the first damn thing, are you?" Slade said, still on her heel. Then, before Callie could answer, she tacked on, "Wayne told you not to."

"I'd already excluded you, Slade. Don't blame him. This kind of crap is seriously dangerous, and these people don't play."

Slade swooped in, and being five inches taller than Callie, reached to block the entryway to the bedroom. "Then all the more reason for you to talk to me. I have nobody to tell out here, and don't even have a vehicle to get anywhere. I'm totally at your disposal to use as you see fit because what else am I to do? And if this endangers Wayne, I have a right."

"He's trying to pass the case to the right federal agency," Callie said.

Slade lowered her arm. "So it's drugs again? Like Indigo?"

"Worse." Callie entered her bedroom and reached for the door. "Please don't dig. I don't want you involved. Wayne doesn't want you involved. It's that important we keep this, as you're so prone to say, on a need-to-know basis."

Her friend stared a hole through her, as if she could put the pieces together if she stared hard enough. "So what are you going to tell Jeb when he comes in tomorrow?"

"Shit!" Rubbing her chin hard, Callie paused and reached for her phone, then halted.

Slade didn't turn smug, but her expression flaunted a satisfaction of seeing something Callie missed. "You tell him not to come and he'll wonder what you're up to. You're either drinking or involved in something you shouldn't be, which will only light a fire under him to get here. But from the look splashed all over you, you do not want your child on this island right now. It's that bad, isn't it?"

Slade was on-the-money right. Sophie would not want her precious Sprite out here, either. She wouldn't want her baby girl within a thousand miles of the trash that trafficked young girls, and she'd hate Callie forever if she didn't redirect their children from visiting.

She'd have to take it on the chin for the greater good. She placed the call. "Jeb?"

"Yeah, Mom. What are you doing up?"

"Slade and I were over at Sophie's," she said, not exactly lying. "What time were you expecting to come in tomorrow? I haven't had a chance to put a thing in the refrigerator."

"Too late," he said. "We're crossing the big bridge right now."

She massaged the worry on her forehead.

What? Slade mouthed, and Callie felt the beginnings of a headache behind her eyes.

But she might be worrying too hard. The chances were slim to none of another drop on the island for days, even weeks. Jeb and Sprite could come, stay, and be gone before that. Who said the trafficking appointment the other night was successful enough to repeat?

The first choice was to keep her son close while he eagle-eye-watched his troubled, unemployed, alcoholic mother for cracks. The second was to send him to Sophie to be the man in the house for her and her daughter. "Need you to stay with Miss Sophie, if you don't mind," she heard herself say.

"Why?" he asked, not in a soft, disappointed manner, but in something more examining.

"Slade's here. It's late. We were getting in bed when I decided to call. It's been a long, long day. On the other hand I doubt Miss Sophie's asleep yet. She was wide-eyed and wound up when we left."

Jeb was accustomed to his mother's shifts and abrupt detours in schedule, but that had been when she was chief or a detective. Now she was a plain mom. He had a right to question. He knew when to question, too.

But he didn't. "Okay," he said, giving her a pass. "However, I'm coming over tomorrow. I want to lay eyes on you, the house, and everything about you, Mom." Then he softened. "I need to see how you're adapting, please. You'd be the same about me."

How could she not understand his plea? Such a genuine, heartfelt spillage of love for her gripped something in her chest. "Yes, I would. Thanks for being patient with me, Jeb. Love you."

"Love you, too, Mom. Bye."

Slade wasn't three feet away, leaning on the doorframe. "That was pretty awesome, Mother Dearest. Almost reduced me to tears. Don't you think you ought to warn Sophie? No doubt in my mind she and Stan jumped back under the covers once we left."

Slade's laugh escaped like a too-fat balloon. Callie wiped Slade's spittle off her chin then dialed Sophie. No answer. Callie left a voice mail of warning, then texted the same.

"Oooh, Sophie's gonna hate you," Slade said, turning toward the guest room.

No, she wouldn't. Sophie always did her thing and made the world adapt to the shock. Callie wasn't even worried about Sprite, who had to be familiar with her mother's ways. The Kodak moment would be Jeb. Stan had been an uncle figure to him since he was born, and this would no doubt burn a different impression on the poor kid's brain. A visual he could never unsee. After that shock, he might not even remember he was supposed to be checking on his poor ol' mom. *I could hope.*

Chapter 28

Callie

CALLIE'S PHONE RANG from deep in a tunnel. An incessant ring, like it had a personality, yelling for her to find it. Buried so comatose in a dream state she couldn't move, she couldn't make sense out of what to do next. Finally, she answered, vision still too funky to read the time, but no sign of sunlight around the edges of her curtains. Her phone said *Caller Unknown*, and she almost didn't answer except telemarketers didn't dare call people this early . . . or this late.

"Hello?" She cleared her throat when she barely heard herself, so she tried again. "Hello?"

"Callie?" the voice whispered.

She sat up in bed, blinking hard. "Annie?" she whispered back though she had no need to, safely tucked in *Windswept*. "What's wrong?"

"When I got home, Armstrong came out of the bushes and told me to grab my weapon, don't change, and get in my patrol car to head to the airstrip. Thank God I didn't wake Daddy. I'm here now."

Callie's feet hit the floor, instinct telling her to throw on clothes and grab her weapon. Reality stopped her at the bathroom door, nightshirt already off and on the floor, reminding her that she wasn't being called to action as chief anymore.

She eased down, bare bottomed on the upholstered chair in the corner. "Same situation?"

"Yeah, but things are more tense. Way more."

The officer's nerves sang across the phone.

"Fill me in best you can," Callie said, already understanding as quiet as it was out there, a call might be overheard. The connection might go dead or Annie mute.

"The plane was already here. Armstrong said when the van comes by, turn away. Last time the driver complained that I tried to look inside." She choked once, then clearly swallowed it down. "Said he almost off'ed me on the spot for doing so. And he said . . . Armstrong said, that if I spoke to anyone, Daddy would die."

Holy shit. "Van go by yet?"

"No. Wait . . . I hear it. Hold on."

Poor girl. She wasn't in Pon Pon anymore.

This wasn't normal. Two nights this close was stupid in anyone's criminal playbook. This was an emergency situation, and the rise in tension an indicator. Or tonight could be a special order worthy of the risk. Callie wanted to go out there so badly she bit the edge of her tongue clenching her teeth.

Listening hard, hand over the other ear, gazing at the carpet, she focused in case someone spoke. In case someone's voice was familiar. In case a bump or shot meant Annie couldn't talk to Callie anymore. Agonizing seconds passed when she really needed to call Mark or Stan . . . especially Wayne. She couldn't roust Slade and make her call Wayne without telling Slade what to tell him.

No predicting how far away Annie's phone was from the exit gate, where it sat, or how far she stood, no, hid, from the driver. Callie had to listen for what could be a firearm quieting Annie for the naïve misstep she'd taken before . . . or took tonight.

The phone thumped, or something thumped, and adrenaline shot up through her like Vesuvius. Tucking in tighter, she listened harder. A vehicle approached, muffled. No telling where Annie had dropped her phone, hopefully in the floorboard of her cruiser or somewhere where its light couldn't be seen.

Someone yelled in the distance yet close enough to hear the words with the night so still.

"*Mira y te mato!*"

Callie had a poor working knowledge of Spanish, much less spoken in such a guttural manner. Though barely able to identify that the man spoke Spanish, her ear still interpreted the words *look* and *kill*.

"I'm not, I'm not," Annie pleaded.

The vehicle's motor revved once, twice, a foot mashing the gas pedal of a braked vehicle to make a point. Then its engine revved again, didn't stop, and waned as it drove into the distance.

Callie waited. No telling who else was there.

Static came across, the phone being moved. "C-c-callie?"

"I'm here, Annie. Are you alone?"

"Y-y-yes." The girl's teeth chattered.

If Callie'd been in her shoes, she'd have been scared too, but also would've instantly been pissed at being so readily intimidated. She'd have then itched to follow the escaping vehicle. But she wasn't Annie, and Annie wasn't her. "Another van?" Callie asked.

"Y-yes." Better, but she remained wary.

"See the tag?"

"God, no. I kept my eyes shut." Tears tried to choke her words, but she self-corrected. "I kept waiting for a bullet in my head."

No possibility of pursuit, and besides, Annie wasn't the person to do it. She had little talent beyond that of a security guard. There might be others waiting along the route. There might be others on the landing strip, able to see she'd disappeared the same time the van did.

"Where's Armstrong?" Callie asked.

"The van's coming back!"

"Look away, Annie. Don't make eye contact!"

Annie didn't reply.

The call went dead.

Callie called Annie's name to no avail.

Who to call now? Who could Callie possibly call?

She had no proof. She had no recording. She had no authority and had never missed it more than now.

Finger hovering over Thomas's number in her favorites, her instinct was to involve him. Should she? The young officer had zero experience in this realm. But what if Annie was bleeding out at this very moment from a gun, a knife, a garroted throat? Thomas lived not far, his rental out on the island. Would he wind up dead on the ground beside his new friend?

Callie couldn't breathe.

She'd lost Seabrook on that road. She couldn't stand to lose another friend.

What was she to do?

Options shot like pinballs in her head. Did she dare call Greer? Good or bad, should he be notified of his lieutenant's intimidation tactics towards his daughter? Annie said Greer could be killed if she talked, a mediocre indication that Greer wasn't involved . . . unless Armstrong played the line just to nail Annie's cooperation . . . maybe even at Greer's direction.

"Callie? What's going on? Why are you sitting there naked?"

But Callie was too busy ticking boxes in her head. Call Mark? Call Stan? Call Wayne, yes, God, yes to that one, but right now she needed to find Annie. Raysor would take too long to get there from Walterboro, but at least he would come running, with the force of the Colleton

County Sheriff's Office at his disposal. They were the safest of everyone she could think of.

Slade squatted in front of her. "Girl, I hope Mark isn't hiding in the closet. If I thought I'd catch a glimpse of him I'd be thrilled, but that's not what's going on here. You're white as a sheet."

"It happened again," she said, as much to herself. Then in a flash of insight, she leaped to get dressed. "Gotta go."

"Now? It's three in the morning. This already sounds dangerous."

"It is," she replied, snatching on clothes, choosing her work shoes out of habit, tying them on.

"Then you can't go alone. Let me go with you."

"Oh, no," Callie replied. "And I'm not going alone," she tacked on, unsure if it was a lie since she hadn't decided yet.

She leaped up and grabbed keys and purse off the credenza, her weapon in a paddle already in her waistband. "I'll call you," and she was out the door. Before she hit the gravel at the bottom of the stairs, she'd dialed Wayne.

"Hang up and call Raysor," he said, by the time she started her car. "Better late than never."

She heaved a breath snatching on her seat belt. "You and I both know that isn't necessarily so, but you call and update him, please. I've got to grab Mark." As much as she wanted to, she couldn't contact the two other Edisto Beach officers who used to work for her. They still worked for Greer. And they'd never dealt with anything like this.

How had her beloved Edisto gone down so fast?

"Call Thomas," Wayne said.

"Can't." She pulled out without explaining why. "Let me go. Gotta wake up Mark."

"Thomas is closest to this. Thomas knows both sides. Thomas is loyal."

She eased off the gas hearing her tires on the asphalt. No point in getting pulled. "Thomas isn't disposable," was the best way she could say she couldn't lose someone near to her. All she could think of was Francis, who'd been her youngest officer before he died on the job, being the hero. Neither her gut nor her heart would allow her other junior officer to put himself out there like this. She still felt responsible.

Wayne couldn't call him either. He didn't have the number, and the only way to get patched through to Thomas would be via dispatch, and Greer might find out as well as Armstrong.

She called Mark turning the corner to his street. "Dress and arm yourself," she said. "We're going out."

No point running up his stairs. Wasn't a minute before he appeared. Even with his slightly gimped leg, he took the steps down two at a time.

"Just you?" fell out of his mouth before he could buckle his belt. No asking for justification. They might have only known each other ten months, but he trusted her instincts, and she'd learned to trust his.

"Just me," she said. "Let's hope this amounts to nothing," she added, taking off toward Jungle Road to head out of the beach town.

Chapter 29

Callie

CALLIE HAD NO plan other than to find Annie. She covered Annie's phone call with Mark, and he offered to call SLED for what that was worth. The crisscross of jurisdictions complicated any crime.

"We've all been blacklisted with our connections," she said. "This all falls on Annie's shoulders. She has to come forward." Assuming there still was an Annie to come forward.

Callie sped up, aware of Pine Landing Road just ahead, she and Mark both scouting for either a van or an Edisto Beach cruiser. They could just as easily be spotted by Armstrong, and Callie had no idea what that would amount to. She was winging this.

Halfway between midnight and dawn, there was no sign of headlights on Highway 174 by the time she took the turn. They were so long after the fact, after Annie's phone call, that Callie didn't attempt to blend in. Not this time of morning, and not with the unknown of Annie's plight hanging over them.

Callie hadn't seen the airstrip, so she wasn't quite sure how far down. Surely it wasn't right on the road. After one wrong dead-end, she backed out and took another. The road went further than she recalled, freshly cut brush along the way. They reached a broad metal farm gate.

"There," Mark said, bailing from the car.

Annie sat on the ground, barely visible in the shrubs behind her cruiser, head between her knees.

"Annie?" he said, rough at first, but when she looked up, he lowered to the ground and took the urgency out of his voice. "Are you all right?"

Callie reached his side. "Are they gone?" she asked quietly, as if they hadn't already made themselves obvious.

Annie whispered, "Yes."

Callie shone a flashlight across the young woman. Annie winced but let Callie take stock of any damage, which appeared to be a goose egg of a knot to the outside over her left brow.

"I'm fine," she said, feeling, tenderly measuring the bruise. "I stayed in the car, so he wouldn't accidently think I wanted to get in the way. Just watching the gate, like Armstrong said. Just following instructions."

She strove to explain how hard she tried to do as asked. For a crime, no less. Comical and tragic.

"He asked for my phone. When he opened his door, I stared down into my lap. He was a man, Hispanic, but a blind person could tell that. He ordered me to turn over the phone, so I held it out through the window . . . and stared to the passenger seat. I heard it crack when he bent it in his hands." Tears started. "He stood there, not leaving, like it was a test to see how long before I turned and clenched my fate. But I didn't." She shook her head once, then a couple times. "I was not going to look at him, no matter what he did." Her deep breath turned into another sob. "He had to have seen I was talking to you."

Callie pushed wet bangs away from her eyes. "If he had, you wouldn't be here talking to us, hon."

She shrugged. Mark helped her up. She looked herself over in the light as though she had to make sure nothing else was hurt.

"Did you lose consciousness?" After a quiet negative from Annie, Callie asked, "Are you nauseous?" Another negative. "Good. Then we'll follow you home." Callie glanced over at Mark, concerned. "Did Armstrong leave you out here like this, Annie?"

"I, um, I tried to look like I held it together when he showed. He'd already seen the plane off and made sure the gate was locked. He told me I was lucky to be alive, calm down, and get home." She seemed better, then quickly welled up with a last thought. "I didn't even look at the plane!"

For a change, Callie agreed with Armstrong. Annie needed to be home in bed, but after all this, she'd either crash at the adrenaline drop or stare at the ceiling till dawn. She wished she could be with the young woman, but she lived with her father. "What will you do about your father?"

"Nothing," she said. "Avoid him. Don't need him reading me, you know?"

Good luck with that. To Callie, Annie's biggest personal weakness was what Greer might notice. Parents read children.

"Go home," Callie said. "Don't give Armstrong a reason to question where you are. And dodge your father."

Sighing and smoothing out her jeans, tucking in her T-shirt as if she had to look presentable first, Annie gave some nervous micro-nods to show she understood. "So what happens now?" she asked, like Callie was in charge.

"We're working on that," she replied. "You don't worry."

Callie's best answer held little substance, but it was the best she had at the moment. She'd call Wayne. She'd update Thomas, emphasizing that he keep his behavior clandestine and normal, but first she'd call Deputy Raysor, telling him not to haul ass to Edisto. He could call off his Colleton dogs for now. They had nothing concrete to pursue, and to show their hand too soon for Armstrong or Greer to see could turn catastrophic.

"I'D FEEL BETTER if you stayed with me," Mark said, after they saw Annie home and returned to Mark's place. They'd hung up from Wayne. They parked at the base of his beach house stairs, Mark clearly not wanting to exit Callie's car. "Armstrong is not who we think he is, and God only knows who Greer answers to. If Annie lived alone I'd have Thomas stay with her, but we can't alert her dad."

From Mary Street she could see straight up to Beach Access Three barely a block away with its blue-black water. The night weighed on her bones. No telling how bad Annie felt. Callie prayed the girl wasn't on duty today.

"I have Slade at the house," she said, too tired to talk much.

He covered her hand with his, laying it on the seat beside him. "She's a big girl. She's aware you went out. And she seems the type to almost envy you having another bed to go to."

"Which is another reason I don't need to leave her alone. We have no idea what or who we're dealing with, and Armstrong's aware she's at my place. He surveils us, Mark. You've seen him. So no, she can't be left alone, especially after tonight."

He hadn't stayed at *Windswept* yet. Callie hadn't asked him to, and he hadn't offered.

"Come here," he said, drawing her over with the hand he held. Wrapping both arms around her, he kissed her temple and cuddled her as tightly and as closely as a front seat would allow. Then with another kiss on her ear, he whispered, "I love you, Sunshine."

She was stunned at the words, but instead of reciting it back rote to him, she tucked that kissed ear into his warmth, re-settling her jaw against his collar, feeling she could stay right there.

He grounded her. Not like Seabrook. Honestly, in some ways better than Seabrook, who'd never been a natural cop—part of what got him killed. Mark, however, had developed a career with SLED. Real investigative work. A real cop. Someone who'd already proven over and over that he grasped where her head went sometimes without her saying the first word.

After kissing his stubbly neck, she eased back, retrieved herself from his embrace, and reached for the ignition.

He didn't bother putting on his seat belt as she left his drive. He knew exactly where she headed, and it was just down the road on Palmetto.

Along the way, both canvassed the driveways and parking areas, the side streets and the gray shadows under palmetto trees that would soon take on the less muted hues of dawn. No one stirred.

At *Windswept*, they took the stairs on the balls of their feet, out of respect for Slade . . . out of respect for this being different.

Tonight the direction of the wind blowing through their relationship had changed, a change that might not have occurred without danger in their midst. This time, this address made it all the more sincere. All the more . . . promising.

Each accustomed to stealth moves, they eased inside, reaching across each other to lock the door, her ultimately letting him do it.

For a second she regressed, noting how the evening had become an aphrodisiac, but he was already here. There was no heat, no rush to undress, no fumbling and stumbling over each other to put skin against skin.

This was more reverent.

She pushed the bedroom door closed, slid off shoes, and led him to Seabrook's old bed. But it really wasn't. She'd traded the headboard, bought new sheets, replaced the spread. The paint went from pale blue to beige, and the nautical theme converted to one of birds.

Seabrook had been a doctor, a person in love with humanity, a person who gave everyone a second chance, making him a mediocre cop at best in some situations, a public servant to admire in others. That doctor side of him had more carved him into that beautiful person, an Edisto favorite son.

He'd brought her mint chocolate-chip ice cream, nudged her toward AA, and orchestrated events so the Town of Edisto Beach allowed him to step down and hire her in his stead, he more than proud. He loved his heritage, his town, and helping others. And he recognized early on she was a much better candidate for chief. He saw what others needed, and he thought of others before himself.

He of all people would totally empathize with this night.

Callie gradually eased him into her past.

Here, lying beside her, was the present. Possibly a future.

Mark slid her to him, his sigh maybe a little shakier than hers. They'd had sex. This wasn't sex. This was the first step of them coming out on the other side of each other's pasts. Tonight, at least hers.

So she gave herself to him. Even in this room once steeped in such harsh history, she softened and focused on Mark's need, concluding he was what the doctor would have ordered for her.

Chapter 30

Slade

CALLIE RODE OFF into the night alone, armed and adrenalized up with no plan or backup which made me call Wayne right out of the chute. Voice mail. Again, voice mail. *Answer, damn it.*

I walked outside, giving Callie time to talk to Wayne, or so I assumed was the reason he ignored my caller ID. I tried sitting on the red swing. Callie always acted like it channeled energy, so, frustrated and impotent I gave it a go. Three pushes in, and it didn't do a damn thing for me.

Impatiently giving that swing a final push for all it was worth, I lifted feet into the seat and dialed and hung up, dialed and hung up like a robot, hell bent on Mr. Lawman to pick up and be aware of what was going on from my perspective. If he wasn't talking to Callie, if he was sprawled in an Atlanta motel bed sleeping through all this personal vexation, I'd be vexed tenfold more.

"Slade," he finally answered.

My toe stopped the swing, almost dumping me, and I returned inside, not of the right mind to whisper, and at three in the morning not needing the neighbors to hear. "She went out alone, Wayne. I tried to go with her. Where is she, and please tell me you two talked."

"Don't—"

"And if you tell me not to get involved, so help me, I'll go hunt her myself."

"You have no car."

"I'll wake up Sophie."

"She won't get involved."

"Then I'll go get her son, Jeb. He's on the island, and all I have to do is tell him his mom is in trouble."

He got quiet.

"Yeah," I said, feeling like I'd played a trump card.

But his chilly reply countered quite well. "You piss me off when you get childish, Slade. The facts are what they are. You are not law enforcement, regardless how much of a superhero you profess to be. We don't have time for games. It's moments like this that you get in the friggin' way." He blew a hard breath, and I couldn't tell if it was for my purpose or his. "Doesn't look good on you, Butterbean."

I tempered things a bit and sank on the sofa, sort of wishing I was back on Callie's swing. "The not knowing is worse, Cowboy. You make me nuts being secretive."

"Don't I know it," he replied, a step off the attitude but not yet down to ground level.

"She is not law enforcement anymore, Wayne. She's rogue. She's as bad as I've ever been."

"She's trained, she's running things by me," he said, "and she took Mark with her."

Well, thank God for that. But what did that mean that she needed backup?

"Will you call me—" and I stopped. Of course he'd call me if something went sideways. Of course he'd call me if I needed to run to Callie's aid after the fact.

But when it came to danger in the moment, he'd call Mark, Stan, Thomas, or Raysor first, and remember me once the dust settled. My concern was I'd be the last person he'd call after everyone else had tried and failed. I got it. I did. Internal investigations were as close as I could get to being an agent, more paper and interviews than anything else, and, bless him, Wayne gave me a longer leash than he should, but I'd proven myself more than once or twice. The reality that I'd aged out of being eligible to go into law enforcement before knowing that's what I wanted to be when I grew up continually stuck in my craw. As a retired cop once told me when they pushed him out the door, stating he was too old to chase bad guys in the field anymore, *Why chase them? Never known a bad guy yet who could outrun a bullet.*

I laughed bittersweetly to myself. Great. Now I was comparing myself to a retired old man. "Just call me when you can," I said.

"I will. I get it, Butterbean."

The feel of hanging up on my nickname offered some solace, but we also hung up leaving me alone and worried again. I wasn't good alone. Not like Callie. Not that she was in all that great a shape these days, but she did her best thinking alone. She was a much deeper well than I cared to be.

I woke up stiff, chilly, and curled in a knot against the arm of the sofa, my phone singing and vibrating under me somewhere. Stirring, I bumped it out on the floor, and I almost toppled over retrieving it. "Hello?"

"She's fine," Wayne said.

"Are . . . things fine?" I asked.

"Not really, but nothing can be done tonight."

Not wanting to re-enter an argument, I didn't ask to be looped in on the details, but neither did I want to hang up. "She's not back yet."

"If she's not back in a half hour, call me. I gotta catch some sleep before tomorrow, babe."

Okay, that made me feel bad. "Go on to bed. Love you."

I hung up, silently vowing to leave him alone, thankful that Callie was with Mark. She ought to just stay at his place, but she'd feel obligated to me being here alone. I could call, but what higher level of nuisance did that make me?

Half of me wanted to wait up, half of me wanted to crawl in bed, so I stayed where I was. Callie would fill me in best she could. I was learning to trust her.

We were only a year into our friendship, but the intensity of our time spent and cases worked together had distilled it into a meaningful one. We were of like minds and like ages, but not like personalities, not by a long shot. She mattered to me, though. It's why I shot down here to pull her sorry ass out of the deep, dark chasm she'd cast herself into. I understood her well enough.

But worse than the burnout, Callie took every lost soul to heart, and who could blame her with her track record of personal loss?

My lids fell shut while typing a note to myself to call my boss in the morning to put me on another week's leave. Best stay down here until my friend stood more firmly on her feet, even if it meant no more than camping on this sofa for her to return home each day from slaying her dragons.

Nestled into the arm, snuggled into the cushion, I deemed the sofa cozy enough to maintain my vigil.

Funny how the tall stairs to these beach houses served as an alert, but even in my fog I stirred at a suspected presence. Like a babysitter caught falling asleep on the job, I hopped up all sloppy and lopsided.

No voices, and the steps sounded like more than one set of feet. I eased toward my guest room, none too pleased with myself at leaving my personal weapon in the glovebox of the truck Wayne had driven off in. He probably took it on purpose.

They entered rather gently, my first impression being their attempt not to wake me. Mark walking her to the door it seemed. Kudos to him. No, oh wait. Damn. He didn't appear to be leaving.

Had things gone that badly? Was she that unstable?

Callie took his hand.

Oh, um, no, clearly not that unstable. I slipped into my room, leaving the door cracked, hugging the wall just inside, darting out of sight in case she checked on me. I prepared to slink under the quilt if need be.

I peered out again. They locked the front door, bumping hands in doing so like two teenagers. The bedroom door barely made a sound as they disappeared inside.

Would you look at that?

Falling into bed, I sank into sleep, so pleased my friend had made something good of the night.

I WOKE, DISORIENTED before pieces clicked together. The memory of last night gelled pretty quickly.

After a shower, omitting the hair to avoid the noise of a dryer, I eased on jeans to generically handle whatever this day was meant for. God forbid anyone tell me what to expect. A fast brush to my hair, and I teased my bedroom door open.

Quiet as a tomb.

With stealth steps through the living room, I stopped at the bedroom door as if I was supposed to hear something. Stepping to the window, I spotted her car parked below, not his. Had he left already?

Did I dare peek in the bedroom and see?

Nope, Mark's keys hung on a sea turtle display of hooks in the kitchen, convincing me otherwise. I was deliriously happy to spot those keys.

So, what now?

Right next to Mark's keys hung the scarf Callie had tied around Lumen's house key for safekeeping, and it called my name. *Oh yeah,* I thought.

There you go, Slade. No one can complain about you taking the boring inventory job off Callie's plate.

Now I needed wheels, but not Callie's, and I had a good suspicion where I could get those wheels if I didn't mind a partner. Stealing Lumen's key, I crept out, easing the front door until it softly latched, and slipped down the steps, remembering how loudly those steps had announced my two friends coming in last night.

While Callie managed some respite from her troubles, I now had a mission to take my mind off the whatever it was I wasn't allowed to participate in.

I couldn't hold back the smile.

Chapter 31

Callie

CALLIE WOKE IN a gradual rise of consciousness, more relaxed than she had been in . . . since she could remember. There was almost something wrong about it.

"Been wondering when you'd open those eyes," Mark said, lying on his side. "It's nine thirty. I was giving you until ten when I had to get up and head to the restaurant."

The warmth of the sheets . . . and him. The laziness of the moment. "Then give me until ten," she said, inching over, sliding an arm beneath his so he'd embrace her.

The kiss turned into more, then more one more time. Then it was ten. Only then did Callie remember Slade, the first glitch in her Nirvana morning. Then she remembered Annie and the night before, and the bubble popped.

With Mark in the shower first, she checked on her guest, promising to follow him in a jiffy. Slade's room was empty, the bed made. Callie hunted for a note, but her best guess was her friend had figured out the unexpected house guest and had given them time, space, and quiet. She was probably sitting at the SeaCow right now, nursing coffee and their Moo Mania special.

She wished Slade lived closer than a hundred fifty miles away.

They had to make the shower quick with El Marko's doors opening at eleven and Mark having played hooky to the prep work. Sophie would forgive him if she were opening, but she stuck to hostessing in the evenings, when all she had to do was chat up the diners and seat them such that they felt special. People-stroking was more her forte.

The rush, the expectation of Wayne's call, hopefully with federal badges on the ground sometime soon, and the need to find Slade and make amends for ignoring her friend, sucked the energy out of any shower action. The day had begun. Time to do grown-up tasks.

"Need me to drive you?" Callie asked as they threw on clothes. He had twenty minutes to get there.

Three knocks sounded on the front door. "Hello? Mom?"

Callie dropped her chin to her chest. "Yeah, kinda forgot he was coming." She tied on her second sneaker and stood, grateful Jeb hadn't been home but once since she'd moved into *Windswept*, meaning he had no key. "Take my car, Mark."

"How will you . . . ?"

"Jeb has his car."

Mark scurried by with a peck on the cheek, then changed his mind and gave one to her lips. "Why does he only come home when we're getting out of bed?"

Exactly what she was thinking. At least it showed she wasn't pining away in a corner as Jeb was prone to think. Or lost in a bottle, his biggest concern.

At the door, Callie let Jeb in as Mark squeezed past. "Hate to rush and not chat, Jeb, but I'm running late to open."

"Sure, man," Jeb replied, watching with a judging eye as Mark galloped down the front stairs and leaped in Callie's car. He turned to his mother. "Does he live here now?"

"Believe it or not, he hasn't stayed under my roof since the last time you caught us at the other house. Come here, give me a hug."

Her arms around his waist, his around her head and shoulders, he towered over her, his height from his father. "You smell good."

"You smell like you just got out of the shower," he said, giving her a smirk at the alternative if he'd arrived a half hour earlier.

"Where's Sprite?" she asked, inviting him back outside and over to the swing. She'd kill for coffee. Her dull head needed caffeine. Mark may have been a catalyst for her, but she hadn't had much good sleep these last few days. The snap in the air helped. "And do you want a cup?"

"She's hanging back, waiting to see if the coast is clear over here," he said. "And no thanks. Had mine over an hour ago. If you need me to take you to breakfast, I'm game. She can meet us there."

"You're on," she said, knowing full well he'd charge the meal on the card she made the payment on. At his vehicle, she almost explained about Mark borrowing her car. It was what it was, and the night had been well worth the morning awkwardness with her son.

Jeb texted his girl the plans.

"Tell Sophie to come, too, if she likes," Callie said, getting into the passenger side of his Jeep. She liked this distraction. Wayne must still be in the middle of his séance with his bosses. She prayed they had made headway, that the late morning hour meant progress, not complications.

"Miss Sophie went out." In a sudden thought, he stopped himself from putting the Jeep into drive. "Speaking of her, a little warning last night would've been nice, Mom. Walking in on Mr. Stan and Miss Sophie was . . . not sure what it was. Memorable? Mind-branding? Nobody likes walking in on two naked old people."

"They aren't old people. They're five and ten years older than me."

"Which means you aren't there yet."

Blessings for backhanded compliments. "Bet Sprite handled it just fine."

His eye roll reflected the child she remembered. "She grew up in a haunted house with a yoga witch," he said. "She's been acclimated, while I, on the other hand, am scarred to the end of my days." He did this explosion gesture with his fingers around his head. "Can't get all that skin out of my head."

The exhibition wouldn't have happened anywhere else, but Sophie didn't lock doors, which she ever deemed someone else's problem. She'd strut bare-assed down Palmetto Road if it served the proper purpose; however, she also had a better body than most thirty-year-olds. Many others in their twenties.

Took them two minutes to reach SeaCow, beating Sprite. Walking across the porch entrance, Callie asked the obvious. "Sophie teaching yoga?" Sometimes Sophie had back-to-back classes, though this was not that time of year.

"No," he said, holding the door open. "She went out with Miss Slade."

That drew Callie up short. At the doorway, she still scoured the small eatery. Slade wasn't at a table as expected, and an uneasiness stirred. "Where would they go?" With a criminal element on and off the island, apprehension one-upped the uneasiness.

Mark had been a brief, extremely pleasant respite from the airstrip last night, but in the light of day, in light of the endless possibilities Callie cared not to list, the fact that nefarious folks walked Edisto Beach in the guise of badges forced her to snap her guard back up. She hadn't the luxury of time or mind space to relive the early morning tryst with Mark. Instead, she preferred being on top of where her favorite people were in times like these, and two of them weren't accounted for.

Jeb gave her a comical, don't-really-care shrug. "They went to another witch house, they said. Who'd have thought there was more than one witchy lady out here? Or maybe I should've figured that out being a sea island and all." He nudged her when she'd blocked the door. "We going in or what?"

Leaving Slade alone unsupervised had become a poor decision. Slade's mind rambled untethered without Wayne. Pair her with Sophie, and no telling what would happen. They weren't buds, but they got off messing with each other, each intrigued with the other's individuality, each one-upping the other. "How long ago did they leave?"

"They left maybe ten minutes before I did. What's the deal?"

Jeb was astute, but fortunately, he saw the morning as no more than three middle-aged women unable to keep up with each other's social schedules. Guess he had a right to think that after finding both his and his girlfriend's mothers in bed with their boyfriends on the same night.

But back to what he'd said. *Witchy* meant Lumen. Not a terrible choice of outing. Callie could see them going to Lumen's, which shouldn't be too disastrous a mission. Slade had clearly fallen in love with those journals, admittedly beautiful in word and art, and Sophie had held a personal relationship with the lady who created them. They could pilfer away the day out there amidst those books and bottles, scarves and beads, and stay out of trouble.

Well, maybe. Sophie and Lumen's weed weren't exactly strangers, which most likely made her a willing participant in Slade's trek.

But at least Slade was occupied in case Wayne came through with ICE.

They assumed a place at a table outside on the porch, Callie's preference from a cop's habit of watching the traffic and strollers, the comers and goers. Plus, Sprite would see them the second she walked past the building next door.

Annie passed in a patrol car, a bit focused on something per her speed, headed east. The girl had to be exhausted. Callie bet Armstrong got his sleep, though. Yet again, she wondered where Greer was. What did he think about his daughter out last night though not on duty? Unless he knew why.

If Callie weren't sitting in front of witnesses, she'd call Thomas. Instead, she texted. *You working today?*

Yes.

Annie update you?

Yes. Pisses me off.

Stay alert. Is A on duty?

Thumbs-down. Armstrong wasn't accounted for. Callie didn't like that.

Boss on duty?

IDK

So, Greer not accounted for either. Interesting.

Keep up with her. Will be in touch.

Thumbs-up.

The coffee came first. Callie ordered toast and a small bowl of grits. She wasn't the three-egg-omelet breakfast person Slade was. Her phone said eleven oh-two, the same as the last time she glanced, then flipped to eleven oh-three. She parked the phone on the table face down to avoid appearing so obvious.

Mark should be kicking things off at the restaurant about now . . . and Wayne should've called. She had the impression he met his higher-ups early, like first thing, and if they gave his warning credence, they'd act. This silence worried her, but the science, business, and politics of law enforcement had turned unpredictable these last couple of years. She'd been away from Boston for going on four years, and cable news told her only snippets of what wreaked havoc with federal agencies. Hopefully, they weren't taking Brice's complaint against the Lawman seriously.

Callie jerked back to the here-and-now. When had Sprite sat down? "Hey. I'm sorry, hon. My mind was a hundred miles away." Actually, more like fifteen. On Pine Landing. She reached for her cup. Damn, her coffee was cold. "How's school?"

"Good."

"Heard y'all walked in on some fun last night," she said, deciding to just throw it out there.

Sprite gave a cocked half grin that reminded Callie of her mother. "Mom's libido runs pretty high. Always has. I quit making apologies for it."

Which made Callie snap a questioning glance at her son.

"Don't," was all he said.

She didn't.

A text came through, and she snatched it up from the table, assuming Wayne.

hrko

Hunting for HRKO on the keyboard, Callie recognized a fumbled attempt to type HELP.

Then xxxxxxxxx.

Both from Slade.

What the heck?

Callie started to call, then opted to text. *You OK?*

Help they took Sophie.

What? Who the hell was *they?*

Clearly Slade didn't feel she could make a phone call in her situation, so a call to her might be dangerous, as would an extended string of texts pinging her phone.

"Got to go," Callie said to her son.

"What's wrong?" Sprite asked.

"Not sure. Something's . . . come up," was all she could say, catching the edge of her plate as she stood, not wanting to say it was Slade because that also meant Sophie.

Jeb rose with her. "You're not a cop anymore, Mom."

"Yeah," she answered, like that needed to be said. "In this case it doesn't matter," she added, when in fact it probably would. But badge or no badge, friends made a difference.

Her phone rang again.

Early on, she'd put the man's number in her contact list, in case she needed him . . . in case he needed her. But for him to call now held an ominous, dangerous feel.

"Hello, Chief Greer," she said, leaving the table in a fast walk to her car. "I don't have time for you."

Chapter 32

Slade

"I HAVEN'T BEEN to Lumen's house in at least two years," Sophie said, her vintage powder-blue Mercedes taking the turn easier than I expected off Jungle Road, carrying us across Scott's Creek. "Not sure if I should've brought sage for this visit, but surely she has some there. We witches always do."

Good thing I liked the scent of sage, but right now, with the top down, chilled briny air filled our sinuses. The side of the road, however, crept by. I even spotted a lizard slither into a ditch. "Funny. I imagined you driving like a bat out of hell."

"Not in this car, baby." Sophie stroked the dashboard. "There's a reason she's lived so long. Same as me and this body, this hair, these nails. . . ." One hand swooped through the air from her head down. "We're both totally spoiled." She held a gaze on me for a second, and I sensed my first zing of the day.

Her self-assured smirk never failed to humor everyone else, but I read a smidge of condescending judgment. Just a hint. Sophie had already baited me for our first verbal exchange of the day, and I wasn't falling for it despite the fact the woman had given me no more than a damn banana for breakfast. My stomach had growled in protest while passing SeaCow, desirous of a plated omelet and hashbrowns. Lumen had a mighty fine garden, though. Maybe there was food there, presumably healthy, but I'd take what I could get.

I hadn't told Sophie about Callie and Mark, not that she hadn't asked—and asked again—and it didn't surprise me that she wouldn't let the subject die. All I'd said was they went out early this morning on something urgent, and I awoke with Callie sequestered in her bedroom.

She chose to fill in the blanks. "He stayed with her. I've seen this coming. You think this is the Mark in love or Mark the protector we're talking about here?" she asked. "Him staying at *Windswept* is huge, girl!"

"Who says he stayed there?"

"You."

"I didn't say he stayed there."

"I read minds, girlfriend."

I snorted. "Keep telling yourself that." But I couldn't help but feel she did.

"So, they spent the night at *Windswept*," she said. "What else?"

"There is no *what else*. I saw them come in last night and go into her bedroom," I replied. "They never even saw me."

And suddenly I'd told her the *what else* she desired.

Slowing at Blue House Lane, she paused before turning and grinning, taking the win.

This trip to Lumen's might not have been the best idea after all.

But we were here. Wayne would be thrilled I was out of Callie's hair. If there wasn't a bookcase of handwritten journals, recipes, potions, and spiritual wisdom at this house, I would've stuck around with Callie, but the universe called me to Lumen's. Not in a Sophie way, but in an I-need-to-get-my-hands-on-these-books way. They were rich in a dozen directions, and they beckoned to me as though possessed. Them, not me. Maybe both. For a nano-second I started to ask Sophie if she felt that Lumen might be speaking through them . . . then caught myself, wondering what I was thinking.

We entered Blue House Lane, taking the silt slower than the as-phalt, giving me enough time to have a thought. "You know Truman Burnett, right?" I asked, noting his mailbox up ahead and willing myself not look across the road from it to where three men had met on the sly, where Lumen accidentally saw them, ran into the woods, and died.

Sophie didn't need to know all that. She'd be claiming to see Lumen's spirit walking down the road.

"Of course I know Truman," Sophie said. "We both signed the will together, silly."

Indeed. "Does he like you?"

Sophie rolled to a stop at the entrance to his drive, staring at me as if I'd grown horns. "Let's see if he likes me," she said, and took the ninety degrees on a dime.

I grabbed the door. "Not exactly what I meant."

But she'd donned a hard pout. "Then you shouldn't have insinuated he doesn't like me."

"That's not what I—"

Why bother? We were here, and Mr. Burnett had heard us. He made his way to the base of his creaky steps, his shotgun coming to rest on the toe of his boot again.

"Hey, Truman!" Sophie hollered, her voice an octave higher in sing-song fashion. "How're you doing?"

Damned if the man didn't melt right there and smile like he was in love.

"Hey, Mr. Burnett," I said, coming around from the other side. He didn't smile as bright for me.

"What y'all need?" he asked, uncertain about the yin and yang of the two ladies before him.

Sophie shrugged. "Ask her," she said and nodded to me. "She's the one who wanted me to pull in."

Unbelievable. *Go with the flow, Slade. Ball's in your court.*

Mr. Burnett held his gaze on me, waiting for whatever this was, and I scrimmaged to give it shape. "I just wondered if you remember more about the day Lumen died," I said, picking a safe topic, seeing nothing wrong with double-checking. "Maybe you remember hearing those men she saw? Any chance you heard Lumen say something?" He hadn't mentioned hearing her before, but neither did I recall anyone asking the question.

His sadness took me aback.

"I'm so sorry," I said. "You must miss her terribly. Clearly, you were the dearest of her friends."

He peered down at his boots. "But I wasn't a friend. I didn't help her when she needed me," he said in a half talk, half whisper. His mourning washed over him like a wave, the folds under his eyes assuming a deeper sag, his shoulders the same.

I wasn't doing a very good job here. "Mr. Truman, excuse me but what do you mean that you didn't help?"

Sophie's expression turned concerning. She didn't understand the why, but she recognized the sorrow and went to him, her short little person enveloping him in an embrace. "Honey," she dragged out, and he laid his stiff shriveled head on her tiny shoulder. "Come here."

"I hear her," he said, his words weak and cracking. "In my mind," he corrected. "And I was too old and too scared to go tend to her." He eased back, readjusting the shotgun to his other boot toe to wipe his forehead with his dominant hand.

A pressure built in my chest in imagining what resided in his. "Mr. Burnett," I said, sighing for his benefit . . . and mine, "no telling what would've happened if you'd made yourself known. And she died of a heart attack. It wasn't like they killed her." I started to say they might've killed him if he'd charged out with his cane slash shotgun demanding explanation.

"She shouted," he said. "She shouted *no*."

What? "What kind of *no*," I asked. "What was she saying no to? Or how did she say it? Angry, afraid, demanding?"

"Protective," he said. "She'd waited in my driveway until she heard what they said, marched out, and told them *no*. Next thing I hear she's dead. Heart attack or not, they didn't like being seen." He pushed his shotgun back and forth like a lever, needing to expel energy.

Sophie's frowns and expressions, brows up and down in her listening, showed an earnest attempt to click pieces together, but having been omitted from the outset, she struggled. "Who are these people you're talking about?" she asked. "And you say they scared Lumen to death? They came out here to . . . do what?"

Mr. Burnett looked to me, as if I'd dropped the ball and it was my place to inform Sophie.

"I don't even know the whole story," I said. "They've cut me out of the loop, too." All truth, but what little I'd learned I'd promised to keep secret.

"Lumen interrupted someone's illegal plan, then," she concluded.

"Sounds like it," I said.

"One of those men was Mexican," Truman added out of the blue.

Whether he spoke Spanish or not didn't matter, even the sound of an accented Latino voice would stand out on the island where other culture dominated, making non-Southern accents memorable.

When we returned, I'd update Callie. No, I'd best text her now. But my attempt showed iffy cell coverage. "We'll . . . pass this on," I said, holding out my phone as if I'd done something.

From her sour expression, Sophie expected me to do more.

"They have something planned today, Soph, and I'm not invited. We'll touch base when we finish at Lumen's." I slipped the phone in my pocket, feeling the scarf-tied key. Somehow going to scout for potions and recipes mattered less, but what else was I to do?

Sophie returned another hug to Mr. Burnett. "We're trying to salvage her home, her things, and her memory," she promised. "Is there anything you'd like us to bring to you, Truman?"

"One of her books," he said. "There's nothing more Lumen Townsend in that house than one of her books."

There was the urgency, at least to me. The three of us standing here recognized how much of that lady was embedded on hundreds of pages in dozens of books. Few people left that much legacy behind. Regardless of what the will said, surely we could snatch one of them for Mr. Burnett, Lumen's last living friend on Edisto Island.

More hugs, then we backed out of the drive, Sophie watching over her seat to avoid a tree, me watching Mr. Burnett standing pitifully alone in that dirt yard under a dark canopy of oaks, pines, and myrtles. Me . . . trying not to cry at the sadness of that poor man.

Suddenly, the day held a bigger mission, a worthy substitute for not being involved with Callie and her three wisemen. Wayne, Mark, and Stan. I was trying hard not to look at things through a bitter lens.

"What is going on?" Sophie said, creeping down Blue House Lane toward Lumen's.

"I wasn't lying. They cut me out," I said.

"But you're aware Lumen died out there after stumbling across some meet-and-greet, right?"

Oh whatever. "Yes. But those men called her death in."

"Who're *those men?*"

"You promise not to broadcast this, right? It could hurt Mr. Burnett."

She didn't promise, instead staring over in a sardonic mock of a look. "You can't begin to know the promises I keep. Behind my reputation as a flighty, laughable soul, a person everyone downplays as shallow and easy to manipulate, stands a woman holding a shit-ton of secrets. I could own this beach, from town council to each and every business owner and real estate agent." She gave me a self-assured smirk. "Already got out of you Armstrong was one of those men, didn't I?"

"Not from me you didn't."

"Now I did."

Either I gave the woman credit for her *savoir faire* or I was a dolt. I chose to give her the credit. Sophie Bianchi wasn't such an empty-minded vessel after all.

We covered the less-than-one-mile stretch with nobody in sight. My stomach growled again, reminding me to check the pantry the second we entered the house.

We parked just off the road, not in the drive, Sophie avoiding any trees that might weep or offer birds a perch to poop onto her vintage leather seats. As we left the vehicle, I surveyed the surroundings. Nobody but those familiar with Lumen would see any magic in this place. The faded painted mailbox, aged and molded macrame hangers of potted ferns in their last days, and dull flowers stenciled over the front door gave subtle promise to the enchantment inside.

Out of habit, I glanced around harder, taking that place in. A heron squawked from behind the house, at the water's edge, irritated at our arrival. Wind whistled through the top of the largest live oak, squirrels rustling, frisky at the cool air while eager to stash acorns for the winter.

Summer out here meant intense humidity and mosquitoes as big as your fingernail. But in the fall, after a cold snap or two took care of errant snakes and annoying gnats, the environment cradled you in its hand which made me want to go around back first. We weren't in a hurry. We had the day. I hadn't even sat on the dock yet.

"Let's see the garden," I said. "When's the last time you've been here? Two years, you said?"

For a change, Sophie didn't seem contrary to my suggestion. "Yeah. What kind of garden?"

With a devious grin, I winked. "Oh, girl, you can't imagine the goodies back there. Come on."

I veered left, slowing right before we reached the corner of the brick. I put my arm out in front of Sophie. "Hold on."

Drawing herself up short, she gripped that same arm. "What? What's wrong?"

Tire tracks headed around the side of the house. There was no driveway to the backyard.

My first thought was Armstrong. My second was whether this vehicle was still there.

"Down," I whispered. We both dropped to a squat, Sophie mimicking my movements when I flattened against the brick wall. Slowly, I moved forward, she doing the same in my shadow. I turned and murmured, "Wait here," after she'd whispered *ouch* scratching her foot on a stray root of a long-dead bush.

The house wasn't but twenty-five feet wide and we'd covered half of that already. Enough for me to see ground and plant life flattened by tires wide enough to belong to a pickup or van, the trail curving around the corner.

In one final scurry, I reached the corner and peered around. I spotted the back end of a dated, worn white van with rust spots along the wheel wells, and a current South Carolina tag.

"Slade," Sophie called, way louder than she should.

Reaching behind me, I palmed the air for her to hush.

"Slade," she called again, in full voice.

I turned in time to see a Latino man behind her, a hand gripping her frosted shag.

Sophie dipped down and twisted, fighting to get loose . . . and I bolted for the dense undergrowth of a natural spread of trees and bushes.

"Slade!" she hollered, the yell cut short as he returned to the front, presumably to haul Sophie inside, away from eyes. Not like there were many eyes out here.

A bad guy would presume I bolted for the highway or the nearest house for help, putting distance between me and him, but something in me said, *Don't let Sophie out of my sight*. Something also told me to crawl up under the dead palmetto fronds scattered helter-skelter so they'd think I was gone.

I'd smelled something wrong . . . just not fast enough.

How stupid to think an empty house wasn't attractive to some criminal type. Criminals were by nature opportunists and improvisers. They did not plan like the average person. They acted on ideas, they capitalized, and they did both better than honest people who couldn't get around their own forthright selves fast enough to think on their feet like that.

My phone showed one bar of service. With one hand I tried to text Callie, the other serving as a trellis for the dead fronds, hiding the light from my phone and giving me no way to shoo whatever that was crawling on my ankle.

Chapter 33

Callie

"WE NEED TO TALK," Greer said, in a forceful tone she hadn't the patience to hear.

"I'm busy," she replied starting up her car, shouting to the Bluetooth.

"Won't take a minute."

"I don't have that minute."

"Then find it!"

The even harsher tone steeled her yet baited her. She yearned to tell this man what she thought of his policing, or rather his lack of. Facebook still rumbled over DUIs not being ticketed, street signs being stolen, and natives watching tourists get away with the small but touchy issues like parking in private yards. God help them all if social media caught wind of an officer or two aiding and abetting human trafficking.

Edisto would never be the same.

But if something happened to Sophie, this island would absolutely lose its mind.

"Chief," she said, "I don't answer to you, and I don't have the time. Something's come up. I'm hanging up now."

Which she did then backed out of her parking place, the text from Slade putting her on an edgier edge. Whether someone had broken into Lumen's place, or Slade struggled to tell Callie something in code, she had no idea, but the unknown of the text and the lack of Slade's ability to clarify threw an urgency over whatever this was.

An Edisto PD cruiser turned into the SeaCow parking lot, nudging to within a foot of Callie's bumper. She put on brakes. Greer got out of his vehicle tight-jawed and challenging.

Sick of this man, Callie got out of hers.

With a glance back to the restaurant's porch, she spotted Jeb with Sprite beside him while a dozen other heads turned to watch. The tourists would wonder why a police cruiser had stopped. The natives would grasp the significance of the before and after beach enforcement finally coming to a confrontation. No doubt phone calls were being made.

"In my car, please, Ms. Morgan. Not in the open."

His intimidation fell short on her. She had somewhere to be. Slade needed her. Greer had ignored everything Callie'd said over the phone, which only spurred her to cast him aside in person.

"Out of my way," she said, standing with hand on her door. "I have an urgent matter."

"Mine's more urgent. I'm serious. We need to—"

"Oh, you're serious. Wow, that makes all the difference in the world, Chief. And for some reason you believe your problem outranks mine without the intel to do so. Well, if you aren't prepared to arrest me, it isn't as critical as you claim. Get your cuffs out or get out of the way."

She hated what she'd said the second she said it . . . not that she didn't mean it.

"I can do that," he said, "but I'd prefer we not."

There they stood in a gravel parking lot, the impasse thick and challenging. Observers stood along the porch deck, and now, observers collected across the street, along the covered walkway that stretched between the pizza place on one end and El Marko's on the other. She wondered when Mark would come out and join them. The moment he did, he'd be over, in defensive mode.

Greer's moustache made him difficult to read, his tone very Western sheriff-like. He stood fast with his body language warning that anyone crossing him had a strong likelihood of losing.

But she didn't care how long he'd policed Pon Pon, South Carolina. Though her years measured two decades less than his, she'd amassed a highly concentrated dose of experience he'd never seen or would ever see.

The air buzzed at the standoff.

"I need your help, Callie," he finally said, revealing his discomfort with the open scrutiny. Whether being in the public's eye or something else, he almost strained at wanting her alone.

She glanced at Slade's incoherent text, worried at how powerful, how scary, how threatening the passing seconds might be for her. Could be nothing. Could be everything. Could be life threatening.

She got back into her car, pulled it forward, and parked. Engine off, she exited and locked the door.

Greer still stood fast, taking her in with his gaze every step as she made her way to his cruiser but around to the other side. "You want to talk to me, huh?" She opened his passenger door.

He watched, wary.

She stood there, one leg inside. "Chief Greer, if you want to talk to me we do it en route to Lumen Townsend's house. We take it 10-18. No lights, no siren." Fast but silent.

She was buckled up by the time he got inside.

"What are we—"

Callie wasn't doing this in the parking lot. "Can you drive and talk at the same time, because I got someplace to be, and I could sure use backup."

He three-pointed the car and pulled onto Jungle Road.

"What are we gonna find out there?" he asked, her issue suddenly becoming his and his own pushed to the background. He'd at least respected her for having a real issue.

She had no idea what they'd find on Blue House Lane and literally had nothing to fill him in on other than the text, but in case she needed police assistance, she had it. He wasn't her choice, but fate landed him in her lap, so she accepted the gift. She'd learn real quick Greer's involvement in the treatment of Lumen Townsend's death. His behavior, his avoidance, his eyes . . . unless the man possessed a keener ability to deceive than she expected, she'd read him.

"Punch it," she said, feeling the need to be there.

He sped up. "Are we needing backup, Ms. Morgan?" Either he trusted her, or he was feeling her out in the same manner as she did him.

"No," she said. "I don't know who to trust around here anymore. But for some reason you crossed my path when I needed help. My need to be there outweighs my doubt about you. Or so I hope."

Greer studied the road, holding fifteen miles above the speed limit. Any more was deadly. Even he understood the danger of hitting one of the massive unforgiving oaks lining the highway.

"Well, if we're it, and it's as bad as you might think, then you best get my backup piece out of the glove box," he said.

Callie opened the box, noting the contents not much different than when she had patrolled in the same car, and retrieved the nine mil. She checked it over, deemed it suitable, then slid it back into its holster and slipped it under her leg.

"You'll have to point me out where to turn," he said. "The name of the road is . . . ?"

"Blue House Lane," she said. "A few miles to go, but it's up on the right. . . ." She paused.

He waited for more.

"Just past Jane Edwards School," she finished.

His head jerked once in recognition. He wasn't familiar with the road, just the school. Everyone knew the school. It sat right on Highway 174 and served as a major landmark in giving directions.

It appeared he hadn't been on the road where Lumen died. The first confirmation that Armstrong had taken care of things there . . . and that Greer had taken his word for it.

The man had flaws, with his biggest one being his trust in Armstrong.

"Listen," he said, "we're gonna be there before I can finish. Suffice to say, I love my daughter."

Callie said nothing. They had seven miles at best to the turn. Best let him say as much as he could.

"I left Pon Pon to get her away from bad influences. I admit part of that influence followed us here."

"The influence being Fox?" she asked.

From the way he sat back in his seat, her mention of Fox shocked him. "Uh, no. Something else we've gotta talk about, apparently, but I mean Armstrong."

"Thought you brought both Annie and Armstrong, making them part of the deal."

"No. Just me and Anna May. Armstrong approached Brice without my knowledge, professing his loyalty to me, so Brice agreed to hire him as well."

That sounded so lame. "You could've told Brice to rescind the offer and blame it on budget." She wasn't a Brice fan, but Greer needed to own his mistakes. "Don't dump this on Brice."

He hesitated. "You're right." The Jane Edwards School was just ahead. "But I was in this too far to stir the pot."

"How deeply are you in *this*?" She didn't mention what *this* might be because he hadn't. The trafficking? Or did he mean something out of Pon Pon?

"I believe they've sucked my daughter into something," he said. "She's nervous. She dodges me, and now she avoids having anything to do with Armstrong. Suddenly, she's going out in the middle of the night. I know of twice," he said. "Thought a boy at first since that Thomas fella has been awful nice to her, but now I'm thinking it ain't that simple."

"The next road to your right," she said.

"I need you to maybe talk to Anna May," he said.

"Already have," she replied. "But we don't have time to discuss it now. Stand by me here and I'll do what I can to help. Screw me over and

I'll hang you out to dry."

"Understood." He didn't bat an eye at Callie appearing more aware of the situation. "So, tell me what we're doing out here before we're in the middle of it and get ambushed."

For that moment, and she hoped it lasted more than a moment, Callie felt she had an ally.

She pointed. "This is the road. Turn in."

He did.

"Pull over . . . right there." She motioned to a spot. "Been here before?" she asked.

He peered down the road, to the left and to the right, his focus never faltering on one area. "No. I take it that matters to you?"

Yes, it did.

She pointed again. "My friend Lumen Townsend died several yards in the brush, right over there. You didn't check it out, did you? You relied totally on Armstrong's accounting, which, by the way, probably didn't mention Troy Fox or an Hispanic man, name unknown to me. Maybe not even to Armstrong, if I were to guess."

Greer took on a contrite expression, almost ashamed.

"We don't have any more time to lay out those details," she said. "Right now, my friend Slade is somewhere near Lumen Townsend's house, and Sophie . . . you remember Sophie."

Of course he did. The woman he wanted Callie to hook him up with.

"Slade said . . . just read this," and she held out her phone.

He read the text. "Who's got her?"

"No idea. Vandals, locals taking advantage of an empty house, not sure, but we have to get her loose. Maybe I know them. Maybe you know them. But this road is a dead-end to water, so we'll be blocking it."

In front of him, for him to read, she texted Slade. *Still there?*

Yes.

Sophie still taken?

Yes.

We're up the road from you. Stay hidden.

Nothing.

Outside Lumen's, right?

Nothing.

Right?

Nothing.

Greer peered up at her once the texting stopped.

"Drive ahead until I tell you to park," she said. "I'll tell you where. Block the road when you do."

He crept along as told. "Didn't mean to step on your toes in moving here, Ms. Morgan. It's clear that Edisto is your world."

"Not the time, Chief." She scouted the roadsides, not sure what she was looking for other than Slade and what she assumed was Sophie's Mercedes.

She wished she had more information.

She hoped Slade wasn't hurt.

She prayed Sophie wasn't taken by the type of people who'd dispose of her.

She beseeched the universe that Sophie professed to love would do something to protect its own.

The distance wasn't a mile, but who said this event, whatever this event was, happened on Lumen's place? Might've happened on the road, before the house, thus the slow creep to get there.

Greer appeared to get it, scouting just as hard as she was.

The house was maybe sixty, seventy yards ahead. "Stop," she said.

She texted Slade again. *We're here. Where are you?*

Slade appeared on the edge of the woods to their left, in a wide-eyed panic scanning the road as if crossing four lanes of interstate during rush hour. It wasn't but thirty feet to their vehicle, but she was afraid to cross.

"What's wrong?" Callie said, immediately scouring ahead, behind, at the woods, hoping to catch a glimpse of whatever danger this was.

A bullet hit the windshield, then a spray of several more hit Greer's side of the car.

Yeah, that was dangerous enough.

Chapter 34

Slade

CALLIE WAS ON her way. Thank God the beach wasn't that far. I could wait that long for my cavalry to arrive.

After shaking three different bugs off my feet and ankles, one of which buried inside my sock, I remained hidden, convinced that maintaining vigil on the house was most critical. One bit of noise, one moment of looking elsewhere could make me miss spotting Sophie or whoever else was inside. In my running into the woods, I'd witnessed nothing. By the time, I reached the trees and turned around, Sophie and her captor were gone, assumed inside since they were nowhere else to be seen and the van remained in place. I wouldn't look away again.

We'd interrupted someone capitalizing on an isolated empty house, the van positioned so they could rob it down to the studs without witnesses. They could take their time, pilfer the pantry, pack loot neatly into whatever Rubbermaid containers they brought with them. Not like in the city where the timing had to be precise, the getaway quicker.

Of course we had to walk up on them. Damn it, I knew better than to approach an empty house and not scan for a threat, and Sophie had paid the price. God, I hoped she used that mouth of hers to talk herself out of a situation. Odds were this guy was a local. She could shame him out of his criminal activity by threatening to tell his mother. She'd be the one on this island who could get away with that. Or tell him that all would be forgiven if he came to yoga and worked on his spirituality.

I didn't want to think about the dark options.

From my vantage, there was but one window, to the kitchen over the sink if I remembered right, and nobody had walked by. There weren't even lights on from what I could tell. I heard nothing. Saw nothing. At first I found that comforting. Then my mind took note of what could be happening in the other rooms, like the bedroom. I didn't want to think about that either.

Get here, Callie.

I hid behind a wider pine so my phone didn't shine from the forest shadows, and I texted Wayne. *Hiding outside Lumen's. Someone snatched Sophie. They are inside the house. Callie is on the way.*

Held my thumb over the send arrow for a while. He'd want to know. But did I want him breaking his neck eating up road from Atlanta? Three hundred miles wasn't quick. Five hours per the speed limit. He'd run twenty miles over that when he could, so I gave him four hours once he left downtown Atlanta.

All that was assuming he wasn't in some meeting. He'd bolt from it, and take about twenty minutes more to get here, but I didn't want him blowing off his higher-ups. While I wanted him here, I didn't like thinking about the method by which he'd arrive. There was good and bad in having a loyal beau.

I deleted the text. No. I couldn't do that to him. He'd fuss later, but he'd get over it, his common sense coming around in the end because I'd already done the smartest thing that I could, which was escape and call the closest help.

Phone put up, I studied the house again. I couldn't believe they'd continue hiding in there for long with me on the loose to contact authorities.

Suddenly, I got what I asked for. The sound of the back door sliding drew my attention though it fronted the river, out of my sight, but I could make out the left back corner of the van. I hadn't heard its doors open, but they could have already been open. Someone might be boarding or loading it to leave. Nobody ever came within my line of vision, though, and the van remained in place. I glanced toward the front, then the back. The front, then the back, not trusting this guy not to distract me.

The sliding door closed. Guess he went back inside.

A text came through. Hoping it was Wayne, just for the soothing effect, I whipped back around the large pine, my back against it, and read.

It was Callie. *Still there?*

Yes, I typed.

Sophie still taken?

Yes.

We're up the road from you. Stay hidden.

Duh. No problem.

A girl's voice sounded behind me, I jerked around. That wasn't Sophie.

Chest against the tree, peering around to the right, I waited for someone to show themselves. The voice hadn't sounded muffled, just as if the door was open, the front door. Then I heard that door slam shut.

What was going on in there? Who were these people?

I feared looking again. Front, then back. Front, then back.

Another text from Callie.

Outside Lumen's, right?

Bark chipped off the tree, right over my head sending me into a crouch, wood shrapnel raining over me. A handgun from the sound.

Peering around the tree would provide a target because he'd clearly figured out where I stood. I tore off into the woods, not toward the road but deeper, to the water, in the hope of throwing him off. I assumed it was a *him*. I assumed it was *the him* who'd taken Sophie. That was my mental image, and that was all the time I was willing to commit to identifying this guy as I hauled ass. Twenty feet in, I veered behind another pine tree wide enough to conceal me.

My lungs about exploded in an effort to remain silent.

A stick snapped, the leaves too moist this time of year to give steps away, and I thanked the heavens for the notice. He'd followed me toward the river. Now I could change course.

My phone texted again in my pocket, and though muted, I cursed the vibration.

"Chi-qui-ta?" My pursuer sang the syllables, hunting side to side, but in the generally opposite direction of where I was.

What now?

Hide and hope for salvation? Or run and pray I found it on my own?

Callie had texted she was up the road. A mile was too far to be any good. A half mile wasn't much better. If she wasn't out on the road where I came out, I'd get a bullet in my back.

Before, I couldn't get my panting under control, afraid of being heard. Now I was frozen, the breath lodged behind a lump in my throat, threatening to suffocate me. Delay was a death sentence. Running held little better odds.

I bolted toward the road. A *crack* of his gun sounded. With no idea how close or how far, I took wide leaps and zigzags, spurring myself to break records in reaching the road.

Another shot, this one hitting the tree ahead and to the right. I hunched shoulders and swerved left.

There. The road. And bless the angels, I saw a car . . . an Edisto

Beach PD cruiser.

The fear of running into the open made me stop at the wood's edge. But I didn't get a foot on the silted road before bullets riddled the side of the car.

I dove into the ditch, hands over my head.

Son of a bitch, that was no handgun.

Chapter 35

Callie

"WE'RE A SITTING duck out here," Greer said, throwing the transmission into gear and pivoting it such that the vehicle blocked the road at an angle, the engine between him and Callie and the direction of gunfire.

They both fell out. Greer on the driver's side. The passenger side toward Lumen's place, Callie scrambled around to take up residence behind the trunk.

"An AK," Greer said, his sidearm drawn and resting on the door hinge.

"Correct," Callie said, half crouched, her piece drawn and resting on the trunk lid. "Slade, get over here."

Her friend popped up to her knees, then to her feet and half ran, half stumbled around the car to squat beside Callie.

"You all right?" Callie asked, with only the slightest glance down.

Slade breathed hard, rolled into a tight ball on the ground. "Yes. That guy has two weapons? Seriously? He came after me with a handgun and a . . . whatever that nasty thing was. I heard the difference."

Callie, like Greer, recognized the repetitive fire of an AK-47, the weapon used by most armies around the world, United States enemies and allies alike. One of the earliest true assault rifles, and, unfortunately, also the choice of many criminal enterprises.

"Pop the trunk," Callie shouted to Greer, remembering the twelve-gauge Remington 870 pump shotgun she kept there.

Greer shook his head. "Not there anymore. We took them out of the vehicles. Brice and the council found them offensive to tourists."

No long gun. Great. Brice never failed to continue being the gift that kept on giving.

Greer took out his radio. "Officer needs assistance, shots fired. Request immediate backup on Blue House Lane on Edisto Island." The message would reach anyone and everyone, and they'd welcome whoever decided to show.

They still didn't see the shooter, and a few seconds had gone by with no signs.

Poised tight against the cruiser, Callie scanned the woods and spoke to Slade. "Who is he?"

Slade shifted her squat.

Callie hissed at her. "Stay down."

"I am," she hissed back. "He's the guy who grabbed Sophie. Hispanic, maybe forty. His van is parked behind the house."

"See anyone else?"

"No. Heard a girl inside though, and it wasn't Sophie."

Callie's first inclination was that the van and Hispanic man equaled the people Annie had gotten involved with, but what would bring them out here? Something went wrong? And they needed a hideaway? Of course, Armstrong had been happy to assist. He'd recently been reminded of an unoccupied house when he'd followed Callie to Lumen's, so why not use it? He probably thought Greer had shut them down with probate and they wouldn't be back.

The house sat between Truman up the road and three families toward the dead-end. Days could go by without anyone going in, a decent place to hide if one only needed a one- or two-night stay. Still a risk, but these people lived for risk.

Sophie and at least one other female were left in the house. Either they were secured or the shooter had a partner. Callie prayed for the former.

Greer's call would send any available Edisto PD officers their way, to include Annie. They'd know soon enough if this guy was the same who had driven the van of human cargo, taking her phone and hitting her. Just as soon as she had a chance to see him.

Charleston SO would arrive too late to be of much good with the island being on the far periphery of their county, but Raysor would arrive from Colleton SO in a heartbeat.

Bullets sprayed from the wood's edge. Slade hunkered and yipped a scream.

Greer and Callie hid, protected, until they got a split-second lull. Both fired back, but the shooter had hidden behind an oak.

They only had handguns. He had thirty to forty rounds for his weapon, if not more.

"Second shooter!" Callie shouted.

Another Hispanic man, in his thirties, ran out the front door and opened fire with another AK.

She shot at him, praying for a lucky hit at a moving target. "He's trying to flank us!"

More shots peppered the vehicle, the sound of the hits going on forever, cutting the car to pieces. At least two tires flat. No doubt the engine was worthless in terms of running but still doing its job as a barricade.

Lights and siren approached up Blue House Lane. Callie's heart tried to leap through her ribs at the sign of hope.

Then it dropped like a rock when the vehicle stopped way too far distant, maybe seventy yards back. Armstrong got out of the car, hugging his door in front of him for cover.

From his tight-jawed scowl, Greer was none too pleased either. Callie presumed, like her, that Greer had already concluded he was fighting for the other side.

Callie returned attention to the second shooter behind a tree on the edge of Lumen's lot. "Armstrong's giving these two guys a chance to kill us first."

Greer got on the radio. "Armstrong, advance and engage."

No answer. Unless he'd already been off the beach for some unknown reason, Armstrong arrived way sooner than he should have simply responding to Greer's call for assistance. He'd already been on his way. He'd been beckoned by more than Greer.

He shut off his siren, but Callie heard another in the distance and prayed for Raysor.

More shots riddled the car, and they stooped lower.

Greer radioed again. "Anna May? Thomas? Need your ETA, and I need it now."

"In sight of you, Chief," Thomas replied, whooping the siren twice to confirm.

"Don't trust Armstrong," Greer said.

Dirt clouds billowed behind the new Edisto car, a foot heavier on the gas than was safe with Armstrong blocking the way.

Annie had the wheel. The car veered right, two tires chancing the shallow ditch, and blew past Armstrong, choking him in her dust, then sliding around to a broadsided stop, parallel to that of Greer's.

She positioned her car to protect her daddy, doubling their defensive fire cover.

Annie bailed to join her father. Thomas fell out the passenger side to join Callie.

Callie tapped Slade on the shoulder. "Go get between the cars."

Slade did as directed but hid further, half crawling under the new vehicle.

With her friend safe, as limited as the options were, Callie nudged Thomas who was cursing Armstrong with language she'd never heard from him. "Armstrong is a piece of shit!" he yelled.

"No argument there."

Armstrong's options were clear, and he was clearly playing those odds in his head right now. He could get back in his car and leave, and hope the bad guys won or were both killed, using some lame excuse that he had to return for more firepower. Or two, he could sit and do nothing and see who had the upper hand before participating. Or three, he could pick a side and fight for a cause.

From his delay to participate, he wasn't too keen on choosing an ally.

The arrival of backup drove the two shooters to escalate their fire, and they slowly advanced. The closer they got, the better the penetration. AK-47s held a strong advantage over the limited ammo of four handguns.

The two adversaries moved closer, peppering the cars, and the four peeled back behind Annie's car, putting two vehicles between them and the overwhelming firepower of AKs at Lumen's, leaving them exposed to Armstrong if he chose to engage.

Callie recognized a coward when she saw one. All bark and no bite. He wasn't putting his bullet in one of them. Forensics. The odds were on the side of the kidnappers anyway.

Annie kept stealing looks back at Armstrong. "The bastard. He thinks we're losing."

But Armstrong could be right. They could lose. They *were* losing.

"They're coming!" Thomas shouted, and shots rained from both of the men at Lumen's.

Someone had to take a chance. Callie scooted forward, to the front of the two cars, listening for a chance. She raised up, and as the first shooter fired at where he thought they had hunched for cover, she placed one mid-center into the man's chest. He dropped.

But in turning back to check on her people, she spotted Armstrong, arm raised holding his Glock, his aim apparent. He couldn't afford for Callie's side to lose.

A shotgun blast cut through the air, then four more.

Not from their direction, but rather toward them, from further up the road.

A banged-up Yamaha Rhino ATV parked center line of Blue House Lane, still running. Truman Burnett stood poised in front of it, shotgun hugging his shoulder.

The second shooter recognized he functioned solo, and semi-automatic or not, without his buddy and Armstrong, the firearms coming at him held more danger than before.

He ran back into the house.

"Our cars are down," Greer shouted.

Thomas hurried back toward Armstrong's cruiser, grabbed Armstrong's firearm off the ground, and got in the car, pulling it forward. He had to step over Armstrong's body to get in, but he wasted no energy in moving the dead officer to the side of the road. Just didn't roll over him.

Slade raced back to Truman.

Tentatively taking to the woods, Annie collected the first shooter's firearm, ensuring he was dead, and slipped to the side of the house where Slade had been, where Sophie had been nabbed. Thomas caught up with her. Callie and Greer kept watch on the front. The house was bracketed.

Annie scooted around the house and shot out the van's tires with the AK. She radioed Greer. "The dead man is the driver from the airstrip last night."

Greer got on his phone, not his radio, and asked for someone by name . . . in three seconds he was put through.

"Who . . . ?" Callie started to ask.

"ICE," he said, before turning away. Someone had come on the phone damn fast to his request.

Puzzled, Callie took interim gazes over at him, sorting the pieces . . . beginning to hear some of them click into place. Just as Greer wasn't informed about Annie, the Edisto team wasn't informed about him. Secrets all around.

The conversation took place in short snippets. "Gun battle with two Mexican traffickers," he said to his contact.

She and Greer hadn't discussed the traffickers.

"One officer down. One perp down," he continued. "One still barricaded in the house, maybe with girls. We've developed into a hostage situation."

He gave directions. People were coming.

Greer had already been working with ICE.

He reached for the PA system mic. "Listen up, you in the house."

He paused. "This is the Edisto Beach Police Chief. The smartest thing you can do is to come out with your hands up."

Nothing.

Minutes went by. Long minutes. If Sophie weren't inside, and goodness knows how many girls, Callie would rest easier and allow herself to wait for the backup with less tension in her neck. But with soft targets at risk, any second could lead to bullets and tragedy.

Greer attempted more calls on the PA system.

Several more minutes. Nothing.

Sirens sounded from Highway 174, and soon Colleton Sheriff's Office cars, three of them, arrived. They exited, armed to the teeth, *all dressed up for the ball* as Raysor called suiting up for an occasion.

The house thoroughly covered, they breached the front and back, Greer with them. Callie remained with Annie's patrol car on the road. She heard Sophie all the way out to where she was.

"Don't shoot, he's gone," she screeched, others squealing behind her. "It's just us girls."

They'd been found zip tied in the bedroom, clustered on the bed, too afraid to open the door when things got quiet. Turned out when shooter number two had run into the house, he'd continued straight out the back, taken to the river, seeking to exit the island.

Freed, Sophie wasted little time running outside, leaving uniforms to see to the other girls. Callie met per partway as she ran into her. "Callie, Callie, where's Slade? Is she all right? Did she get help or did she . . . ?" She started crying. "They didn't shoot her, did they?"

Callie wrapped arms around her, giving her back some of the comfort she'd given her so many times in the past. "No, they didn't touch her. She's fine and up the road with Mr. Burnett."

With Callie not being a uniform, she sat with Sophie in the car while the others checked the hostages and hunted for the escapee. In between soothing Sophie, she coaxed answers to questions, like what had they said in front of her, and if she understood their plans. Sophie was fluent in Spanish, but then so were the girls, and the two men had isolated them to the bedroom so they heard none of their captors' talk. Not so great for the ICE authorities who were on their way but good for Sophie's sanity. She'd walked in on something she knew nothing about. She didn't need the nightmares.

Funny, Callie had to remind Sophie to call Stan. The jury was out on whether theirs was a real thing or not. One could say that they hadn't been an item long enough for her to feel obligated to touch base with him, but one could also say that Sophie wasn't a commitment sort of gal. Sophie often confided in Callie she'd never marry again, which meant sleepovers only, and she'd see gentlemen when she felt the urge. Callie decided this might be a topic she refused to discuss with her old Boston captain to keep their friendship intact. Still, he needed a call from Sophie, regardless of what level of love this was they possessed.

Callie, however, did what she usually did when needing to update friends and family that all was okay. She texted. Jeb shot back all kinds of questions, and she told him they had to wait. Mark, however, answered short and sweet once he heard she was alive and well. "Call me when you can leave, and I'll meet you at the house."

She loved how *the house* meant *Windswept* now.

Raysor put his guys to traversing the roads, hunting for the escapee. The guy had at least headed north, in the proper direction to get off the island, or so the signs indicated. The other way would've taken him in and out of coves, cays, and inlets until he reached the beach, and people, and too much potential for mayhem. It appeared their fugitive had a geographical knowledge of Edisto Island.

Like always, they'd blocked the Big Bridge as the only driving road off the island, just in case he snared a car or, God forbid, kidnapped a driver. Standard procedure when someone dodged authorities. If he chose to steal a boat, however, he stood a better chance of escape. All these officers and deputies could do was pursue the routes they knew they could control.

Thank God only the bad guys had died this time.

Chapter 36

Slade

BULLETS . . . ALL around us. When Callie ordered me to hang behind that second car, I didn't argue.

But to see that son-of-a-bitch Armstrong staring me down . . . with everyone else occupied and me being one of the people he didn't particularly like . . . I ate dirt crawling under the car. Hands over my ears, I cringed behind a wheel. This wasn't real. This wasn't real.

I couldn't keep my eyes shut, though. The fear of what might creep up on me saw to that. Like a movie where every time you blinked the ghoul was ten feet closer, I wasn't letting Armstrong slip up on me.

From the first time he'd showed up to intimidate us, I'd read him as nothing but a bully, yet here he was hiding from the fight. His choice to stand back meant he'd watch his allies die and not miss a beat telling other authorities how hard he fought.

But he stood there . . . until he drew his sidearm.

"Callie!" I screamed, only for her unable to hear, too focused to think of me other than hidden and safe.

Who the hell was he aiming at?

I twisted to follow his gaze. Surely, he wasn't drawing down on . . . us?

A different shot fired, a piece I hadn't heard yet in all the commotion. Armstrong jerked forward, into his car door. The rebound slung his piece ten feet ahead of him, the gun dropping with an abrupt stop into a silted rut.

What . . . ?

Four more shots rang out, just like the first. Armstrong jerked again, then again, then with a shocked stare at me, slumped to the ground.

Wait. The shots came from *behind* him, *up* Blue House Lane. Which was it? More bad guys or more cops? The way Armstrong played both sides, who could say, which had me shaking from my hiding place behind a wheel.

Half of me wanted to ball up and shut down. If friendlies were coming that'd be fine, but what if more enemy came at the beckon of that kidnapper. The not knowing stopped me from playing the victim. While I couldn't see, I had to keep watching. They'd make themselves known. Surely they would.

Who shot Armstrong . . . who was Armstrong aiming for . . . what in heaven was happening?

Hands trembling, fingers trying to find purchase in the rubber tire, I wanted Wayne so damn bad. I wanted Callie. I wanted to be out of here. I'd seen my share of danger, but unarmed like this left me like a damn pig in a tiny corral, good for nothing but a slaughter.

From Greer's car, feet came and went, running by me toward Armstrong. Edisto feet from the uniform. They didn't run far before those feet became legs, became a back, and finally became Thomas. He checked for a pulse on Armstrong, then stepped over the officer's body and retrieved the car, pulling it forward, around the incapacitated other cruisers, and parked it in front of the house.

Truman Burnett's rundown ATV sat parked front and center now, he in a wide stance in front of it, that old shotgun butt on the toe of his boot, his hand holding the barrel like a walking stick, like he had back at the house.

Wriggling out, I didn't waste time dusting myself off, and I ran toward Mr. Burnett. He was armed, and he was further away . . . and apparently he was willing to kill someone if they needed killing.

The old man opened his arms as I came running, and, God help me, I ran into those arms and hugged him until I worried I'd break the feeble ninety-year-old man in two.

Chapter 37

Callie

WITHIN AN HOUR of Raysor's arrival, uniforms and badges of all shapes and sizes blocked Blue House Lane with Greer in the midst of it all. Trucks, SUVs, and two ambulances, with about a half dozen different emblems on the doors arrived to jump into a fray that had long dissipated.

Medics checked Sophie and the girls first, after one officially deemed Armstrong dead. Then they gave the rest a once-over, finding cuts here and there, a gash on the back of Greer's hand he couldn't remember getting. Slade still sat in the ATV with Mr. Burnett, and agents spoke with them there. A medic bandaged her forehead and its triplet of cuts from shrapnel of the missed shots.

God bless that old man.

Callie couldn't imagine what might've happened if she'd arrived alone, without Greer. He wasn't near the creature she'd imagined him to be, but he wasn't a total hero either. ICE had him off to the side, someone with a notepad speaking to someone else, most likely in some level of headquarters. She pieced some of this together, but over the next day or two, she'd arrange a tête-à-tête with the current Chief of Edisto PD and complete the story.

He may not have meant for this package of evil to follow him here, but it damn sure had. Had to be some guilt there. Had to be some regret. But from what she gathered from snippets and the quickness of the feds pulling him aside, he'd tried to do the right thing about his former shortcomings. Edisto Beach would be totally unforgiving if they connected him to any of this, and she couldn't help wondering how loyal a friend Brice would be. Love him or hate him, Brice LeGrand put Edisto first.

"That ought to be you talking to the authorities instead of him," Sophie said, not having a clue what was going on other than bad guys had trespassed in Lumen's house with kidnapped girls.

"Appreciate the allegiance, Soph, but he's where he ought to be. He's pretty key in the history of all this. Without him, I'd have walked in by myself, and truthfully, you, me, and Slade might not be breathing right now." She couldn't have Sophie hating on the man. Not after what he'd done to help save her.

Nobody was ever a hundred percent hero, and even the devils had their good moments.

Callie bet Greer would never land that wished-for date with Sophie now.

Which made Callie remember whom Sophie dated at present. "Did you call Stan?"

"Yeah." She grimaced. "He's rather protective, isn't he?"

"You wanted to test drive a badge."

Callie's adrenaline had finally come down after an earlier moment of the shakes. Sophie continued chattering, probably her manner of dealing with the aftershocks. She talked herself almost stupid, covering every detail of her kidnappers, the six girls, and their stories. Part of her own rush, and part of just who she was.

Per what Sophie learned, the girls had been promised the sun and the moon and a better way of life and been told once they established themselves in the states they could call for their families to join them. Ages fifteen to nineteen, one having left a child behind, one hoping to bring her mother with cancer.

Even after some settling, out of the blue Sophie exclaimed, "We all could've died!"

"But you didn't," Callie said, giving the woman yet another hug.

Sophie was finally grasping the tragedy that had been averted. These girls and Sophie would've never seen home or family again. A tragedy interrupted because Armstrong had lied to Greer about when Lumen died and Greer had accidentally told Callie.

Assuming that had been an accident at all. On the other hand, he'd tried to push her away from Edisto, scare her out of being involved. Her interpretation of Greer's behavior remained hazy.

She scanned the Townsend acreage, had already walked the perimeter, just because she felt she needed to. The second shooter's tracks had already been identified, and the manhunt was on. Maybe she sought to feel Lumen's presence, to capture some of the gentleness she'd exuded in life. The peace of her place had been shot to ribbons . . . literally. The woman had to be turning over in her . . . well, guess she didn't have a grave yet.

Once authorities arrived she wasn't allowed inside, and expecting such, she hadn't gone inside to start with. Wouldn't be able to today, at least not until they processed the crime scene. A scene riddled with bullets outside and trashed with food wrappers and dirty dishes inside from what she'd seen peeking in the window. She bet her right arm they'd found whatever pot stash there might've been, a stash that Sophie might've so nicely removed herself. Closing her eyes, she tried to remember the house like it was, because once investigators finished with it, the character would be destroyed.

She sighed at the loss and turned attentive to her friend, trying to act like Sophie's babbling meant everything in the world.

Raysor remained out with his people, Thomas with him. Greer still counselled with ICE.

Squinting up the road, Callie noted the ATV gone, most likely back to Mr. Burnett's. Slade would take care of the man, and no doubt he'd take care of her. Somehow, Callie didn't see Slade so quick to come back down to Lumen's, even with the all-clear sign. The recipe journals she'd grabbed the first time might be the limit of her interest.

She hadn't heard the pickup pull in . . . couldn't with so many other vehicles, but she recognized that voice calling his woman from a hundred yards away. "Slade!"

Callie headed toward him, Wayne not seeing her as he asked one person, then another where Slade was, none of them able to say much since she'd taken off with Mr. Burnett. Law enforcement would be back to speak to Truman again, but he'd saved lives. A righteous shoot without a doubt.

Wayne finally spotted her. "Callie, where's Slade?"

"She's with Truman Burnett," she said. "She's fine."

He had the manners to hold off running off to Slade right away, though Callie could read the urgency in his body language. "Are you okay? Is Sophie okay?" He hesitated. "Did anyone who matters get hurt?"

"Armstrong is dead. The rest are fine."

He ran both hands up into his hair. "Good God, Callie, I never would've left if I'd known."

"You could not have known, Lawman," she said, snaring one of Slade's nicknames for him if for no reason other than to calm him. *Cowboy* seemed too personal for anyone to use but Slade. Then grinning through the relief, the melancholy, and the incessant nagging in her head of what might've happened, she reached to give the big man a hug. He hugged her as if she were Slade, and she let him, because right now she damn sure could use a hug from Mark.

Chapter 38

Callie

THE NEXT MORNING Greer agreed to meet with Callie, but only with her alone. She got it. And she respected that he understood she was owed more of the details to justify the jeopardy her friends endured. Then there was Thomas not getting his promotion and Raysor losing his position at the beach, which felt little more than vindictive. Probably a Brice move, but he used Greer to do it, and Greer had gone along.

Too many questions.

In light of yesterday, she was willing to cut him some slack. If he hadn't come with her to Lumen's yesterday, there might not even be a today for her and her friends. He'd reached out to her first, in broad daylight, and she had to give him that.

She left Wayne and Slade at *Windswept* with Mark and Jeb, promising to rejoin them in an hour or so. Jeb had turned protective again and made noises about taking a gap semester, and Callie wasn't having it. Her friends offered to continue that dialogue with him in her absence, with assurances Callie had their support. To skip school would only complicate her life and postpone his. Jeb had to learn he wasn't the only man in his mother's life, and far from her only protector. Delaying his adulthood only served to make Callie feel less of a mother. All that sounded better coming from third parties.

She'd make sure Stan underlined that later.

Wayne wasn't leaving Slade's side, and he trusted Callie to fill him in later. Mark wanted to be there when she returned, not sure what frame of mind she'd come back in, or so Callie assumed, plus he'd come to appreciate Callie's friends and hadn't much time with them short of the case.

It was time for everyone to take a deep breath.

Stan was being what Sophie called *smothering*, having even attended yoga with her. Sophie had dropped a string of texts to Callie not long ago, asking if he'd haunt her like this all day. Callie grinned, typing, *yes,* then added, *be careful what you wish for.*

Callie would've taken the class just to see the big man bend and twist places he'd never bent and twisted before, but Greer was the priority. It was ten in the morning, and Sophie might even be done with yoga, but if Stan came to *Windswept*, Sophie would have to as well, then the group would turn into a Stan and Sophie show. Sprite would tag along because her mother and Jeb were there. A domino effect.

Callie met Greer at the station, his suggestion and, frankly, the most private place she could think of without someone seeing them and wondering what was up. Even if seen together, one could easily justify the old and new chief comparing notes over any of an assortment of issues. Edisto Beach wasn't much familiar with what had gone down on Blue House Lane or the airstrip off Pine Island, nor how involved their police force had been in a human trafficking ring. Even if they heard about illegals and a shootout, best they never find out the whole tale.

ICE controlled the narrative in the news. Armstrong went down as one of the bad guys, with little more detail than he'd been sucked into the dark side by the lure of easy money. Greer was painted more of a hero. Callie wasn't mentioned at all, which she could easily live with. Edistonians would chew on Armstrong for a long while and praise their new chief for seeing through it all and calling in the backup.

Pon Pon was put on the map, though, as the birthplace of the players and the possible origination of Armstrong's criminal exploitation. An investigation was launched there, but the feds weren't as open to the public and press as local or state law enforcement about their plans, so it would probably take indictments to explain more. Callie no doubt expected that activity in the future, unless Fox was stupid enough to talk to reporters.

Callie just hoped that Greer remained Annie's father to public eyes and nobody learned of Fox. The girl didn't need that.

But Edistonians were open-minded and forgiving souls to those who lived full-time amongst them, tending not to care what people did once they left, crossing the big bridge to the mainland. Plus, they'd experienced such a turnover of cops in the last few months they wouldn't even miss Armstrong.

Greer must've been watching for her arrival because he had two hot cups of coffee waiting in his office. Marie wasn't at her desk, and no officers were at the small station. Good for him.

He shut the door when she entered. The room had a welcome feel for her, a bit warmer than usual but comforting. Taking the chair across from the chief's desk interrupted that feeling, but things were what they were. The coffee was still good, though. *Thanks, Marie.*

Greer sat behind the desk, rearing back like he'd spent decades in that chair instead of six weeks. Then he seemed to catch himself, remembering who his visitor was and how every way he moved, everything he touched, she'd mirrored not long before. He sat straight into a benign pose. "Thanks for meeting here, Ms. Morgan. Has to seem odd for you."

"No problem," she said, ill at ease at both their discomforts. She had him at more of a disadvantage than he realized, but no point embarrassing the man. She'd rather hear everything from him. She'd rather measure if everything he said matched what she'd learned.

They each sipped coffee, and Callie sensed Greer wasn't quite sure how to start, so she did. "On the way to Lumen Townsend's, you started telling me about Annie. You left Pon Pon for her sake, to get her away from bad sorts, one of which was Armstrong."

He sighed, not in a release sort of way but as if still toting a heavy load. "When you left this chair, Ms. Morgan, it was as if the sky opened up for me. Here was a chance. As you may have heard, Brice LeGrand and I go back to college. He went because his parents made him, and I went to decide what I wanted to be. Both of us wound up back in our hometowns, doing what our parents wanted us to do, but we kept in touch. Pon Pon and Edisto Beach aren't far enough apart to lose touch." He gave her a sorrowful grin. "I'm aware of your mother's prior relationship with Brice. I'm aware of when you were born. And I'm aware of your secret lineage between your father the mayor and an Edisto native." He shook his head at the clear and apparent fact Brice readily gossiped. Then he gave a flippant wave to the room. "And I definitely heard about your arrival here, and you assuming this role."

None of this embarrassed her. She'd endured her life being fileted and displayed to the community for ages. "You have me at a disadvantage, Mr. Greer. I'm not much familiar with your past other than your affiliation with Brice, which doesn't exactly place you in the best light."

"Call me Lamar."

As her mother had taught her, one didn't use a first name before being invited to do so, especially with elders. "Lamar," she said, awkward at the invitation. Like the military, law enforcement used last names a lot. Raysor, Seabrook. "Mind if I just call you Greer?" she asked.

He nodded in consent.

"So, Greer, start with Annie."

"Anna May is my daughter, even if she's not blood kin. For years I thought her my own, but I suspected as time went on that while her mother was my wife, her father was Troy Fox. His name suits him. He's manipulative, and in a small town like Pon Pon, that's powerful. I loved that little town, grew up in it, but my family wasn't Pon Pon royalty like his. Like a slow-growing poison, he wormed his way into most of the town's enterprises. He'd been a county councilman, but he couldn't quite get away with as much there, or rather, he wasn't as savvy as he thought he was, and once he was about to get in trouble about mismanaged contracts, he decided not to run again. One term. Empowered and better educated at how power works, he took a stronger hold of Pon Pon."

She showed no response, just a guest and her coffee. But she wasn't that forgiving. He'd been a head cop for a long time. He had strong control. He had the means to stop some of Fox's ways and he hadn't.

"Fox sucked in Armstrong." He studied his cup at that point. "However, I cannot deny Armstrong was loyal to me as well. He may have even assumed I wanted what Fox wanted, because we were two of maybe five people in the town who ran everything. But he crossed lines. Armstrong, I mean."

"Being a member of that small tight cadre of people sort goes against you, Greer," she said, unable to swallow his coming out of this clean and noble.

He couldn't look at her, ironically studying the framed commendations on his wall instead, as if they helped to cling to the fact he'd been good in his life, too. "We have a history," he said.

Callie hushed, hoping he'd share. She'd appreciate an understanding. She wasn't comfortable with this image she had of him, as if he'd escaped the gavel somehow.

"When my wife was dying of cancer, I was a mess," he said. "She'd strayed with Fox in our earlier days, part of which was my fault, part hers, but mostly Fox's. Anyway, we managed to think of Anna May first. For some odd reason, the effort brought us closer together."

He took a breath. Callie did, too. He didn't seem a man who readily cut himself open for just anyone.

"But when Neila was failing, I devoted myself to tending her. Anna May was torn between work and her mother, and I made her work to keep her sanity. But—" He stopped, remembering. "Armstrong stepped up. He managed my daughter on the job, training her, keeping her attention on her work to take some of her mind off her mother. He stepped into my place on so many occasions to the point I practically threw him the reins."

"For how long?" she softly asked.

"For almost two years," he replied, just as low. "Fox capitalized on him during that time, and I overlooked a lot, not having the energy . . . not even the desire, to chastise a man who'd been so good to me for so long." He paused again, finally able to bring his gaze up to hers. "I'm not proud of it, and I'm not excusing him. It is what it is, and if they decide to blame me for looking the other way in Pon Pon, I'll take whatever comes."

In those few minutes, Callie's opinion of the man shifted. He wasn't clean, but he wasn't dirty, either. He was simply human. And he'd put family first. He just hadn't the substance to juggle it all.

"What about Annie?" she asked.

He stared at her hard now. "I was hoping she could stay here."

Odd thing to say. "Why wouldn't she be able to? Everyone likes her. None of this will stick to her. I'm sure of it."

"Oh, I don't know. Who knows?" he concluded, returning attention to the cold empty cup in his hands.

"SLED had a file on him. You, too," she said. "It's part of how we started wondering."

"I know. Not surprised you dug that up, either. From everything I've heard about you, and now, everything I've learned firsthand, you're good at this job, Ms. Morgan. Very good. Brice is a fool."

That came unexpectedly out of left field. "I'm honored, Greer."

"You were a fool as well letting him coerce you out of this job."

To that she couldn't argue. She had come to that conclusion some time ago. Between Brice and her demons, she'd lost direction, but that's not why they were here. "Brice told you I resigned, and you jumped to remove your daughter from bad influences. Can't hold that against you."

"Appreciate that," he replied. "This will be hard for her. Armstrong worked at taking her under his wing. No doubt he expected to assume the role of Pon Pon Chief of Police once I retired until I threw them coming here. She grew up admiring him, unaware of how he abused his power. Admittedly, I might've sheltered her from a lot of that reality."

"Like a good father," she said.

"But not like a good chief," he replied.

True that.

She'd hate to have to juggle motherhood and chief if Jeb were one of her officers. But her son wasn't a law enforcement fan. Made her feel sorry for Greer.

"Then Brice hired Armstrong," she said. "You assumed Armstrong wanted your job. Why didn't he stay in Pon Pon if he did?"

"Good question, but Fox drove that," he said. "I didn't learn of their collaboration until after we'd all moved here. Armstrong kept disappearing. Thomas tried to talk to me, but I refused to hear, thinking him too loyal to you to accept a different policing style."

Callie sadly heard that. Greer had been in such a rut in Pon Pon he'd lost his ability to read people. That had cost him.

He took a heavy breath. "A part of me welcomed Armstrong. He'd help make the transition easier, I told myself. He'd be further from Fox, less tempted to be distracted, and he could start fresh and focus on policing. All that dirty politics would be behind him."

"He didn't fit in here," she said. "Too much of a bully." She didn't say Greer should've seen that. Truly this chief had not had the insight everyone gave him. Like she'd told Mark, and like she'd discussed with Wayne, the length of time in the job didn't exactly make you smarter at the work. It could make you complacent.

Greer could tell himself he had tried to save Armstrong, but he'd grossly and irresponsibly underestimated the man's intentions. To his credit, he appeared to see that now, just too late for it to matter.

"Armstrong lied to Brice to come here," he continued. "Said I had to bring Anna May but I hadn't wanted to push Brice into hiring him, too. So Brice did me a favor and hired him. The deed was done before I was made aware."

"Welcome to the world of Brice," she said.

"He definitely has a dumbass side."

They gave their camaraderie a moment to gel.

He sighed with a growl behind it. "Did not recognize the depth of evil Fox was involved in. When I smelled the rot, and because my assistant chief of so many years might be involved, I deemed myself too close to investigate. I couldn't surveil him. Too obvious. I chose to call ICE because more Hispanic males were making appearances in town when they weren't tourists, residents, or employed anywhere I could tell. I suspected narcotics at first, then quickly thought about trafficking. The transfer to Edisto was to put it behind me and leave it to them to handle. When Armstrong followed, ICE took note."

His voice cracked on the end. Greer was grappling with demons and would for some time.

"That why you lied to me about Lumen's death that night at dinner?" she asked.

The man slowly shook his head, unable to return her gaze. "It was a desperate man's plea for help," he said. "Armstrong was lying to me. I felt it. ICE warned me to not involve anyone, but you held such a reputation I reached out anyway, immediately regretting it. You didn't deserve any of this."

She'd pieced this part together last night. "That's why you went on the offensive, trying to shake me loose of the querying I was doing." She scoffed a sad laugh. "Going to my mother was primo, Greer. First-rate try. You just didn't understand the family dynamics."

"Guess not."

This man had erred in his judgment so many times he could hardly stand himself.

"When did you see he'd dragged in Annie in the Edisto enterprise?" she asked.

"When she came back that night with a knot on her head. I backed her in a corner for explanation. That wasn't like my girl to get involved in something like this. Armstrong at first posed to her the situation as legit, some affluent renter coming in or something in that vein, and before she could read the situation, she was up to her neck in it."

"Yes," Callie said. "She came to me after the first time. I did research. Mark went to SLED. Wayne Largo took it to his federal people."

He quieted. "Armstrong was helping Fox to expand his Pon Pon operation to someplace closer to the coast."

"Or change locations if he felt you were on top of things in Pon Pon," she said, trying in some small way to make him feel better. But they both knew he hadn't fought this hard enough. Fox wouldn't have spread to Edisto if he'd seen Greer as more of a threat in Pon Pon.

"When I pulled into SeaCow, I was coming to you to ask for help with Anna May," he said. "And there you were ten steps ahead of me." He eased back in his chair, as if tired of the storytelling, as if tired of his life.

"There will be no case against her," she said, hoping to console the parent in him.

"I could always say she was on the inside, helping me gather intel," he added.

"And she came to Thomas, then to me, seeking a way out. That's when we sent Wayne to ICE. She's going to be all right, Greer. She's not the first cop to take an off-the-books security gig, but when she identified criminal activity she came straight to law enforcement, to Thomas."

The man, old enough to be Callie's father, teared.

She didn't say he wasn't at fault. All she could do was sit there, staring down, trying not to embarrass the man who had a lot of reasons to feel embarrassed.

She guessed the rest. Crime had gone up here because Armstrong didn't give a damn about policing Edisto Beach. He was so busy running interference to keep Fox's enterprise a secret. He just didn't bother. He limited Thomas and Annie to specific, minor duties. He bent Greer's ear day in and day out, making assurances, and Greer had his hands tied due to ICE.

Maybe being harsh on weed had been a way to police Edisto without interfering with the freedom ICE wanted to catch Armstrong

"They'll catch Fox," she said.

"Yea," he said. "*They* will catch Fox."

She couldn't argue with him there. They would succeed. They'd already caught the second shooter, found half drowned holding onto a boat he'd tried to use in his escape.

But the two chiefs sitting in the room had come to the same conclusion. Greer had made their job a lot harder than it had needed to be.

Chapter 39

Callie

"I'M NOT BELIEVING this," Jeb said, leaning in the bedroom doorway watching his mom put the finishing touches to her clothes.

"You thought you'd won," she said with a mother's smirk. "I get it. But the job runs deeper than that."

"Tell me something I don't know."

She went to him, hands on his chest, peering ten inches up into that gorgeous, young man's eyes, he trying so terribly hard to look disapproving. "Admit it, son. You're proud of me. You could ride a garbage truck and I'd be proud of you." She grinned, having backed him in a corner.

"Yeah, I guess," he said.

"Come on. We'll be late. If Mark doesn't get here—"

A knock sounded at the front door.

"He's here," Jeb said, disappearing to answer.

His and Mark's joint worry over Callie had united them, and the discussion they'd had the morning after the Lumen house shootout had somehow taken hold. Jeb had accepted Seabrook once upon a time only to lose him. He'd been reluctant to accept another. This trust in Mark was a good solid baby step.

She stepped out of the bedroom and presented herself.

Mark saluted the uniform.

Jeb took note, unable to hold back an approving smile. "We're gonna be late," he said, going for the car keys on the kitchen hanger.

"I'll drive her," Mark said, hand on the boy's arm. "You go tend to your girl." He turned to Callie. "I'll tend to mine."

He didn't have to tell Jeb twice.

Once Jeb disappeared, they followed, stopping on the porch to lock up. Callie stood there with key in hand. "I'm as nervous as the first time," she said.

"Wish I'd been there," he said. "I would've liked to have seen you then."

She allowed herself to fall back to that day, and who had been there. "Might sound weird, but I wish you'd known Seabrook. And Francis." Just a few months after taking office she'd lost both officers, both friends, within a week of each other.

She'd told herself not to do that anymore. She'd lost people . . . and she'd lose more people, but she had a better grip on the circumstances wearing the badge. These ten weeks without it had taught her that.

"Let's go," he said, waiting for her to lock up, then took her hand to lead her back to the life she loved.

The assembly room at the government complex wasn't big, so when there was an event like a critical town council meeting, they packed the room and stood against the walls. This was a standing-room day per the cars. The temperature was crisp, the sun radiant, and when she took her sunglasses off inside, she couldn't immediately see.

But when she could, she almost gasped. She'd been sworn in before. She'd been held accountable here. She'd been recognized and awarded here. She'd appeared in this room more times than she could count. This time, however, felt different.

Greer resigned the day after he met with Callie, and he left town, people unsure where he went and if he'd return. Annie knew he'd returned to Pon Pon to help clean up what he hadn't before, but she kept the knowledge between her heart and Callie's. Her daddy had been used, some could argue too willingly, and despite his efforts to repent and cooperate in the case, he saw himself as the reason for what had happened at Lumen's. He'd work with ICE to nail Fox who hid in his country manor behind a criminal defense attorney out of Charleston.

Annie was the only living person other than Fox who could add a smattering of whats, whys, and hows of what little she'd witnessed and heard. ICE would have her in and out of their offices for a while. For instance, she was aware the cache of human cargo that had wound up in Lumen's place was for a certain celebrity; a last-minute order, and a mix-up in ground transportation had forced them to overnight at Lumen's.

Nobody needed to hear any of that, though. Greer knew that better than anyone.

Edisto Beach didn't need its naïve, Eden-istic bubble popped.

But the why didn't matter to Edistonians who petitioned the council to rehire Callie. They began begging her to come back the day

Greer left. Like . . . phone calls, texts, and night-time knocks on her door begging.

They really hadn't needed to. The first phone call from the mayor was all it took for her to say yes.

The double doors bumped people when she tried to enter the gathering. People had to part to let her in.

She meant to arrive earlier, to avoid any sort of grand entrance, but she couldn't find this and that for her uniform, having lost a lot of her wardrobe in the fire that had taken her home on Jungle Road. Even after Annie had cannibalized her father's uniform and accessories to supplement, she fell short, but Mark had convinced her that nobody would notice. She had no choice but to agree.

Both her mothers were there, alongside Jeb, Sprite, Sophie, and, yes, Stan beside her. Still together. FBI Agent Knox sat a few rows back, in full suit and tie, like he didn't stand out. Raysor had dressed himself to the nines and brought along the Colleton County Sheriff who'd already agreed to let Raysor come back to Edisto Beach. After all, Edisto was an officer down with Armstrong gone.

Ms. Hanson from Jungle Road and Monty Bartow who lived with her now, the young man she'd saved on her last case. The Edisto Fire Department, all of them. Thomas and Annie stood against the wall near the front, part audience and part security, in dress uniform. Annie had made no noise about leaving Edisto, with Callie assuming Thomas having had something to do with that.

The list went on and on. Old friends who'd driven to the beach, and others who'd been here the entire time. A choke lodged in her throat at the sign of Truman Burnett, for a change with a cane propped on the toe of his shoe in lieu of his old shotgun. Slade and Wayne sat next to him, probably his escorts. He'd avenged Lumen by killing Armstrong and hadn't thought twice about the right and wrong of it . . . because it could only be right.

So many allies. She'd forgotten she had so many friends. She made her way down front, doing her best to breathe.

It wasn't until she stopped scanning the crowd, each resident clearly projecting appreciation, that she bothered taking note of the tables in front.

She didn't particularly want to see Brice LeGrand, but there he sat, front and center. He made eye contact, but his expression remained empty. That was okay. He knew that she knew he'd brought Armstrong to Edisto, and while he hadn't been made privy to the details, he recognized that he'd been a major catalyst to this mess. He might not be familiar with the whole story, but he was aware of enough for his reputation to fall on the bad side of things . . . if people learned.

Today, he welcomed her back, at least in front of these people. She didn't want to know how the council vote had played out. The bottom line was the council had signed off.

There were small speeches—not necessary, in her opinion. Some praised her. Some praised Edisto Beach. Some even praised Greer for serving well as *temporary* chief, the rewritten story being spun up and down the beach. She didn't hear half of the presentations, just pasted the obligatory smile, hands folded before her, because if she let them loose they'd tremble.

"You got this," Mark said, leaning over. "Look at this room. You've got this top to bottom."

Finally, they called her up. Jeb rose and strode forward. Bless him for disliking law enforcement yet being so noble as to pin her badge back on after the mayor swore her in. His big hug showed he meant it.

"Speech," someone called out. A few more echoed the same. The room clapped, slowed, then clapped harder when she asked for the mic. She let the applause die down.

"I cannot begin to explain the importance of this moment. It's more than being accepted by you, for which I am mightily grateful. It's me accepting myself."

The room went vacuum silent. Mark had a fixed gaze on her, urging her on.

"It's me accepting that I am not perfect. I can try to be perfect, but God won't dare let me wear that mantle." She chuckled then sobered. "Because God knows I can't wear it well."

She threw her shoulders back a little more. "Today, you welcome me back, and I cannot begin to express how deeply that touches me. Deeply, y'all," she said, empty hand in a fist over her heart, coincidentally over the badge Jeb had just pinned. Small applause went around the room. She remained in the position, and when the sound died, she tapped the badge again with the same fist and held it there.

"New officers at police academies learn to use guns, handcuffs, batons, flashlights, vests, and so many other pieces of equipment. They pass exercises, exams, and tests. They must get a grip on their physical, mental, and psychological self. They put on a uniform for the first time, but it comes without this . . . a badge."

She patted it one more time, then lowered her hand. "The public deems it accoutrement, insignia, a symbol of authority granted by taking an oath. Some see it as nothing more than a simple means of identification, but those who accept the wearing of a badge promise to defend, remain loyal, and serve. It's a chivalry thing. An agreement to maintain order and hold self and others accountable to the laws and community served."

All eyes were on her though she'd never been much of a speech maker. She'd never entertained the press, thus never held the first press conference since coming to Edisto Beach. Higher-ups did them in Boston. Everyone here couldn't help but recognize a different Callie.

"I could have an ID card instead," she said. "I could wear a lanyard around my neck with my photo on it to confirm identity. But this badge . . ."—she tapped it—"is a visible sign that I've sworn to be a person of integrity, of a certain character, committed to providing safety and security to Edisto Beach. And I will never betray this badge . . . nor you."

The audience leaped to its feet, the applause a roar in the confinement. It wasn't until people began to come forward and Mark handed her a tissue, did she feel the tears. It wasn't until then it registered with her just how badly she needed to be Police Chief of Edisto Beach.

Someone took the mic from her and made it squawk. "Everyone, we have refreshments in the bay of the Fire Department next door. You are welcome to move the festivities over there."

Took her a half hour to get there herself and another two hours to speak to everyone before the gathering fizzled out.

Mark pulled her up a chair at the bay entrance, to feel the breeze and catch her breath. Jeb brought her a lemonade and a water, not sure what she wanted. Suddenly parched, she drank down the water, then wilted into the seat and sipped on the other.

"I'm going on with Sprite," Jeb said. "I'm staying at Miss Sophie's house tonight if that's okay. We're playing poker with her and Mr. Stan. You and Mark are welcome to come."

That visual made her laugh. "Thanks, son, but I'm exhausted. Y'all have fun."

Tables folded in the background, people cleaning up the final dregs of appetizers and dirty paper cups. Mark pulled up his own chair.

"That . . . was intense," she said. "I'm half deaf from the noise, and my throat almost hurts."

Mark smiled . . . an exceptionally beautiful smile, she thought. "I've never seen you so happy," he said.

"You never know what you've got till it's gone," she said. "How many times does crap have to happen to me before I appreciate that?"

The unsaid *times* being her husband, her father, her job in Boston, Seabrook, and ultimately her job here on the beach. Most people learned this lesson after one loss, maybe two. "Somehow I'm particularly hard-headed in that regard," she said.

Thomas saluted from the parking lot before he left.

She returned the gesture. "My first action tomorrow will be to promote him."

Mark scooted his chair to touching hers and reached around to squeeze her to him. "Edisto Beach looks mighty honored to have you back."

"I so appreciate that," she said, leaning into the squeeze.

He added low enough for the people behind them not to hear, "I so want to sleep with you tonight."

She laughed quietly. This time she didn't think twice about it. His house or *Windswept*, it didn't matter. Unless she had a house full of guests. "What about Slade and Wayne?" She'd spoken at length with them. Slade wasn't quite as eager to take home witchy recipe books anymore.

"They were delivering Mr. Burnett back to his house and heading home from there," he said.

After promoting Thomas, Callie would reach back out again to Lumen's sister, Lovey Townsend Walker, the rightful heir, and put a bug in her ear that Mr. Burnett deserved something from the estate as Lumen's last best friend. There'd been some talk of Lovey moving back down to the island. She'd regretted selling her land years ago, and with her husband deceased she had no reason to stay in New Jersey. She could be Truman's new friend.

Mark touching her badge brought her back to the present. "That speech was pretty awesome," he said.

He of all people, a retired SLED agent, would understand the heartfelt level of those words. That badge mattered, and it meant more than the average person understood.

The event had dragged out from four to seven, and the autumn sun was trying to fade. "I have a place to be," she said. "And I want you with me."

"You want to change first?" he said.

She grinned. "Not at all."

She drove though. She needed to be the one to drive. They left the beach, crossed the causeway, and headed up Highway 174. Five or six miles out, he asked, "We going to Lumen's?"

"No."

When she didn't volunteer, he asked, "We going by Truman's?"

"No."

But they were headed that way. Wasn't long before she pulled into the parking lot of the Presbyterian Church. She parked and shut off the car, sitting a moment as she always did each time she came. She'd never come in uniform before.

Familiar with the importance of the place, Mark softly asked, "Want me to sit here?" The joy in him had been replaced by something more respectful.

"No." She reached over and took his hand. "I want you to come with me." She kissed his palm and let go, exiting the car. He got out and joined her, and they made their way past the front of the church with its fat tall columns and wide stairs, the autumn wreath on the door, and around to the path leading into the cemetery. Making their way past the Mikells and the Baileys, the Hopkinsons and Jenkinses, Callie led him to the Seabrooks.

He'd never been there before.

"Mike," she said, touching the top of the headstone. "This is Mark. He's good, he's kind, and he's dear to me now."

She hushed, soaking in the moment, not looking back at Mark. She'd come to know him deeply enough to appreciate he understood how much she needed this without a discussion. She dropped to her knees, like always, rubbing her hand across the grass.

For a change she didn't crave to crawl atop it, or worse, crawl down into the dirt with him. This was a visit. This was an introduction. This was closing one door so she could open another.

Mark's hand brushed down over her hair to her jaw, as he moved to stand against her. They remained still for a couple of minutes.

Finally, she stood, brushing off her slacks, then slipped an arm around Mark's waist. He returned the gesture. "Thank you for that," he said.

"Thank you for being patient with me," she replied. "Let's go back."

He gave a questioning glance.

"Yes, I mean *Windswept*," she said. "The ghost is gone."

She let him drive back. "We don't need to eat anything, Mr. El Marko, sir."

"You didn't get two bites back at the station. Too busy talking to people," he said. "Let me stop at the restaurant a quick second and grab us some tacos."

"I have food. Besides, there's something I wanted to run by you. Head on home." She said *home* on purpose.

They parked and sat in the car, the beach house rising high above them. "Sure there's nothing I can get for you—"

"I've decided to rebuild *Chelsea Morning*," she said.

He waited for more, and when there was no more, said, "Excellent. Glad to hear it."

"There's more," she said.

"Okay. I'm all ears."

She unbelted, shifted in her seat, and took him all in, wanting him to see her well when she said this. "By the time *Chelsea Morning* is built, I want you to move in with me."

Again he waited for more. "Um, I'm . . . um . . . wow."

"No pressure," she said.

"Not feeling any pressure," he promised.

"So, deal?"

"What if I—"

She reached over and yanked him to her, kissing him hard. A long-time hard kiss. She finally backed away and smiled.

"Deal," he whispered.

Chelsea Morning had been about white and blue, pastels and sea colors, the palette her mother preferred. Callie hadn't cared about decorating, but amidst all this, she made up her mind how her new home would look. It would be a darker nautical blue, with white trim and shutters . . . with a splash of red—the old swing from *Windswept* anchored on the new front porch.

Seabrook would be totally fine with that.

The End

Acknowledgements

Of course I thank my publisher, led by the illustrious Debra Dixon. I so wish we'd married up earlier in both our careers.

I thank my husband who is the most loyal person on the planet. Then my two sons. One who reads my work religiously, and the other who ensures I remain fit by training me in his gym. And to my beautiful daughter-in-law who is the first to send me heart emojis when I've done something well.

And to my fans, especially my Chapin fans, who keep telling me they cannot wait for my next release. What a glorious combo of pressure and love.

About the Author

C. HOPE CLARK holds a fascination with the mystery genre and is author of the *Carolina Slade Mystery Series,* and the *Craven County Mystery Series* as well as the *Edisto Island Series,* all three set in her home state of South Carolina. In her previous federal life, she performed administrative investigations and married the agent she met on a bribery investigation. She enjoys nothing more than editing her books on the back porch with him, overlooking the lake with bourbons in hand. She can be found either on the banks of Lake Murray or Edisto Beach with one or two dachshunds in her lap. Hope is also editor of the award-winning FundsforWriters.com.

C. Hope Clark
Website: chopeclark.com
Twitter: twitter.com/hopeclark
Facebook: facebook.com/chopeclark
Goodreads: goodreads.com/hopeclark
Bookbub: bookbub.com/authors/c-hope-clark
Editor, FundsforWriters: fundsforwriters.com

CPSIA information can be obtained
at www.ICGtesting.com
Printed in the USA
LVHW050006120523
746751LV00004B/249

9 781610 261821